BUTLER'S JUSTICE

A Monroe T. Lovett Novel

PERRYPERRETT

Other Books by Perry Perrett

To Kathie...

BUTLER'S JUSTICE

A Monroe T. Lovett Novel

PERRYPERRETT

Chapter 1

Three Lane County Sheriff's vehicles sped through the dense early morning fog, responding to a 9-1-1 call of shots fired at 202 Castle Hill Drive. This address was very familiar. It was the home of Marcus Butler, Jr. The three deputies drove with only their overhead lights flashing, their intensity subdued by the fog. They didn't use their sirens though. The sound might alert a possible perpetrator.

In the moments leading up to the call, tension in the master bedroom soared as the three persons in the room heatedly shouted at each other. This situation had been building for some time, and now it had reached the point of eruption. What began as a calm discussion was over. One of the three paced, stopping just inside the doorway to the walk-in closet. Out of the corner of the eye, a 12-gauge shotgun was propped against the wall inside the closet, within arm's reach. Another look. *Why not grab it?* Maybe it will make the point this affair needs to end—and end now.

A marriage was in trouble. But not just any marriage. This was the Butler family, the most powerful family in Lane County. A family's reputation was on the line. Someone had to do something before it all came crashing down. Accusations resumed as the three tried to make their point, all at the same time, yelling, but none heard over the other's shouts. A confrontation was moving in the wrong direction.

Then, everything went silent. The three stood, looking at each other. Anger, more like rage, radiated from the person standing at the closet door. The other two could only wonder what might happen next. Was it over? Had the argument ended? Perhaps the three might come to a peaceful understanding.

Wrong.

Filled with indignation, the 12-gauge pump action shotgun looked even more inviting. Now that's when the whole situation deteriorated.

With a quick reach, the person grabbed the shotgun, swung it around, and yelled at one of them, "Get out! Get out of the house, now!" The advice was taken. Now just two remained. Anger overcame reason, with the gun pointed at the other, the one seen as the root of the problem—the girlfriend.

Chh-Chhk.

That sound, the sound of a shell inserted into the receiver of the shotgun changed everything. An intense argument just took the next step and was now close to a dire ending. At this point, both could walk away. However, one rarely walks away, as emotions overcome prudence. Once prudence makes its exodus, loathsome reasoning leads one to savagery. Savagery ends in death.

A gravel drive wound through the trees opening to a large lawn and a single-story ranch home with an exterior of brick and dark stained cedar, also enclosed by woods. At a little past 8:00, the three sheriff's cars eased up the drive. The sound of gravel crunching under the tires echoed through the quiet morning. They met a pickup coming toward them. The driver of the lead vehicle, Deputy Reed, recognized the driver of the truck and motioned for him to turn around. He sat for a moment staring at the deputies who were ready to act. Realizing there was nowhere to go, the guy in the pickup put the truck in reverse and backed up, stopping in front of the house.

Cautious, the deputies got out of their vehicles. They surveyed the house from the safety of their patrol cars. The driver of the lead patrol car pointed at the truck telling the driver, "Stay put, Junior." The young man dropped his head back as he sat behind the wheel of his truck. Turning to a deputy in the second car, he gestured toward the pickup, ordering the deputy, "Stay with him. And don't let him leave."

Deputy Reed sent three other deputies to the back of the house while he and his partner eased to the front of the home. Finding nothing outside, the investigation moved to the home's interior. Reed gently checked the front door. The door was closed but not latched. Normally, they would call out, announcing their presence; however, not this time. Silence was necessary for their protection.

One deputy remained outside the front door while another watched the back of the house as Reed and his partner entered, searching through the house. Seeing nothing in the living room, dining room, and kitchen area, the two deputies made their way down the hall, clearing each room, until they reached the master bedroom. They stepped into the room, first the veteran cop, followed by his rookie partner. The odor of the recently fired shotgun was strong in the air. The bloodied body of a young woman in her early twenties was lying on the floor. Blood saturated the carpeted floor and drenched the body. A shotgun shell was lying a few feet from her. Deputy Reed looked inside the sizeable walk-in closet, which had its own sitting area, to ensure no one was there. Looking down, he saw four additional shotgun shells lying on the floor.

"Clear," Deputy Reed said with an exhale to his partner while holstering his .40 caliber pistol.

Frozen by the gruesomeness, the rookie stood there gawking at the body—his first murder. And it was repulsive. Suppressing his sudden up-heave, the young deputy put his hand over his mouth, rushed from the house, and vomited in the front yard.

Deputy Reed, after watching the rookie's exit, said, "I've gotta make a call." Pulling his phone from a case on his duty belt, he pushed the speed dial for Detective Carson.

About fifteen minutes later, the detective arrived at the crime scene. He saw the pickup truck but paid it no mind. The deputy watching it pointed at the house, telling the generally cranky Detective Ben Carson, "They're in the bedroom." Carson nodded slightly and parked in front of the house.

An ambulance pulled up as Carson made his way inside the house.

Having regained his composure, the rookie deputy was back in the bedroom. Unwilling to look at the body, he pulled back the sheet for Carson to see the body. Lifeless hazel eyes stared back from the mutilated body of a light brown woman. She was dressed only in a black bra and panties. Black hair topped her five feet, six inches, slender body.

Detective Carson scrunched his face and turned his head at first sight, but then knelt to get a better look at the repugnant scene. He examined the girl's mutilated face. Due to the amount of damage to her face, he didn't recognize her at first. After studying her features, as best he could, he blurted out, "It's the Miller girl. This ain't gonna be good." He looked over the young woman's bloody body and said, "Somebody definitely wanted this girl dead." He stood up with a grunt. "Was this sheet over the body when you found her?" Carson asked. He knew if the killer placed it there, then it meant remorse.

"No. I put it on her when I came back in," the rookie replied.

"Have you ever heard of cross contamination?" Carson asked.

"Yeah."

3

"Then remove it," Carson told him. He looked around, noticing the bed was unmade. There were no apparent signs of a struggle. "Makes no sense," he mumbled.

The rookie began pulling the sheet from the body.

"Carefully," Carson instructed, with a scowl.

"Huh?" the fledgling deputy asked.

"Carefully. Be careful how you remove the sheet, son." Carson carped. "And bag it. We might need it now." Then, with a slight wave of his hand, he told the deputy, "Never mind, leave it for forensics." Using his phone, the detective began taking some pictures. "Where do we get these guys?" he muttered under his breath, glancing at the young deputy.

Carson walked over to the wall and looked at several small bullet holes where some of the buckshot had penetrated.

The Lane County Sheriff's Department was small and did not have a full-time Crime Scene Unit like some of the larger departments. Detective Carson had only attended a series of classes in crime scene investigation and evidence collection a few years earlier in Jackson. For anything more complex, like this, they called in additional assistance from the state's forensics lab.

"Who was first on the scene?" asked Carson as he looked around at the room.

Deputy Reed popped his hand up. "Me. Well, me and the up-chucker here," he said pointing to the rookie.

"You call for forensics?" Carson asked, writing his notes.

"Yeah. Barnes is on his way. Probably be a while, though," Reed answered.

"Why?"

"Said he hadn't showered yet."

"Stevens?" Carson asked.

"The doc is on her way," Reed answered.

"Well, don't touch anything until Mr. Clean gets here. And tell the doc to check for sexual intercourse," Carson said, scouring the room for additional clues. "Anyone else here when you arrived?"

Reed motioned with his head toward the front of the house where the patrol cars and other emergency vehicles sat parked. "The Butler kid was out front. *Said* he had just pulled up when I asked him."

"Said?"

"Saw him when we pulled into the drive. He was leaving," Reed said.

"Great." Carson took a deep breath and then asked, "Anyone called his dad?"

"Not that I know of."

"Someone needs—Never mind, I'll call Marcus myself."

Another deputy called from the large walk-in closet, "Detective."

"What?" Carson answered.

"You might want to see this," the deputy in the closet said.

He began walking to the deputy's location. When Carson got to the closet, he looked in and said, "This closet's larger than my bedroom."

"This bedroom's large than my whole apartment," Reed remarked.

"Detective?"

"I'm coming," Carson said, looking at the deputy standing near the rear of the closet.

"Looks like we've got the murder weapon," the deputy said, tapping his foot next to the barrel of a 12-gauge shotgun sticking out from under a row of hanging clothes.

Making sure not to destroy any possible evidence, with care Carson knelt and examined the firearm. The odor of spent gunpowder was very perceptible. "Recently fired," he said, looking up at the deputy. "You're right. I do believe this is likely our murder weapon. See these smear marks here?" he said, pointing at the stock.

"Yeah," the deputy answered.

"Looks like someone tried to wipe it down, so don't touch it. And mark those four empties on the floor there," Carson said, laying the shotgun back on the floor. Getting up, he walked to where the four additional empty shells were located. He stood to get a line of sight to the bedroom. "No doubt the killer stood about here," he said, staring at the body on the floor. "And then, walked over for a close shot to the face."

It was time to have a conversation with Marcus Butler, Jr., the young man sitting in the pickup. Before he left the house, he told Reed, "Call out front and tell 'em to inform the ambulance guys this is definitely one for the coroner."

"Got it," Reed said.

Marcus Junior was leaning against the front of his truck where a deputy was keeping an eye on him. Carson headed straight to the young man. "Junior, what the hell were you thinking?"

"I didn't—," he answered.

This wasn't just some kid. This was the son of a good friend. Carson put his finger in his face and said, "You'd better tell me the truth, you hear me?"

"Sure."

Fuming, the heavyset detective glowered at the twenty-four-year-old, whose dark blonde hair kept falling over his eyes. Each time he would brush his hair back with his hand. Carson could see his hand trembling. "Did you do this?" Carson asked.

"No. I wouldn't—"

"Hey, everybody knows—" Angry, Carson stopped midsentence. Junior remained silent. Finally, Carson asked, "Do you know who did?"

Marcus Jr. hesitated, looked down at the ground, and then answered, "N-no."

"Look, somebody called 9-1-1. We can trace that number."

"Wasn't me," Junior said, as he looked away, avoiding eye contact with Carson. "I just got here," the young man said.

"Funny, I've got six deputies who'll testify that you were leaving when they arrived."

"Nope. Like I said, I just got here," Junior maintained.

"You didn't make the call?"

"No. A sheriff's car came flying down the drive before I could even—"

"You could even what?"

"Before I . . . I'm done talking. I ain't saying anything else until I talk to my dad."

Carson stared at the former high school star athlete. He knew he wouldn't tell him anything more. "Alright. Go. Get out of here. But, not too far. You hear me. We need to talk later."

Junior nodded his head and then jumped into his truck. He sped away as deputies watched and a little confused by his departure.

Deputy Reed exited the house and walked up to Carson looking at the dust flying from behind the pickup and asked, "Why'd you let the boy go? You know he knows something."

"Yeah. I know. Just let me handle this. Got it?"

"Alright. You handle it," Reed said, a little confused by Carson's actions. "You gonna call the sheriff?"

"No. You call him," Carson snapped as he headed back inside to finish processing the crime scene, leaving Deputy Reed standing there.

After completing his investigation, Detective Carson got back into his SUV and left. He made the drive back down to the main road. Nearing the county road, he saw a pickup waiting at the entry of the driveway. He pulled up next to the truck. The two men remained in their respective vehicles as they talked.

"The boy looks guilty, Marcus," Carson said.

"He didn't do it."

"And you know this, how? If not him, who?"

"I'll get you a name."

"Get me a name? What? You gonna pull one from the phone book, Marcus?"

"Of course not."

"Hey, this looks bad for Junior."

"Don't you think I know that, Ben? I need to check on something. If it's what I believe, then I'll have you a name. This thing's been building for some time."

"Building?"

"Like I said, let me do some checking. Make some calls."

"Alright. But for now, the boy's my number one suspect," Carson said, and then drove off.

Chapter 2

Bear one another's burdens, and thereby fulfill the law of Christ
(Galatians 6:2)

Monroe Lovett parked his Camaro on the street like he had almost every morning for the last several weeks. Slowly, he got out and ambled up the sidewalk toward his office, 101 Poplar Street. Passing by the windows of Christi's Coffee House, he didn't look in. Right now, he didn't care. Failure filled his thoughts—failure as an attorney, failure at life in general. His thoughts were on how he had talked Debbie into making this move. Going to his office was the last thing he wanted to do today. Fighting his own demons of despair and discouragement, each step was a struggle to not turn around and go back home, or even somewhere else altogether. Any place seemed better than where he was. But where?

No. Monroe felt stuck, stuck in Peregrine, Mississippi. Peregrine was a small town with its own uniqueness. He chose this town to make his transformation, to start anew on the advice of an old law school friend. Some friend, he thought. Peregrine was the typical rural county seat town, with the stately courthouse set in the center of the old town square with a few shops and businesses on all four sides, each with its own distinct exterior. However, there seemed to be mostly lawyers. Monroe would drive around occasionally and try to memorize their names. He hadn't worked up the courage to visit any of them. Dreams of spending days entrenched in a battle with another attorney were just that, dreams. He had yet to step into the courtroom since the move here. Monroe had vowed he would not go in the courtroom until his first case. The way things were going, he began to think that day might never come.

A car rushed by him, shaking Monroe from his momentary self-pity. Looking up, he saw Jack at the building's entry. "That looks nice," Monroe commented, as he walked up to the front of the 1940's burgundy colored brick building. He had hired Jack to paint his name on the glass door. If nothing else, it would look better than the paper sign taped to the glass.

"Thanks, Mr. Lovett," Jack responded as he kept at his work. With a steady hand, he painted the W of the word law with precision.

Monroe stood on the sidewalk admiring his own name where Jack had stenciled it on the exterior glass entry door of the building—Monroe T. Lovett, Attorney-at-Law. When Monroe chose this place for his office, it seemed like the perfect location, situated on one of the four corners of the town square, with the courthouse across the street. Like a few other attorneys who wanted the place, he thought the corner office would aid him in attracting new clients, clients needing a defense lawyer. Now he would take any client. A simple will construction or a mechanic's lien would be a welcomed sight. A few days earlier, Monroe had even brushed up on the latest bankruptcy law just in case. However, he'd promised himself he would not take a divorce case. Family law was not his forte, and he didn't care to get in the middle of other people's family problems. Ministry had burned him out. Unfortunately, not a single person had made the journey to seek out Monroe's legal services, and money was running thin. Part of him wanted to tell Jack to remove his name from the glass door. But he didn't. Fighting his despair, Monroe clung to what little hope remained.

"Mr. Lovett, how long you been a lawyer?" Jack asked in his black southern drawl as he finished.

"Good question," Monroe answered. He thought for a moment. "Let's see, I rightly don't know how to answer that question, Jack. Well, I started pastoring—"

"You was a preacher?" Jack asked, surprised by Monroe's revelation.

"Yes. Yes, I was, in a previous life, before moving here to Peregrine." Now Monroe was beginning to question his decision. Things weren't going the way he thought they would.

Jack stepped back from the door. "There's you go, Mr. Lovett. It's finished." He stood for a moment and appreciated his handiwork. Jackson Taylor, or as everybody called him, Jack, was an all-around handyman in the small Mississippi town. The sixty-two-year-old black man always wore a pair of faded jean overalls. They fit more comfortably over his round belly. "Maybes I should've put Reverend on there," he chuckled.

"Looks good. But no, no reverend. How long till it's dry?" Monroe asked.

9

"Couple hours," Jack said, and then chuckled, rubbing his hand over the thinning short gray curly hair atop his dark brown face, a face that beamed with a smile, revealing his pearly whites. "A preacher?" He waggled his head. "What makes you become a preacher, and then a lawyer, Mr. Lovett?"

"Actually, I was a lawyer, a preacher, and now a lawyer again. Or, maybe you could say I've always been a lawyer," Monroe answered him with a somewhat amused look on his face. "And Jack."

"Yes, Mr. Lovett?"

"You can call me Monroe."

Jack just sort of stared at Monroe for a couple of seconds and then hooked his thumbs in the top of his faded, well-worn overalls. "Okay," he answered. He continued his stare and laughed, "You not sure what you are, are you?"

"It's a long story," Monroe chuckled. To be honest, he just wanted to retreat to his office. "Maybe I'll tell you about it one day, but"— Monroe pointed to his watch and then at the top of the building where his office was located— "I've got to go."

"Oh, okay, Mr. Lovett. I mean, Monroe," Jack said with a smile. He closed the jar of black paint. "Maybe you can tells me that story someday over a cup of coffee," he suggested as he pointed to Christi's, the coffee shop occupying the downstairs of the building.

"Sure, I'd like that," Monroe said, opening the building's door, the one opposite the one Jack was painting on, ready to head upstairs to his office. The aroma of freshly brewed coffee advanced a rather large-framed man as he hurried through the door Monroe was holding open, almost running into Monroe.

"Morning," Monroe said with a quick step back.

Jack flashed a friendly smile at the man.

Dressed in tan khakis and a dress shirt, the man had a phone next to his ear. He nodded at Monroe. Then he looked at Jack and said, "Hello, Jack." He was noticeably involved in a serious conversation. Jack nodded with a smile. The man stopped at the edge of the sidewalk as a car drove by. Before ending his call, he told the person on the other end, "Tell him, I'm on my way. I'm just across the square." He then darted toward a black and gray four-door heavy-duty four-wheel drive pickup truck.

"Guess he's in a hurry," Monroe said, watching the man. He began to step through the door and then turned back. "Jack, who was that?"

"That? That was Mr. Butler."

"Marcus Butler?"

"Yes, sir. He's a powerful man. A hard man, that Mr. Butler. Yes, sir, he's a powerful man in Lane County. Everybody, well almost everybody, respects him. They do what he tells 'em."

"Thanks," Monroe said as the truck speed away.

Fighting past the allure of cinnamon and sugar permeating the entryway of the old building, Monroe headed up the wooden staircase located directly across from the opened door of Christi's.

Debbie heard the buzzing while sitting at her desk in the outer office of Monroe's law office located at the top of the stairs. It alerted her someone was coming up the stairs, although, the squeaky steps were a better forewarning than any buzzer.

Several coats of paint covered the plaster walls of the renovated building. The current color was maroon. New fluorescent lights installed in the antiquated light fixtures illuminated the stairway and the short hall outside Monroe's upstairs location.

He knew Debbie would be wondering where he had been. He was running late. It was unlike him. After a quick jog up the stairs, Monroe walked through the door into the main office. A new odor smacked his olfactory senses: new paint barely covering the smell of stale cigarettes. A chain-smoking CPA was the previous occupant for more than ten years, and evidence of his tenure remained.

Debbie gazed at the tall, lean Monroe as he emerged through the door. A smile appeared as she saw her man.

"Hey, hon," Monroe said to his wife, Debbie, as he closed the door behind him. She was also his secretary. One thing he could count on, seeing Debbie's smile invariably brightened his day—usually.

She sat at a 1950's time-period desk left for the current tenant to use. It was free, and Monroe needed it. Debbie pushed back from her desk and asked, "Where have you been? You left the house before I did."

"I got caught up at the gas station. You know, it's funny—"

"What? You huffing from climbing the stairs. Maybe you should start exercising."

"No. Now, if you'd let me finish." He grinned and pointed back toward the staircase. "Yeah, those are—"

"Tough on an old guy," Debbie said with a giggle. The zingers were flying today.

"What's with the sarcasm?" he asked.

"I'm not being sarcastic. Just stating the truth, sweetie," Debbie said, with a shrewd little grin. "So, you were at the gas station."

"Like I was saying, whenever someone hears I used to be a pastor, they start telling me, you know—"

"Personal stuff."

"Yeah. Like I care who stubbed their big toe."

"You're in the South. People talk. Talk a lot."

He walked over, bent down, and gave Debbie a kiss. "You have very kissable lips, you know," he said, resting his forehead on hers, looking into her bright green eyes.

She placed her hand on his cheek and told him, "You know, I could look into those baby blues every day."

He chuckled, as he stood back up straight.

Debbie, in one smooth motion, stood up and pressed her five feet, eight-inch lean feminine body up next to her husband's. One small kiss was not enough for her. No. She gave him a long passionate kiss as she ran her fingers through his sandy-colored hair.

"Umm . . . What's gotten into you?" he asked, fiddling with her long dark auburn tresses, gazing into her eyes.

Monroe and Debbie met as freshman in college. He saw her in the school's bistro and fell in love on the spot. After some convincing, she agreed to go out on a date. That's when she fell in love with him. The rest is history, as they say, over twenty years of marriage and no kids, and best friends for life.

"Just love my man, that's all," she answered, touching his chin with her finger.

"Then, I guess I am one lucky man," he said with a slight pop to her bottom followed by an affectionate squeeze. Letting Debbie know how much he cared for her was always important to him.

"Hey!" she giggled.

"Any calls?"

"No, not yet."

"Not yet." He smiled at her. "Always the optimist, aren't you?"

"Somebody has to be. Remember, you believed this was God's plan." She had watched Monroe's slow downward spiral over the last few days.

"The way John made it sound when he told me about this place— people were lined up, needing attorneys." John was the law school friend of Monroe's who talked him into moving to Peregrine. The two kept in touch over the years. "Probably why he moved to Atlanta," Monroe said with a touch of sarcasm. "I mean, look around this place. Throw a rock in any direction, you'll hit a lawyer."

"They may not be lined up, but they're going to come."

Monroe pointed at the stairs again, "I guess all my clients will be young, or in shape," Monroe said, and began walking toward his office.

"Maybe you should put in an elevator. Increase your clientele," she yelled to him as he walked down the twenty-foot hall to his office.

"Yeah, like they're busting down the doors now," he replied over his shoulder as he entered his office.

Monroe and Debbie moved to Peregrine, Mississippi, from Ohio. For nineteen years, Monroe pastored a small church he had started near Lake Erie while still working for a prestigious law firm near Toledo. Once the church was up and going, Monroe left the law firm and devoted his energy to the church. Several years passed and then he began feeling the urge to leave, but he was unsure of what else to do, or where to go. Pastoring didn't seem to fit anymore. Going back into law was never on his radar, but he also never thought he would leave the ministry. Stranger yet, Monroe's plans never involved him moving below the Mason-Dixon.

Boxes lined the walls—boxes full of legal books and journals. Many of them not opened in years. Monroe let out a sigh as he dropped into his distressed brown leather executive chair. It sat behind his large, solid oak desk. It was a gift from his parents when he graduated from law school. He began fiddling with his pen. *Click. Click-click. Click.*

Debbie laughed to herself when she heard the clicking. As she adjusted the stapler, she hollered, "You know, since you don't have any court cases, you could unpack your—"

"Yeah, yeah, yeah—I'll get to them." *Click.* "I'll get to them . . ." he replied, then made a mocking gesture with his mouth.

"I heard that," she said.

Leaning over the side of his chair, he looked out the door into the hall. *How did she—?*

"Because I'm a woman. And your wife."

He sat straight up, astonished.

Debbie's hint had little impact. He figured, unpacking the boxes only meant repacking them later. Monroe spun his chair around to face the window behind him. Looking out from his office located on the corner of the town's square, he had an unobstructed view of the courthouse. The prestigious building sat with four large, white columns positioned at the top of the steps. Built in an era long past, the courthouse's dark red brick and white trim still looked almost new. There was an old bell tower atop the building. He stared at it for several minutes. People were entering and exiting, but none of them made the short trek across the street to his petty law firm.

He smirked as he scrutinized the large brick building. With a slight waggle of his head, he thought, *Maybe I should have stayed in Ohio. Mississippi? How did I end up here? I could've found another church. Another city. Or state. Or, maybe, I could have—*

Bzzz . . .

Someone was coming up the stairs. He spun his chair back around.

Debbie watched the door with anticipation.

The door opened.

In walked a young woman. Debbie eyed her. *Dark brown hair. She's young. Pretty.* Wearing a light blue sundress, with white and yellow flowers decorating the cotton dress with spaghetti straps looped over her shoulders, the melancholy woman closed the door behind her. Her countenance, and the fact she was looking more at the floor than at Debbie, gave away her apprehensiveness.

Monroe strained his ears trying to hear. *Probably someone lost.*

"Hello. Can I help you?" Debbie asked, noticing her somber appearance.

"I need to see . . . speak with, with Mr. Lovett," she said with a soft timidity.

Debbie pointed in the direction of four light-colored wood chairs, the sort of chairs used in libraries years ago. They sat in the corner, two on each wall with a small table between them. "Have a seat over there," Debbie told her. "I'll go see if Mr. Lovett can see you." It was just a formality. Debbie knew quite well Monroe could see the woman, but she played the part to perfection.

The young woman did as Debbie asked. She sat down in a chair nearest the corner with her knees tight together. She crossed her arms firmly against her body and fixed her gaze on the old pine floor beneath her feet. Clearly nervous, she sat.

Debbie got up. Quickly glancing at her, Debbie's intuition told her something was wrong. She hurried down the hall and into her husband's office. She pushed the door shut behind her. "Monroe," Debbie said in a loud whisper.

"A client?"

"I don't know. I didn't ask. She just said she needed to speak with you. She looks like . . . from her bloodshot eyes that she's been up crying all night."

"Okay. Give me a couple of minutes, then bring her in."

Debbie walked back towards the woman. She smiled at her and said, "He'll be with you in a minute."

Instead of sitting down, Debbie walked over and sat down next to her. "What's your name?" she asked.

"Ashley."

"You have a last name, Ashley?"

"Butler."

Monroe hurried to straighten his office. *Should've unpacked, Monroe.*

Knock-knock.

He scurried back to his desk and straightened some papers, and then fell into his chair. "Come, come in," he answered, attempting to catch his breath.

The door opened. "Mr. Lovett," Debbie said in a professional tone. "This is Ashley Butler."

Standing, Monroe said, "Ashley, please have a seat," motioning to one of the brown faux leather chairs sitting in front of his desk. He snuck Debbie a wink. He'd never heard her call him Mr. Lovett before, and well, he liked it. He sat back down as Debbie walked out, closing the door behind her.

"Miss Butler, what can I do for you?" Monroe asked.

"Mrs.," Ashley informed him.

"Okay. Mrs., it is. Why do you need to see me?"

"I believe . . . I think . . . I might need a lawyer."

"First, how old are you?" Monroe asked. Ashley looked young to him.

"Twenty-two," she answered.

"You do know I'm a defense attorney?" Monroe told her. As soon as the words came out of his mouth, he thought, *how stupid.* At this point, he would take just about any case.

"Yeah. I-I know. That's why I'm here."

"Have you been arrested?"

"No. Not yet."

"Excuse me, I'm a little confused. Why do you say, *not yet?*"

"I believe I will . . . that they're gonna arrest me, arrest me for murder," Ashley said with a sniffle.

"Murder?"

Her eyes filled with tears as she looked down at the rug covering the wood-planked floor. She turned her face so as not to look directly at Monroe and then answered, "Yes. For kill . . . killing my husband's girlfriend."

Monroe leaned forward. "Wait. Did you say your husband's *girlfriend*?"

"Yeah." She wiped the tears from her cheeks. "She's . . . they found her this morning. Marcus told me it was over b'tween 'em, but . . ."

Must have been the sirens I heard early this morning? Monroe thought as he looked for a tissue. "Is Marcus your husband?"

"Uh-huh. Two days ago, he—" she began crying.

With urgency, Monroe looked for a tissue. "And, why do you believe they are going to arrest you?"

She took a deep breath as she struggled to gain control of her tears. "Cause my father-in-law is Marcus But—"

"Marcus Butler." Monroe quickly put two-and-two together. Marcus Butler owned Butler Transportation and ran most of the county with his power and money. He knew the name and reputation of the man. He'd seen the man earlier. And that was as close as the two had ever come to meeting. "Marcus Butler, he's your father-in-law?"

"Yeah."

"And your husband's girlfriend is . . ."

"Dead."

"And, you believe they will, are going to arrest you for killing her?"

Ashley nodded, saying, "Ye—"

"Wait, before you answer," he said, putting his hand up. Monroe opened a drawer and removed a sheet of paper. He handed it to her. "If you want me to represent you, I need you to read and sign this agreement. It states you have retained me as your attorney."

Ashley turned and looked away. She mumbled, "I don't have any money. Junior handles all the money, and I can't get to any of it."

Monroe, with a comforting tone, told Ashley, "Mrs. Butler—Ashley. The most important thing is you have proper representation. There's nothing in this agreement about money or fees. It only states that I have the authority to act as your attorney. That you're giving me permission to represent you."

She picked up the document and looked at the Attorney-Client Agreement. She didn't read it. In her mind, there was no need. She needed help, and Monroe was it for her. "Okay, I need a pen."

"You should read it," Monroe said.

"I did."

He knew she didn't. Why push the issue? The girl needed help, and he needed a client. She was too afraid. All he saw was a young woman who needed an advocate, someone, to come along beside her, to help bear her burden. Monroe was that person, and he realized it.

"Here," Monroe said, handing her a pen.

She signed the agreement and handed it back to him.

Monroe looked at the signature. "Okay. Good. Now tell me, why do you believe they are going to *arrest* you? Why you?"

"Because—"

Knock! Knock! Knock! The door rattled from the rapping.

"Hold on," Monroe shouted.

Ignoring him, two deputies walked in. Debbie was on their heels. "I tried to explain, but they wouldn't listen," Debbie said.

"Mr. Lovett, we're here to arrest Mrs. Butler," Deputy Reed said.

Monroe jumped to his feet. "Hold on one minute. Mrs. Butler is my client, and we were—"

"Counselor, I don't care what you were doing. We have a warrant for Mrs. Butler here, and we're arresting your client—period. You can come down to the sheriff's office if you want," Reed said, gently grabbing Ashley by the arm. "Please stand up, Ashley." She obeyed Reed and began crying. "Ashley Butler, you're under arrest for the murder of Julie Miller. You have the right—"

"Ashley, don't say anything, not a word until I get down there. Okay?" Monroe directed as the deputies continued their duty.

She nodded in agreement, but her face showed her fear as Reed finished explaining her rights.

"There. Your lawyer can't say we didn't inform you of your rights," Reed said.

Debbie watched, open-mouthed, as the whole scene unfolded in front of her.

"And, Ashley . . . stay calm," Monroe said, trying to hide his own anxiety. "Everything's going to be fine. You're going to be okay."

Deputy Reed finished handcuffing Ashley. "They're not too tight, are they?" he asked her.

Ashley, looking down, shook her head no.

Reed and his rookie partner escorted Ashley from the office as Monroe and Debbie stood watching, not believing what was happening before their eyes. They looked at each other and then hurried to the building's entrance as they watched the two deputies put the young, sobbing Ashley into the back seat of the patrol car.

"I guess you've got a client now," Debbie said.

"Yeah. I guess I do. And that's only half the story."

Chapter 3

Opening his briefcase, Monroe tossed a legal pad inside. He stared into the old leather attaché, took a deep breath and thought, *Well, I hope you're ready for this, Monroe.* He closed the case with a big exhale. Sure, this is what he came to Peregrine to do, but now it was real, it was happening—his first case. You would think his slowly rising dejection would now turn to joy, but in all honesty, anxiety was his number one emotion at the moment. Easing back into the legal system was more of his agenda, not a full-blown murder case.

Turning to leave, Monroe stopped and peered out the window again at the Lane County Courthouse. Did it feel like a dream fulfilled? It was more like a nightmare. However, before he entered the courtroom, Monroe must go to the sheriff's department where Ashley is being booked for murder.

Gripping his briefcase, Monroe was ready to go see his client. He made it all the way to his office door and then suddenly stopped. Turning around, he thought about what was in his briefcase and returned to his desk. Monroe re-opened the case. *Yeah, need to get rid of that.* He tore off the first two pages of the legal pad. *Don't need bad cartoon doodles.* Crumpling the two sheets, he tossed them into the trashcan.

Hurriedly, he walked down the hall and stopped at Debbie's desk. She was still in shock. Monroe looked at Debbie and told her, "I love you."

"I love you too, Monroe."

"Wish me luck," he said, giving Debbie a quick peck on the lips.

Debbie looked into his eyes and said, "You're Monroe T. Lovett. You don't need luck." She was trying to hide her own anxiety from him.

"Thanks," he said with a loud exhale. Monroe shot down the stairs, focusing on his first case. As he reached the sidewalk outside the building, he stopped, turned around, and ran back upstairs and into the office.

Confused to see him, Debbie asked, "What'd you forget?"

Monroe put his hand up, gesturing for her to hold on while he caught his breath. He then told her, "This, this morning . . . I read in Acts 20:35, 'In everything I showed you that by working hard in this manner you must help the weak and remember the words of the Lord Jesus, that He Himself said, "It is more blessed to give than to receive."' Is that wild or what?"

"Wow," Debbie said with a little amazement in her voice.

"Well, I didn't think much of it then, but now, well, I do believe God was trying to tell me something."

"So, do I. Monroe, you'll be fine." Debbie pointed at the door and said, "Now go . . ."

Stares fixed onto Monroe as he walked into the Lane County Sheriff's Department. He didn't know any of the deputies or the sheriff, but news of his arrival had made it through the department. They didn't think much of defense attorneys. This was their first look at him. He was more interested in the department's modernity. *Wow, they're up-to-date*, he mused to himself as he scanned the squad room.

Two uniformed deputies were sitting at desks. They just watched him, more out of curiosity than anything else did. Two other deputies stood in the back observing Monroe as he continued to admire the department's furnishings: computers and two forty-two inch flat screens mounted on the wall. *Not bad. Not bad at all.*

One of the deputies in the back of the main squad room leaned over and asked the other, "Who is this guy?"

The other shrugged. Eyeing Monroe, he responded, "He's the new defense attorney. I think his name is Lovett."

In a very distinctive Mississippi drawl, Monroe heard from another part of the room, "Hey, look boys; we got us a Yankee lawyer in here."

Monroe snapped his head around to see Detective Carson approaching him from the opposite side of the counter as he walked from a hallway, chuckling. The other deputies snickered at Carson's remark. Monroe's first impression of the fat detective was not a good one. "Excuse me?" he asked.

"Oh, I guess he's hard of hearing too," Carson said, laughing. "Typical for a *de-fense* lawyer. They never want to hear the truth of their client's guilt. And a Yankee defense lawyer, well . . ."

Stay calm, Monroe. He's the typical cynical cop. Monroe, with a fixed stare, fought back his own snide remarks, and replied, "I'm Monroe Lovett. I'm looking for my client—"

"Yeah, I know who you're looking for, Counselor. Who else would defend a guilty—?"

"Your opinion. I'll let a jury decide *if* we get that far. Now, where's Mrs. Butler?"

"Whatever," Carson said with a sneer. "She's still being booked. You can wait for her in the interrogation room." Carson buzzed Monroe in. "Follow me."

Monroe followed Carson through the squad room. He could feel the stares from the other cops. The detective led him down a hall, stopped and pointed to an empty room. "You can wait in there."

"Thanks," Monroe said. He placed his briefcase on the table and asked. "Coffee?"

"What?"

"Coffee. Is there any coffee? Surely, there's coffee in a police station. It's in all the movies," Monroe said with a grin. If he wanted to make friends with the sheriff's office, then he was starting on the wrong foot.

"Movies, huh," Carson sniped with a waggle of his head. "First, you need to learn the difference between a police station and a sheriff's office. And second, yeah, down the hall, to the left there's coffee. Maybe there's a donut in there, too. C'mon, I'll show you."

Entering the break room, Monroe asked, "Detective?"

"What now?"

"Did you question Marcus Jr.?"

"Yes."

"And?"

"And, it ain't *none* of your business," Carson barked. He pointed to the other side of the break room. "Coffee's right there," Carson said, and then left the room.

Monroe stood there a moment. *Nice guy.* He scanned the break room for the coffee pot hid in the corner behind several vending machines. *What? I thought he said donuts.* He thought as he poured some coffee into a white Styrofoam cup. He then walked back down the hall to the small interview room. Sitting down, Monroe sipped the coffee. "Aw, now that's horrible," he mumbled. He tossed the full cup of coffee into the waste can.

Monroe sat, waiting.

Half an hour later Detective Carson arrived with Ashley. She appeared dispirited and drawn, much worse than she did when Monroe first met her in his office. "Mrs. Butler," Monroe said, standing up.

Ashley stood slumped, wearing green and white striped coveralls. She had handcuffs attached to a chain and affixed to shackles fastened around her ankles.

"Detective, are these necessary?" Monroe said pointing to the restraints.

"She's a murderess."

"Charged. She's only been charged, Detective," Monroe stated emphatically, not seeing a killer, but a girl who needed help.

"Well, they're staying on. Policy," Carson said. Handing Monroe a folder he said, "Here."

Monroe took the folder from Carson, glaring at the detective as he left the interrogation room. Ashley started crying as she sat down in the chair facing Monroe's chair. Monroe set the folder down and began looking for a box of tissues. "Tissue? Tissue?" he mumbled as he searched. He sat down. "I'm sorry, but—"

"It's o-okay," Ashley said, slurring her words as she wiped her tears with her sleeve.

Opening his briefcase, Monroe removed the sole object inside, his legal pad, and laid it next to the folder. His hand shook as he clicked his pen. *Monroe, hold it together. What do I ask her? Remember law school. You've done this before*— He tried to think back all those years. *Nothing. Zilch. Great.* Finally, he said, "First thing, let's see, you are accused of murdering—I don't even know the woman's name." Monroe opened the folder handed to him by Detective Carson, which contained the arrest report.

"Julie," Ashley said.

"Huh?"

"Julie. The whore's name is, *was*, Julie."

Knock.

Carson opened the door as Monroe observed Ashley's animosity.

"Yes, Detective?" Monroe asked brusquely.

Carson walked over to the table where Monroe and Ashley were sitting. Laying several pieces of paper in front of Monroe the crabby detective tersely said, "Here."

Monroe snatched the papers from the table. "What's this?"

"Her confession."

"Her *what*?" Monroe asked crossly.

Motionless, Ashley shrunk away from Carson's presence and started crying again.

"She didn't—" Monroe turned and looked at Ashley. "Ashley, did you sign a confession?"

After a quick look at the detective, she nodded yes. Monroe saw her reaction, her fear of Carson.

"Detective?" Monroe asked, holding the confession in front of Carson, his hand quivering. His quivering was not fear. He was mad. "Why wasn't I called before—?"

"Everyone knows she did it," Carson said, looking down at Ashley. He was unfazed by Monroe's anger. "All I know is this—she signed it," the detective said with a brief sardonic grin.

"You can't . . . this is . . . No! No. This is wrong," Monroe declared, ripping the papers into several pieces and then throwing them across the room. "Now, get out while I speak with my client."

Monroe's theatrics didn't fluster Carson. "Fine. We've got copies," he snapped and then left the room.

Ashley sat sniffling as Monroe sat back down, trying to regain his composure. He picked up his pen and, with a deep breath, he said, "You shouldn't have signed that." He thought for a moment. "Did you tell them you did it?"

Slightly bobbing her head back and forth, she answered, "Sort of."

"But . . . Why would you?"

"I was confused," answered Ashley, her voice trembling as she spoke. "They told me it would be easier if I signed it."

Angered by what she told him, Monroe asked, "Did they read you your—? Wait, they did in my office." He strove to regain his composure. "Who told you?"

Visibly afraid, she sat with her body drawn in, staring down at the table. She didn't answer. He could see Ashley's fear as she shivered sporadically, but the room was not cold, not even cool. Running through her mind were questions. Why trust him? Why trust anybody? All she could see was Monroe's anger, unsure if it was at her or Carson. Maybe it was both. She clammed up.

He realized he had to earn this girl's trust, to convince her to allow him to figuratively take her by the hand and lead her through this process. Leaning across the table, Monroe calmly asked, "Ashley, I'm not upset with you. But why didn't you tell them I was your attorney?"

His softened demeanor helped, a little. She answered, "I don't—like I said, I was confused. I thought—I don't know."

"Okay. It's fine," he said reassuringly. Pointing at the ripped sheets of paper laying on the floor, Monroe asked, "Did you write out your confession?"

She shook head no.

"Who wrote it, then?"

She shrugged, answering, "You don't know how things work 'round here."

"What do you mean?" he asked, confounded by her remark.

Ashley clammed up again and her eyes flooding with tears. She knew more than she was letting on or telling him at least. That's how he saw it. He tried to comprehend everything. Then her reaction to Carson dawned on him. Monroe leaned over so he could see Ashley's face, and she his. "So, you're telling me you didn't write the confession?"

Tears streaming from her eyes, and with a slight nod, she answered, "Y-yeah." Ashley pulled her knees up tight to her torso with her arms wrapped around them.

"And that's the truth?"

"Yeah. But it don't matter," she said, burying her face in her knees, sniffling.

"Okay. I believe you," Monroe said. He weighed the possibility of dealing with a corrupt system if what she was telling him was the truth. Should he really believe this girl? Maybe she was lying to him. Why not dupe a new lawyer and try to get away with killing her husband's lover? Monroe looked at the obviously troubled young woman sitting across from him, studying her demeanor. What else could he do, except believe her? He thought the best thing for him to do was to get as much information as he could and uncover the truth. A single thought came to him, *Do your job and represent your client, Monroe.*

After pausing for a moment, allowing them both to relax a little, he said, "Ashley, you came to me this morning believing I could help you. That means you are going to trust me, one step at a time."

She glanced up at him, but only briefly. Barely long enough to make any eye contact, but it was sufficient for him. He asked, "Where were you early this morning, between five and eight?"

Without looking at Monroe, she answered, "With a friend."

"Male or female friend?"

She shifted her look to the side, staring at the wall through watery eyes.

"Male?"

She didn't answer.

"Ashley, you have to tell me the truth," Monroe said, altering his position to look at her face. "I'm not going to judge you. I'm here to help. And I want to help you. But you must answer my questions for me to do so. Okay?"

She nodded yes.

"Male?"

"Yeah, a guy."

"What's his name?"

"Billy. Billy Jenkins."

"How do you know him?"

"He and Marcus Jr. were friends. Went to school together."

"Were?"

"They don't get along anymore."

"Where were you and this Billy?"

"His place."

Her answer didn't sit well with Monroe. Now the question of her own infidelity came into play. "How did you get there?"

"I drove."

"Alright. What time did you leave Billy's place?"

"Early. Don't rightly remember the exact time. It was around sunrise because I remember the sun was just coming up when I left."

Monroe thought for a minute and said, "That would have been around six."

"I guess. Like I said, I don't remember."

"Okay." Her vagueness about Billy caused Monroe to develop some doubts of his own concerning what actually happened. She had the time to kill Julie. She had a very good reason to do so. Intently looking at Ashley, he said, "You do know that is before they found Julie Miller?"

"Mr. Lovett, if you want me to feel bad 'bout her bein' dead, well, then, I don't," Ashley blurted out. She lifted her face and for the first time and looked straight into Monroe's eyes she said, "Julie ruined my marriage. I'm glad she's dead."

Taken back, Monroe didn't know how to respond at first. He set his pen down and asked, "Did you kill Julie? If you did, then I will still represent you. But you must tell me the truth, Ashley." With a hint of confusion, he said, "Right now, I'm not sure what to believe."

Through eyes filled with both anger and fear, Ashley, answered, "No."

"Okay. I believe you," Monroe responded. No doubt, she was an emotional wreck. She came to him for help. There was only one direction for him to go—forward. Clutching his pen, he asked, "What were you and Billy doing, you know, *before* you left his place?"

"Not that!"

"Sorry, I had to ask."

"We talked. That's all. But we didn't have sex or anything. You've gotta believe me, Mr. Lovett. Me and Billy aren't like that. We're just friends, good friends. We just talked, talked about my—Marcus Jr. and that—Julie."

"How long were Junior and Julie seeing each other?"

"A few weeks. Maybe a month. I don't know. I wasn't exactly keeping count of the days my husband was sleeping with another woman."

Monroe jotted down some notes and then asked, "How did Billy, you know, how did he feel about the situation?"

"Made him angry."

"Angry how?"

"No. Billy would never."

"Why not? You said he and Marcus didn't get along."

"Billy didn't kill Julie."

"But they didn't get along, right. Maybe Billy felt he needed to do something," Monroe pressed.

"No," Ashley huffed. "No, he didn't do it. I just know . . . Billy would never—"

"What did you do after you left Billy's? Did you go for a ride? Call anyone?"

"Drove around town for a while and then came to your place."

Monroe quickly recounted his morning and then jotted down *9:20 am; Ashley first arrived at my office.* "What made you come to see me?"

"Billy called. Told me he heard about Julie and said I needed a lawyer because they were looking for me."

"How would Billy know that?"

"He's got a buddy who's a cop. Chad something. Don't remember his last name. Anyway, he likes to brag to Billy about his job and such."

"I need Billy's address?"

26

"I don't want Billy to get drug into this, Mr. Lovett."

"It's too late for that, Ashley."

She placed her feet back on the floor, and her eyes began to dry. She sniffed and said, "I'm not sure of the number, but it's the third trailer on the left out on Coon Hunter's Road."

"Color?"

"He's white."

"No. The trailer?"

"Oh. It's . . . I think it's brown and white. But, the white ain't really white no more cause of the mold growing on it."

"Where does Billy work?"

"He didn't do it, I'm tellin' you."

"Look, I need to speak with Billy. His testimony can help you."

"He's a painter. Does odd jobs 'round town."

Great. "Okay, I'm going to leave. I'm going to speak with Billy," Monroe said, placing his notepad inside the attaché case. He stood up to go call a deputy to come and get Ashley. "They're going to take you to the county jail until your arraignment hearing."

"I know. I've been in jail before."

"For what?" Monroe asked, walking to the door.

"Fighting. But that girl had it coming to her. Anyways, that was a long time ago."

Great. "How long ago?"

"Three years, I think."

Monroe opened the door and motioned for the deputy to come and get Ashley. There was a brief silence as they waited. He looked over at the young woman. He could see her distress. "Ashley?"

She looked up. Her eyes looked empty. Monroe looked straight into her emptiness and said, "We're going to prove your innocence, okay?"

She gave a forced smile and nodded. The rest of her said she didn't believe him.

"Is there anyone I can call for you? You know, a family member to post bond?"

"No."

"You don't have any family?" Monroe found this hard to believe.

"No."

"There's no one I can call? Parents? Siblings? No one?"

"Nah. Both of my parents . . . I don't have . . . there's nobody. I ain't got no one—"

"Alright," Monroe said, concerned over her apparent lack of support. He wasn't buying her family story, but for now, he took her at her word. "I'll see you at your arraignment hearing."

She began to cry as the loneliness of her situation overwhelmed her. "I-I ain't got any—"

"Hey, Ashley, you have me. You came to me for help, and I'm going to help you. But, you've got to trust me. Okay?"

"Trust? Ain't nobody worth trusting. My own husband cheated on me."

"Well, you can trust me. I promise," Monroe assured her. "Okay?"

"Whatever."

This was no time to push the issue of trust. Monroe dropped the subject, telling Ashley, "And don't talk to anyone. They're watching every move you make and listening to every word you say. When they take you to your cell, take a nap. Read a book, if they'll let you. Read the Bible. It always works for me. Get some rest. But don't, don't sign *anything* or talk to *anyone* but me, not even other inmates, okay? Understand?"

"Uh-huh," she answered with a sniffle.

"I'll see you later. I'm sure I'll have more questions," he said. Monroe left there feeling very green, like a first-year law clerk. The rust was there, and he knew it. He motioned for the female deputy to enter the room. Monroe watched as she led Ashley away. *Monroe, I hope you're not in over your head.* He glanced up at the ceiling. *God, I need some help*

Chapter 4

Upon returning to his law office, Monroe hurried upstairs. With a quick nod of her head, Debbie shifted her husband's attention as he entered to the gentleman seated in one of the chairs. Monroe stopped, dead in his tracks, and gave a quick glance. *I don't recognize him.* Monroe, cautious, walked over to the man.

The man stood to greet Monroe. At five feet, ten inches tall, with slicked-back black hair, the man was a few inches shorter than Monroe was. Extending his hand to Monroe, he said, "Robert Breaux. District Attorney, Robert Breaux."

"Hello. Monroe Lovett," Monroe replied, cautiously greeting Breaux.

Known for his stylish garb, Breaux was dressed in a tailored gray suit with dark blue pinstripes, gold watch, and a college class ring. "Can we talk, Mr. Lovett?" Breaux asked, giving Monroe a quick once-over. He was not too impressed with the blue jeans, untucked long-sleeved red dress shirt, and scuffed loafers.

"Sure,"—Monroe motioned down the hall— "in my office."

Breaux picked up his briefcase and followed Monroe. *He doesn't dress like a lawyer*, Breaux assessed. He glanced at Debbie. "Ma'am."

The two men walked down the hall. No doubt, this was not a "welcome to our town meeting" from the local district attorney.

"Please close the door," Monroe said. Stepping behind his desk, Monroe pointed to one of the two guest chairs. "Have a seat, Mr. Breaux."

"Thank you," Breaux said, surveying the office as he sat down. He glanced at the empty walls looking for diplomas. They were still in a box. With a hint of pride, Breaux said, "Ole Miss, class of eighty-six. You?"

"Who?"

"Ole Miss. You know, the University of Mississippi."

"Oh . . ." Monroe said, appearing as if he were trying to figure out where Breaux was talking about, that is until he saw Breaux's vexation. "No, I'm kidding. I've heard of Ole Miss. But the look on your face was priceless."

"Ha. Funny," Breaux said, forcing a smile. He gestured to the empty walls. "You? I don't see—"

Growing impatient, Monroe said, "Look, I'm sure you didn't come here to compare law schools."

"No. No, I didn't," Breaux replied. He swirled his finger around as he looked at the office and said, "Nice place. Close to the courthouse."

"Yes, it is." Monroe leaned forward, resting his forearms on his desk. "Is there a reason you're here, Mr. Breaux? I know you didn't come here to admire my office, either. I thought we'd meet tomorrow morning, at the arraignment hearing."

"We'll meet again later, but you just need to know, your client is guilty, Mr. Lovett. Or may I call you Monroe?"

"You know,"—Monroe said, leaning back in his chair— "that's what everybody keeps telling me. Which leads me to believe she's innocent. And it's Mr. Lovett."

Breaux reached into his attaché and removed a brown envelope. Handing it to Monroe, he said, "Here, look at this."

"What this?"

"The confession your client signed . . . *and* pictures from the crime scene. Along with a preliminary report."

"You guys are moving fast on this one, aren't you? Got everything all wrapped up in a neat little package," Monroe said, removing and studying the photos. He pitched the confession to the side. *Same as the last one.*

Breaux sat quietly, waiting for Monroe. He impatiently said, "Surely, after you've had time to think it over—you'll agree, your client, Mrs. Butler, is guilty." He leaned back with an arrogant posture. "Look, I understand, Mr. Lovett, you want to help this girl. But look at the evidence. She and the victim have a past, a bad past. She can't account for her whereabouts. The confession alone . . . And—"

"Have you spoken with her?"

"No. You know I can't without you present."

"Exactly. Then, how do you know where she was or wasn't at the time of the murder?"

"Her husband, Marcus Jr., said she and the victim had a fight last night. Things got out of hand, and one thing led to another. There are witnesses who will testify to her being out all night, and that she and the victim had a past, a bad past."

"Hearsay. Marital privilege."

"True. However, we still can connect the dots for a jury. And who do you think they'll believe?"

"All fruit from the poison tree. Still hearsay. Admit it, you have nothing."

"Mr. Lovett, look. You need to know something about your client. She's known to frequent the bars, to remain out all night, doing who knows what. She's been arrested before for fighting."

"So, says you. Besides, none of it's admissible in a trial. And besides, last time I checked, going to bars is not a crime."

"This is a small town, Mr. Lovett. Now, I don't know what they taught you in law school, but down here, her past will be on the minds of the jurors. She's already guilty in their eyes. Plus, those pictures will make a big impression on the jurors."

Trying not to let his emotions show, Monroe said, "I'll ask for a change of venue."

"Good luck. Judge Harper will laugh you out of his courtroom."

Monroe sat, staring at Breaux. *I smell a railroad job here.*

"First-degree murder, Mr. Lovett. Is your client's life worth you making a mistake?"

"First-degree murder?"

"I'll tell you what. I'll take the death penalty off the plate if she agrees to a deal."

Losing this case could cause him Ashley's life. Take the deal, and at least she lives. He quickly weighed his options, Ashley's options. Breaux was moving fast with this case. Something didn't feel right. He couldn't put his finger on it. "No. No deal."

Breaux stood up. "I'll leave you to look that over,"—he pointed to the confession— "Give you time to . . . to think things over. I'm sure that when I see you at three this afternoon, by then, you'll see your client's guilt, and let this case progress quickly—save the taxpayers some money, and take the deal."

"Three?" Monroe exclaimed, bounding to his feet. "But, I thought—"

"Judge Harper had an opening at three this afternoon. So, I jumped on it. An arraignment hearing won't take long. I'm sure you'll be ready by then." Breaux walked to the door and grabbed the knob. He looked back and winked. "See you at three, Counselor." Breaux walked down the hall, leaving Monroe standing frozen in his tracks, livid. As Breaux passed Debbie, he nodded. "Ma'am."

Debbie watched the district attorney walk out. She waited for the door to close before she jumped up and rushed down the hall to her husband's office. She entered and plopped down in the buttery-leather reading chair next to the wall. "Well?"

"You know I can't talk about a case," he answered.

"Must not be good. You look mad," she said. "Hypothetically speaking?"

He walked over to Debbie, took her hand, and drew her from the chair. Monroe then sat down in the chair pulling Debbie into his lap. He looked into her green eyes and said, "Hypothetically, I've got problems, big problems. But your face and smile make them all disappear."

In a small, dark jail cell, Ashley sat on an old squeaky metal bed, with her back to the corner, and with her knees pulled to her chest. She was crying—sobbing at times, feeling alone and abandoned. Her body trembled from her crying. Of the six cells in the small county jail, hers was the only one occupied. Her sobs went unheard, unnoticed. By now, her hair was stringy, wet from her own tears, and her eyes puffy.

Freedom seemed like a dream long past to Ashley. She wiped her nose thinking, *My life's a nightmare.* Her marriage to Marcus Butler, Jr., she believed, would be a new start in life, a chance to put a horrid past behind her. The Butlers had money and power, though she didn't know it when she met Junior. She wondered, *Where's Junior? Why haven't I heard from him?*

Monroe's promises seem a half world away from her. She'd heard promises before, from so many people, and every single one of them had failed her. *Why should he be any different than the rest of 'em?* she thought, remembering Monroe asking her to trust him.

Through her tears, and the shivers of her body, feeling she had hit rock bottom, prayed a simple little prayer, *Please God, please help me.*

She laid down, curled up in a ball, pulling the covers up over her.

Chapter 5

Sunlight penetrated the aged glass panes of the large oak stained wood framed windows mounted in the old courthouse, casting rays of light directly onto the defense's table where Monroe sat. He bounced his leg, waiting for the hearing to begin. His plan of finding and speaking with Billy would have to wait until later. Looking up at the judge's bench, Monroe strained through the sun's glare and dust particles to see if something was about to start. There were no apparent indications anyone was doing anything. He looked up at the clock, 3:07. *C'mon,* he thought as the judge and clerk shuffled papers and stacks of file folders. They spoke quietly to one another, but their conversation seemed more casual than anything pertaining to the work at hand. Monroe gave a quick glance in Breaux's direction to see his reaction to the late start. Breaux appeared to be napping. *Glad he's relaxed.*

"Next case," Judge Harper said, tapping the gavel.

Finally, Monroe thought.

A deputy entered the courtroom from a side door with Ashley, again wearing the green and white striped coveralls. Lane County had not installed the safety-glass partitions to shield the public from the inmates. Ashley walked in plain view of all who were present. The shackles clanked as she shuffled her feet. A deputy escorted Ashley to a chair next to Monroe.

Ashley glanced over the courtroom, but neither Marcus Jr. nor any other Butler family members were there. Only about ten people were scattered around the small courtroom. She swiftly dropped her head when she made eye contact with Julie's parents. They glared at Ashley, fixated with hatred in their eyes. Who could blame them? All they saw was their daughter's killer.

Monroe saw her reaction. He asked, "What's wrong?" He had no clue of Julie's parents.

"Julie's parents. They're—I just didn't think they'd be here."

He glanced over his shoulder at the grief-stricken couple. He had seen them earlier but did not connect them with Julie. *They're white?*

"Read the charges," ordered Judge Harper.

Monroe nudged Ashley to stand as the clerk announced the case.

"The State of Mississippi versus Ashley Butler," the clerk read aloud. "One count of murder in the first degree. And one count of aggravated assault in the first degree, in the death of Julie Miller."

"I see this is a death-penalty case, Mr. Breaux," Harper said.

"Yes, Your Honor," Breaux answered.

"How does the defendant plead?" Harper asked.

"Monroe Lovett for the defense," Monroe said.

"Tell your client to enter a plea," Harper said.

"Not guilty," Ashley answered despondently.

"Thank you," Harper said.

Monroe and Ashley sat back down.

"Mr. Breaux?" Harper asked.

"Your Honor," Breaux answered, "due to the *heinous* nature of this crime, the state asks that the defendant be remanded without bail as per the seriousness and extreme gravity of this offense. Mrs. Butler has no known family, and is a possible flight risk if allowed to go free on her own recognizance."

Harper lifted the gavel, ready to grant the prosecution's request.

Ashley made no visible response to the request. All hope seemed gone to her in her mind. A single tear rolled down her cheek.

"Your Honor?" Monroe asked, standing. He figured why not give it a shot.

"Yes?" Harper answered.

"The defense asks that the charges against Ashley Butler be dropped."

"On what basis, Mister . . .?"

"Lovett, Your Honor. Monroe Lovett."

"Mr. Lovett. Yes. That's right, you just told me. Sorry, I forgot," Judge Harper said with a smile. "You're our new defense attorney here in Lane County." Judge Harper leaned forward. The sunlight reflected off his shiny dark brown head. Only the sides of his head had any resemblance of hair, albeit gray, with a little black mixed in. "So, tell me, on what grounds should I *drop* the charges against your client?"

"Because they're all circumstantial at best, Your Honor. The prosecution hasn't presented a shred of physical evidence. All I've seen is hearsay and, and innuendos."

"Your Honor, the defendant signed a confession," Breaux said.

"Without my knowing," Monroe countered.

"Mr. Breaux, is this true?" Harper asked.

"Your Honor, Mrs. Butler knew what she was signing. It's her confession," Breaux replied. "In addition, the defendant never informed anyone she had retained an attorney."

"Mrs. Butler was arrested in my office," Monroe declared. "Surely, the sheriff's department and the prosecution are smart enough to put two and two together and ascertain that I am her attorney."

"Mr. Breaux, did you know the defendant had retained counsel?" Harper asked.

"Me personally? No," Breaux answered.

Not giving Harper time to reflect on Breaux's response, Monroe requested, "The defense asks that the confession be suppressed since it was signed without counsel present."

Before Harper could respond to Monroe's request, Breaux stated, "Her fingerprints *are* on the murder weapon, Your Honor."

"I haven't seen any fingerprint report," declared Monroe.

"We just got the report moments before the hearing, Your Honor," Breaux stated.

Julie's parents watched tentatively, worried the Butler name and Monroe's pleas might be enough to release Ashley. Ashley sat, unsure of what was going to happen next, her leg twitching. She assumed her fate was sealed, but not in the same way the Millers did. She also knew the Butlers, and those not showing told all she needed to know—she was alone.

Judge Harper mulled over the two attorneys' arguments. "The confession stays, for now."

"But, Your Honor?" Monroe appealed.

"Mr. Lovett, that's why we're having a trial," Harper declared. "Your request is denied. Your client was informed of her rights, and she signed the confession."

Monroe looked dejected by Harper's ruling as he sat back down in his seat, unsure of his next move.

Breaux grinned as he glanced over at Monroe. He sat down with an air of confidence.

Mr. and Mrs. Miller both breathed a sigh of relief.

"Bail?" Monroe asked. "You didn't rule on bail. I ask the defendant be released on her own recognizance."

"Bail, Your Honor?" Breaux asked as he stood. "Obviously our new attorney doesn't realize the seriousness of these charges. Just look at how the man dresses. He doesn't respect this court or these proceedings."

"How do my clothes have anything to do with my client's bail?" Monroe asked, glaring at Breaux.

Judge Harper rolled his eyes at Breaux's remark and then thought for a moment before answering, "One million dollars for bail, or bond. It *is* first-degree murder."

Breaux did not object. He knew Ashley did not have the money, nor a means to obtain a bond. "A trial date, Your Honor?" Breaux asked.

"I've looked at the evidence and all of the reports. Sixty days." Harper said, grabbing the gavel again, ready to end the hearing.

"Your Honor, sixty days?" Monroe exclaimed as he promptly rose to his feet again. "The defense needs more than sixty days. I mean—"

"Mr. Lovett, have you read the case against your client?" Harper asked. "Sixty days is plenty of time."

Ashley's anxiety was evident. She cut her eyes up at Monroe. *I am going to prison for the rest of my life. It's hopeless.* She sunk back in her chair and rubbed the tears from her face.

"You mean the fictional account against my client? The coerced confession by the sheriff's deputies?" Monroe asked, looking for any help he could get at this point. "I haven't seen this so-called fingerprint report the prosecution has mentioned. Is this how things are done here in Lane County?"

"Watch yourself, Mr. Lovett," Harper sharply said. He shifted his gaze to Breaux. Peering over the top of his reading glasses, he inquired, "Mr. Breaux is there a reason you haven't given the fingerprint report to the defense?"

Breaux stammered, "Well, no, Your Honor. Has Mr. Lovett filed for discovery? I haven't seen it. Maybe being a preacher all those years, he's forgotten—"

"Mr. Breaux, stop the song and dance and give Mr. Lovett everything by four-thirty today," Harper ordered.

"Yes, Your Honor," Breaux replied.

"Bailiff," Judge Harper called. "Have Mrs. Butler returned to the county jail. And, Mr. Lovett?"

"Yes, Your Honor?"

"Find something more appropriate to wear to my court," Harper said.

"Yes. I will," Monroe conceded, looking down at his casual attire.

Before Ashley left, Monroe leaned over and whispered, "Remember what I told you. Talk to only me, okay? This isn't over. Nothing happened today that I did not expect."

She mumbled, "Okay. But, I'm done."

"No, you're not, Ashley. Trust me," he said with a gentle smile. "I'll see you Monday, okay?"

Ashley slightly nodded her head and said, "Okay," as a female deputy assisted her to her feet and began to escort the dejected young woman from the courtroom. Before she made it to the door, Julie's mother leaped to her feet and began yelling, "I hope you go to hell! I hope you go to hell, you murderer! You killed my baby! You killed my Julie!"

Her husband reached over and took hold of the raging mother, pulling her back down into her chair. If looks could kill, Ashley would have dropped dead at that moment.

Mr. Miller looked at Breaux and said loud enough for all in the courtroom to overhear, "You better make sure that girl doesn't get away with killing our Julie. You hear me? Do you?"

Monroe and others in the courtroom observed the Millers, startled by the outburst. Ashley stood emotionless.

After the Millers had quieted and a deputy ushered them from the courtroom, Breaux walked over to Monroe. "Crazy, huh?" he said, motioning with his head in the direction of the Millers. "Here," Breaux said with a sardonic smirk plastered across his face as he handed Monroe an envelope.

"What's this?"

"Fingerprint analysis."

"Why didn't—?"

"Mr. Lovett, you need to learn how things work here. Learn to play ball on our terms," Breaux said, patting Monroe on the shoulder before he walked from the courtroom.

Monroe stood there for a moment, fuming. He mumbled, "How things work. Maybe it's time for things to change."

Breaux exited the courthouse feeling good about his case—a slam-dunk in his mind. A young woman, professionally dressed, looking to be in her late twenties, greeted the prosecutor as she stepped out from behind one of the large white fluted columns as he walked out the door. "Mr. Breaux, my name is Amy Cabrera from the Ledger in Jackson. May I ask you a couple of questions regarding this case?"

Breaux stopped when he saw her. "Hello," he replied, a little startled. He was not one to shy away from the opportunity to enhance his public persona. Moreover, being familiar with the statewide circulation of the paper, Breaux said, "Sure."

Seeing the two and perceiving who Amy was, Monroe slipped by in a rush, unnoticed by the reporter. He had better things to do than to give an interview.

Amy asked, "Mr. Breaux, how is it the sheriff's department was able to make an arrest so quickly in this horrible murder?"

"You would have to ask them that. I'm not at liberty to speak on their behalf."

"I did. A Detective Carson said someone had given them a tip, which led to Mrs. Butler's arrest. He referred me to you. So?" she insisted.

Carson's referral was not what Breaux wanted to hear. "Look, the accused had the motive and opportunity to commit this horrible crime. The evidence, which I cannot disclose to you at this time, will prove she murdered Julie Miller. It was a logical conclusion that presented itself to the detective on the case and my office. We acted quickly before she tried to flee. After she was arrested, she signed a confession."

"Why such an early trial date? Doesn't it hinder the defense's ability to prepare his case?" Amy pressed.

"It's not my job to help the defense. I have a murderer off the streets and plan to keep her that way. There's no sense in needlessly spending the taxpayers' dollars. Now, if you will excuse me," Breaux told Amy as he stepped around her, and then quickly escaped.

"But, I have another question," she yelled as he fled, scurrying down the sidewalk.

Successfully getting past the reporter, Monroe's next order of business, talk to Billy Jenkins. He shoved the large brown envelope Breaux had handed him into his briefcase and hurried to get into his car, a 1968 fully restored blue Chevrolet Camaro SS.

Knowing just the street name, Monroe entered Coon Hunters Road into the map application on his smartphone. It was a couple miles out of town. He drove out trying to decide how to handle Billy. Part of him wanted to treat him as a viable witness, an alibi for Ashley. Although, he had a deep-seated inkling Billy made a very good suspect and Monroe wanted to cast the blame on him. After locating the road, he began searching out Jenkins's mobile home. Driving slowly, he counted the number of mobile homes. *This must be it.* He pulled into the compacted dirt and grass driveway and parked.

After sitting and observing the place, Monroe got out and walked to the door. *This isn't a pastoral house call.* Three wooden steps led up to the front door. Monroe didn't use them. He stepped around them to the side, knocked, and stepped back several feet while waiting.

No answer.

He banged again, harder this time.

Nothing.

He listened for any sounds but didn't hear anything. Monroe walked around the tatty mobile home, examining it as he made his way to the back. *No signs of life.*

"Hey! He's not home." Monroe heard a man call from his left and behind him.

Monroe turned fast. An older man wearing jeans, a plaid shirt, a western-style straw hat, and sporting a bushy gray mustache was leaning on a shovel.

Monroe walked over. "Hello, I'm Monroe Lovett," he said, extending his hand.

"So, you are," the old guy responded, but not returning the handshake.

Okay . . . Withdrawing his hand, Monroe pulled a small notebook from his pocket.

"You a government man?"

"No," Monroe chuckled.

"Then, why you here?"

"I'm looking for Mr. Jenkins. Do you know when he'll be back?"

"Nope," the old man answered. "Left early this morning. I yelled to him, but he didn't answer. Kind of odd. Billy always speaks. You sure you're not a government man?"

"Yes, I'm sure," Monroe laughed. "I'm an attorney."

"Lovett? Oh yeah, I heard about you. Just as bad," quipped the old man. "Billy usually stops and talks, but not today. Seemed to be in a hurry."

Monroe struggled to write down what the old man was telling him. "I'm sorry. I didn't catch your name."

"Didn't tell you. Don't know you," the old guy said, leaning on the shovel.

"I told you, I'm Monroe Lovett."

Adjusting his straw hat, the man said, "Don't mean I know you. Just your name. Means nothing to me."

Not wanting to agitate the man, Monroe asked, "Did you see anything else?"

"Nope. Now—if you're through asking me questions—I've got work to do. Something lawyers and preachers know nothing about." The old man chuckled, "Yeah, that's right, I knew was a preacher too."

"Thank you." Monroe laughed under his breath. Continuing to chuckle and waggling his head, he strolled back to his car.

Sitting in his car, Monroe replayed the day in his head from the time Ashley showed up in his office. *Something's not kosher here.*

Reaching into his briefcase, he grabbed the envelope Breaux gave him and removed its contents. It was the updated preliminary arrest report with the fingerprint analysis. He began reading. "Witness. Witness." He scanned further down the report until he reached the fingerprint information. "Two fingerprints; right thumb and index finger, found on the shotgun, blah, blah, blah, are a perfect match for Ashley Butler." He threw the report down onto the passenger seat. *Crap! I need an expert.* All he could think was how everywhere he turned he hit a brick wall.

He looked over at the report laying on the passenger's seat. He picked it up and looked at it again. Something caught his eye that he'd missed before. "Who made the 9-1-1 call?" He grabbed his phone and typed Ashley's address into the map application. Quickly backing from the drive, he hurried to the location.

Monroe made the same drive up the gravel driveway the deputies had, but no one was there when he arrived. He looked at the time. It took sixteen minutes to get there from Billy's. It was more than enough time for Ashley to do the same.

After parking, he got out, stood for a few seconds, and noticed how quiet it was. There was no road noise, no noise from neighbors. He walked toward the house. A piece of yellow crime scene tape was across the front door. Not a problem; he had no intention of going inside. The crime scene photos were enough for him. No, he wanted to figure out who might have made the call to the sheriff's office. Why would they be close enough to hear the shots? There were no open hunting seasons. It was early summer.

Removing his phone from his pocket, he opened the map program again and switched it to satellite. Trees, nothing but trees surrounded the home. The closest house was more than a mile away. "Who made that call?" he mumbled to himself. *Junior? Maybe Billy, after he shot her, he felt some sense of remorse*

Chapter 6

A dark green moss covered much of the old, weather-grayed, oak boards on the outside walls of the hunting cabin. It was small, one room, just large enough for four hunters, and hidden deep in the dense woods. Only a handful of people knew of its existence. The cabin was miles from anywhere.

A light rain fell from a passing storm cloud. It was close to midnight. Heavy clouds and a new moon, along with the density of the trees, made the cabin almost impossible to spot on such a dark night. Only those who knew of its location could find it under the current conditions. Moreover, due to its remote locale, no one would hear what was going on inside.

Three men were inside. One of them, dreadfully nervous, sat in a chair donning a thick black cloth hood over his head. His hands and ankles bound with gray duct tape. Breathing was heavy and rapid through his nose with tape wrapped around his head and face prohibiting him from breathing through his mouth or speaking. Sweat, more from fear than the heat, rolled down his face underneath the black cotton cloth.

He could hear the other two men moving, but they did not say anything. Using his best effort, he tried to ask, "Who are you?" However, his words were indistinguishable garble. Three times, he asked the same imperceptible question.

"Quiet," one of the men harshly demanded through gritted teeth.

The other man motioned, emphatically, for his co-abductor to remain quiet. He then made a cutting-like hand gesture for the first man to remove the tape from the man's mouth.

"Why?" the other mouthed.

Pointing to his watch and then to the door, he indicated a third person would be there soon.

Doing as requested, he cut the tape, releasing its pressure, allowing the hooded captor a little more freedom. After a loud inhalation, the hooded man asked, "Wh-where am I?"

No response.

With his breathing and heart rate increasing and nearing hyperventilation, he asked, "Who, who are you guys? And wh-why did you bring me here? I haven't d-done anything."

Still, there was no response from the two men. They stood in the corner waiting. Their instructions were to bring the man to the deer camp and wait. They waited, not saying anything more to him, or each other. One of the two men, the one who told him to be quiet and removed the tape, became jittery. He started pacing back and forth, as their captive continued to beg for answers. Seeing his accomplice's nervousness, the other motioned for him to calm down.

Tap-tap-tap, lightly on the door.

Walking to the door, the calm captor peeked through a window to see who was there.

"Help!" screamed the hooded man.

"I told you to keep quiet," said the jumpy one, slapping the man across his face.

"I know that voice," he responded.

Again, the edgy one slapped him. This time almost knocking him from the chair he sat in.

Unlocking the door, the more composed man allowed the newcomer to enter. A man with a dark complexion, very unshaven, and shoulder length hair entered the cabin. "What the hell's going on in here?" he asked, glaring at the nervous accomplice before grabbing a chair and sitting down. He positioned himself directly in front of the hooded man. No doubt, he was the person in charge. The other two took a position against the wall, acting as spectators.

Clearing his throat, the boss asked, "So, boy, the question is, what do I do with you?"

"Noth-nothing. Let me go. The joke's over. Ha, ha, you guys got me."

"This ain't no joke. Now, why would you do that to that girl?"

"Girl? What girl? Do what?" he asked, looking around, trying to see through the hood. But it was useless.

"You hear that boys? What girl? He won't even man up and admit he knows her." The man opened a knife. Three and a half inches of razor-sharp steel clicked and locked open. The sound of the click was unmistakable. He deliberately rubbed it over the face of his extremely frightened captive.

"P-please . . . don't hurt me," the hooded man begged. "I didn't do anything . . ."

"Didn't do anything," the man chuckled. "Oh, I think we've moved beyond hurt," he said, sliding the knife blade underneath the trembling man's upper thigh. The stainless-steel blade cut through his jeans and lacerated him just next to his crotch.

"Oomph! Oh God, please . . ." he begged, his eyes tightly shut in anticipation of the worse.

The other two watched, not speaking or doing anything. Even the fidgety man did not make a sound.

"You'd best be still, boy before you lose something," the merciless interrogator told him with a devious chuckled.

"You m-must have the w-wrong guy," the frightened man pleaded, perspiring. "Yeah. That's it. You've got the wrong man. I haven't seen you. You can take me somewhere and let me go. I won't tell, I promise."

Bending next to the kidnapped man's ear, his knife-wielding captor whispered, "Oh, I've got the right person. But, for some reason, I don't b'lieve a word you're tellin' me, boy. You know what I'm talking 'bout." A wiggle of the blade; it sliced a little deeper into the trembling thigh as he said, raising his voice, "Now tell me, how could you do that to that poor girl?"

"Ow . . ." groaned the man as he gritted his teeth. Blood began to soak his jeans. "I didn't do anything," he cried.

"I promise, before we're done, you gonna tell me what I want." He pushed the blade deeper into his leg.

"Oh . . .!" he screamed as his breathing increase with intensity. "No-no-no-no— Please . . . Please don't. Please. Please. Ple-ease . . .," the abducted man cried as blood flowed from the wound. It saturated his jeans and began to puddle in the chair beneath him. Drops of his blood began to fall to the floor as the blade dug deeper. "No . . .!" he wailed as the blade hit bone. However, he could scream and yell all he wanted. No one could hear him—no one.

Debbie woke up and noticed Monroe was not in bed. She got up and saw light coming from the living room. With a sluggish stagger, she made her way down the hall. She saw Monroe's head sticking up just above the back of the couch. She stopped. "Monroe . . ." she said softly. He didn't respond.

Louder, she called, "Monroe?" Again, there was no response. Hesitantly, she eased over to him. Debbie reached over and touched his shoulder.

He jumped. "What?" he said, spinning around.

Debbie hopped back. "Oh!" She grabbed the top of her chest. "You scared me."

"Scared you?" He tried to catch his breath. "I must've fallen asleep." He was awake now.

"Why are you in here?"

"Couldn't sleep. I got up and came—trying to clear my head."

Debbie walked around the couch and sat down next to him. "The case?" she asked, pulling her feet under her.

"No. Our finances . . . Wondering if I am cut out to defend this girl," Monroe said, running his fingers through his hair. "I don't know, maybe I'm out of my league. Too many years away from—"

"Honey, the Brooks told us we could stay here rent free for as long as we need. And you *do* know what you're doing."

Monroe slowly pulled his hands down over his face. He looked over at Debbie and said, "But, the first case I get, my client doesn't have any money. I'm not even sure—"

"Yes. But, she is a client. The money will come. And, we've still got money in the bank."

"But—*this* girl—she needs a better attorney. A better attorney than me."

"Blah, blah, blah. Well, you should've made that decision before we made this move. All I heard from you was, 'How great it would be to defend people who need help.' Well, here's your chance. God answered your prayer."

"I know. I know . . . And there's—"

"And there's nothing." She leaned over and grabbed Monroe's hand. "You worry too much, sweetie."

"Debbie, I'm not even sure she's innocent anymore," he said, leaning back, turning to look at Debbie.

"Why do you say that?"

"I can't say. If I'm wrong about her, then, well . . . I'm not sure if this, this whole situation, the case, the practice, everything, is going to work."

"It's going to be fine."

"But if she's innocent . . . and I mess up, losing this case, they will put a needle in Ashley's arm. I don't know if I can live with that."

Debbie squeezed Monroe's hand. "This will work. Trust God. He believes in your ability, or he wouldn't have brought you here. Honey, I believe in you."

"Do you?"

"Yes."

"You're just saying that to make me feel better."

"No, I'm not."

Monroe exhaled. Looking at Debbie, he whined, "Do you know the judge told me to wear more appropriate clothes?"

"You poor thing," she said with a slight frown and pouty lips. "I'll take care of that for you. We'll show that mean ole judge.

Chapter 7

Friday morning Peregrine started to show signs of life as people began moving about on the very warm and humid Mississippi morning. The previous night's rain and clouds were gone, replaced by hot sunshine. Steam rose from the ground as the rainwater evaporated, making it feel sticky. In summer, even the concrete sweats—everything sweats. Your shirt sticks to your back, and you struggle to breathe. It's summer in the Deep South.

Sheriff Austin was having his usual cup of coffee at the local combination gas station/convenience store/hole-in-the-wall on the edge of town. Just as he lifted the hot java to his mouth, a call blasted from the radio handset clipped to his shirt epaulet, "Dispatch to Sheriff Austin. Copy?"

Sheriff Austin almost spilled the steaming hot liquid. He sat the cup down. "What now?" he mumbled. Pressing the button on his radio mike, he responded, "This is Austin. Go ahead."

"Sheriff, we've got a 10-79 near the old Johnson cutoff on County Road 156."

"Can't Detective Carson handle it?"

"He's the one who requested you. It's another possible 10-76, Sheriff."

Austin jumped up, tossed the coffee in the trashcan, and then trotted to his patrol car. *Great. All I need is another murder.* Other patrons sitting inside overheard the call. They wondered what those codes meant. They figured it must have been bad, since the sheriff left in such haste.

No siren blaring, just flashing blue grill lights, Austin raced down the back roads until he arrived at Carson's location. Austin was the newly elected Lane County Sheriff promising to keep the citizens safe. Now, he wondered how two murders in a matter of days would play on the minds of the people. Only four months on the job, and this was not a good start.

Two other deputies along with Carson were already on the scene when Austin arrived. The slightly podgy sheriff threw the car in park and bounded from his car. He asked Carson, "Why didn't I hear the call go out on this? Who's running—?"

"It came early, Sheriff. Everyone thought it was a simple 'drunk passed out' call until Deputy Reed and his rookie arrived. Reed called me. You know, not to rouse anyone. Too many people listen to their scanners and report everything that happens."

"Okay," Austin agreed as he took a deep breath. "The last thing we need right now is the local gossip society spreading rumors."

"Anyway, I called dispatch when I saw what—well, you can see for yourself," Carson said, pointing with his thumb over his shoulder in the direction of the crime scene.

"See what?"

"It's bad. Really bad," Carson said as both men walked toward the scene.

Reed was standing with his back to the ditch several feet behind him. He had his hand over his nose and mouth. Austin saw the look on Reed's face. It told him whatever was in that ditch was not something he wanted to see. Deputy Reed saw Austin. "It's bad, Sheriff. Really bad."

"Yeah, that's what I've been told. What is it that's so bad?" Austin looked around. "Where's your rookie?"

"Over there throwing up his breakfast," Reed said, pointing in the direction of a small stand of trees on the opposite side of the road. "Sheriff, I don't know how I catch these cases," Reed choked out, allowing Austin to get a look.

Just then, the stench smacked Austin. "Oh, that . . . that . . ." he choked as he reached into his back pocket and removed a handkerchief. Placing it over his nose, he leaned over close to Reed, whispering, "You should've called me first, deputy. Now, what's the cause of that smell?"

Carson overheard Austin and smirked disrespectfully behind Austin's back. The two had a recent past. Both had run for sheriff, and Austin won. Carson saw it as a rejection by his community. In his mind, the people had turned him down, a slap in the face. It still stuck in his craw. Austin may be his boss, but he did not like the man, purely because he saw Austin as taking his rightful job.

"Sorry, Sheriff. It won't happen again," Reed said. He then stepped aside for Austin to get a look below. "It's down there," he said, gesturing into the ditch.

Austin looked at both Carson and Reed, but primarily at Carson. "I know I'm still new around here, but I expect to be called first on something like this. Got it?" They both nodded yes. Being a non-local was not easy for Austin, but he was more than qualified to run the Lane County Sheriff's Department. Eighteen years of experience in a large city prepared him. Austin and his wife moved to Lane County for the rural life. It was a quiet county situated in a heavily wooded part of Mississippi and with very little crime.

Austin took a few steps toward the deep trench. Before he saw the scene, the stench penetrated his handkerchief. "Oh, my . . ." he said, turning his head, the odor strangling him. He worked to catch his breath, coughing several times, as did Carson and Reed.

"I warned you," Carson said, with his hand covering his nose.

Peering down into the ditch, Austin saw the smoldering remains of a body. Snapping his head back, he asked, "Do we know—?"

"No," Carson answered.

"Oh . . ." Austin coughed. "Let's move back so we can talk," Austin told Carson, still choking. Reed took it he too could move to a better spot, away from the smoldering flesh. Moving several feet away, Austin asked, "Have you called the M.E.?"

"She's on her way," Carson answered as he looked at the time on his phone. "It's been about ten minutes."

The sound of a vehicle coming down the road got their attention. "There she is," Austin said, seeing the van.

After the van had stopped, Carson walked up and warned Dr. Stevens about the scene. Somehow, Carson felt that seeing a charred body would bother the female examiner. She just put up with the detective, usually ignoring him. Stevens got a whiff of the smell and grabbed a medical mask from her van.

Deputy Reed turned to his pallid partner, who had returned, but still feeling a little queasy, and told him under his breath, "I always like when Dr. Stevens shows up."

"I bet your wife doesn't agree," the rookie replied.

"You're so funny, rookie. But, if you knew anything, you would know I'm single. Never married."

"You know, I do have a name. Chad Watters. You can call me Deputy Watters, or even Chad."

"Rookie's good enough for now," Reed replied as he moved back a couple of feet. "Your breath smells like vomit."

Watters smirked, ignoring Reed's last remark. He knew he was only trying to get under his skin. He gestured with his head in Stevens's direction and said, "She's a doctor, you know. And you're a—"

"A what? A little ole deputy. So, what are you saying?" Reed asked, his eyes remaining glued on Stevens.

"She's out of your league. A doctor. Educated. And she's a former homecoming queen. Good luck, lover-boy."

"I'll have you know I have a bachelor's in criminal justice, you dimwit," Reed said sarcastically and then returned to appreciating the curvaceous doctor. "I put her at five feet and nine, or maybe ten inches. I like 'em tall."

"But, you're only, what, five nine?"

"Five ten. And so?" Reed said without taking his eyes off Stevens. "Look at how her black hair drapes over her shoulders. And those blue eyes. I could stare into those—"

"Man, there's something seriously wrong with you," Watters said.

Dr. Stevens walked over to Austin. Pulling the mask away from her face, she asked, "Where's my body, Sheriff?"

"Doc, it's not pretty," Austin warned, pointing toward the ditch.

"Never mind. I can follow my nose." She headed straight to the body. Walking toward Reed, she said, "Getting a good look, Deputy Reed?"

"No. I mean . . . I was just—" stammered Reed with an embarrassed look painted across his face.

She laughed.

Struggling to regain his composure, Reed said, "Over here, Doc."

After inching her way down to the body, she yelled, "Appears to be a male." She took care to get a close look at the victim's face. "But I can't tell who it is by looking. The face has been badly burned. Looks like someone took a knife or something to his face, too. We'll need dental records and DNA to make a positive ID." Dr. Stevens motioned for her two assistants, telling them, "Bring a bag." Standing up, she started to climb back up and out of the ditch. Her foot slipped, and she just about fell onto the burnt cadaver. After catching herself, she extended her hand up and asked, "Deputy Reed, can you give me a hand?"

"Yeah, sure," he said, clutching her hand. He pulled her up. "There you go." Stevens stopped about three inches from Reed. He gazed into her blue eyes as she removed the mask.

"You can let go now," she said with a playful smile.

"Oh. Sorry."

"Don't be," she told him, and then walked back over to Austin and Carson.

Reed stood there with a silly grin on his face.

"Huh, maybe I was wrong," Watters said.

When Dr. Stevens reached Sheriff Austin, he asked, "How long?"

"Give me a few days. Could be weeks or more. The body's burnt badly. It will affect the time of death. I'll need the state lab to run some tests."

"Call me when you get *something*, Doc," Austin said as the two techs placed the body in the van.

Removing her gloves, she said to Austin, "Right now, all I've got is a burnt dead body–male."

"Okay. Got it," Austin replied.

"If there's nothing else, Sheriff?" she asked.

"No. That's all I have. You call forensics?" Austin asked Carson.

"Yeah. I gave Barnes a call," he answered. "Should be here soon."

Dr. Stevens got back in her van and pulled away. Austin turned to Carson and told him, "Find out who did this, Ben."

"I'll do my best, Sheriff. But we still have the Miller case."

"That's in the hands of the lawyers now," Austin said. He gave Carson an intent stare and told him, "You deal with this one. You hear me? And keep me in the loop."

"Yeah, Sheriff, I hear you," Carson replied.

Austin walked back to his car in a huff, muttering to himself, "Two freaking murders in one week. There haven't been two murders around here in years. Now, this. What in God's name is going on?" Austin knew people and county leaders would be asking those same questions. In the back of his mind was job security. He opened his car door and yelled back to Carson, "Find out who did this."

Carson acknowledged him with a slight wave while muttering, "You're in the loop.

Chapter 8

Immersed in deep thought, pondering his best defense strategy, Monroe is startled when Debbie knocked on his office door. "What?" he hollered. He needed the time to work on his case, not deal with interruptions.

She pushed the door open and then rushed to one of the chairs across from him. Plopping down, wide-eyed, with a look of having the latest word on the street, excitedly asked, "Have you heard?"

"Heard what? I've been here all morning. I haven't heard anything," Monroe responded somewhat displeased by the intrusion.

"They found another body this morning."

Now his displeasure turned to curiosity. "Who found?"

"Sheriff's deputies. And get this—it was burnt to – a – crisp," she said, making a yuck-face.

Sure enough, this intrigued Monroe. "I wonder who—?"

"Don't know. No one does. But it's the talk of the town."

"How did *you* come to hear about it?" Monroe asked with curiosity. "You sure it's not just some gossip?"

"Yes, I'm sure." She pointed in the direction of the coffee shop. "I heard it downstairs in Christi's. Everybody knows about it."

"Oh, well, that makes it legit," he said with a cynical smirk and a roll of his eyes.

"Would you listen before giving your *authoritative* decision?" Debbie popped, giving Monroe an angry-face.

Monroe assumed an interested posture. He leaned back in his chair, crossed his legs, and interlaced his fingers just below his chin. To ensure Debbie believed he looked interested, he even squinted his eyes a little while making a serious expression.

Ignoring his antics, which were nothing new to her, she said, "From what I heard, Deputy Reed, he's the short thin, but not too short, just shorter than you, but not real thin, deputy that came in here to arrest Ashley. I'm sure you remember him. You know, he did all the talking." Monroe fought to keep a straight face. "Well, he came in to get some coffee down in Christi's, and a muffin. Blueberry I think, or was it—?"

Monroe's patience was growing thin. He snapped his fingers and said, "Debbie. Stay focused, babe."

Debbie raised her right eyebrow and shot him a look. He'd seen it before and just waited for her to continue. She did, telling him, "Well anyway, Reed told a few people in the coffee shop downstairs they found a body, all burnt."

"And?" he asked, holding his hands out and his palms up.

"Make up your mind. Do you want the short version or the long version?"

Frustrated, Monroe clenched his jaw and glared at his wife. Using a slow diction, he told her, "I want the significant details, not a list of what he ordered."

Debbie began to give him the pertinent details, telling him everything Reed had spilled to the inquisitive crowd downstairs. "And, that's it. They're waiting on the coroner's report."

"Interesting."

"That's all you've got to say? Interesting?"

"Yes," Monroe answered with a slight shrug.

Debbie, thinking he would want to discuss it more or even offer his own conjecture, felt flustered by Monroe's lack of curiosity. However, he had issues that are more pressing. She popped to her feet and made a hasty return to her desk. He chuckled at her exaggerated body language as he watched her leave.

With this new bit of information, he found it hard to refocus as the gears in his head started to turn. He thought aloud, "I wonder if this has anything to do with my case? And, if so, how? It's time to do a little snooping around downstairs."

Passing by Debbie's desks, he said, "I'm going to get a cup of coffee."

Pointing to a half-full coffee pot sitting in the corner, she said, "We've got coffee—"

"Not the same."

"You're gonna go nose around, aren't you?" she asked with a laugh.

He didn't respond. Debbie watched the door close and said under her breath, "He ain't fooling no one."

Hoping to get the latest scuttlebutt, Monroe walked into Christi's. A quick scan for a familiar face, he didn't see anyone. *Somebody's . . . got to . . .* he thought as he re-surveyed the room again. Only two people were in the coffee house. Sitting in the corner was an elderly couple looking to be in their eighties. *I doubt they know anything.*

With his balloon deflated, Monroe ordered a cup of coffee at the counter and sat down in the booth next to a window overlooking the town square. He took a sip of the black java as he tried to clear his mind. *Just stick to your case, Monroe. Just stick with your case.*

"Morning," a man said from over Monroe's shoulder.

Monroe turned but did not recognize the face behind the voice. "May I help you?"

"No. But I may be able to help you," the stranger informed. Pointing to the opposite side of the booth he asked, "May I join you, Mr. Lovett?"

Reluctantly Monroe said, "Sure. I guess."

The man sat down as Monroe studied him. "Hot today, isn't it?" the man asked.

"Yes. It is."

"They say it's going to get even hotter over the next few days."

"Did you come over here to give me a weather report?"

"No. Just making small talk."

"I'm not looking for small talk, Mister—. What is your name, by the way?"

"Hermann, Ed Hermann. But, you can call me Herm."

"Well, Mr. Hermann."

"Herm."

"Well, Herm, you said you can help me," Monroe said, unsure who this man was and why he just showed up. One thing he learned over the years was to be careful whom you trust; especially, when they say they can help you. Usually, an all-too-friendly stranger's advice is not advice, but a warning in disguise. Monroe thought, *Listen cautiously to the man. Keep your guard up and defenses in place.* Monroe sat his coffee down. "Okay, speak."

"Your client's innocent," Herm said, taking a sip of his ice-cold sweet tea.

"And, you know this how?"

"Got a gut feeling."

"Sorry, Mr.—Herm—but your gut feeling is not allowed as evidence in court. Do you have any real evidence?"

"I know. And no, I don't. At least not at the moment. You're going to have to trust me," Herm said, taking another drink from his glass of tea.

"Trust you? Why? I don't even know you," Monroe flippantly said.

"I love the way Christi brews her tea. I need to ask her what brand this is." Herm sat the glass on the table. "I just don't believe the girl has the moxie, you know, the ability to kill."

Monroe studied Herm trying to figure out his angle. His own gut said the man seemed okay. He'd been wrong before, and this was no time to be wrong. He decided to proceed cautiously, feel Herm out. "Either the husband, Marcus Jr. or Billy Jenkins did it," Monroe replied with confidence.

"Even if Junior did it, he's got an airtight alibi." Herm thought for a moment. "But the Jenkins kid . . .?"

"What's Junior's alibi?" Monroe asked, now a little more interested. Then he stopped himself. "Wait. Why am I even talking about this with you?"

"Jenkins, huh? Believe me, Junior will have an alibi." Herm took another drink of his tea. He knew Monroe would be guarded. "Because you know I can help you."

"And where or who is this coming from? How do I know you weren't sent here to throw me off?"

"As I said, you've got to trust me."

"I heard you the first time. Are we even having the same conversation?" Monroe asked, sitting there, still sizing up Herm. The word 'alibi' kept floating around in his head. "So, how tight is Junior's alibi?"

"Umm . . ." Herm said with a back and forth wave of his hand, indicating it was so-so.

"Not airtight, then?"

"See, we are having the same conversation," Herm said, swirling his ice tea. "I'm telling you, my instinct is telling me—"

"As I said, your gut, instinct, or whatever you want to call it, isn't evidence. Nor is any made-up alibi for Marcus Jr. Plus, there's a problem, she—"

"She signed a confession. I know."

"Then he does have an alibi—her confession? But it's not good enough," Monroe said.

"Yeah, but—"

"But nothing."

"Let me finish. I should've worded it better. He *will* have an airtight alibi. I know his family and friends well enough. The confession is only part of it. You see, by the time you get to court, Junior, well, he will have been in the Arctic, or Africa, or who knows where for all of that week, no matter what they're saying now."

"Half of the sheriff's deputies saw him the morning of—"

"Won't matter. Believe me."

"Then, who? Who do you think did it?" Monroe asked, growing a little annoyed at what appeared to be a cat and mouse game by Herm.

"Not sure yet. That's why I'm here. To help you."

Leaning forward across the table, Monroe said in a lowered voice so no one could hear him, "You're telling me I'm wrong, but you haven't a clue who did it? How is this helping me?"

"Yep. You pretty much got it."

Monroe leaned back and looked out the window. "At this moment, I think you're the town nut. Is that it? Or did Breaux send you to mess with me? Well, you can tell him, or whomever, I'm not playing the game."

"No, it's nothing like that," Herm answered with a chuckle. "I promise, what I have to offer will be an asset for you. And, as for Robert Breaux, I don't trust the man. Now, we need to get to work on our case."

"We? Our?" Monroe asked, chuckling and becoming more irritated. "You seem pretty confident. I'm even more convinced that you're crazy."

"Because I trust you, Mr. Lovett." Herm finished the last of his tea as the ice rattled in the glass.

"What is your background? You some wanna-be private-eye, or something?" Before Herm could answer, Monroe's cell phone rang. He looked at the screen, saw it was Debbie, and said, "I need to take this."

Herm stood up and said, "I'll be in touch. I look forward to working with you."

Then, he started walking away.

"I'm not looking for a partner," Monroe said, covering the phone as he watched Herm depart. "I said, I'm not—" *Who does he think he is?* Lifting his cup of coffee, he took a sip. "Oh, that's cold."

"What's cold?" Debbie asked.

"Nothing. Look, we'll talk later, okay? There's something I need to do right now."

"Okay," Debbie replied and then hung up.

After reflecting briefly on his conversation with Herm, Monroe decided to go outside to find him, or at least see where he went. He still had questions for Herm. On the sidewalk, he scanned the area. He didn't see Herm anywhere. It was as if the man had vanished. From behind Monroe, Jack rounded the corner of the building carrying his tool bag, almost running into Monroe.

"Mr. Lovett. How's you doing, sir?" Jack asked with his signature smile.

"I'm fine, Jack," Monroe answered. He was more interested in trying to spot Herm.

"You looking for someone, Mr. Lovett?"

"Yes. A man named Ed Hermann. Goes by Herm." By now, Monroe was even more curious who this stranger was.

"Oh, Mr. Hermann. Nice man."

"Do you know him?" Monroe asked, continuing to look for where he went. *Maybe he might drive by,* Monroe thought as he looked around. However, he didn't see him.

"Just see him around town every occasionally. Nice man."

"Yeah, you said that. Is he from here?"

"Was from here. Moved away. Now moved back, not that long ago. He stays in an apartment above the hardware store. But he doesn't stays there much, though. He leaves early and comes home late. Not sure where he goes, though."

"And you know all this, how?"

"Cause I'm in the hardware store alls the time, Mr. Lovett. The owner tells me everything that happens there. But, that's all I know 'bout Mr. Herm. He keeps to himself."

"Thanks, Jack," Monroe said with a pat on Jack's shoulder. He turned to head back upstairs. "Later, Jack."

"You have a good day, Mr. Lovett," Jack said, and then went about his business.

"Yeah, you too," Monroe said, walking back in the building. Taking his time walking up the steps he wondered who this Herm was. *Why would he show up offering his assistance? Why now? Seemed fishy, too fishy.* Monroe decided to speak with Sheriff Austin about him.

Chapter 9

After repeated efforts to track down Sheriff Austin, Monroe spotted a black Dodge Charger parked outside the building of the Prosecutor's office on the opposite side of the town square from his own. The words Lane County Sheriff stenciled in dark gold on the rear fender were the giveaway. All the other patrol cars had full markings and overhead lights.

Inside the building, the cool air was refreshing. The morning heat had given way to just simply hot. A simple black plastic sign with white lettering had District Attorney's Office on it, with an arrow pointing upstairs. Monroe trotted up the gray rubber covered steps. Reaching the top, he scanned the hallway for the correct door. "There it is," he muttered, spotting a door on his right, Breaux's name conspicuously painted on the clouded glass inlay of the door.

As he entered, a woman in her early thirties greeted him, "Hello. May I help you?"

"I'm Monroe Lovett. I need to see Mr. Breaux."

"I was just getting ready to call you, Mr. Lovett," she replied, holding the phone's handset.

"Well, here I am. I'm psychic, you know."

She didn't crack a smile.

I guess you don't, he thought as he stood there with a blank look on his face.

She placed the telephone handset back in its cradle. "Mr. Breaux needs to speak with you. He and Sheriff Austin are waiting." Getting up from behind her desk, she motioned for Monroe to follow as she told him to do so. He followed her down the short hall, looking around at the other offices. All he could think now was how it must be nice to have assistants in addition to local law enforcement to prepare a case. Breaux's secretary tapped on the door, showed him in, and then closed the door after leaving.

Sheriff Austin was sitting on a dark green leather couch to Monroe's left. Breaux stood between his black leather desk chair and a walnut executive desk. He was holding several sheets of paper.

With its dark blue carpet, beige painted walls covered with Breaux's diplomas and accomplishments, and walnut shelves, the office screamed, "Look at me!" One shelf specifically caught Monroe's eye. It was devoted to several pictures of Breaux's family. He sensed Austin and Breaux seemed troubled by his visit.

Breaux disregarded all pleasantries. Straight to the point, he said, "Mr. Lovett, please have a seat." He gestured to a chair across from himself.

Monroe did as requested. "Your secretary said you wanted to see me."

"Yes. I'll let Sheriff Austin fill you in," Breaux said, signaling for Austin to proceed.

"Mr. Lovett, I thought we might meet under more pleasant circumstances," Austin said as he opened a folder and removed a document.

"Me, too."

"Here," Austin said, handing the document to Monroe.

"What's this?"

"It's a preliminary report on a call we got this morning."

"The burnt body?"

"News travels fast," Breaux said.

"It was the latest in Christi's," Monroe said, looking up at the prosecutor. "At least, that's what I heard."

"Reed," Austin said, pressing his lips together. He knew it didn't really matter who let the news out; someone would have leaked eventually. "Anyway, while we're still awaiting the coroner's official report, we found a wallet with a driver's license near the body. It was also burnt, but we were able to make out the name."

Monroe quickly scanned the report as Austin spoke. Before Austin could tell him the name on the license, Monroe blurted out, "William Jenkins? That was Billy Jenkins they found?" Ashley's leading alibi just showing up dead was not the kind of news he wanted to hear. Monroe's heart sank. A lump swelled in his throat. The sudden feeling of doom overcame him as he stared at Jenkins's name. This meant he had to rethink his theory. How would he convince a jury that Jenkins committed the murder, and Ashley didn't?

"Yes, we believe so," Austin answered.

"Mr. Lovett, I knew Jenkins was someone you wanted to speak with about your case. That's why I requested for you to be told the news firsthand," Breaux said.

"Yeah, I, I went out to see him after the hearing yesterday, but he wasn't there," Monroe said. Mystified, he sat, fixated on Jenkins's name. "The old man next door told me he hadn't seen Billy. Well, I take that back. He told me he saw him—" Then he looked up at Breaux and asked, "How did you know I wanted to speak with Jenkins?"

"The old man, his neighbor, called me," Austin answered. "Welcome to a small town. People get a bit nosy. Told me you were out snooping around."

"I know this almost certainly puts a big hole in your defense, Mr. Lovett," Breaux said with a bit of arrogance. "Now, I'm not going to ask for your decision now, but I think we both know where your case stands now."

"What do you mean?" Monroe asked. In his mind, he was already beginning to reevaluate his strategy. He still had a case. He just needed to figure out what it was. The gears were already turning as he began postulating why, why kill this guy? If he could figure out the "why" for Jenkins's death, then he might have the answer for Ashley's acquittal. Of course, he recognized this wouldn't be easy.

"Mrs. Butler's signed confession for one." Smugly, Breaux said, "Man one, with minimum sentencing. I assure you, I'll try to get her into the best—"

"No," Monroe adamantly insisted with a furrowed brow. Everyone seemed all too quick to convict Ashley. This did not sit well with Monroe. Striving to restrain his anger, he glared at Breaux. "Who do you work for, the Butler family or the people?"

"I won't dignify that question with an answer," Breaux retorted. "As I said, we know where your case stands."

"No," Monroe said, pointing at Breaux. "*We* don't. As I see it, no different than it did before."

Sheriff Austin took the role of spectator as the two attorneys went at each other.

Breaux fired back, "If you want to go to trial, then fine by me. I was just offering."

"Thanks for the *offer*," Monroe said sarcastically.

Both men realized they were getting a little too heated and each settled their emotions. Austin chuckled, "This was just getting good." Neither one responded to his wisecrack.

"Take some time. Think it over. Talk it over with your client," Breaux said, sitting down.

Monroe knew the real meaning behind Breaux's offer. He'd met plenty of 'Breauxs' over the years. He was a prosecutor, and all he wanted was a conviction. A conviction would pad his résumé and help him climb the political ladder. Of course, an acquittal would help his own reputation. "I actually came here for another reason," he said, wanting to dodge any further discussion about the case and deals.

"What's that?" Breaux asked, grabbing a cigar from his humidor. "Cigar?" He offered one to Monroe. "They're some of the best."

Monroe looked at Breaux and said, "Government building," indicating their location with his finger.

"I open the window. No one suspects a thing," Breaux chortled.

Tired of Breaux's arrogance, Monroe turned his attention to Austin and asked him, "What do you know about Ed Hermann, Sheriff?"

"Retired police detective from New Orleans. Met him a few weeks ago. Told me his family is from here."

"Grew up here. Sold the family home several years ago," Breaux said.

Austin continued, "He rents a place above the hardware store. Why do you ask?"

"Just wondering," Monroe answered nonchalantly. "Ran into him earlier."

"As far as I know, he's a good man," Austin said. "He's a former cop. Can't dislike that."

Monroe held up the preliminary report detailing the findings of the body found earlier and asked, "Can I keep this?"

"Sure, I'll keep you updated if anything changes," Austin told him.

"Thanks," Monroe said, standing up.

"Monroe," Breaux said.

"Yeah?"

"You know, we're not enemies here."

"Enemies? Not sure, yet. Opponents? Yes." He walked to the door. "Thank you, gentlemen," he said, leaving. He then stepped back into the office.

"Forget something?" Breaux asked.

"Yeah, who allowed Mrs. Butler to sign a confession without me being consulted?" Monroe asked. He thought he might do a little fishing and perhaps get a bite.

Breaux, with a wily smirk, replied, "Check the report I gave you." He motioned toward Monroe holding the cigar in his one hand and a lighter in the other. "I believe you'll see her signed attorney waiver."

"You're railroading my client," Monroe said, departing. He walked past the secretary's desk, telling her, "You have a nice day?"

"Thanks," she replied. "He offered you a cigar?"

Monroe stopped and answered, "Yes. How'd you know?" Monroe pointed to Breaux's office. "He said—"

"He thinks nobody knows," she said, rolling her eyes. "But, just so you know, when he offers you one of his expensive cigars, it means he believes he's won the case."

"Well, he can believe all he wants. Have a good day," Monroe said, leaving.

With Monroe gone, Breaux looked at Sheriff Austin and told him, "Mr. Lovett's case is over. He'll realize it. He'll see it." Breaux chuckled as he lit the cigar, relishing in his supposed easy victory. "Chalk up another win."

"You know, I wouldn't count my chickens just yet," Austin gibed.

"What do you mean, Sheriff?"

"He's not going to roll over just because you tell him to. The man's a bulldog. I've seen that look before."

"Well, maybe someone needs to explain the rules, put a leash on the dog. Convey to him how things work around here." Breaux pointed at Austin, making a sweeping motion with the hand holding the cigar that ended with him pointing at the door. "Maybe you can take care of it."

"I don't work for you," Austin retorted.

"Funny, Sheriff. Real funny." Breaux opened his window, waving his hand, trying to get the smoke out.

Austin rose to his feet. "Maybe your days of being king of the hill are coming to an end. You can explain whatever rules you want to explain to yourself." He walked to the door. "I've got to get out of here before I get lung cancer." Before leaving, he glanced back and said to Breaux as he pointed to the preliminary M. E.'s report, "Looks like you've got a new case, *Mr. DA*."

Breaux sneered as Austin left. He took a long draw from the cigar. *We'll see who the big dog is.*

Taking his time, the defense attorney strolled back to his office. Too much was on his mind for him to notice the hot, muggy, heavy air. Monroe contemplated his next move. One thing stuck in his mind—the signed confession. *How do I get past it?*

After his protracted trek and slow climb up the stairs, Monroe emerged at the top of the staircase and entered the office. His inner deliberation was evident.

"You okay?" Debbie asked, seeing him.

"Yeah. Yeah, sure. I'm fine."

She didn't believe him but knew better than to ask. He wouldn't tell her anything, no matter how much she persisted. Instead, she grabbed a small, white, postal box on her desk, she handed it to him. "Here."

"What's this?" Monroe asked, looking at it. Another surprise was not something he was looking for now, especially if it was bad news.

Giddy and almost bouncing out of her chair, she said, "Look inside. It'll cheer you up."

Monroe peaked into the box. He held the box away to get a better view inside. Its contents stunned him. He looked at the address on the front. It read, 101 Poplar St. "Who sent this?" he asked, puzzled by what he saw.

"According to the label, I guess we did," Debbie answered, smiling big. She didn't care who sent the package because the contents thrilled her.

"I can see that," he replied skeptically. "But I know we didn't send this to ourselves."

"It's twenty—thousand—dollars," she said, electrified and still overtly excited. "There's a letter. More like a note."

"Calm down," he said. Monroe reached into the box and removed the ten bundles of $20 bills. Each bundle had the standard violet-colored banking strap around it. Nothing seemed odd, except for the fact he was holding it. Stupefied, he removed the sheet of paper and placed the twenty-grand back into the box. He read aloud, "Dear Mr. Lovett, This should cover your expenses to defend Ashley Butler." He flipped the piece of paper over, but there was nothing else, no name nor signature. He looked at Debbie, "I wonder who—?"

"Who cares!" she said in a loud whisper and with a big smile.

"Well, I'll keep the note. You take the money to the bank."

"All of it?" she asked wide-eyed. She was hoping Monroe would let her spend some of it. Possibly, he would tell her to go shopping, buy something for herself.

"Yes. All of it," Monroe said. "Then again, maybe I should—"

"You don't trust me?"

"Yeah, I trust you," he said, looking at the note again. He started to walk to his office, but suddenly spun back around to Debbie's desk. Leaning over, he opened the bottom drawer of her desk and removed the new bank bag, the kind with a locking zipper. This was the first time they had needed it. Debbie watched as he took the money from the box and placed it in the bag. He filled out a deposit slip, writing $20,000 in the line for cash. Then he placed the deposit slip inside the bag and locked it.

"You don't trust me, do you?" Debbie asked, making a sad puppy-dog like face. If her lower lip pouched out any further, Monroe would trip over it.

He fought laughing at her. "No, it's not that," Monroe said. He held the box up. "I want to keep this box." With the bag locked, he held it up with the twenty-grand inside. Shaking it a little, he said, "Somebody knows who sent this money and I want to know who."

"Who cares? Monroe, this is from God."

"I'm not sure about that. Sometimes what appears to be from God is from the devil himself. I'll hold off judgment until later." Too many weird things were happening at once for Monroe's comfort. Herm popped up offering to help. His key alibi for Ashley was dead. Now, money was appearing from an unknown source. If anything, Monroe's radar was on high alert.

"Well, then we'll take the *devil's* money and use it for good," Debbie said, taking the money bag from Monroe.

Monroe chuckled at her persistence, bent over, and kissed Debbie's forehead. "Always looking for the silver lining. That's why I love you, baby."

He placed the letter back into the box and the moneybag key in his pocket, and then told her, "Now, go make the deposit."

"I saw that," Debbie said, referring to the key. "How will they get the money out at the bank?"

"They have a key at the bank."

"Huh!" she huffed. "Monroe, you don't trust me."

"With that much money. No." He turned to walk to his office. "Now go."

Chapter 10

"Why was the body left on the side of the road for just anybody to find?" Marcus Butler Sr. yelled. He paced, flashing angry glances at the two men there with him. "Why did you kill him?" He stopped and glowered at the two men. Things were getting out of hand in his mind. "Why do such a thing? . . . Idiots!"

The three men were in a vacant office building. One of Butler's failed enterprises once occupied the empty structure. Being located down a small gravel road made the place an ideal meeting spot. Five old chairs and a beat-up metal desk were the only pieces of furniture in the dilapidated concrete block building.

"Sir?" asked one of Butler's gofers, apparently confused by the rant. So was the other man.

"Kill him? Why?" Butler asked as he resumed his pacing.

Both men were more afraid of the overbearing Butler than respectful of him. "Kill who?" the other underling asked.

"And burn him?" Butler roared. Stopping in his tracks, he stared down the men. "What were you two . . . thinking?" he asked with a dramatic wave of his arm.

"Mr. Butler, we didn't kill nobody," both claimed, puzzled looks on their faces.

Butler huffed as he scrutinized them. "I said . . . talk to him."

Ring . . . Ring . . . Butler checked his phone. It was a missed call from Junior.

"Mr. Butler, we didn't—"

"Hold on," Butler snapped. He tried to call back, but no one answered. He muttered, "Must have lost his signal."

The building's door swung open.

Butler whirled around.

Joe Galliard, the fourth person invited to this little secretive summit, entered. "Joe," Butler exclaimed, "What were you thinking? You said you were just going to ask some questions."

"I did," Galliard said, stepping into the office. "I was doing what Mr. Roueché told me to do." He took the final drag from his cigarette, flicked it back through the doorway, and then shut the door behind him.

"Kill him? Kill him?" Butler demanded.

Still shaking in their boots, the two men with Butler looked at each other. They were used to doing Butler's dirty work, occasionally putting pressure on someone, but nothing ever involved serious criminal activity. However, hearing of someone killed made the two men feel queasy.

"Look, the boy's dead," Galliard said, blowing smoke from his nostrils. "Ain't nothing we can do 'bout it now," Galliard chuckled as he walked across the room, smirking at the two pawns. He could see their faces drained of color.

Sweating, fearful, and ready to piss their pants, the two lackeys swallowed hard as they watched Galliard.

"But why involve these two?" Butler asked, pointing at them.

"Who? These two chuckleheads?" Galliard said, laughing. He snarled at them, just to watch them flinch. They did. "Naw, they weren't with me. I use professionals, not, not—what do you call pups like these two?"

Butler angrily stomped over to Galliard. Galliard was unfazed. With his jaw clenched tightly, a livid Butler said, "I—didn't—tell you . . . to *kill* anybody."

Galliard laughed in Butler's face. "I don't take orders from you, you hear me? You're lucky that— Don't matter now, like I said, it's done."

Butler's scowl said, "Drop dead." Discretion told him to back down. Circumstances were already worse than he desired. He walked over to the rickety old desk. A piece of rebar was laying on it. He seized it and bobbled it a few times in his hand as if he were trying to get a better grip. His discretion gave way to hostility.

Wham!

Butler struck the desk in his anger. His two puppets jumped. Galliard didn't blink. He simply looked at the exasperated man. Calming Butler was essential for Galliard. The last thing he wanted was for the large man to decide to use the piece of steel to hit someone, to hit him. Galliard put his hands up motioning for Butler to settle down as he explained, "Look, he saw me. B'lieve me, I did what needed to be done. Okay. Relax."

Butler took a deep breath and chunked the piece of rebar to the floor. It rolled over next to Galliard's foot. Galliard looked down at the piece of steel. He put his foot on top of it. He looked up at Butler acutely and said, "And understand this, I work for Mr. Roueché, not you." With a disdained chuckle, he said, "The boy was a liability. And Mr. Roueché doesn't like liabilities."

Butler glanced at the rebar under Galliard's foot. He also noticed a slight bulge under Galliard's shirt, the shape of a pistol. "Fine. It's done."

Galliard kicked the piece of rebar over to the wall and sat down in a chair sitting in the corner of the room, a few feet behind him. Reaching inside the top of his boot, he removed a pack of cigarettes. He removed one, lit it, took a long drag, and slowly exhaled the smoke.

Butler sat down across the room from him. He leaned forward and said, "Joe, this complicates matters."

"How?" he asked smugly. "Nothing's changed."

"My boy? Marcus Jr.?"

"What about him?"

"How is he? I haven't heard from him. His mother's worried."

"Don't worry about him. He hasn't called me either. He's smart. He's staying out of sight."

Butler watched Galliard enjoy his smoke. The other two men were relieved they were off the hook. Growing weary of Galliard, Butler pointed at him and said, "This better not come back on me, you hear?"

"Don't worry. I got everything covered. Everything." He took another drag from his cigarette. "Look, Mr. Roueché wants you to convince Carson to use him as a firearms expert. You think you can handle that?"

"Shouldn't be a problem. But why?"

"Because I'm not sure prison fits you. If you want your name free from this, then do what you're told."

Back in Peregrine, in his upstairs office, Monroe studied the letter with its simple message. He mumbled, "Who would send this much money, and why?"

Still confused by such a large sum suddenly showing up, he picked the box up to examine the inside, as if he had missed something. He didn't. To him, it all seemed strange, a little too strange.

He looked at the postmark. "Jackson. Huh."

"This case is getting weirder by the minute," he mumbled as he leaned back in his chair.

Chapter 11

Staring at the clock, it was 4:32 Monday morning, Monroe couldn't go back to sleep. He thought it would be a good idea to get an early start. Slowly, he sat up on the side of the bed and rubbed his face. He was still tired. He looked back over his shoulder at Debbie. She was still asleep. He gently patted her rear end. He didn't wish to wake her. She moaned a little as she tugged the covers up, pulling them over her head. Only a few locks of her hair were showing. Monroe smiled as he looked at her. She still had a couple hours before she had to get up. Before leaving, Monroe gave her a light kiss on her head. She softly mumbled, "Goodbye."

The drive to his office didn't take long. There's not much traffic at this time of the morning in Peregrine. Monroe checked the time on his phone, 5:53. Unlike most mornings, he parked near the entrance. Normally, the early morning crowd beats him to the good spots. Pulling himself from the car, he walked into the corner building. He never had to unlock it because Christi got there way before the sun came up. The aroma of fresh coffee got his attention. *Coffee. Yes, I need caffeine.* Stepping into Christi's, he glanced around, noticing there were only two people in the shop. "Business slow?" he asked Christi.

"Naw. It'll pick up in a little while," the petite brunette answered, handing him his coffee. "You want a cinnamon roll with that? They're just out of the oven," she said while removing the freshly baked rolls from the glass case. A combined cinnamon and sugar aroma floated up to Monroe's nostrils. He inhaled. "Sure. How can I say no? The sugar and caffeine might give me a good *jolt* this morning."

"Morning, Mr. Lovett," a gum-smacking waitress said as she walked by.

"Good morning," he replied as he secured his coffee and pastry in his hand and then headed upstairs. Locking his main office door behind him, Monroe ambled down the hall to his office.

With an exhale, he plopped down into his chair. The copy of the 9-1-1 tape on his desk caught his eye. He picked it up, stared at it, and laid it back down. He knew he needed to listen to it, but he wasn't in the mood. Something about the case was bothering him, but he just couldn't put his finger on it. He had listened to the recording once, but he didn't hear anything that might help.

The hot java seemed more inviting than the recording, so he took a sip as he leaned back in his desk chair, closing his eyes. He cracked one eye open, looking back at the recorder. *You need to listen to the tape, Monroe.* He reached for it again. *I know, but . . .* he thought as he changed his mind.

Feeling like he was in over his head with Ashley's case, the preacher turned defense attorney slowly moved his chair around facing the window behind him. Through half-opened eyes, he peered out the window at the courthouse. The sun was piercing through the early morning clouds; its rays emblazed the old brass embellished clock set atop the courthouse.

It wasn't too long ago that Monroe dreamed of a headline-grabbing case. He would have people all over the county, maybe the state, calling him, calling Monroe Lovett to represent them. Days turned into weeks, as he anticipated his first client walking up those stairs. She finally did. This wasn't what he had envisioned. Monroe took a deep breath and muttered, "Monroe, maybe you should've stayed in church work."

A short nap before starting the workday would be nice, but that little voice in his head said no. Too much work to get done. Monroe reached over and picked up his notes from his meeting with Ashley. *There's got to be something here. What am I missing?* He flipped the pages back and forth. He sat up straight and said, "How did Ashley end up at Billy's?" He drew a blank. His mind was tired from long hours. He looked up at the clock Debbie had hung on the wall. "Six eighteen. Hmm, I think I will finish my coffee first." Quiet. Peaceful. Monroe's eyes slowly closed as his grip on the cup of coffee loosened, gradually sliding from his grip.

Bzzz . . .

Startled, he sat up, spilling some of his coffee. "You've got to be— Son-of-a—?" Monroe griped as he pulled some tissues from the box on his desk, dabbing up the spilled java. After Ashley's first meeting, he bought several boxes.

Bzzz . . . Bzzz . . .

"Yeah, I hear you!" he hollered. *Who would be here this early?* Right now, he hated that buzzer. His desk dry, Monroe hurried to the door. As he rounded the corner, he saw Herm standing on the opposite side of the wooden door's glass inlay. Monroe unlocked the door.

"Morning, Mr. Lovett," Herm said with a smile. "You know, you should put a doorbell or something up here. I'm about out of breath from going up and down the stairs to trigger that buzzer."

"Absolutely, I'll get right on it," Monroe retorted. "It's kind of early for—how did you know I was here?"

"Christi told me." A stop at Christi's for coffee was part of Herm's morning routine. Gesturing in the direction of Monroe's office, he asked, "Can I?"

He could see the man wasn't going to take no for an answer. "Sure. Why not?" Monroe responded, still a little flustered.

Herm followed Monroe. Looking around the office as they walked, He commented, "I like what you did with the place. I remember when it was a smoke-filled dump. I looked at this place when I moved back, but it's not really set up for living in."

"I didn't do anything to it. The owner did. And it's still the same dump. Just with a fresh coat of paint and new carpet," Monroe responded. He was not in the mood for an early morning conversation about building remodeling.

"Well, it looks nice anyway."

"Have a seat," Monroe said, pointing to a chair.

Herm looked at the chair and then spotted the couch. He went to the couch instead, still gawking at the remodel. Monroe watched as Herm ignored his invite to sit in the chair. "This is comfortable," Herm commented, feeling the couch's cushions as if he was in a furniture store.

"Well, did you come here to admire the place and my couch, or do you have something on your mind?" Monroe asked.

"Straight to the point. Alright," Herm said with a slight grin. Over twenty years in police work taught him to read people. "Thought I would check in with you about our last conversation."

A dilemma was facing Monroe. On the one hand, he didn't know if he could trust this guy. However, on the other hand, it would be nice to have someone with his experience. "What do you want from me, Mr. Hermann?"

"Nothing. Just to help. And please, as I told you, I prefer Herm."

"Yes. Yes, you did. Or, maybe you prefer Detective Herm? Heard you retired from the New Orleans PD."

"Did your homework, good," Herm chuckled. "But Herm is fine. I'm retired. So, you can drop the 'detective'."

Growing a bit exasperated, and still not trusting Herm, Monroe asked, "Why do you want to help, as you say?"

"Like I told you. I think the girl's innocent. I want to help. That's it."

"That's it?"

"Yep."

"How? How do you know? I really don't have time for games. Don't like games. And this is starting to feel like a game to me." The look on Monroe's face confirmed what he was saying.

Herm could see he was getting under Monroe's skin a little, but he didn't care. "Just my—"

"Yeah, I know . . . your gut, your freaking gut," Monroe said acerbically, trying to contain his impatience.

"Hasn't let me down in twenty years."

"What makes you think I need help?"

Herm had been waiting for this question. "Let's see, you're an ex-preacher who has never *really* practiced as a defense attorney. Barely even been in a courtroom."

"What makes you think that?"

"You clerked for Don Mecker in Cleveland—not bad, but still no real trial experience—after graduating from—"

Raising his hand up to stop him, Monroe said, "Okay. I get it."

"No, I want to finish the story. I like it." Monroe consented. "You started a small church, Grace Community Church. You were there for seven years, two months, one week and four days. And now, you are here in Peregrine, Mississippi. Miss anything?"

Monroe knew he had nailed him. "No, that about covers it. Minus a *few* minute details. How did you—?"

"As you said, I was a detective, Mr. Lovett. I have sources, sources who can help you. Look—to be honest—I need something to do to . . . keep me busy. I spent most of my career putting people behind bars. Now, at this point in my life, I want to help those stay out who don't deserve to be put away. And . . ."

"And still put the bad guys away."

"Yep."

Monroe considered Herm's offer as they sat looking at each other. The two remained locked in a stare, eyeing each other for what seemed like several minutes. To allow Herm to work with him would mean trusting a total stranger. Only one issue bothered him, a single question. How tight was he with Butler? Trusting Herm would entail allowing him access to inside information on the case.

"Well? I don't want to sit here looking at you all day," Herm stated.

Monroe chuckled at Herm's uneasiness. "I have to admit, your expertise would serve as a great help. I'll have to get Ashley to sign off on allowing you access to her case file, but that shouldn't be a problem."

"So?"

"Okay, you're in. But—"

"I know, I have to earn your trust. I understand."

"Something like that." From the corner of his eye, Monroe saw the 9-1-1 tape. He reached over and picked it up. "Listen to this. It's the 9-1-1 call. Tell me what you think."

"Alright."

Monroe played the recording.

"9-1-1, how may I help you?"

"Yes, I would like to report a shooting—a gunshot at the Butler residence, 202 Castle Hill Drive."

"What is your name, sir?"

Silence.

"Sir?" the 9-1-1 operator asked.

Silence.

"Hello?" the operator asked again.

Monroe turned the tape player off. "That's it."

"Definitely didn't want their voice to be recognized," Herm said, rubbing his chin. "Is there a number?"

"Throw away cell."

"Figures."

"Does the voice sound familiar?"

"It's hard to tell," Herm answered as the wheels turned in his head. "No. No, I can't place it."

"I've got to go see Ashley," Monroe said, looking at the clock on the wall. "Can you be back here at, let's say, ten thirty?"

"Yep. I'll see you in a couple hours," Herm said, rising to his feet.

The two men shook hands to seal their arrangement. "Bring me something that can help," Monroe said.

"I'll do my best," Herm chuckled and then left.

Watching Herm leave, Monroe said under his breath, "*Please* bring me something."

A few minutes later, Debbie arrived at the Lovett Law Firm. She made her way to Monroe's office. She spotted the cinnamon roll. "Ooo . . . Did you get that for me?" Debbie asked, wide-eyed, licking her lips.

Monroe looked at the roll. He'd forgotten about the pastry. "Yes. Yes, I did. Christi made them fresh this morning. Thought you might want one," he told her with a beaming smile.

"Liar," she responded as she snatched up the roll.

Monroe walked over to Debbie. "Hey, can I at least have a bite?" he asked, snuggling up close to her and placing his hands on her hips.

"Me or the roll?" she asked with an impish little smile. She held the sweet treat up next to her face, looking at him with a, *choose one or the other*, expression.

Monroe looked deep into her eyes as he pulled her closer to him. He leaned in close to her face. "The roll," he said, taking a quick bite.

Debbie giggled.

He gave her a quick kiss leaving some of the icing on her lips. Monroe watched with desire as Debbie sensually licked her lips.

He took a deep breath and slowly backed away a little, eyeing her from head to toe. Exhaling, he said, "I so badly want to stay here, you know."

"Then . . . stay," she said rather suggestively.

"I can't," Monroe replied regrettably. "I need . . . to go see my client. But I will take a rain check."

Debbie took a bite of the cinnamon roll and said as she chewed, "We'll see."

A little musty and in need of a fresh coat of paint, the concrete room felt uncomfortable for someone not used to it—an icy ambiance. This was as close to jail Monroe wanted to be. He sat at a table, fidgeting as he waited. He took a few deep breaths trying to calm his nerves. Then, after what seemed like forever, the steel door echoed as it squeaked open. He looked up and saw an emotionless female deputy escorting Ashley into the room. Ashley sat down at the table in a chair opposite him. He just watched.

"Give me your hands," the deputy said.

Ashley complied, and the deputy locked the chain to a steel ring attached to the table. The callous-looking deputy then took a position behind Ashley, standing against the wall. Monroe glanced up to the deputy. With a quick, single head gesture, he let her know she could leave. The deputy complied, but her smirk said the opposite. Metal contacting metal boomed as the door slammed and the key turned in the lock.

It was evident Ashley had not slept much. He eyes appeared sunken with dark circles beneath them, though they were a bit hidden by her messy, tangled dark brown hair, draping down just over her shoulders. She sat with her thin, frail body drawn in. She showed every sign of someone who had given up—defeated.

Monroe, with concern, asked, "You okay, Ashley?"

"Yeah," Ashley answered, but her voice was very soft.

"Why don't I believe you? Have you eaten anything?" he asked. She didn't answer. "Ashley, you have to keep your strength up."

She sniffled. "Heard 'bout Billy. I'm done. What does it matter?"

"No, you're not."

"I'll change my plea to guilty. Save you a bunch of trouble. I already signed the confession."

Monroe wasn't about to let her give up. "Ashley, look at me."

Ashley just stared at the table.

"Ashley!"

She jumped, startled by Monroe's raising his voice. "What?" she answered with a swift glance at him, but then she quickly returned her stare to the table.

"Look at me, Ashley."

Brushing her hair from her face, she slowly raised her eyes to meet his. With sincerity, he said, "This isn't over. Yes, Billy is, is *likely* dead. But I have other options." *Though I don't know what they are*, Monroe thought, fighting to prevent Ashley from seeing his uncertainty. "And I . . . I have some help." He reached into his briefcase and removed a notepad along with a permission form. "I'll need you to sign this," he said, clicking his pen.

"Help?"

"Yes, help."

"But I ain't got no money."

"Not a problem. It's covered."

"Who—?"

"Doesn't matter," he assured her with a smile. "He's a retired police detective who believes you're innocent. All I need is your signature allowing Herm access to your case file," Monroe said, placing the permission agreement in front of Ashley. He set his pen on it.

"Herm?"

"His name is Ed Hermann."

"Sounds like an old man."

"He's not that old."

"Is he from here?"

"Yes and no. He grew up here but moved away. Now he's back."

"From where?"

"New Orleans."

Restrained by the chain, she picked up the pen and signed the document. Her bleakness was obvious. The thought of Herm being from Peregrine didn't give her much comfort. Ashley was losing hope, losing the will to fight for her freedom. She signed to appease her lawyer.

Monroe hadn't lost hope. Seeing Ashley's despondency invigorated him even more to help her. Her appearance drew a single question to his mind—was she suicidal? For a moment, he considered calling a psychologist but decided to wait until after their conversation was over to make a final decision. He told her, "Ashley, you're not done. You have to trust me."

"That's what you keep saying."

"Trust is all we've got. You need to trust me. I have to trust Herm and God."

"Easier said than done." To her, God seemed far away. She was beginning to wonder if God had given up on her too.

"I know, but believe me, God is going to get us through this. He's all we've got right now," Monroe said. His inner pastor voice told him to continue counseling her, but the attorney in him said press forward. He decided to listen to the attorney in him and said, "Look, I've got some more questions about that night. Where did you meet Billy the night—?"

"Swatters."

"Swatters?"

"Swatters. I ran into Billy at Swatters. It's a bar on the edge of town. It's a local hangout. Swatter owns it."

Monroe shook his head a little trying to comprehend what Ashley was telling him. Getting used to Southern nicknames was still something he was learning. "Did anyone see you?"

"Sure. Plenty of people."

"Here, write down their names," Monroe said, pushing his notepad over to Ashley. "And why did you leave with Billy?"

"Cause me and Junior had a fight."

"A fight?"

"It was more like an argument. Anyway, he left with,"—Ashley got angry as she thought about the whole situation— "he left with Julie."

"But you left with Billy?"

"Yeah. So?"

"Why didn't you just go home?" he asked, thinking it would have been the obvious place for her to go.

"Cause that's where Junior and Julie went."

"And you know this, how?"

"That's where they always go when . . . Do I have to talk about this?"

"Yes, if you want me to prove your innocence."

She looked away in frustration and then said, "Every time the two of 'em hooked up, they went to our house," Her eyes began to tear up. "So, usually I would go to a friend's. The other night I went to Billy's."

"Okay. Sounds good to me," Monroe said, satisfied with Ashley's explanation. He pointed to the notepad. "The names. I need those names."

She picked up the pen and thought for a moment, trying to remember who was there. As she jotted some names, she asked, "Mr. Lovett, can I ask you a question?"

"Sure. Anything."

"Do you really think you can get me off?"

"Ashley, I'm not here to get you off."

"Huh?" she asked with a puzzled expression. "But I thought that's what you did. You know, get people off."

"Are you guilty?"

"No. But—"

"But, nothing. I'm here to prove your innocence. I believe you're innocent."

A slight smile breached her listless face. "I am. I just didn't think anyone would believe me. And Mr. Butler won't—"

"Don't worry about Mr. Butler. Just know that I do."

"Do what?"

"I believe you, Ashley."

"But what 'bout my confession? The judge said—"

"Forget about it," Monroe assured her, even though, he knew a signed confession was a major hurdle to clear. That alone could prove the greatest

76

piece of evidence the jury utilized to convict Ashley. "I will prove your innocence. I'm sure I can convince the jury you signed it while under extreme duress. That you were coerced."

"Ha. Good luck. Ain't nobody in the county gonna believe you."

"Do you believe me?"

"I think." She studied him a little. "Maybe?"

"But you came to my office."

"You were the closest lawyer."

Her answer took Monroe back a little. He figured he had her full confidence, that she had sought him out. *So much for that*, he thought as he slumped in his seat. However, this wasn't about him, and he knew it. Promptly recovering, he assured her, "Don't lose hope, Ashley. I'm going to fight for you. Not just me. You have Debbie and now Herm fighting for you, too."

Ashley's eyes became moist and then she began to cry a little.

"I thought it would make you feel better," Monroe said, scrambling to think of something to say to stop the tears.

"You don't understand," Ashley said, struggling to wipe the tears from her face with her restrained hands. "No one's ever said that to me before." Finally, someone showed an interest in Ashley as a person, not merely as someone to use and set aside like a piece of property.

He could only speculate as to what this girl had been through in her short life. Looking at her face, Monroe got a glimpse of deep pain. He desired to ask but knew he shouldn't press his luck. "Here," Monroe said, handing her a tissue from his briefcase. "I've learned to keep these close by since I met you." He smiled at her.

"Thanks," she replied, taking the tissue. She even laughed a little, again covering her past pain.

"One more question," Monroe said as she wiped her tears. "Did Junior ever abuse you?"

Ashley sniffled. "He's never hit me if that's what you mean."

"How about anything else?"

"He yelled at me sometimes. But that's just the way he is. His daddy's the same."

Monroe finished writing down his notes. "Is there anything you want to ask me?"

"Why? Why you doing this?"

"Because you asked," Monroe answered with a warm smile.

"Do you really believe God cares, you know, 'bout this, 'bout me?"

"Yes. Yes, I do, Ashley."

Chapter 12

Detective Carson didn't see Herm standing in the doorway. A couple of minutes passed as Herm leaned against the doorframe with his arms crossed, calmly watching the detective. Carson had his head buried in a file folder. A cup, half-full of coffee, sat on one side of his desk and a partially eaten pastry next to it.

"You're still just as ugly as I remembered," Herm chuckled.

Carson yanked his head up. He didn't recognize the voice; however, seeing the face brought back memories. "I heard you were back," Carson said, closing the folder. "You know, you're not Mr. GQ yourself?" he said, standing, motioning for Herm to come in.

Herm jabbed at the detective as he walked over, "Better looking than you. I always have been."

"Long time no see, Ed," Carson replied, extending a hand.

Herm could sense Carson's apprehension. However, he needed information and playing nice meant he might get something. "Yes indeed. Yes indeed, it has been," he replied as he shook Carson's hand. "But call me Herm."

"Herm?"

"I picked it up down in New Orleans."

"Okay. Herm it is."

The two men had attended school together from kindergarten all the way through high school. After graduation, Herm enlisted in the Air Force as a member of the Security Police. He finished his enlistment and then moved to New Orleans, where he got a position with the city's police department.

Carson, on the other hand, went to a junior college earning an associate's degree in criminal justice. After graduation, he got a position as a Lane County sheriff's deputy.

"Have a seat," Carson said, gesturing to a chair as he sat back down. Herm sat down as requested. The detective looked at his old school friend with a slight frown. He scratched his chin and said, "All those years. And now you just move back. No phone calls, nothing." He let out a little contemptuous chuckle. "Yeah," he exhaled, "long time no see. So, tell me, why now? Why move back here?"

Herm smirked at Carson, fighting back his aggravation at Carson's interrogation style. "Maybe this was a mistake," he said as he started to stand.

"No," Carson said, indicating for him to remain seated. "You're here now. Don't mean to—just curious."

"Look, I know I left and didn't keep in touch. But—life got complicated."

"Complicated. Complicated how?"

"Long story. Maybe some other time."

"Okay. Didn't mean to pull the bad cop routine on you," Carson said. "Habit, isn't it?"

"Yeah, I guess it is. So, why *are* you here?"

"Retired. Needed a quiet place to live, away from city life. Figured Peregrine was the perfect spot. But—"

"But, what?"

"This Butler case. It got my attention. It's why I'm here. I've offered my services to the girl's lawyer."

"So, you're working for Lovett. Marcus won't like it."

"Who cares what Marcus Butler likes?"

"Oh . . . I don't know, just about everybody in Lane County. Things have changed over the years."

"Oh well," Herm said, pointing to Carson's desk. "Got anything you can give me?"

Carson sat and stared at Herm for a few seconds as he mulled over the request. He knew Herm understood the process and wouldn't expect much. But figured he would play along with the fishing routine. "Well, I guess it can't hurt to give you this," he answered, handing him a copy of a report. "You can have this."

Herm looked over the information. "Anything else?"

"Nope," Carson snipped. "You'll get more when your new boss gets it."

"Okay. I'll leave you to your work," Herm said, standing with the report in hand. He walked to the door as Carson watched. Then he stopped, looking back at Carson, and chided his old friend, "You need to lay off the donuts, Ben. Really, lay off the donuts."

Carson scoffed at him. He picked up the pastry and took a spiteful bite.

With the report given him by Carson, Herm headed to Monroe's office.

Hearing the buzzer, Debbie watched for the door to open. A couple of seconds later, a tall, large-framed man entered. He had a gentle smile. "Hello. May I help you?" Debbie asked him.

"Yes, you can. I'm here to see your husband."

"Is he expecting you?"

"Yes."

"Okay, I'll go check with him," she said, jumping up and headed to Monroe's office.

"Tell him it's— Mrs.? My name—Ed . . . Herm . . . Oh well, he said as she scuttled down the hall. Herm took a seat in the small sitting area, grabbing a magazine as he waited.

Knock-knock-knock at Monroe's door.

Monroe called out, "Come."

Debbie entered and closed the door behind her.

"Yes?" Monroe asked.

"There's a man here to see you."

"Who?"

"Appears to be maybe, oh, I don't know, maybe in his late forties. Well-groomed hair, and—"

"A name, not a description."

"I forgot to ask. All I saw were his bushy eyebrows and his eyes, his blue eyes just seemed to look right through me. But comforting."

"Tell Herm to come on back."

"You know him?" she asked, pointing back in the direction of the reception area.

"Yes."

"Oh . . ." she said, easing down into a chair. "Who is he?"

"Debbie. Go tell Herm he can come back, please. I'll tell you later."

Debbie popped back up, gave him a peeved look, and sashayed away. Monroe watched her. His gaze lingered on one distinct part of her body, and a mischievous grin quickly emerged on his face.

"You wish," she said, not turning around.

"How does she—?"

Herm was thumbing through a magazine when Debbie returned. "Hello," she said.

He stood up and held up the magazine. "I'll tell Monroe to get some updated reading material."

She extended her hand. "I'm Debbie, Monroe's wife."

"Yes, I know. We met a few minutes ago."

Slightly embarrassed, and with a smiled, she said, "You can go on back," gesturing toward Monroe's office.

"Thanks," he said, and then proceeded back. Debbie watched him, pondering who he might be. She thought of Googling his name, but Herm wasn't much to go on. Her curiosity would have to wait.

Rap-Rap on the doorframe.

"Herm, come on in," Monroe said, waving him inside.

Herm entered and closed the door. He opened a folder and said, "Here," handing Monroe a sheet of paper.

"What's this?"

"It's a preliminary report Carson gave me from his gun expert, a guy named Jason Daniels. But I suppose you already have it." Herm sat down on the couch. "I like this couch. Where'd you get it?"

"No, I don't. Haven't heard of him," Monroe said, trying to place the name. "Any relation to Christi Daniels from downstairs?" He glanced over at Herm. "It's not for sale. And, I don't remember."

"Her husband. He's good. Knows his stuff," Herm said, as he got comfortable. "Too bad, I wouldn't mind having one like it. Would you consider—?"

"No, the couch isn't for sale," Monroe said, reading the report. "So how good is he?"

"Like I said, knows his stuff. Check his answer to the last question," Herm said, pointing at the sheet of paper.

Monroe found the statement. He read aloud, "After reviewing the forensics report given me concerning the shotgun retrieved by Lane County Sheriff's Department, the firearm could have fired the shots that killed the deceased. However, a more proper examination will be required to make a final determination."

"That's not good."

"This isn't conclusive. He said, 'could have.' The next sentence contends he hasn't personally examined the shotgun. Besides, any shotgun *could have* fired buckshot." Monroe placed the sheet in the folder on his desk.

"I guess," Herm said, seemingly more interested in the couch. "However, in a small town, one owned by Marcus Butler, that's pretty convincing. But what do I know? You're the lawyer."

"How much sway does he have?" Monroe asked. He then picked up and handed Herm the crime scene photos. Here, look at these. But I warn you, they're pretty gruesome."

"Enough to make your opinion a non-issue," Herm answered as he took hold of the photos. "I was a homicide detective, you know." He studied the photos, and then said, "Oh my. Somebody wanted this girl dead." He turned the photos, attempting to get a better look. "How many times was she shot?"

"Five buckshot shells were found on the floor. Four just inside a walk-in closet, and one a couple feet from the victim."

Still scrutinizing the photos, Herm surmised, "This was personal, Monroe—very personal."

"Why do you say that?"

"Shot several times and the last to the face. The first probably was enough to kill her. The second for sure. But up close, and to the face—makes it personal, very personal."

Monroe took a deep breath. "Ashley?"

"Her or anybody else who wanted this girl dead. Best to wait for the expert's report," Herm suggested handing the photos back to Monroe.

Monroe laid them back on his desk. "Change of subject. Heard of a place called Swatters?"

"I've seen it. Why?"

"Ashley told me that's where she first hooked up with that kid, Billy, that night. They were all there the other night; her, Marcus Jr., Billy, and Julie. We need to speak with some of the witnesses to corroborate her statement. Maybe someone will tell us something they didn't say to the police. You want to go with me?"

"When?"

"Now."

"Nobody's there now," Herm chuckled. No doubt, Monroe was green when it came to matters of speaking with people who hang out in clubs. "It's too early," Herm said, pointing to the clock. It was a little before eleven. "I doubt they're even open."

"When then?"

"Between four and five this afternoon at the earliest."

Monroe thought for a moment. "Maybe we should go at seven or so?"

"Four-thirty is better. Less crowded."

"Alright. You're the expert."

"I'll stop by your place and pick you up. I've got a couple things to check on before then," Herm said.

"Before you go, now that you've had time to think about it, what do you think of Billy killing Julie?"

"Who knows?" Herm shrugged. "Anything's possible at this point." He got up and began walking to the door. "I wouldn't rule him out."

"So, who killed him and why?"

"Maybe Junior. Revenge for Julie."

"Huh, I hadn't thought of that."

Herm waved. "See, you do need me. Later."

"Alright," Monroe said.

A few minutes later, Debbie flounced in, dropping an unopened letter on his desk as she sat down.

"Who's it from?"

"The return address is the Coroner's office. Mr. Hermann seems like a nice man."

He opened it with haste. "I've been waiting for this." He unfolded the official report. It was concerning Julie Miller. He began reading it.

"Well?" Debbie asked.

"Seminal fluid found in the victim."

"Who's?"

"There's no DNA match. Probably Junior's."

"Too many details for me," Debbie said.

"You asked," Monroe said, continuing to scrutinize the report. "There it is."

"What?"

"Time of death. Between 6:30 and 7:30 am."

"Is that important?"

"Yes, but it's not good for Ashley." He refolded the report and tossed it onto his desk. Debbie saw his frustration, got up, and walked around to Monroe. "What are you doing?" he asked, reaching over and turning the crime scene photos over so she wouldn't see them.

She didn't answer him but glided into his lap. She kissed him and told him, "I love you, you know."

Monroe took a deep breath as he licked his lips. "Debbie, the door is unlocked. Somebody might—"

"We're not going to do that, silly. Can't I just give my husband a kiss and tell him I love him without him thinking of *that*?"

"Yeah, but, you know—"

"No, I don't," Debbie said, kissing his nose. Then got up and walked toward the door.

"But, I'm a guy. You started the launch sequence . . ." he pleaded with a juvenile grin on his face.

Debbie giggled, "Pour some water on that fire," and kept walking.

Chapter 13

Shadowy and with the odor of stale beer, Swatters sat about a mile from town. Few houses were close to the local bar, the tavern's proprietor owned most of the adjacent property. Monroe and Herm parked and then entered the dive. This was nothing new for Herm, but for Monroe, it was a completely fresh experience. Being a Monday, they didn't expect much as far as speaking with witnesses, but with a short time to prepare a defense, anything would help. Standing in the doorway, their shadows laid long across the tavern's floor.

Behind the bar, there stood a female bartender in her mid-thirties, an attractive blonde. She wore a pale T-shirt and faded jeans. Glancing over at the two men, she curtly said, "In or out. We're not here to air condition the parking lot."

In the back corner, five people sat around a table, two men, and three females. They gave a brief look before resuming their conversation.

Closing the door, Monroe and Herm walked over to the brash barmaid.

She asked, "What can I get you?" Before either man could answer, with a quick once-over, she said, "Never mind. Who you looking for?"

"That obvious?" Monroe asked.

"He's a cop," she said, pointing at Herm. "You? You're a lawyer or a preacher. But most preachers—"

"How—?" Monroe asked.

"Because she's seen guys like me a hundred times. You . . . you just look like a lawyer," Herm said with a slight grin. "You especially look like a preacher."

Monroe smirked at Herm.

"Must be a lawyer. Ain't no preacher gonna come up in here. Well, maybe that one who came in here back when . . . when was that?" she reminisced.

"Don't care," Herm said.

She shot daggers at him. "So, who you looking for?"

"Swatter," Monroe answered.

"He's upstairs. Busy."

"Go tell him to get unbusy," Herm said, not in the mood for the runaround.

"He might be sleeping."

"Look, go wake him, or I'll call Sheriff Austin to come down here," Monroe said in a stern tone.

"Fine, I'll get him," the crusty barmaid growled as she left to retrieve Swatter.

Herm chuckled, "Woo . . . Call Sheriff Austin?"

"It worked, didn't it?"

"Okay, I'll give you that one."

From the back room, a man's voice griped, "Who's looking for me?" Subsequently, a stockily built man, with a dark complexion, shoulder length hair, and a full beard strolled through a tattered curtain covering the doorway to the back. Swatter was wearing swimming trunks and a T-shirt with a hole under one armpit. And he was not in a good mood.

"You Swatter?" asked Monroe.

"Yeah. What's it to you?"

"I have some questions for you."

"You're right," Swatter said to the barmaid, "he's a lawyer. They've always got questions. Them and cops, but never any answers."

Ignoring Swatters sarcasm, Monroe asked, "Was Ashley and Marcus Butler, Jr. here last Wednesday night, the night before Julie Miller was found dead?"

"Could you be more specific?" Swatter responded with a chortle. "I always wanted to do that." He looked at Monroe and asked, "How's it feel?"

"Sir?" Monroe retorted.

"Don't have much of a sense of humor, do you?" Swatter said with a laugh. Feigning being thoughtful, he exhaled and stroked his beard. "Not sure."

"Not sure, or not saying?" Herm asked. He wasn't sure if Marcus Butler had his hooks in Swatter.

Swatter eyed Herm over and answered, "Oh yeah . . . I remember now. I talked to them for a few minutes. But it was busy that night. Two-dollar beer night. It's the only way to compete with the churches," he said, chuckling.

"They sat at that table over there," the barmaid said, pointing to a table across the room.

"What did you talk about?" Herm asked Swatter.

"Nothing much. Just chit-chat."

"How about Billy Jenkins?" Monroe asked. "Was he here that night?"

"Yeah," the barmaid answered. "He was at the table next to Ashley and Junior."

"How about Julie, was she here?" Monroe asked.

"Yeah," Swatter answered.

"How were they acting? You know, anything unusual, out of the ordinary?" Herm asked the barmaid.

"They talked," she said with a shrug of her shoulders.

"People come here to relax, have a good time," Swatter said.

"Did anything happen that night?" Monroe asked.

"Nope," Swatter answered.

"So, nothing unusual? No argument? Fights?" Herm asked.

Swatter and the barmaid looked at each other. "I do remember"—she stopped and quickly glanced at Swatter— "No, not that I saw," she answered.

"Look, I don't think Ashley did it," Swatter said.

"Why?" Monroe asked.

"Cause she ain't that kind of girl. Ashley's . . . Ashley just ain't no killer."

"So, what time did they get here and when did they leave?" Herm asked.

Growing frustrated with the questions, Swatter answered, "Look, dude, I don't keep time cards on my customers. People come. People go," he said with animated gestures. "I don't ask 'em to write down when they get here. I don't record their conversations. I don't ask 'em where they're going when they walk out the door," he persisted, pointing to the front door. Pausing, he took a deep breath. "Now, if the two of you are finished, Lisa here"—pointing at the barmaid with his thumb like a hitchhiker thumbing a ride— "can get you a drink. But, if you're not drinking, then feel free to leave. You're making my customers feel *uneasy*."

Monroe looked around the small tavern. "All five of them, I guess," he quipped.

Swatter turned and headed back through the door from which he emerged.

"So, you two want that drink?" Lisa asked nervously.

"No thanks," Monroe said. "Lisa, do you still have any credit card receipts from that night?"

"We don't accept credit cards or checks. Swatter runs a cash-only business. He says he doesn't trust banks or the government."

"Thanks," Monroe said, patting the bar. He and Herm walked out, back into the hot Mississippi heat. After the door had closed behind them, Monroe looked at Herm and said, "That went well."

"Yep."

"How do you guys deal with this?" he asked, grimacing from the sun's late afternoon rays beating down on him.

"Talking with guys like him?"

"No. I've dealt with much worse in church work. I mean this heat."

"Just wait until the humidity kicks in in July," Herm said.

"It gets worse?"

"Oh yeah. Oh . . . yeah."

"I've moved to purgatory," Monroe griped, reaching into his blazer pocket removing a small piece of paper. "Here," he said, handing it to Herm.

"What's this?"

"The other names Ashley gave me. Maybe a few of them could be of some help, but I doubt it."

"Makes two of us. I guess I'm definitely working for you now."

"As long as you work for expenses, coffee, and an occasional donut."

"I'll do you one better."

"Yeah?"

"You keep the donuts. But I do like cupcakes."

"Deal," Monroe said, opening the car door. "Now, let's go. Get out of this heat."

Herm agreed as he walked around to the driver's side of his Chrysler 300.

Chapter 14

After you have suffered for a little while, the God of all grace, who called you to His eternal glory in Christ, will Himself perfect, confirm, strengthen and establish you.
(1 Peter 5:10)

That evening Debbie and Monroe were dining on one of their favorite dinners, pizza, and beer. Monroe grabbed a slice and sat back down on the couch to watch a baseball game. The Rangers were playing the Indians in Cleveland.

Debbie took a sip of her beer and then asked, "Monroe?"

His focus remained on the game. "Huh?" he answered as he chewed his bite of bacon pizza.

"Who do you think—?"

"C'mon, ump," he protested, pointing at the TV. "He was safe."

"Monroe, are you listening to me?"

"Yeah," he said, not taking his eyes off the game.

"Who do you think sent us the money?"

Monroe stopped chewing and cut his eyes over at Debbie. His look said, *"I don't want to talk about it."* He turned back to the game and resumed his chewing.

"You're not getting off that easy. You can watch your game *and* answer my question."

He swallowed and said to her, "I don't know, and . . . right now, I don't care."

"You've got to be curious," she said, and then gulped another mouthful of cold ale.

"Nope," he said, taking another large bite of pizza. He reached over and grabbed his own beer, a dark stout.

"Then, why did you keep the box if you aren't the slightest bit curious?" Debbie persisted. She wasn't going to let this go.

Monroe dropped his head back and then placed the paper plate, with a partially eaten slice of pizza, on the couch complaining, "I'm glad this is good cold." He pushed the mute button on the remote. Rubbing his face, he explained, "Look, I don't know who sent it. The return address is our office. It was postmarked, Jackson. So, there's no way to trace it back. I don't know why I kept it, I just did. You asked if I'm curious. Yes. Yes, sweetie, I am. But there's no way to trace the money. Okay, you happy now?"

"So, who would want to give us twenty thousand dollars? And, why? Sure, at first, I was thrilled. But after I thought about it, well, I began to feel uneasy."

"Deb . . . I. Don't. Know." Monroe knew he should've stopped there, but he didn't. "See, that's the problem with you women, you allow your feelings to get in the way."

Debbie's eyebrow shot straight up. Her green eyes drew a bead aimed dead on him. But he sat there unfazed. This was nothing new for him. Deciding to ignore his goading remark, she asked, "Is it legal to keep it?"

"Sure," he shrugged "We show it as payment for Ashley Butler's case along with the note that came with it. Everything's documented. Everything's fine."

"Why not just keep the cash?"

"I wish I had. But, we've already deposited the money. Now, we need a paper trail."

"Oh."

"Enough with the questions," Monroe said, picked up his slice of pizza. "Now, can we finish our dinner and not discuss business?" Monroe then took a large bite of pizza.

"If you say it's fine, I believe you."

"It's fine," he mumbled as he chewed.

They finished their pizza and beer with little more than small talk, mostly about the game.

Later in the evening, after dark, Monroe sat up from lying on the couch and said, "I almost forgot, it's trash night."

"I'll help you," Debbie said.

"No. I'll do it."

He gathered the bags, threw them into the large, green, plastic can, and wheeled it to the street, the whole time griping how much he hated taking the trash out. Monroe sat the cans in place and then looked up at the night sky for a moment. Gazing up, he heard a vehicle speeding towards him from down the street. At first, he didn't think anything of it, until it came to a sliding stopped behind him, loose pieces of asphalt and pebbles grinding beneath the tires.

Before Monroe could turn around, two large men seized him and threw him into the back of the paneled van. A third man, smaller in stature, was the driver. He stomped the accelerator to the floor, and the van sped away.

As the van raced down the street, one of the men slid a hood over Monroe's face. Pitch black was all he saw as his heart pumped hard and fast.

Monroe attempted to scream, but before letting out a sound, one of them wrapped duct tape tightly around his head several times, covering his mouth. The other man yanked Monroe's hands around behind his back, clasping them together, and bound them with duct tape. He groaned from the strain on his shoulders. They also taped his feet together and then rolled him to the back of the van.

Oh God! Who? What? Debbie! "Ohm! Ohm!" *Just relax. Relax. Try to listen. Maybe someone saw. They'll call the police. Yeah, everything's going to be fine.* Monroe attempted to yell through his taped mouth, "Who . . .?"

A punch landed on the right side of his torso. A perfect liver shot.

"Ugg!" Monroe let out as he curled into the fetal position, struggling to remain conscious. A piercing pain shot through his side as he endeavored to catch his breath.

"No talking," one of the men ordered.

Chapter 15

"Where is he?" Debbie asked under her breath as she was in the kitchen cleaning out the dishwasher. "Take the trash to the street," she mumbled. "How long does it take?" Curious of Monroe's whereabouts, she walked to the front door droning, "Probably talking to a neighbor," Debbie stepped out onto the porch. While holding the door open, she peered into the dark. Not seeing him, she eased to the edge of the porch, letting the door close behind her. Looking around, she called, "Monroe . . . Monroe . . ."

There was no response.

Only the sound of crickets and other insects rang in the small neighborhood. Growing more concerned, Debbie walked into the front yard, looking up and down the street for her husband. She called out again, but louder, "Mon—roe . . ."

Again, there was no response.

No one was outside. It was too warm and muggy—sticky. Cool air conditioning kept most everyone inside. Monroe was gone. Vanished. "Monroe . . . Where are you?" she whined as her anxiety increased. *Maybe I should call Herm*, she thought and then turned to go make the call. She stopped. *I don't have his number. Great.* "Humph!" she shrieked under her breath, not realizing Monroe's phone contained Herm's number. Nor did she think to check.

Fretting, she looked around, hoping he would come walking from one of their neighbor's homes. He didn't. *Maybe I should call the police. But what if he comes back. They'd laugh at me.* Debbie stood in the front yard just off the edge of the porch, looking, waiting. *Maybe, he walked down the street.* She walked toward the street where the trash cans were sitting.

"Ouch!" Debbie screamed as she grabbed her left foot while standing on her right. "Dang stickers," she grumbled while hopping on her right foot and pulling the tiny thorns from the bottom of her left foot. "I'm going to kill him when he gets back," she muttered, even more frustrated.

A neighbor across the street heard Debbie and pulled back the blinds to peek out at the noise. Seeing Debbie doing her one-legged dance next to the garbage cans, he thought nothing of the sight and went back to watching his TV show.

Having freed her foot of the tiny briars, she found a spot clear of them to stand. Upset and concerned, she squealed quietly, "Monroe! Where . . . are . . . you . . . ?"

Dragged from the van, Monroe landed on the ground with a thud. Grabbing his feet, the two men pulled him over the damp ground covered with dead leaves and pine needles and weeds toward the small cabin. Every time he hit a root sticking up from the ground, he felt it, right where he took the punch to his side. They stopped while one of the men unlatched the door and pushed it open with his foot. Monroe could only imagine what or why this was taking place. All he figured, it had something to do with Ashley. With a hard tug, they yanked him through the doorway. His head smacked the doorjamb. "Ugh . . ." he moaned.

Once inside, they lifted him up to his feet and dropped him into a chair. "Sit," one of them said.

Monroe sniffed, trying to get a feel for where he was. Mustiness and woodsy odors filled his nose. No doubt, he was somewhere deep in the woods. He listened. The tree frogs' trilling echoed loudly. Locusts clacked and buzzed. The two noises combined was almost deafening at times on this warm humid still Mississippi night. His captors remained silent as they watched him. Their job was done for now.

Mosquitos buzzed around him as perspiration soaked through the hood. The pain in his side throbbed with each breath, causing Monroe to squirm in the chair. One of the men kicked the chair. "Stay still. You fall out, I ain't picking you up."

Turning his head in the direction of the voice, Monroe squinted, trying to see through the dark cloth, but the thick black cotton material blocked even the light from the single bright bulb hanging from the ceiling. Not wanting another punch, Monroe did as he was told.

Squeak, as the door opened and closed.

Monroe snapped his head around. He could hear two sets of footsteps.

The two men walked over to where he was sitting. Neither man spoke at first. Time passed with only soft whispering, but Monroe could not hear what they were saying. A chair was dragged across the floor by one of them and stopped in front of Monroe. He sensed someone sit down and lean close to him.

"Hello, Mr. Lovett," Joe Galliard said, pulling on a pair of leather gloves. "Now I know you can't see what I'm doing. But, I believe you need to know. I'm putting on a pair of gloves to protect my hands."

Monroe's breathing became heavy. He knew exactly what Galliard meant.

"Mr. Lovett, this is your only warning, okay?"

Monroe didn't move. He braced for what might come next.

"Ashley Butler, she's going to change her plea to guilty. You understand me?"

Monroe remained silent. Even if he wanted to respond, speaking was almost impossible with the tightness of the tape around his face. Monroe tilted his head slightly trying to identify the voice, but it didn't seem familiar to him.

Galliard chuckled. "I get it, you can't speak. Just nod your head if you understand."

Monroe refused to acknowledge him.

A punch to Monroe's side, the same side as before, doubled him over in pain. He let out a loud moaned as his eyes opened wide, and as he squirmed in agony.

"How hard is it for you to understand?" Galliard asked. "This doesn't have to be painful. Just assure us she will change her plea and nothing else will happen. All you have to do is go to Breaux's office tomorrow and request the change. You do it, and life goes on. No one will blame you."

Heavy breathing—but no response came from Monroe.

Galliard removed a knife from his boot. *Click*, as the blade locked open.

One of the other men chuckled.

Monroe recognized the sound, too.

Easing the blade beneath the tape, Galliard cut the tape from around Monroe's face.

"Who—?" Monroe asked.

"Shut up," Galliard said with a slap to the face. Monroe did. "Tell the girl—change her plea to guilty, you got it? You walk away. New clients will come. Do you understand what I'm saying? Don't be stupid."

Monroe looked away.

Becoming impatient, Galliard said, "Mr. Lovett, do what we ask, and we'll leave you and your pretty wife alone. Am I making myself clear?" Another blow to his side—the same spot.

"Oww . . .! Oh, God . . .!" Monroe wailed, writhing in pain. He wheezed, "Don't, don't you touch, touch my—"

Galliard threw a punched to the same spot as previously. "Don't tell me what to do. For all you know, we have Debbie right now."

"Oh . . . God . . .!" Monroe wailed, grimacing and contorting in pain. "How, how do I know I can trust you?" he asked, struggling to say each word.

"Oh, God ain't gonna help you now," Galliard said, mockingly.

Another man from across the room growled, "Do what you're told. You have my word."

Monroe turned to face the man. *That voice?* "I can't—."

Infuriated, Galliard threw three more quick and hard blows to Monroe's side. Each one compounded the damage of the previous.

Monroe's eyes widened and filled with tears with each strike. He had never felt this much pain, ever. His fists clenched as every muscle in his body tightened. He twisted in pain, falling forward in the chair. "Umm . . .!"

Galliard pushed Monroe so that he was sitting up straight. "Breathe. Breathe. Go ahead, Mr. Lovett. It's okay to scream." He glanced over at the other man and waggled his head. His expression said he didn't believe Monroe would cave.

Coughing and breathing hard with pain radiating through his body, Monroe wheezed, "Who . . . who are you?"

One of the men who snatched Monroe from the street moved toward him, drawing his fist back to deliver another strike, "Let me at him. He'll do what you want, or else, Mr.—"

Galliard jumped up, grabbed the man, and covered his mouth before he could hit Monroe or call out a name. He shoved the man against the wall with force and a loud thump, as the man hit the wall. With intensity, Galliard glowered into the man's eyes. "You stay out of this," Galliard said with a lowered voice through gritted teeth. "Understand?"

"Yeah," he muttered, reaching around to rub the back of his head.

Galliard spent several more minutes pressing Monroe to agree to change Ashley's plea but got nowhere. Monroe remained adamant until the torturous intimidation stopped. Enraged, Galliard slapped Monroe.

"This is getting us nowhere," Marcus Butler said from across the room.

"So, what do you want to do with him?" Galliard asked.

Butler replied in a loud whisper, "Take him home," motioning to the two large men who kidnapped Monroe.

They pulled him from the chair. Pain careening through his torso, Monroe struggled to stand.

"Don't do anything else to him. You understand me?" Galliard told them as he removed the gloves and rubbed his own hand, the one used to throw the blows into Monroe's rib cage.

"Yes sir," answered the one with a new headache.

Lugging Monroe outside, they put him back into the van.

With only Butler and Galliard left in the room, Galliard asked, "So, now what?"

"Don't know."

"Aren't you concerned he might recognize your voice?"

"Why? We've never talked."

"Thank you, Mrs. Lovett," Deputy Reed said, closing his notebook and placed it in his shirt pocket. Deputy Watters was standing next to him. Reed told Debbie, "I'll have everyone be on the lookout for your husband. If you don't hear back by morning, call us, okay?"

"You probably think I'm just an anxious wife?" Debbie asked. She had become very concerned by now. It was almost midnight.

"No, ma'am. I completely understand." Reed said, offering a consoling smile. "Hopefully, Mr. Lovett is talking with someone and hasn't realized the time."

"He did use to be a preacher, and, well, we all know how much they talk," Watters said, followed by an awkward chuckle.

Reed gave Watters a quizzical look, and then the two deputies left the Lovett house. Debbie closed and locked the door. Worried, she sat down on the couch. Bouncing her knee and biting her lower lip, she was upset and unsure about what she should do. They hadn't made any friends except for Herm. None of their family lived close by, so calling them would be of no use. "Monroe . . . where are you?" she sighed.

Walking back to their car, Watters asked, "Where do you think he is?"

"Who knows? I'm sure he'll show up soon," Reed said, opening the patrol car door. "And by the way, your preacher statement was stupid."

"I know."

"Let's go get something to eat. Man, I hate working midnights," Reed griped as he got into the car.

During the van ride, Monroe laid there, trying not to move. Every bump sent pulsating, excruciating pain shooting through his side. He struggled to paint a mental image of the route with each turn, but the throbbing was too much, causing him to lose track of the turns and direction of each one. Staying alive was more of a concern at this point.

One of the men moved closer to him.

Is this it? Maybe their instructions were code to kill me. Monroe prepared himself for the worst. He squeezed his eyes tightly like someone readying themselves for a hard hit.

Grabbing Monroe, the man rolled him over on his stomach.

"Oh . . .!" Monroe moaned from the pain.

Click. There was that knife sound again.

Monroe flinched. He gritted his teeth and held his breath, awaiting a stab or cut.

"You scared?" the guy whispered maliciously.

God, please take care of Debbie if I don't make it.

The knife blade slid between Monroe's hands. Monroe squeezed his eyes harder.

There was a dull popping sound. The tape was loose.

Monroe exhaled.

Next, the man cut the tape from around Monroe's ankles.

The second man slid the van's side door open as the vehicle slowed. Yanked up, in one swift movement, one man tossed Monroe from the van as the other snatched the black hood off his head.

Monroe hit the ground hard, rolling several times. With each roll, he felt burning and stinging in his side.

The van sped away.

As he rolled along over the ground, Monroe caught a glimpse of the van as he stopped. Slowly, he rolled onto his back, and he was looking up at the stars. Monroe didn't move at first. Turning his head, he mumbled, "I'm home. Thank you, God." Then he remembered Galliard's warning about Debbie. Panicky, he moaned, "Debbie?"

Laboring, he got to his knees. Shaky and wobbling, he stood up. "Ow!" He grimaced as he wiped the dirt and grass off his face and clothes.

Holding his side, he staggered to the front door. "Deb! Debbie!" Monroe yelled as he pounded the door. He prayed she opened the door, unharmed.

Debbie was pacing in the living room when she heard him. She ran to the door and flung it open.

Monroe was standing there with clothes scruffy and dirty, with pain in his face.

Terrified, she gazed at him. "Monroe! Where, where have you been? Look at—what happened to you? Monroe . . .?" She exclaimed as she began to cry.

Wincing in pain from the blows to his side, he said, "Help me inside."

Instead, she threw her arms around him, clutching him around his torso.

"Ouch . . .!" he screamed, recoiling, his knees buckled. "Um . . .!" he moaned excruciatingly.

She stepped back and saw him grab his side. "You're hurt."

"Ye-ah."

"Is it bad?" Debbie asked, assisting him to the couch.

He inched down. "Someone grabbed me when I took the trash out."

"Grabbed you? Who? And where?" she asked, jumpy.

"I don't know. But one of the voices . . . it sounded familiar. I know I've heard it somewhere before." He contorted his face with each word, with each syllable. "Re-recently."

"I'm calling a doctor?"

"I think I need to go to the hospital?"

"What did they do to you?"

"Punches. Several punches to my side," he said, writhing in agony.

"Mon . . . roe . . ." she said, crying even more.

"Deb . . . bie . . ." he mocked with a chuckle that quickly turned into pain. "Oh, oh, oh . . ."

"This is no time to be funny."

"I agree. Don't make me laugh."

"I didn't. You did."

He put his hand up, needing a moment.

She stared at him.

At least, in ministry, he never got beat up. He was threatened a time or two. However, no one ever beat him up—physically, that is.

"Hospital," Monroe moaned. "Let's go."

"Let me get my purse."

As she drove toward the nearest hospital in Jackson, Debbie asked, "Do you think it was Mr. Breaux?"

"No. He's not this stupid. Stupid, but not this stupid."

"Detective Carson?"

"No."

"Maybe some of his friends. Maybe—?"

"No, no, no . . ." he said, grabbing his side, moaning.

"It must really hurt."

Monroe gave her the stupid question look. "Excruciating."

"You wouldn't tell me if you knew who it was, would you?"

Monroe's patience with Debbie's interrogation was running low. He clutched his side. The pain worsened with each breath he took, with each bump in the road. He pulled his shirt up.

Debbie glanced and gasped.

The car swerved.

"Just drive," he said. He looked down. A large bruise was beginning to form, about seven inches in diameter.

Soon they arrived at the ER. After a short wait, a nurse took Monroe to a room and helped him remove his dark blue, and now grimy, t-shirt.

"Oh my," Debbie exclaimed. She bent over to get a closer look at her husband's contusion. It was beginning to show its colors. Reaching over, she gently touched it.

Monroe flinched in pain.

Debbie got her first clear look at his side. "Mon-roe . . .," she said, beginning to cry again.

"Don't cry."

The doctor entered the room. "That looks bad," the doctor said, looking at the contusion. "How did this happen?"

"Got jumped," Monroe answered.

"Jumped?"

"Yeah. Two guys jumped me."

"Let's get a CT," the doctor instructed the nurse. "Got jumped, huh?" he said, observing the dirt and stains on Monroe's clothes.

"Okay," the nurse replied as the doctor left the room.

After several minutes inside the donut-shaped CT machine, a tech returned Monroe to the room where he stretched out on the bed. The tech lowered the lights before leaving. He and Debbie were alone in the room. Staring at the ceiling Monroe said, "This is stupid. I wonder who would do this to me. Why did I move to the South?"

"Dummy, they beat people up in other places, too," Debbie said.

"I know."

A half hour passed as the two sat in silence in the darkened room. The gravity of the situation had them both disconcerted, questioning why and who. Soon, the doctor and nurse entered the room. The nurse turned up the lights. Monroe covered his eyes.

"I looked at your CT, Mr. Lovett. Nothing's broken. No internal bleeding. However, you took some acute blows right here," the doctor said, pointing to an area on Monroe's side, to the darkest area of the large bruise. "I guess your attackers didn't like this one side," he said with a hint of sarcasm. It was obvious, he didn't believe Monroe's story, but Monroe didn't care.

"Then I'll live?" Monroe asked with his own sarcastically.

"You'll live. Here's a prescription for the pain," the physician said, handing it to Monroe. "If you notice it getting worse, then come back here or go to your doctor."

"Thanks, Doc."

Debbie and Monroe returned home after getting the prescription filled. She got him some ice, and he took the medication. It helped some, but it was a short sleepless night for the most part.

Chapter 16

Someone knocking at the front door of the Lovett home startled Monroe awake. It's early the next morning. He was still groggy from the painkillers and wasn't sure if he was dreaming or not. "What time is it?" Monroe grumbled. He attempted to get out of bed. "Ow . . ." he groaned. His side was tight, and the pain was more intense than the night before. Slowly, he sat up on the side of the bed. Gingerly, he stood up, holding his side. Peeking through the curtains, he saw the sheriff's car in the driveway. He squinted to see, but his eyes were still too blurry to see anything more.

There was knocking again, but louder.

"Yeah . . . I'm coming," he said, but not loud enough for anyone to hear. He didn't want to wake Debbie.

"Who?" Debbie moaned as she rolled over, but not opening her eyes.

"Looks like Sheriff Austin. I think. Go back to sleep."

She pulled the covers over her head.

Monroe walked to the front door, moving delicately with each step. Before opening the door, he looked out the side window. Sheriff Austin stood ready to knock again. Monroe opened the door and asked, "Is there a problem, Sheriff?"

Sheriff Austin noticed Monroe holding his side. Seeing the large area of discoloration, he pointed and asked, "You okay?"

"Yeah, I'm fine," Monroe answered. "Why would you ask?" He didn't think about the fact he wasn't wearing a shirt.

"Your wife called us last night. Said you were missing. Thought I'd stop by and check to make sure everything's okay. And by the looks of that bruise there—" he said, pointing at Monroe's side— "and the pain on your face, well . . ."

"No. Everything's fine."

"That's funny," Austin chuckled and then pointed down the street. "Because one of your neighbors called reporting he saw a van drive down the street late last night. And here's the real funny part, he saw you fly out and roll across the yard. Now, unless you've been practicing your superhero moves, I'd say you're hiding something."

"No superhero stuff here, Sheriff," Monroe said, squinting from the sun's blinding as it reflected off Austin's car windshield into his eyes.

"What about those scratches on your face?" Austin asked, pointing with a circular motion at Monroe's face. There was one thing Austin knew; when someone had been assaulted.

Monroe dropped his head. He knew he couldn't continue to deny the truth any longer. No doubt, it would soon become public knowledge. He just nodded his head as he looked at Austin. "Had a conversation, but don't ask me who with, because I never saw them."

"Didn't get a look?"

"No, more like they put a hood over my head. I couldn't see anything."

"Recognize any of their voices?"

"Not sure."

"Not sure, or not saying?"

"Not sure. One of the men, he didn't say much, but his voice—his voice sounded familiar."

"Familiar how?"

"Don't know. I can't place it. But I'm sure I've heard it before."

"Okay. How about you coming down to the station later, give a statement?"

"To you or Carson?"

"Me."

"Okay."

"If I'm going to arrest someone, I want it to stick," Austin said. "I'll be in my office all morning," Austin said, stepping from the porch and walking to his car.

Monroe remained in the doorway as he watched Austin get into his car and back from the driveway. Austin pulled forward, and then stopped his car on the street and let down his window. He called out to Monroe, "Work on remembering that voice, Mr. Lovett."

"I will," he responded with a wave. Monroe noticed a neighbor, the same neighbor who heard Debbie the night before. The man was standing in his driveway staring in Monroe's direction. Monroe closed the door.

103

He walked to the kitchen. Feeling the pain, he grabbed the coffee and began thinking about his interrogation and beating just hours earlier. He worked hard to place the voice. The more he endeavored to recall it, the angrier he got. He just couldn't place it. He knew he had heard it before. "Who was it?" he mumbled as he squeezed the bag of coffee. "I know that voice."

He didn't hear Debbie walk into the kitchen. Monroe's back was to her. She eased up, slid her arms around him, and gave him a slight embrace.

He spun around, letting out, "Ouch!" as Debbie jumped back. He doubled over in pain, dropping the bag of coffee onto the countertop. Popping open, grounds of coffee spilled out across the countertop.

"I'm sorry. I'm sorry. I'm sorry. I'm so sorry. Monroe, I didn't mean . . ." Debbie said, wearing blue satin pajamas, shaking her hands rapidly like a bird flapping its wings, while making her own pain-face. "I forgot about your side."

"Forgot? How could you forget?" he said, holding his side and wincing in pain.

"I said I'm sorry."

"I know. It's just—I was trying to—never mind," he said, still cringing.

Pointing at the spilled coffee, and eager to lighten the mood, she said, "You know, you have to put it in the filter."

Monroe looked at the coffee and then at Debbie. He wasn't in the mood for jokes. He responded, "We'll stop at Christi's."

"What did Sheriff Austin want?"

"Follow-up to your call last night. You didn't tell me you called the sheriff's office."

"Well, that's good to hear. What did you expect? Was I supposed to sit and wait until your new friends tossed you into the front yard after play time?"

"No. You did the right thing, I guess."

"You guess?"

Monroe changed gears. He knew Debbie was right. He stood up straight trying to stretch his side a little. "You know what bugs me?"

"No. What?"

"Why do they want Ashley to change her plea?"

"Is that what they wanted?"

"Yeah. And after last night, I'm even more convinced she's innocent. I mean, why anyone would go to this much trouble unless they're trying to cover up something."

"Could be," she said.

The two stood there a minute not saying anything. Monroe tried again to place the voice as he worked to stretch his side, but the pain was too much. He pondered why they wanted Ashley's conviction so bad.

Debbie moved close to Monroe. "Does it hurt bad?" she asked, caressing his side with a featherlike touch.

He snapped from chewing on the previous night's events. "Huh? Yeah, it's pretty sore."

"Too sore?" she said with a little smile.

A smile emerged on Monroe's face. "You gonna be gentle?"

"I can't make any promises," she said, running her finger down the middle of his chest. "You game?"

"Oh, I'm game," he said, turning to clean the coffee off the counter. "Oh-h-h!" he yelled, bending over in pain.

"Never mind. One part of you might be willing," she said, pointing at a particular zone of his body, "but the rest of you ain't ready."

Trying to ignore his pain, Monroe settled into his desk chair and began working on Ashley's case. He kept questioning, why and who wanted this case to go away, to vanish, without any concern for Ashley's future. However, many girls like Ashley are pushed aside by society, by those who do not wish to have their neat little lives disturbed. And someone's neat little life was being disturbed.

A soft knock at the door preceded Debbie's entrance. "Hey, Herm is here to see you."

"Alright, tell him to come on back," Monroe replied as he squirmed from the ache in his side.

Debbie saw it on his face. She walked over to his desk. "You take your pill?"

He shot her look. "I'm fine."

"Fine? You're about to screw yourself through the floor by the way you're twisting."

Monroe knew she was right. He reached into his desk and pulled out his bottle of pain meds. "Will you get me some water?"

"Sure."

"And tell Herm to come on back."

"Okay," Debbie said, walking to the front office area.

A few moments later, Herm entered with a slight smile on his face and a bottle of water in his hand. "Here," he said, handing Monroe the water. "Heard about your little *encounter* last night."

"Who told you?"

"Ran into Deputy Reed."

"Great, now the whole town will hear about it."

"Probably," Herm laughed. "So, who'd you piss off?"

"I guess someone who wants this case to go away," Monroe said, removing a pill from the bottle. He popped it into his mouth.

"No doubt," Herm said, opening a folder. "More on that later. Look at this."

"What is it?" Monroe answered with a groan, reaching for the sheet of paper. He took a drink of water and swallowed his pain pill.

"The name of an independent forensic investigator."

Monroe looked it over. "Dr. Bryan Michaels?"

"He works out of Jackson. Supposed to be one of the best around. I took the liberty of contacting him."

"Not a problem," he said, watching Herm dropped into his favorite spot on the couch. "Anything else?" Monroe asked.

"Yeah. I spoke with the people on the list you gave me."

"And?"

"And, nothing. Personally, I think they were pretty hammered that night."

"Probably still are," Monroe said with a touch of sarcasm. He attempted to stretch but recoiled in pain. "Ow! I feel like we're hitting a brick wall."

"You think maybe the girl is guilty? I mean—"

"No. Why would someone do this,"—Monroe said, pointing to his side— "if she's guilty?"

"Let's see. She had a motive, the opportunity, and means to do it."

"And . . .?"

"And she did sign a confession."

"Forced to sign. What? Have you changed your mind now?" Monroe asked, wondering if he'd made a mistake taking on Herm.

"No. Just making sure you're still committed after last night," Herm said, pointing to Monroe's side. "So, how are you going to convince a jury otherwise, Counselor?"

"Good question," Monroe answered, taking a deep breath and then moaning from the pain.

Both sat in silence for a moment, contemplating the situation. Believing, or even knowing, the accused is innocent wasn't adequate substantiation. Monroe had offered to prove Ashley's innocence. Now, he just had to figure out how to do it.

"So, about last night. Who do you think wants this to go away?" Herm asked.

"I've got my suspicions."

"Me, too. But, like everything else, it's just a gut feeling."

"Same here," Monroe said, anger etched on his face. He inhaled, and with pain in his face he said, "Man that hurts." He softly rubbed his side. "Oh well, maybe we should find a way to prove what we believe. If we focus on last night, we'll lose perspective on the case."

"Alright," Herm said, but he still was wondering about Monroe's battering. "You sure you're okay?"

"Yes," Monroe answered tersely. He didn't desire to dwell on his issues. The case took precedence with him. "Here's a question for you. Has anyone seen the younger Mr. Butler, Marcus Jr.?"

"Not that I know. Carson spoke with him at the crime scene, but then the boy disappeared."

"More like fallen off the planet. Sure, would like to speak with him. I have some questions about his whereabouts at the time of the murder. If he and Billy don't get along, then either of them makes a good suspect."

"But the evidence and confession finger your client. Ashley had opportunity and motive to murder Julie Miller."

"Herm, you're not helping."

"Sorry, the old cynical detective in me comes out at times."

"Put it back."

"Now, back to last night. You never said what they wanted."

"They want Ashley to change her plea to guilty. Threatened to hurt Debbie. But don't say anything to her, got it?"

"Understand." Herm pointed in Debbie's direction. "I'll keep a close eye on her when you're not around."

"Thanks." Monroe gestured to the newspaper on his desk with the headline: **BURNT BODY FOUND IN DITCH**. "Think they might do more if there's a next time?"

Holding up a finger, Herm said, "First, we don't even know if the two are related." Then he raised another finger stating, "Second, let's make sure there's not a 'next time'." He pointed at Monroe and said, "Look, you need to watch your back. Stay in public places. Don't venture out too far at night."

A little agitated, Monroe replied, "I went to put the trash on the road, Herm."

"Notice anything unusual?"

"Yeah. I heard a vehicle speeding toward me and looked up and saw the van coming at me."

"And you stood there. Didn't move."

Monroe reflected for a moment. "Yeah . . . Your point?"

"I'm just saying. Put the trash out early while there's still plenty of daylight. Pay attention to your surroundings. That's all."

Monroe grew frustrated with talking about the experience. Herm sensed it, got up, and walked across to the other side the office. Admiring the master carpentry of the old built-in maple bookcases, he said, "Monroe, let me play detective for a moment?"

"What do you mean?"

"About last night—"

"Herm . . ."

"I know you don't want to, but bear with me. Tell me what you can remember after they grabbed you."

"I just went over all of this at the sheriff's office a little while ago. I'm tired of talking about it."

"Doesn't matter. The more you tell it, the more details you'll remember. So?"

Reluctantly, Monroe began to retell what he could remember as Herm listened carefully. He recounted everything to the retired detective, every sound and smell he could remember. "There, that's it," Monroe said.

"Okay then."

"That's it?"

"Yep. For now. Gives me something to go on, to work with. Now, you go back to doing your lawyer stuff."

Chapter 17

A visit to Breaux's office seemed appropriate. Monroe had stewed for a couple days, and now was the time to try to get a question answered. Heading across the town square, he walked past the courthouse, giving it a glance. He knew the occasion was drawing near when he would be fighting for Ashley's freedom inside, for her very life. The thought made him even more determined.

No trot up the stairs this time, his side was still sore. After a brief hello, Breaux's secretary led the defense attorney back. The DA's office door was open. "Mr. Lovett is here to see you," she said as Monroe entered. He closed the door behind him.

"Have a seat, Monroe." Breaux could see Monroe had something on his mind. "What can I do for you?"

"Got a question, Robert," Monroe responded, easing down in a chair across from Breaux.

"What kind of question?"

"Where's Marcus Jr.?"

"Why? He didn't have anything to do with this," Breaux answered, a bit annoyed by Monroe's question.

Breaux's response was unexpected. Monroe went to lean forward, but his discomfort caused him to remain sitting upright. Heatedly, he spouted with a wave of his hand, "Nothing to do—how do you know that? I mean, shouldn't someone at least question him? Or, is someone else pulling your strings?"

Ticked by the accusation, and his feathers ruffled, Breaux retorted, "No one is, as you say, *pulling* my strings." He worked to regain his composure. Clearing his throat, he said, "Heard you had a tad bit of a run-in the other night. Maybe it's got you, you know, a bit upset, but—"

"Deflect all you want, Robert, but I want to speak with Marcus Jr."

Breaux leaned forward, resting his arms on his desk. "Detective Carson spoke with the young man. Told me Junior wasn't there when it happened."

"And you believe him?"

"Yes. Yes, I do." Struggling to remain calm, Breaux said, "You want to talk with the boy, you find him. I'm not going to do your job for you."

Monroe wanted to leap forward and put his finger in Breaux's face, but his throbbing rib cage restrained him. It was probably for the best. He knew Breaux was right about finding Junior. Intently glaring at Breaux, and with all the contempt he could muster, Monroe asked, "Why don't I believe you, Robert?"

"That's your problem." Breaux also worked to fight back his anger. Monroe could see his jaw muscles tightening. Breaux, after taking a deep breath, said, "Look—you're new here in Lane County. You're pushing buttons with your . . . your less than hospitable ways. And, from the way you're wincing, there's no doubt you've made some folks around here upset."

"Upset? Less than hospitable? Hah!" Monroe laughed, as he looked away and then back at Breaux. He couldn't believe Breaux was accusing him of being inhospitable. "Is this how you southern folk welcome newcomers?"

"No, we usually—" Breaux said, chuckling. Rethinking his response, he scratched the back of his head, and said, "Look, Sheriff Austin will find out who did that to you," Breaux said, pointing his pen at Monroe's side. "You focus on your case. Make a good show for the girl, and I'm sure more people will come to you. As for your assault, we will prosecute your attackers."

Monroe knew this conversation was getting him nowhere. He stood up with a not-so-happy expression as he stared at Breaux. He walked toward the door as Breaux watched with a condescending grin. Monroe stopped and turned back, and said, "So, I guess you're saying I'm not going to get the opportunity to speak with Marcus Jr."

Breaux, with his sardonic grin, replied, "Like I said, you want to speak with him, you find him."

"Yeah," Monroe replied, nodding and pursing of his lips. "And, don't you worry about the other night or my side," he said, with a soft rub of his torso. "You need to worry about losing this case," He then opened the door and left.

Breaux laughed to himself and then muttered, "The man's got a few things to learn. Yes sir, a few things to learn."

Stepping out onto the sidewalk, Monroe stood for a few seconds and said under his breath, "That went well." He noticed the sun reflecting off the sign over the sheriff's department. *Why not*, he thought and headed straight over. *Maybe Sheriff Austin will give me some info on Junior.* With each step, the pain in his side throbbed, but he didn't care. He was on a mission.

Entering the building, he saw Carson standing at the counter looking through the mail. Carson saw Monroe and said, "Well, if it ain't our Yankee Doodle Dandy defense attorney." Others in the room heard the comment and snickered.

"Funny, real funny, Detective Carson," Monroe replied. He walked over closer to the rotund detective and asked him, "What are the chances of me getting to speak with Marcus Jr.?"

"I've been asking myself the same question, Mr. Lovett."

That's odd, Monroe thought. "I thought you questioned him?"

"At the crime scene. But no, I haven't seen him since. It seems the young man has disappeared."

"Have you asked his father of his whereabouts?"

"Yes, but Marcus told me he hasn't seen him either."

"Believe him? I mean, a woman's found dead in Junior's house, and now he is missing. To me, it makes him a prime suspect, even more of one than his wife."

Carson took a deep breath. He knew Monroe had a point, but he didn't have time to help the defense. In his mind, he had a viable suspect in custody. "Look, Counselor, it's not my job to do your job. If you believe Mrs. Butler is innocent, then prove it. She signed a confession. To me, it makes her guilty."

"That's right . . . forget the facts and where the evidence leads you. Just put the girl away, right." He looked dead into Carson's eyes and asked him, "Who else talked to Ashley before I got here when you booked her?"

Carson shuffled the envelopes he was holding, while returning Monroe's stare, and said, "Like I said, I'm not doing your job for you." The two remained locked in a tense stare-down for a moment. He slapped the counter with the mail to break the silence and said to Monroe, "Look, you don't"— he huffed with a wave of his hand— "never mind."

"What made you arrest my client so quickly? I mean, within a couple hours of finding the victim, you had an arrest warrant issued. You knew where she was and apparently had a confession in hand when she got here," Monroe said, getting louder as he spoke.

Carson stood there silent as he listened to the accusations. He took exception to the diatribe. He put a finger in Monroe's face and started to say something, but noticed everyone in the room was watching. He thought better of it as he stood silently shaking his fat finger at Monroe, and then he turned and walked away.

"Well, I guess our conversation is *over*."

Monroe also noticed all the eyes fixed on him. Instead of pushing the subject, he turned to leave. When he did, he almost ran over Sheriff Austin, who was walking through the front door.

"Wow," Austin chuckled, stepping out of Monroe's way. "Mr. Lovett, how's your side?" Austin then noticed the tension in the room.

"Still sore," Monroe said in a suspicious tone. "Have you arrested anyone?"

"No. Not yet," Austin answered. He had no clue why Monroe was angry.

"Funny, isn't it?"

"What's that, Mr. Lovett? What's going on here?"

"Don't worry about it," Monroe said, attempting to calm himself. He crossed his arms and said, "It's taking you longer to arrest the person who assaulted me than it did to arrest Ashley Butler for murder. I would think your deputies would have taken greater measures to find a murderer than a simple assault."

"Small town, Mr. Lovett," Austin said. He was getting a little irritated with Monroe's insinuations. "Things work differently in a small town. Plus, no one has walked in to sign a confession."

"Small town. I'm sure that's all it is, Sheriff. Makes a great excuse, doesn't it?"

"Now look here, Mr. Lovett, I'm not making excuses. But you making accusations won't help matters. Give me something more, and we'll investigate it."

"Yeah," Monroe huffed and then stepped past Austin and left.

Austin just waggled his head as he wondered what had him so upset.

While walking across the town square, Monroe noticed a van looking eerily like the one from the other night. He pulled his smartphone from his pocket and took a quick picture before it drove out of sight. Attempting to block the bright sunlight, he tried to look at the photo, but it was too bright to make out anything. Monroe hurried back to his office hoping to get a better look at the photo. With each step, he grimaced from the pain. Once inside the building, he stared at the photo. "Too small," he murmured.

"Excuse me?" a female voice said.

"It's—hey?" he said, looking up seeing Debbie.

"Hey sweetie," Debbie said with a smile. "What's too small?"

"This photo. I need my laptop."

"How's your side?"

"Fine," he answered looking back at his phone.

"Must be important," she said, pointing at the phone. "Want something from Christi's while we're down here? I was just getting ready to—"

"Maybe I can enlarge it enough to see the plate," he muttered.

"Plate?" She motioned with her finger between them and asked, "Are we in the same conversation here?"

"Love you," Monroe said, heading up the staircase.

"Love you, too," she replied. "I'm going to go and get me—" she pointed into Christi's. "Oh, never mind. The man's in another world."

Reaching his office, Monroe downloaded the photo onto his laptop. He opened the file and zeroed in on the license plate. It was blurry, but he could make out a tag number. After writing it down, he called Herm.

"Hello, Monroe," Herm answered.

"Herm, are you able to run a license plate for me?"

"Yeah. Sure. What is it?"

"I'll text it to you."

Things were not adding up for Monroe as he poured over Ashley's growing case file. More questions than answers. He reread her confession. One statement stood out, *I pulled the trigger on the twelve-gauge shotgun and murdered Julie Miller*. It seemed too well written for Ashley. He had missed it before. Staring at the statement, he realized he had assumed she was forced to write out her confession. He had listened to people telling him all kind of things over the years, and they never used legal terms. For him, Ashley would write something more along the lines of, *I shot her*, or *I killed her. Someone wrote this for her. But who? At the very least, she was coached.* He mumbled, "I need to ask Ashley—"

Buzz . . .

He heard the main office door open and close. Monroe strained to hear someone. *Where's Debbie? Christi's.* There were no sounds. Monroe looked for something to use as a weapon as his heart raced. *I'm not going without a fight this time.* Monroe bent down, looking in a drawer for anything to use.

Herm entered. "Hey."

"What?" Monroe barked, popping his head up. Spinning around he saw Herm. Monroe struggled to catch his breath. Putting his hand to his chest and flinching from the pain in his ribcage, he glared at him. Herm started laughing at Monroe's reaction. "What were you thinking?" Monroe asked, still trying to lower his heart rate.

With a chortle, Herm pointed at Monroe's hand, and asked, "What, were you going to fight me with your pen?"

Monroe was holding his pen like one would hold a knife ready to strike someone. "Hey, you can kill someone with a pen."

Herm pulled his sports coat back to reveal a Sig .40 caliber pistol tucked under his arm. "Not much of a match for this."

"So, that's why you wear a jacket all the time. Are you allowed—?"

"Got a concealed carry permit. Can carry it any and everywhere. Well, except to court."

"Is there a reason you wanted to scare the bejesus out of me?" he asked, sitting down.

"Not really," Herm said, walking over and dropping into his usual seat on the couch. "Just thought it would be fun."

Monroe smirked at him. "Were you able to get anything from the plate number?"

"Yes, I was."

"And?"

"You're not going to believe this—Butler Transportation."

"You're kidding."

"Wish I was. But, here's the thing. It was reported stolen in Jackson a couple weeks ago."

"Stolen?"

"Yep."

Both men sat pondering this tidbit of information. Herm could see the wheels spinning in Monroe's head. Opening his prescription bottle, Monroe dumped a pill into his hand and then popped it into his mouth. He swallowed it without water and looked at Herm. "Herm, you think Butler had anything to do with this?" referring to his side.

"He has the money." Herm waggled his head, tightened his lips, and then said, "But Marcus—something like this? Why?"

"Assure Ashley's conviction."

"You're reaching."

"I believe he'll buy the jury if he has to."

"Monroe, you need more than a tag number from a stolen van. Maybe someone is after the Butler family. You ever think about that? Maybe your pain meds are affecting your head."

"No, my head's fine."

"Then you should"—Herm waved his hand around— "look at all the angles."

"So, what are you saying?"

"We need to make sure we have enough evidence to ensure Ashley's acquittal," Herm answered.

"But I want to make sure the guilty party goes to jail. I don't care who it is. I've been looking over Ashley's confession, someone else wrote it. We need to find out who."

Herm chuckled. "You do know you're a *defense* attorney, right?"

"What's your point?"

Herm stared at Monroe. He knew Monroe was right. He also knew his own old feelings and friendships were getting in his way. "Look, I got you the tag info."

Seeing the tension in Herm's face, Monroe knew it was too soon to stress their new friendship. "We'll let the evidence speak for itself, alright?"

"Okay."

Monroe closed his laptop and stuck it in his backpack/carrying case and stood up. "But for now, I'm going home."

"Home? It's three in the afternoon. Plus, I just got here."

"Want a drink then?" Monroe said as he walked over and removed a bottle of Kentucky bourbon from a cabinet.

"You just took a pain pill," Herm said, pointing toward Monroe's desk.

"So," Monroe said as he poured.

"You're not supposed—sure, pour me one."

"Don't tell Debbie," Monroe said as he finished pouring the drinks.

"Tell me what?" Debbie asked, walking into the office. She saw the two glasses in Monroe's hands. Sharply, she said, "Monroe T. Lovett, you know better."

Monroe stood there looking like a kid with his hand caught in the cookie jar look. He stuck one glass toward Debbie. She walked over, took it, and then took a sip. He handed the other to Herm, who was laughing at him.

Crickets were chirping as Monroe and Debbie sat on their porch swing on the back patio. The conversation was minimal as they swung back and forth. Debbie inquired, "Overheard you and Herm speaking this afternoon before I walked in, catching you trying to be bad. Anyway, Monroe, is everything going to be okay?"

"Yeah." He cut his eyes over at her. "And, you're not supposed to eavesdrop."

Debbie made a guilty face. "Do you think Marcus Butler is involved?"

"It's just a theory. Herm's probably right." He didn't want Debbie to worry more than she already was. He knew she tended to villainize anyone she thought was against him.

"Well, I'm worried. Worried for you. For us," she said, laying her head over on his shoulder. She gently rubbed his upper arm.

Monroe heard the concern in Debbie's words. Reaching over, he took her hand in his, telling her, "Well, don't be." He remembered Galliard's warning. The last thing he wanted was for something to happen to Debbie. She didn't see it, but Monroe's eyes watered a little. He took a deep breath and said, "Everything's gonna be fine. There's no need to worry."

"Have you *forgotten* about your side? What they did to you?" Her eyes filled with tears as she envisioned Monroe's assault, imagining what happened.

Clearing his throat, he said, "They were just trying to scare me."

Debbie wiped a tear from her cheek. "Well, they scare me. I'm plenty scared. And you should be, too."

"Scared? No. Cautious? Yes. But I have a job to do, dear." He reached up, put his arm around Debbie, and pulled her close. "And Ashley Butler is counting on me to do it

Chapter 18

With its New Orleans-style wrought iron railings and weathered chartreuse painted brick exterior, the 1940s building was home to the Pearl Café. Once inside, the walls were exposed brick with stained concrete floors. The wood tables and chairs showed their years of use but added to the restaurant's ambiance. A bar was in the back corner where a bartender was busy making drinks. As a prominent downtown Jackson eatery, people packed the place during the lunch hour, and it was lunchtime. Today, the crowd provided the perfect spot for someone desiring to go unnoticed, and one someone was Marcus Butler. He sat across the table from his eating companion, Joe Galliard. Butler stared at his half-eaten club sandwich. Up until this point, their conversation had been terse.

A few weeks had passed since Ashley's arrest, and the trial was nearing. The last time they were together was in the cabin with Monroe. This was to be their final meeting. "Lose your appetite?" Galliard asked, taking a drink of his beer.

"This has gotten out of hand," Butler stated.

"You said you wanted to know, didn't you?"

"But . . . do you realize . . . my whole life, everything I've worked for . . . do you understand, I could lose it all?" Butler said angrily.

Wearing a dark baseball-style cap, sunglasses, and sporting a goatee, Galliard replied, "Hey. You're not the only one with something to lose here. I've got my own business." Pointing at Butler, he stated, "Your business . . . is not my problem."

That last statement angered Butler even more as he snapped, "A simple—"

Galliard leaned across the table and said in a lowered voice, "Hey, not so loud. All I did was contact you with a message that someone had a very important piece of information you needed to know. You made the deal."

"But the girl remains resolute. Or maybe I should say it's her lawyer—" Butler said angrily while shaking his head. "You said, 'rough him up a little, threaten him, he'll agree . . . that she would—'"

"Let it go . . . Get over it."

"Get over it? Get over it, he says," Butler complained gesturing with both hands toward Galliard.

"I tried to tell you before. Now, let things run their course. Mr. Roueché said he's got everything under control. Did you do what he asked?" Galliard continued to eat his burger, unfazed.

"Yeah. Yeah, he's in," Butler replied as he sat there, trying to come to grips with how everything was spiraling out of control. One bit of information sent Butler seeking for answers. Now, people were dying. Moreover, he was right in the middle. "My son?" Butler asked, tapping his plate with a cold french-fry.

"What about him?"

"Have you heard from him, because I haven't?"

"Not lately. I'm sure he's fine. You told him to keep low, right? I'm sure when this is over, he'll resurface."

There's an awkward moment of silence. Butler watched Galliard as he took another swig of his brew. "What about that lawyer . . . Lovett?" Butler asked.

"Back to him again? C'mon Marcus, let it go."

"Just wish he would play ball like we thought. Maybe I should—"

"I sure thought he would cave."

"You going to take another try at him?"

"No."

"Why not?"

"Because Roueché told me not to," insisted Galliard. "He said we should've—Just drop it, Marcus."

"Drop it?" Butler asked under his breath. "I can't."

"What's that?"

"Nothing. Nothing . . ."

After a couple of moments, Butler reached down, grabbing a brown attaché case. He slid it from under the table and across to Galliard. "Here's what you came for. Now take it. And tell your boss he's paid in full."

Grabbing the case, Galliard said, "I'll give him your message." He finished his drink and then said, "Next month. Here. Lunch again."

"No. No more lunches. I've paid every penny. I'm done with your lunches."

"What?" Galliard asked with a smile. "You don't want your little secret to get out, do you?"

Gritting his teeth, Butler shouted, "We. Had . . .!" People heard him and started to look. He realized he was getting loud and lowered his voice. With a lowered voice he said, "We had an agreement. I paid for information. Now, this is the last payment, as agreed."

"Well, let's just say, the terms have changed," Galliard said. He wanted his piece of the pie.

"Changed. Changed how?"

"That agreement, it was with Roueché," Galliard said, leaning across the table with an uncompromising stare. "Now, now you have an agreement with me. I think you can handle a hundred more. Got it?" He leaned back, wiped his mouth with his napkin, and then dropped it next to his plate.

Angered, Butler slammed the table with a hammer fist with such violence that everything on the table vaulted. Silverware on Galliard's plate jangled. People close by jumped, turning to see the commotion.

"Sorry," Butler told everyone, motioning with his hands for them to go back to eating. Forcing a smile, he said, "I just got some disturbing news."

With an arrogant wink, Galliard told him, "Lunch. Next month. I'll wait for your call."

Reluctant and livid, Butler nodded, almost biting a hole through the inside of his cheek. If looks could kill, then Galliard would have been a dead man.

Galliard laughed, got up, and walked away. Butler sat there smoldering with rage, watching his money walk away. There was a pain in the pit of his stomach, an aching his sandwich could not relieve.

Butler's cell phone rang.

He jumped.

Pulling it from his pocket, he saw his wife's name on the screen. "Yeah?" he answered attempting to sound as if nothing were wrong.

"Where are you?" she asked, nonplussed by his abruptness.

"In Jackson."

"Jackson?"

"Yes, dear. Jackson. I had a meeting with a sales rep, a lunch meeting."

"Where're you eating?"

"Does it matter?"

"No. I guess not."

Butler just wanted to get his wife off the phone. "Is there a reason you called?"

"I was just wondering if you'd heard from Marcus Jr.? I'm worried."

"No."

"Well . . . Hold on, I just got a text." Butler wanted to hang up but waited for his wife. He drummed the table with his fingers. Growing impatient, he took a deep breath, and let it out slowly as he looked at his watch. Anyone else and he would've ended the call. Finally, Darlene said, "Marcus!"

"What?"

"It was from Junior."

"Where is he? How is he? When is he coming back? Did he say?"

"No. All he said is he's fine, and he'll be back after everything blows over."

"That's all?" he asked with anticipation.

"Yes. I replied, but he hasn't sent me anything yet."

Butler thought for a moment. He was still angry at Galliard. "O-kay . . . I'll talk to you later."

"Love you. Bye," Darlene said.

Without responding, he hung up. Galliard's demand stuck in his craw. Fuming and too impatient to wait for the tab, Butler placed enough cash to cover the bill and a tip on the table. He swallowed the last of his watered-down bourbon and glanced at Galliard's now empty chair. "Doesn't even pay for his own lunch," he griped as he got up. Outraged, he stormed out of the café. Upon reaching his pickup, still incensed, he slammed the hood of the truck with an open palm.

Another meeting was taking place that same day, but this one was in the Lane County jail. Monroe had returned to visit with Ashley. Again, he sat waiting in the same cold, gray room. The door opened, and a female deputy accompanied Ashley inside. Ashley appeared to be in better spirits. She sat down across the table from Monroe. "Hello, Mr. Lovett." She looked up at the deputy. "No shackles?"

"I think you'll be okay," the deputy answered. She gave Ashley a little smile and then left.

"Hello Ashley," Monroe said. "This is probably a stupid question, but how are you doing?"

"I guess, okay." She rolled her eyes slightly. "I am in jail, but—"

"Point taken," Monroe replied with a chuckle.

Ashley leaned forward. She asked, pointing at the scratches on his face, "What happened? I heard someone beat you up."

"Nothing that matters," Monroe answered. "Wait—you heard about it in here?"

"Oh yeah. This place is a rumor mill. The deputies."

Not wanting to talk about his unfortunate experience, Monroe dropped the subject. Like the visits before, he pulled out his trusty legal pad.

She giggled.

"What's so funny?"

"It's just—you know—you and that notepad. Is that all you carry in your bookcase?"

"Attaché."

"What?"

"It's an attaché case."

"Oh . . . okay," Ashley replied with a shrug.

"Well, I have to take notes, you know," he said, a little embarrassed.

There wasn't much time before the trial and Monroe needed to go over a few things with Ashley. After touching on the fine points of the case, and reassured Ashley was ready for trial, Monroe asked, "Ashley, I know I've probably asked you this before, but did you write out your confession?"

"I don't remember . . . that whole morning's a blur," she answered looking down at the table.

Monroe wasn't sure if she was being completely honest with him, so he pushed, saying, "Try. It's important."

She sat quietly at first, but then answered, "Like I said, it's a blur."

"Okay," he said with a disappointed look on his face. He could see her body language said something different. He thought if he could get her to tell him something, anything, then it might help. It didn't look like that was going to happen, at least not now. Knowing he had a lot to do before the trial, Monroe told her, "We've got less than two weeks before we go to trial. If you can remember, it would be very helpful to your case, Ashley."

Ashley didn't say anything.

"Alright," he said, shrugging. "Tell me, have you heard from or seen Marcus Jr.?"

"No. Why? Have you?"

"No. I wish. Just wondering, thinking maybe he's tried to contact you."

"Coward's probably hiding somewhere."

"Do you know where that might be?"

"No. His daddy might know. But I doubt he'd tell you."

"I really only have one more question. Tell me, have you ever fired Junior's shotgun?"

"Plenty times. We did some target shooting a few weeks before, before—well, you know. He was sighting in his slug barrel."

"Thanks, Ashley. Keep your spirits up. I know it must be tough in here, but try to focus on being free in a few weeks," Monroe said, standing up. He walked to the door and informed the deputy he was ready to leave. "I'll be in touch, Ashley. We're working hard for you."

"Mr. Lovett?"

"Yes, Ashley."

"It was that fat detective."

"What do you mean?" Monroe asked with puzzlement on his face.

"He gave me the confession. Said . . . he told me that if I signed it that it would make things easier for me."

"Detective Carson, he gave you the confession to sign? Already written for you?"

"Yeah," Ashley said. Monroe could see her nervousness by the way her hand was trembling. He knew she was taking a step toward trusting him.

"Ashley, this is important. Thank you."

"I trust you, Mr. Lovett. You're the only one I trust."

Fighting back his own apprehension and doubts concerning his own competency, he replied, "Thanks, Ashley. I mean it." He smiled. "Now, let's work on getting you out of here and back to living life again."

Chapter 19

Detective Carson impatiently waited in Breaux's office. The prosecutor was talking on the phone. Carson's smacking of a manila folder against his leg irritated Breaux. Several times, he cut his eyes over at Carson, but the detective continued with his smacking of the folder, even letting out a loud huff a few times to display his displeasure. At last, the prosecutor ended the call.

"Here," Carson said, shoving the folder at Breaux.

"What's this?" Breaux asked, clearly irritated with Carson.

"Final report from the gun expert."

"Daniels?"

Carson cleared his throat, answering, "No. It's from another expert. A new guy. I trust him more than Daniels."

"What's wrong with Daniels?"

"Just thought I would bring in some fresh eyes for a change. Someone, not bias."

"Who?"

"Roueché, Fichard Roueché."

"Was this your idea, or Austin's?"

"Mine. He's supposed to be good. His report confirms the shotgun, in all likelihood, fired the fatal shot. That's what you want, right?"

"As long as he knows what he's talking about," Breaux said, skimming the report. "Everything looks okay." He quickly looked at the included copies of some certificates "Looks like he's got all the right credentials," he said, setting the folder on his desk. "Is that all?"

Carson thought for a second and then said, "Let's see, we've got witnesses to an argument, motive, opportunity, and a murder weapon with prints, and, the icing on the cake, a signed confession. It looks like I've handed you a case that is open and shut. The Butler girl will go away, and we can focus on our next case—the burnt body." Carson looked down as he straightened his thin black tie with a sense of self-satisfaction.

"It's not shut until the jury comes back with a guilty verdict."

"Or she changes—"

"You can forget that," Breaux chuckled as he tossed the folder onto his desk. "Lovett's not going to allow it."

"Your problem, not mine."

Breaux picked up another folder and asked, "As far as the burnt body goes, got any clues?"

"Nothing yet. The coroner's report will help."

"Then I guess we're done here."

"Fine . . . I can take a hint." Carson got up, adjusted his pants, and holstered pistol. He departed. Breaux watched the detective walk away. He looked back at the folder with Roueché's information and report. He wasn't happy with the change but trusted Carson.

Across the picturesque downtown square of Peregrine, Monroe was sitting in his office, making some final notes before going to jury selection. This process would be routine for him, but with one little glitch, Breaux knew the people here—he did not. A consultant would be nice, but he just couldn't justify spending the cash. He thought of asking Herm but changed his mind. Now he questioned his decision. With no background on the potential jurors, they were still just names to Monroe. He would ask some questions, attempt to make a quick educated guess, but he was leaning on faith. The one thing that concerned him, many of them worked for Butler Transportation, and that presented an issue for him. The way he saw it, they likely would agree with whatever Mr. Butler wanted—a guilty verdict.

Debbie rapped lightly on the door.

"Yes?" he answered.

She walked in, pushed the door to, and sat down.

"Something I can help you with?" Monroe asked her. He could tell by the look on her face she was bored, but he had work to do. She wasn't going anywhere, and he knew it.

"How's it coming?" Debbie asked, making small talk. He looked at her with his head cocked to the side a little. She could read his mind. "I'm bothering you, aren't I?"

"No. Not at all," he said, forcing a smile. "I've got time for you, always."

"I'll leave you alone," she said, slowly getting up.

He didn't want to ignore his wife, but he also needed to work on the case. The pressing challenge he faced was how to do both. Debbie stood there looking at him. She didn't want to leave. Monroe felt conflicted. *What do I do?* "No, what is it?" he asked.

"Nothing really. It's just that you've been so busy lately. You know, I was just hoping—"

Tap-Tap-Tap at the door. It opened a little. "Hello? Anyone here?" Herm asked, peeking in. "I'm not disturbing you two, am I?"

"No, not at all. Come on in," Monroe said.

Debbie saw the look on Monroe's face. *So much for that.* She sighed, "I'll leave you two alone."

"Debbie?" Monroe asked, seeing her disappointment.

"What."

"I didn't hear the buzzer when Herm came up."

"I know," she answered rather bluntly. "I disconnected it."

"Why?"

"Didn't like it," she sniped, standing at the office door.

"Well, reconnect it, please," Monroe said.

"Fine," she exhaled.

"We'll do something tonight, okay."

"Promise?"

"Yes," Monroe answered with a wink.

Herm dropped onto the couch. "She's mad," he said, gesturing in Debbie's direction.

"No. Not mad. Just—never mind. What can I do you for?"

"How's the ribcage?" Herm asked.

"It's fine. I take it you're here for a reason."

"Have you heard?" Herm asked.

"Heard what?"

"The prosecution has a new gun expert. He's not using Daniels."

"Why not?" Monroe asked with a perplexed look on his face. "I thought he was supposed to be the best around the area."

"He is, as far as I know. Maybe *we* should talk to him?"

"Maybe *we* should."

"There's only one problem. He's out of town for the next several days. I spoke with Christi before coming up here. She told me he went on a fishing trip to Florida since Carson decided not to use him. He's *supposed* to be back the day before the trial starts."

"That's not good. Won't give us much time," Monroe said, pondering the change. "You say that Carson made this decision?"

"Yep."

"That's odd, don't you think?"

"For Carson? Nothing surprises me about him."

"Ashley told me Carson gave her the confession, already written."

"You believe her?" Herm asked, surprised by the statement.

"Do you?"

"That's a pretty blatant accusation."

"You didn't answer my question, Herm," Monroe said with a little more force to his tone.

Herm rubbed his chin as he digested Ashley's claim. This was a childhood friend, a fellow cop. Inside, the blue wall was slowly rising. Monroe could see it. Then Herm relaxed and said, "Yeah. Unfortunately, I do, Monroe."

Monroe felt relieved with Herm's answer. The last thing he needed right now was a disagreement with his investigator. "You know, proving it will be difficult."

"Nearly impossible. Of course, unless you offer him food."

Monroe laughed. He gestured with his hand, asking, "So, what do you know about this new guy?"

"Roueché?" Herm answered with a slight shake of his head. "Never heard of him."

"*Go-ye* what?"

"Roueché. It's Cajun."

Monroe shook his head as he said, "I'll never get used to some of the names down here."

"Oh, this is nothing," Herm said, chuckling. "This is an easy one."

"Well, anyway, something's fishy here."

"You think?" Herm said flippantly. "Anyway, from what I've heard, he confirms the shooting with the shotgun found at the scene. I'm sure a copy of the report is coming."

"Did we expect anything else?"

"Guess not. But we need to speak with Daniels. Get his story."

"The sooner, the better," Monroe said, tapping his pen on the desk. The wheels were turning as he attempted to figure out the real motive in this case. Why frame Ashley?

"You know," Herm said, "this case reminds me of another case I worked. Several years ago, there was this guy who was charged with the murder of his friend. And—"

"And Herm, I don't have time for a story."

Shooting Monroe a disgruntled smirk, Herm said, "Fine. I'm out of here, then."

Chapter 20

In just under 24 hours, the murder trial of Ashley Butler would begin. Monroe's defense was, well, it was lacking. A sliver of hope, along with circumstantial holes in the prosecution's case he would attempt to use, along with Ashley's denial, was all he possessed. At this point, he had nothing concrete. His alternative theory of the crime was either Marcus Jr. or Billy committed the crime. However, Billy was dead, and Junior was nonexistent, to which no one seemed to care. A mountain of evidence stood before him. Monroe wouldn't say it, but he was beginning to doubt his promise to Ashley, to prove her innocence. Sure, his gut told him she was innocent. However, the evidence pointed to her culpability. He had scorned Breaux about not following the evidence. Maybe he did. Moreover, when it came to the confession, it was Ashley's word against Carson's. With Carson being a local, Ashley's word was nil. Monroe knew who the jury would believe. It was looking bleak.

Standing, staring out his office window, Monroe gazed at one thing, the large courthouse; the same courthouse that once brought excitement and anticipation for him, now its grandeur conjured up anxiety, apprehension, and unrest. Facing the jury, or a judge, was not an issue with Monroe. Nor was it going head-to-head with Robert Breaux. No, his problem was his phobia of failure. He did not like to fail, especially in the eyes of others. Had he failed before? Yes. He'd even done so in the public's view. He just didn't like it and would do just about anything to avoid it.

Knocking rattled the door behind Monroe. Startled, he answered, "Come in." Herm eased in. His appearance said it all—a new problem. Without speaking a word, he just ambled over and flopped down on the couch. "What's wrong?" Monroe asked. Herm didn't say a word. "Well?" Monroe pushed. He could read Herm's despondent appearance.

"Daniels," Herm said dejectedly.

"What about him?" Monroe asked, with a hint of concern.

"He's not back," Herm said with a frustrating wave of his hand that finished with a flop on his knee.

"What? Where is he?"

Herm took a deep breath and then said, "I spoke with Christi. Asked her where he was. She said she talked to him last night, and get this, he told her the fishing, *the fishing* has picked up, and he was staying a little longer than planned. She asked him if he was going to make it back in time for the start of the trial."

"And?" Monroe asked, swallowing hard. In his mind, all he could envision was Daniels not making it back at all. Like a scene from a movie playing in his head, he saw his whole case falling apart, with the jury finding Ashley guilty.

Herm sank deeper into the sofa almost becoming one with the leather. "Daniels said he hoped, *hoped* to, but couldn't make any promises."

Monroe became red-faced. "You have got to be *kidding* me!" Dropping into his chair, he asked, "What about Michaels? Have you heard anything from him? You said we would hear from him before the trial. Dammit, Herm."

"Look, I called his office this morning, Monroe. All I got was his voicemail. It said he was still out of town," Herm replied, embarrassed. He knew he had made promises to Monroe.

Everything inside Monroe wanted to leap across the room and choke the man. The only thing stopping him was that sinking feeling in his gut, that feeling of failing big, on his first case. Blow this, and no one will use him. "Well, that's par for the course with this case. We'll go to trial, hope and pray Daniels makes it back, and Michaels contacts us. If not, well, I'll look like a fool. Breaux will parade me around town as his latest trophy." He thought for a moment and then said, "I'll talk to Judge Harper. Maybe he'll give me an extension due to unforeseen circumstances."

"You think he'll allow it?"

"No. Are you kidding?"

Feeling partly responsible, Herm said, "I apologize, Monroe. I didn't think—"

"No, no. It's not your fault." Monroe rubbed his forehead. Herm saw a different look in Monroe's face. "It's this case, Herm. It's this—blasted case," Monroe said with a wave of his hand. Like a speeding bullet, Monroe's mind raced to him having to face Breaux, the judge, and twelve jurors, somehow trusting the truth would come out amid all the lies and an apparent cover-up. He blurted out, "Why would Marcus Jr. just disappear? I can't stop wondering about that, Herm. It doesn't make sense to me."

"Yeah, I know. It's been bugging me, too."

"So where do you think he is?"

"That's the $64,000 question, isn't it? Even if dear ole daddy told him to vamoose, I'd think he would try to contact Ashley—something," Herm said, pointing in the direction of the county jail.

"Let's start poking around, ask some questions, and see if we can find out where Marcus Jr. is."

"What do you think I've been doing?"

"Huh, I'm beginning to wonder that myself."

"Funny. Real funny, Monroe," Herm responded. "People say they saw him here, or there, but nothing solid. I even had someone say they saw the kid in Jackson."

"Well?"

"Just rumors. That's all. No real leads. One thing you learn, people think they know and see lots of things. But they don't."

"You sure?" Monroe asked.

Herm didn't answer. If it weren't for Monroe's frustration with the case, he would rip into him with a lecture on his experience. However, he let Monroe's questions slide.

There was a tapping at the door, a much-needed distraction for the two men as they sat eying each other. Before Monroe could say anything, Debbie walked in with a note in her hand. She could sense the tension.

Monroe sternly asked her, "Did you ever think we might be discussing something confidential?"

"Yeah, that's why I knocked. And I thought you might want this," she said, handing the note to her husband.

Monroe looked at the note, and then said to Herm, "Daniels is on his way back."

"Hey, some good news," Herm said, throwing his hands up in the air.

Monroe looked at Debbie, and contritely said, "Thanks, babe. Sorry about, you know."

"You're welcome, sweetie," she answered giving him an air-kiss before turning to leave. She knew the stress he was undergoing. Walking out the door, she said over her shoulder, "It just means your tab for tonight is growing."

"Things are getting too mushy in here for me," Herm said, shaking his head.

With Debbie gone, Monroe said, "You know, Herm, I haven't heard you say anything about a wife. You married?"

"Nope. No time for a wife."

"What, you're in your late forties?"

"Forty-eight. And your point?"

"You're a little rough around the edges. But, I think we could—"

"Stop right there," Herm said, putting his hand up, his palm facing Monroe. "Don't even think about trying to hook me up. I don't know of anyone who would want this worn-out, middle-aged, hung out to dry, old man, anyway," he chuckled.

"Eh, you're probably right."

Later that afternoon, Debbie was sifting through the mail. One piece caught her eye, an envelope addressed from Bryan Michaels. She took it directly to Monroe. Barging through the door, she said, "Monroe, you got something from Michaels."

"What did I tell you about barging in here?"

She stood there glaring at him, one hand on her hip, and holding the envelope for him with the other. Her theatrics didn't faze him. He thought it was cute. He took the envelope from her, ripped it open, and then read it to himself.

"So, what does it say?" Debbie asked.

"He needs to examine the shotgun and crime scene evidence."

"That's it?"

"Yeah. Basically." Monroe flipped the piece of paper, looking at both sides as if he were expecting to find something else. "A phone call or email would have sufficed." Monroe handed the letter back to Debbie. "Here, stick this in the case file." He slumped back into his chair. "Michaels needs to see the gun, but oh, wait a minute, Michaels isn't here is he? And who knows when he'll be back. Great. Just—great."

Sensing her husband's frustration, Debbie said, "Monroe, it'll work out. You must trust God with this. Remember, he brought you here."

"I'm beginning to wonder if he brought me, or— "

"Don't even finish that sentence, Mister," Debbie snapped.

Frustrated, Monroe knew Debbie was correct. "Anyhow, I've got to figure out how to prove Ashley's innocent. So, you can go back to doing whatever it was you were doing."

Debbie looked at him with a raised eyebrow and said, "I have one more thing for you."

"I hope it's good."

She walked back to the office door and reached out into the hall. "Here you go. I got your suit dry-cleaned, and all pressed," she said, swinging it around to show him. "I even got you a new shirt and tie."

"Hey, that looks good, honey. But when did you—?"

"I have my ways," she drolly said. "Now that mean ole judge won't fuss at you."

"Thanks. I really mean it. Thank you, honey."

"You're welcome. Now I will go back to *doing* what I was doing."

"Okay, got it. I'm sorry," Monroe said as Debbie sauntered away.

Monroe leaned back in his chair and stared up at the ceiling. He rubbed his hands over his face and then ran them over the top of his head, stopping as he grabbed his hair, giving it a slight tug. *Why, oh why, did I do this? There has to be another way to make a living.*

Chapter 21

Packed to capacity, the whispering and undertones from the gallery in the small courtroom echoed into the hallway. Increased anticipation of the trial had caused a mingling of rumors, gossip, and questions in the small town of Peregrine. Many were asking why this girl would sign a confession and then plead not guilty? Where was her husband? How could something this terrible happen in such a quiet town, to such a nice family as the Millers? Those questions and more drew the people into the courtroom for answers. However, the one thing that stood out to many people was the lack of Butler family support for Ashley.

Monroe was sitting at the defense table. He took a deep breath and exhaled slowly. *Calm down, Monroe. Just relax.*

Debbie was sitting behind her husband in the first row of seats in the courtroom. She leaned forward, placed her hand on Monroe's shoulder, and whispered, "You'll do fine."

He turned and winked at her. "Shouldn't you be at the office?" he asked with a questioning look. "What if someone calls?"

She giggled. "Transferred it to my cell, just in case that one telemarketer calls."

"Funny," Monroe said, smirking a little before turning back around.

A door in the far corner of the courtroom opened. Ashley entered, escorted by a deputy. She was wearing a conservative, but not old-fashioned, dark blue dress with white trim. Her appearance was very stylish. Debbie assisted her with her hair earlier. No doubt, she did not look like the same girl Monroe had visited in the jail over the last several weeks.

The door slammed behind her.

Ashley jumped.

Silence imbued the courtroom. Only breathing and the hum of four ceiling fans pierced through the quiet. She felt their stares, condemning scowls, and frowns. They seemed more like daggers to her. Seeing the rubberneckers, she felt discomfited, and she shifted her eyes to Monroe as she walked. Each step reverberated in the small courtroom as her heels clacked when making contact with the old wood floor.

A chair screeched across the floor. It was Monroe's as he stood. He pulled Ashley's chair out for her. Timid, Ashley sat down next to Monroe.

The buzzing of voices resumed.

Taking it all in, Breaux sat with confident haughtiness. How could he lose such an easy case? He glanced over at Monroe. *No way he thinks he has a snowball's chance in hell. But, he's got to start somewhere, and it might as well be losing to me.* The prosecutor chuckled under his breath. In his mind, he had given Monroe a way out. That offer was off the table. Monroe wasn't interested in Breaux and never noticed him, except seeing him when he first arrived. The two only exchanged a subtle nod.

Leaning over, Monroe asked Ashley, "How are you doing?" *Stupid question, Monroe.*

"I guess, okay. Considering . . ." Ashley answered with a half roll of her eyes. She was fidgeting in her seat.

"My bad. Sorry," Monroe said. "Remember everything we talked about. Don't give the jury any signs you are guilty. Don't react to the testimony. Just remain calm no matter how bad they paint you, okay."

She nodded, yes.

He reached into his briefcase and removed an extra notepad. "Here," Monroe said, placing it on the table in front of her. "You can take your own notes. It'll help."

"How many of those things do you carry in there?" Ashley asked.

Debbie overheard her and giggled, "More than you can imagine, sweetie."

A door opened in the opposite corner of the courtroom from where Ashley had entered. A deputy held the door open for the jury to enter the jury box, eight women, and four men. Monroe had done all he could to make the selections he wanted on the jury, but unfortunately for him and Ashley, seven of the jurors worked for Butler. Judge Harper had denied his motion to exclude any of them.

"All rise," the bailiff announced. "The Court of Lane County is now in session, the Honorable Judge Ronald Harper presiding."

Everyone remained standing until Harper entered and took his seat on the bench. Harper gaveled and said, "Bailiff, call today's calendar."

"Your Honor, today's case is the State of Mississippi versus Ashley Butler for one count each, murder in the first degree, and one count of aggravated assault in the first degree."

Monroe swallowed hard and took a deep breath as he attempted to slow his heart rate.

Silence embodied the once vibrant courtroom.

Judge Harper perused the gallery. Faces full of expectation looked back at him. None of the Butler family was present. That surprised him. Julie Miller's parents sat behind the prosecution. That didn't.

Straight-faced, Harper centered his attention on the front two tables. "Mr. Breaux, Mr. Lovett, I trust both the prosecution and the defense are prepared," Harper stated as he peered over his black-framed reading glasses.

Both men nodded and answered, Breaux and then Monroe, "Yes, Your Honor."

Turning his attention to the jury, Judge Harper said, "Members of the jury, I want to remind you this is a death-penalty case. Do not take this case lightly. You were chosen to judge this case based on the evidence, and nothing else. Understand?"

Several members of the jury nodded slightly. A couple of them just sat, staring forward.

"Is the prosecution ready to make its opening statement?" Harper asked.

"Yes, I am, Your Honor," Breaux answered, standing with an air of smugness.

"Please proceed," Harper instructed.

"Your Honor, ladies and gentlemen of the jury, and those here in this court today, this is a simple case," Breaux said as he began. It was easy to ascertain he had rehearsed the speech. Walking around to the front of his table to speak directly to the jury, he continued, "The District Attorney's Office will provide and demonstrate the culpability of the defendant, Ashley Butler, and that she did have the opportunity, motive, and the means to commit the act of murder in the first degree against a . . . a defenseless victim, Julie Miller.

"We will show this court that Mrs. Butler did, without regard for human life, brutally and viciously at point-blank range, shoot, not once, but five times, killing the defenseless victim, Julie Miller, with a 12-gauge shotgun."

Monroe gave a quick glance at Ashley. She sat, showing no emotion, listening to Breaux like any other spectator. It was all surreal to her.

"We will provide witnesses," Breaux said, "who will attest to the defendant's motive to murder of Ms. Miller because of an *alleged* extra-marital affair between Ms. Miller and the defendant's husband." Breaux looked at Ashley, and then around the courtroom, where there was no sign of Marcus Jr. "That this *alleged* affair drove the defendant, Ashley Butler, to commit the heinous act of murder." He paused, turned slightly, giving the jury an opportunity to look at Ashley.

As hard as she tried, with the mention of the affair, Ashley could not veil her emotions as they flooded over her. Breaux's remarks stung. She fixed her glower dead onto the prosecuting attorney.

Monroe noticed and readjusted his position in his chair, attempting to hide her from the jury. He quickly scribbled a note and smiled as he slid it over to her. It read, *Stay calm!!!*

Ashley read it. She licked and pursed her lips and then looked down struggling to act composed.

Harper cleared his throat, urging Breaux to continue.

Breaux had made his point. Grinning a little, he continued, "We will demonstrate the defendant's alibi only provides evidence to her own murderous intentions. That, in fact, her excuse is nothing more than a lie, because firstly, it cannot be corroborated. And secondly, her own signed confession *negates it*. She only offered an alibi after she realized her own guilt and the consequences of her actions.

"We will provide witnesses who will testify to arguments that Mrs. Butler had with the deceased over an extended period of time. In addition, we have witnesses who will provide testimony to an argument between Mrs. Butler and her husband the night prior to her committing this murder. Members of the jury, after you hear and see the evidence, you will be left with only one conclusion—Ashley Butler is guilty. Guilty of murder in the first degree.

Ashley fought back the tears as her eyes filled. Monroe pushed a small box of tissues over to her.

"Thank you, Your Honor, and members of the jury," Breaux said, and then walked back to his chair and sat down.

Whereas Breaux was imparting his opening remarks to convict Ashley, even before any evidence was furnished, all Monroe could think about was where his two key experts, Daniels and Michaels, were. Sure, they're testifying was still a few days away, probably a week at best. Both had assured him they would be ready by the time the trial began. Now, neither one was on hand. On top of that, he wasn't even sure if their testimonies would help. His fear was their findings might verify the prosecution's case.

"Mr. Lovett, nice suit," Judge Harper stated with a slight grin. Most in the courtroom did not get Harper's inside joke. Monroe turned and gave Debbie a quick smile. "Does the defense wish to give an opening statement at this time?"

Monroe stood, buttoned his dark blue pinstripe suit coat, and replied, "Your Honor, the defense desires to wait until the prosecution rests their case before making any opening statements. Thank you."

"Objection, Your Honor," Breaux said.

"Overruled."

"But, Your Honor—" Breaux insisted.

"I'll set precedent, Mr. Breaux," Judge Harper said.

After sitting back down, Monroe glanced at Ashley, giving her a reassuring smile.

Judge Harper turned his attention back to Breaux, and said, "Then, the prosecution may proceed with its case."

Seated a few chairs down the front row, not far from Debbie, the wide-eyed female reporter from the Ledger, Amy, took down every word with eagerness. No doubt, this was one of her first assignments, a big story for her. However, for most, it was still a local feature, a possible love affair gone bad. She knew adding a few adjectives in just the right places meant her story could move her up the ladder of success.

Rising to his feet again, Breaux played the 9-1-1 call for the court. Everyone listened. Breaux was setting his timeline of events. Next, he called Deputy Reed to the stand. His questions set the story up for the prosecution's case. After Breaux had concluded with Deputy Reed, Monroe was ready to ask his questions. "Deputy Reed," Monroe asked, "did you Mirandize the defendant?"

"Yes. I do believe it was in your office," he answered with a slight chuckle and a glance at the jury.

A few people laughed at Reed's response.

Monroe ignored Reed's comedic response. "Did you ask her if she wanted her attorney when you handed her a confession to sign?"

"No. Wait. I never handed her anything to sign," Reed answered, but without the wit. He shuffled a little in the witness chair. "But, to answer your question, I did not ask her if she wanted her attorney. I even went over her rights again."

"And she didn't ask for an attorney?"

"She informed me she waved her rights."

Monroe looked at him with skepticism. "I find that hard to believe." He looked around at the jury and then asked, "Who else, besides yourself, spoke with the defendant once you got her to the sheriff's department?"

"Detective Carson."

"Did anyone else have contact with her?"

"I don't know."

"Who wrote out her confession?"

"Objection," Breaux stated. "No confession has been offered into evidence."

"Your Honor, the prosecution made mention of a confession in his opening statement."

"True. The prosecution's motion is denied."

Breaux did not react to the ruling.

Monroe thought for a moment and then said, "I'm finished with this witness for now. Permission to recall the witness, if needed, later?"

"Granted," Judge Harper answered.

Monroe sat down.

Breaux took his cue from the judge for him to proceed. His assistant began to set up a large easel on which he began placing several enlarged photos of the crime scene: A half-naked female, her body riddled with bullet holes and covered in blood, most of her face obliterated, blood splatters on the bedding, the walls and the carpet soaked with the victim's blood and pieces of flesh. Each picture presented a different angle of the body, as it lay lifeless. Her light brown skin appeared translucent as she lay in a puddle of blood. Julie's hazel eyes were visible, but there was no life in them.

Several gasps from the courtroom and a couple of jurors even whispered, "Oh my." Others seated in the gallery made their own sounds of disgust. Two people jumped up and hurried from the courtroom with a hand covering their mouths.

Julie's parents looked away in shock. Mrs. Miller began crying. Photos of their daughter's dead body lying on the blood-soaked carpet of the defendant's bedroom were too much. Sure, Breaux had informed them of this, but nothing could really prepare the grieving parents to see this gruesomeness.

Ashley turned away, heaving a little as she covered her mouth. Monroe grabbed a trashcan and slid it over to her. He hoped some of the jurors saw how the photos bothered her. Maybe they might question how someone could commit such a ghastly act.

Breaux allowed the pictures to speak for themselves for a moment. He then said, "The prosecution calls Detective Benedict Carson to the stand."

Sworn in, Carson sat down and pulled out his notebook. He looked nervous.

"Detective Carson," Breaux said as he began his questioning, "Would you please explain to this court what you found the morning you were called to the residence of Marcus Butler, Jr. and Ashley Butler?"

Uneasy, Carson fumbled with his notebook as he searched for the correct page. He cleared his throat a couple of times. Reading word-for-word from his notes he said, "Upon entering the bedroom, the master bedroom," he clarified, "the body of the victim was lying on the floor. Several bullet wounds—"

"How many wounds were there, Detective?" Breaux asked.

"The victim had *six* in her chest. Two in her right arm. Three in her left arm. And, three in her lower abdomen," Carson recounted. He swallowed hard and described, "I was unable to ascertain the number to her face. Most likely, it was a close shot. Very close. I believe the coroner can provide more details."

The courtroom door opened. Herm walked in, followed by Jason Daniels. It was obvious he had just returned from his trip, dressed as if he had just walked off the boat wearing a blue fishing shirt, tan cargo shorts, and a ball cap. His flip-flops echoed through the courtroom as he walked. Monroe didn't care how he was dressed. A sense of relief came over him just knowing one of his key experts was here. Judge Harper gave him a glance.

Breaux noticed also, and for a moment, he wondered why Daniels was with Herm. Then he turned his attention back to Carson.

Standing room only forced the two men to find a spot in the back of the courtroom. Daniels stared intently at the photos, studying every detail of the shot pattern, especially those to her chest. One pellet entered just above her left breast. A second entry point was below her right rib cage. Two penetrated the victim's chest over the heart, and another entered below her sternum. The other entry wounds also caught his attention. He asked Herm for a piece of paper. Herm reached into his breast pocket, removed a small notebook, and handed it to Daniels. He wrote a quick note and asked Herm to get it to Monroe.

Breaux completed his questioning of the detective with one final question. "Detective Carson, what prompted you to seek the arrest of the defendant, Ashley Butler?"

Herm eased through the courtroom and handed the note to Monroe.

Carson answered, "Besides the *obvious* motive of the adultery between the defendant's husband and the deceased—"

Now everyone, including Breaux, expected a hearsay objection from the defense due to the lack of any evidence presented at this point. Monroe remained silent as he read the note from Daniels. Even Debbie muttered while keeping her mouth mostly closed, but loud enough for those close by, including Amy from the Ledger, to hear her say, "Object, Monroe, object!"

However, Monroe did nothing. He wasn't listening, but reading, "*Mr. Lovett, ask Carson if something about the shot pattern on the victim's torso seems odd to him.*"

Breaux, noticing Monroe's distraction, motioned to Carson. "Please finish."

"We found a 12-gauge shotgun in the residence belonging to the defendant's husband." Feeling more comfortable, Carson explained, "Well, these kinds of cases lead you to a jealous spouse first. We obtained Mrs. Butler's fingerprints, *which* we have on file, and compared them with the prints on the murder weapon."

"And what were your findings, Detective," Breaux asked.

"They matched."

"They matched," Breaux reiterated. "Then what?"

"Everything about this case led us to believe the murder was committed with extreme prejudice by the defendant."

"Extreme prejudice," Breaux emphasized as he lifted the bagged and tagged 12-gauge shotgun for all to see, with an evidence tag dangling from it. He asked Carson, "This shotgun? Is this the murder weapon you recovered from the crime scene, Detective Carson?"

"Yes, it is."

"Detective," Breaux continued, "was there anything else?"

"An anonymous tip. The person said the defendant was spotted leaving the crime scene around the time of the shooting."

Monroe, surprised by Carson's answer, snapped his head up, and stated, "Objection. The defense was never informed of there being an anonymous tipster."

Harper looked down at Carson and asked, "Detective, please explain why this was not provided to the defense."

Carson swallowed hard. "It must have been an oversight, Your Honor. I ask for the court's forgiveness."

"Overruled, Mr. Lovett," Harper declared. "Detective, please get a copy of the report to the defense by the noon break." Carson nodded that he understood as Harper said, "The prosecution may continue."

It was not the ruling Monroe wanted.

Sheriff Austin was observing the proceedings from the back of the courtroom. He did not like Carson's apparent misstep.

"Detective Carson, what did you do next?" Breaux asked.

"I had two deputies arrest the defendant and bring her in for questioning. It was at that time she gave us a full confession."

"This confession?" Breaux said, lifting it into the air for all to see. "The prosecution wishes to submit the defendant's signed confession into evidence."

"Your Honor," Monroe said, "the defense restates its objection to the confession being allowed as evidence."

Breaux, chuckling, said, "Judge, this matter has *already* been settled by an earlier ruling made by you. The defense knows this."

"Your objection is noted, Mr. Lovett," Harper said. "However, the confession remains."

"But, Judge—," Monroe exclaimed.

"But nothing, Mr. Lovett," Harper warned.

Breaux strutted over and placed the confession on the evidence table as if he were positioning a first-place trophy for all to admire. He turned and walked back to his seat. "That's all for this witness," he said, taking his seat.

"Mr. Lovett?" Judge Harper asked.

Monroe didn't respond. He appeared to be mentally elsewhere.

Again, and a little louder, Judge Harper asked, "Mr. Lovett?"

"Yes, Your Honor?" Monroe responded.

Debbie rolled her eyes and thought to herself, *Great Monroe, your first day in court, and you're already in trouble.*

"Do you have any questions for this witness?" Harper asked, motioning in Carson's direction.

"Yes, I do, Your Honor," Monroe said, standing. He looked down at the note in his hand. "Detective, is there anything about the shot pattern in the victim's torso that seems odd to you?" he asked, pointing at the photos and making a swirling motion with his hand.

Carson studied the photos, and then answered, "No, not really."

"Detective Carson, did you perform a GSR test on Mrs. Butler?"

Carson did not answer immediately.

"Detective?" insisted Monroe.

"No. No, we didn't."

Breaux fought to hide his own anger. He looked at the jury. Several jurors had perplexed expressions on their faces.

"So, there's no way you can prove Mrs. Butler fired that shotgun, or any gun, in or around the day Julie Miller was murdered?"

Carson shifted in his chair, answering, "No."

"Detective Carson, did you encounter any other person or persons at the crime scene?"

Breaux shuffled in his chair as he glared at Carson. The detective wouldn't return Breaux's look. He stared straight at Monroe and answered, "Yes. Marcus Butler, Jr. was in the driveway."

"Detective, did you question Marcus Butler, Jr.?"

"Yes. But there was nothing suspicious about his answers. So, I let him leave."

"Detective Carson, do you know the whereabouts of Marcus Butler, Jr.?"

"No. No, I do not."

Monroe looked at the jurors with a look of suspicion on his own face. "Detective," he continued, "can you state, without any doubt, Marcus Butler, Jr. did not kill the victim?"

"Objection," Breaux said. "Marcus Butler, Jr. is not on trial here."

"Overruled," Judge Harper responded. "Answer the question, Detective."

Carson weighed the best way to answer. He looked to the back of the courtroom where Sheriff Austin was standing, waiting for his response. He answered, "Without any doubt? Well, no. I guess not."

Breaux glowered at Carson with his lips tightened. His anger was evident. The assistant sitting next to him whispered, "Let it go, Robert. Let it go." Breaux listened and relaxed.

"Your Honor," Monroe requested, "I would like for the court to rule that the interview with Marcus Butler, Jr. be removed from the detective's report. And, more importantly—"

"Objection," demanded Breaux. He popped to his feet. "On what grounds? That testimony was obtained by a sheriff's detective. To remove it would undermine the integrity of local law enforcement," he exclaimed with a swing of his arm.

"Your Honor," Monroe responded while turning to give Breaux a quick glance, "how can the defense cross-examine a witness who cannot be produced by the prosecution?" Monroe raised his hand with his finger pointing straight up. "Besides, what testimony? All Detective Carson did was ask Mr. Butler if he killed the victim. To which, the young man answered, no. I do not see any *testimony*. What I do see is a cover-up."

Harper pointed at Monroe and said, "Your last statement is out of order, Mr. Lovett. I will warn you only once to keep your personal opinions to yourself and restrain yourself from making such remarks."

"Yes, Your Honor," Monroe answered. "But how is my client supposed to get a fair trial if the court allows fictitious testimony?" He wanted to insert doubt into the minds of the jurors of blunders by law enforcement and the prosecution.

Harper pondered Monroe's argument. Breaux felt confident. Judge Harper had always given leeway to the prosecution, so why not this time. The Judge then answered, "Objection overruled. The interview of Mr. Marcus Butler, Jr. will be stricken from the record. The jury may not consider it. And—"

"Your Honor?" pleaded Breaux.

"If the prosecution can produce the witness, then the interview can be resubmitted when he appears on the stand," Harper pointedly told Breaux. Turning to the defense table, he said, "Now, Mr. Lovett, please continue." He was going to tell the jury to disregard Monroe's last statement about a cover-up, but Breaux's interruption caused him to forget.

Monroe then asked, "Detective, did Ashley Butler write her confession, the one submitted to the court, herself?"

"She signed it," Carson answered.

"She signed it. That's not what I asked, Detective. I asked you, did she *write* it?"

"I would say that if she signed it, then she must've written it," Carson answered, flustered by Monroe's insistence.

"You're not too good at lying, are you?"

"Ob-jection!" Breaux exclaimed, pointing at Monroe as he rose to his feet. "The defense is badgering . . . harassing, this witness well beyond any allowable—"

"Enough with the histrionics, Mr. Breaux," Harper said, shifting his attention to the defense table. "Mr. Lovett, your quasi-question is out of line in my court."

"The defense apologizes," Monroe replied. He then refocused on Detective Carson who was sitting in the witness chair with this harsh scowl on his face. Beads of sweat were popping out on his forehead, with his glare aimed accurately at the defense lawyer. Monroe was making him look corrupt in front of the very people whom he had grown up around and now served as a law enforcement officer. The jarhead Marine-style haircut could not hide the red glow from his anger. It was about to get worse.

Ignoring the livid detective, Monroe, unconcerned about Carson's reputation, asked, "Did you write out the confession for Mrs. Butler, Detective?"

Before Breaux could object, Carson blurted out, "No," with disdain in his voice.

"Then who did, Detective?"

Carson sat for a second, squeezing his lips tightly, with his thin mustache touching his lower lip. He realized he had to fight back his rage. It wasn't working. He gently stroked his mustache, answering, "She wrote it."

Laughing under his breath, Monroe shook his head. He knew Carson was lying, but also knew he would not admit to it. He also knew Carson would deny everything. In the detective's mind, he was doing the right thing. Monroe laid his notes down on the table and said, "Nothing more for the witness, Your Honor. However, the defense reserves the right to recall this witness, if need be, at a later date."

"Granted," Judge Harper said, and then stated, "Let's take a fifteen-minute break."

Carson soared from the chair, sneering at Monroe as he stormed past him.

"Good job, Detective," Monroe said with a hint of sarcasm and a smile as Carson hurried away.

Not far from him, the reporter, Amy, walked up to Monroe and asked, "Mr. Lovett, can you answer a few questions?"

"My client is innocent. That's all you need to know. Beyond that, I have nothing more to add."

Amy looked at Ashley, hoping to get something. "Mrs. Butler, can you—?"

Monroe stepped between Ashley and Amy. With a piercing stare, he sternly told the reporter, "No questions for my client, young lady. I've given you all you're going to get. Do you understand?"

A deputy saw the confrontation and took a few steps in their direction. Amy saw him and backed away. Monroe's firmness stunned the young reporter. He didn't care. Ashley saw Monroe and was glad to see him protect her. It was something new for her.

Chapter 22

The trial resumed, and Judge Harper was back behind the bench. He wasted no time as he said, "Call your next witness, Mr. Breaux."

"The prosecution calls Brandi Grayson."

"Objection, Your Honor," Monroe contended as he rose to his feet. "This witness is not on the prosecution's witness list."

Judge Harper looked at his clerk, who indicated Monroe was correct. "Mr. Breaux, you care to explain?"

"Your Honor, I sent an updated witness list," Breaux answered with a feigned look of shock.

Harper weighed the situation for a moment and replied, "I'll allow the witness."

"Your Honor, this is the second occurrence of the prosecution offering evidence that has not been provided to the defense," Monroe said. He pointed in what would be the direction of Sheriff Austin in the rear of the courtroom and stated, "Three, if you count Detective Carson's so-called forgetfulness."

"Noted, Mr. Lovett," Harper said. He motioned at the prosecution's table and said, "Please continue, Mr. Breaux."

Dismayed, Monroe dropped back into his chair. Leaning over to Ashley, he asked her, "Do you know Brandi?"

"Yes."

"And?"

"And, that's it. I know her. We're not friends or anything."

Brandi sat down. To say she appeared nervous would be an understatement. She was edgy, visibly trembling.

Breaux opened a folder containing a list of questions. "Ms. Grayson," he asked, "could you please tell this court what you witnessed between the defendant and Marcus Butler, Jr. the night before the murder of Julie Miller?"

"Her," she answered, pointing at Ashley, but not looking at her, "and Marcus Jr. had a loud argument at Swatters."

Monroe glanced at Ashley. She appeared okay, but he wasn't sure.

Breaux asked, "Please, tell us what you witnessed that evening."

Brandi took a deep breath and with timidity answered, "Ashley, she jumped out of her chair, and she began, like, yelling at Junior, 'I'm gonna kill that bitch. Do you, do you hear me?'"

"Objection," Monroe stated. "Calls for speculation. The witness did not state a name, but only a bitch. That could be any female. There's been no connection made between the deceased and the defendant, nor her husband."

Judge Harper asked, "Mr. Breaux, can your witness testify as to who the . . . the *bitch* was?"

Breaux looked at Brandi, then back to Harper. Monroe, along with every other person in the courtroom, stared at Breaux.

"Well, Mr. Breaux?" Harper persisted.

Brandi, ever so slightly, waggled her head in the negative.

"No, Your Honor. No, she can't," Breaux admitted. "But—"

"But nothing. The objection is sustained," Harper said.

"Your Honor," Breaux said, "the witness can, however, speak to Marcus Butler, Jr.'s reaction."

"Your Honor—," Monroe exclaimed.

Before Monroe could say anything more, Harper put his hand up and ruled, "I'll allow the witness to testify to what she heard from the defendant and to Mr. Butler's actions. And his actions only."

"What did Marcus Butler, Jr. do when the defendant yelled at him?" Breaux asked.

"He just sat there staring at Ashley."

"What happened next?"

"Ashley stormed out of Swatters. She looked really mad."

Monroe whispered to Ashley, "This isn't what you told me."

"Because it didn't happen like that. At least not how she's telling it. It wasn't even a big deal. We argued, but Junior left before I did."

Monroe hid his aggravation. He was angry, not with Ashley, but with Breaux's tactics and Harper allowing the testimony.

Breaux turned to Monroe and said, "Your witness."

Monroe was still listening to Ashley.

"Mr. Lovett?" Harper said.

"Yes, Your Honor."

"Please pay attention. Do you care to question this witness?"

Unable to prepare any questions, Monroe considered asking for a recess and time to prepare. Who would blame him? Harper almost certainly would allow it. However, he pushed forward. "Yes. Yes, I do," he replied. "I was just consulting with my client since I did not have time to prepare for this witness."

Judge Harper knew Monroe had a point, and said, "Then, please, proceed."

Monroe slowly rose to his feet and gave Breaux a pointed glance. Then directing his attention to the witness, he asked, "Ms. Grayson, have you ever been so mad, so *angry* with someone, that you said you wanted to kill them? And remember, you're under oath."

Brandi sat, looking like she never heard the question.

"Ms. Grayson?" Monroe asked.

She looked at Breaux, who sat waiting for her answer. She remained silent.

Monroe said, noticing her looking to Breaux. "Ms. Grayson, the prosecutor can't answer the question for you."

She looked at Monroe but did not say anything. The young woman had a deer-in-the-headlights look on her face.

"You have to answer the question," Judge Harper told her.

"Ever?" she asked.

"Just answer Mr. Lovett's question," Harper explained.

She looked back at Monroe, tilting her head slightly as she thought, and then answered, "Yeah, I'm sure I have at some point."

"Are you sure that's how things happened that night, the way you testified moments ago, while under oath?" Monroe asked. "I mean, have you been coached how to answer?"

"Objection," Breaux demanded.

"I'll withdraw the second part of the question, Your Honor," Monroe said.

"The witness will answer the first part of the question," Harper replied.

Young Brandi began to withdraw physically as she pulled her arms in and slouched a little. With her voice shaking, she answered, "I-I think so?"

"You think, or you know?" Monroe pressed.

"I think, but—"

"Ms. Grayson," Monroe interjected before she could continue her thought, "do you have any proof Ashley Butler murdered Julie Miller?"

"Only what I heard that night."

"Your Honor, I ask the witness's answer be stricken from the record?" Monroe asked. "And that you inform the witness to answer the question, as asked."

"Objection," Breaux said.

"Overruled. Strike the witness's answer." Judge Harper then instructed the witness, "Please answer the question."

"I'm not sure," Brandi stammered.

"I asked, do you have any proof—" Monroe said.

"Asked and answered," piped Breaux. "The witness stated she's not sure."

"I'll withdraw the question, Your Honor," Monroe said. Giving Brandi a look of skepticism, he asked, "Are you sure the defendant left Swatters before Marcus Jr., and that she stormed out?"

"I-I think so," Brandi answered.

"Think so, or know?"

"I, I, well . . ."

"Never mind," Monroe said, sitting down. "It is apparent this witness has nothing to add to these proceedings, and the prosecution is wasting this court's time by presenting her to this court."

"The defense is testifying, Your Honor," Breaux expressed.

"I apologize to the court," Monroe said. "It's just that shenanigans like this seem juvenile and petty."

"Judge, are you going to allow the defense to insult me, and this court?" Breaux shouted as he jumped up, his chair sliding back, only stopping when it hit the wood balustrade a few feet behind him. The smacking sound echoed.

Judge Harper warned both attorneys, telling them, "I've had enough of you two. Mr. Lovett, I don't need you offering your opinion about how I run my court. And Mr. Breaux, I suggest you make sure the rest of your case is presented appropriately." Both accepted Harper's reprimand.

"One last question, Ms. Grayson," Monroe said. "Who is paying you for your testimony, and how much?"

"Objection."

"Withdrawn," Monroe said. With a wave of his hand, he said, "I'm done with this witness."

"The witness is dismissed," the judge said. Harper then looked at the clock. The time was a couple minutes before noon. He said, "Court is adjourned until two this afternoon."

Still wondering why Monroe did not object during Carson's testimony, Debbie stood up, shot Monroe a quizzical look, and said to him, "I'm going back to the office."

"Lunch?"

"I'll get something at Christi's," she answered snappishly.

Monroe asked, "What?"

She raised her eyebrow and said, "You know what. You're a better attorney than that." She then turned and walked away. He chuckled, knowing what she meant.

Monroe turned his attention back to Ashley. "You holding up okay?"

"No, I don't think so," she answered. "This is hard." Glancing at Debbie as she left the courtroom, she asked, "She okay?"

"Oh yeah," Monroe answered. "Everything's going to be fine. Trust me, okay? We're poking holes in their case."

She nodded yes, as the deputy led her away.

With the courtroom mostly empty, Herm and Daniels approached Monroe. Herm asked, "Why didn't you object?"

"When?" Monroe asked.

"When Carson—never mind," Herm said.

Monroe grinned, chuckled, and said, "Oh, the affair thing? Later."

"Alright," Herm said.

Monroe shrugged his shoulders and looked at Daniels. "Mr. Daniels, I presume," he said, extending his hand.

Daniels returned the handshake, responding, "Yes, Mr. Lovett, Jason Daniels. I do apologize for getting here late, but when the fish are biting like they were, well, you have to stay as long as you can."

"So, why did you have me ask that question?" Monroe asked him.

"Just a hunch. But, before I answer, I would like to inspect the shotgun and the crime scene," Daniels commented. "I wanted you to have Carson's answer on record in the event my hunch is right. If I'm wrong, then it doesn't matter."

"Hunch?" Herm asked.

"I'll tell you if I'm right," Daniels replied.

"I have a Mr. Bryan Michaels coming tomorrow," Monroe said. He glanced at Herm and said, "I hope." Herm didn't respond. Monroe proposed to Daniels, "Possibly, the two of you can look at the shotgun together."

"I've heard of Michaels. Tomorrow shouldn't be a problem. Just give me a call. Herm's got my number," Daniels said. He grasped the front of his shirt and gave it a tugged, pulling it away from his body saying, "I'd like to get out of these. So, I'll catch you later." He turned and left, leaving Herm and Monroe alone in the courtroom.

Looking around to make sure no one could hear them, Herm said, lowering his voice, "I've been doing that *poking around* you asked me to do."

"Yeah?" Monroe said, also lowering his voice.

"Well, get this. I've been able to ascertain that Butler Sr. has been making some large cash withdrawals."

"And this affects our case how?"

"Look, you asked me to poke around, and this is what I've found, so far," Herm answered. "A *friend* ran the Butler name using a computer program that I don't understand. Anyway, this *friend* found some large cash withdrawals. To me, it means something's up."

"And how do you know this means something?" Monroe asked.

"Believe me, I know. I've investigated some crazy stuff before. Like the case when—"

"Herm, not now," Monroe said.

Herm smirked at Monroe. Monroe didn't care. He had one thing on his mind—the case. "Look, there has to be a tie between the murder and Butler, but where? There must be. I'm starting to think Billy—"

"Billy what?"

"Never mind. If Butler's involved, then we need proof. More proof. There must be a tie with Junior. Maybe he's protecting Junior?"

"That's what I was thinking. But, we need a motive. I mean, why kill the woman who's sleeping with you?"

"Keep digging. I don't care how deep you have to go."

"You do realize who you're dealing with in Marcus Butler?"

"Yes. But my client's life is on the line. We can't let her down," Monroe said, closing his attaché.

"Okay. It's your ribcage."

"Hilarious, Herm. But what if they grab you next time?"

"'That's not funny."

"You want to go get some lunch? I'm buying."

"You're buying? Sure."

As the two men walked from the courtroom, Herm joked, "What happened, you strike it rich?"

"Yeah, something like that," Monroe answered, nonchalantly. "Maybe I'll let you finish telling your story."

"What story?"

"Never mind."

Chapter 23

Juanita's Diner was busy at lunch. The waitress brought Monroe and Herm their orders. After placing the two plates on the table, she turned to Monroe and asked, "You think you gonna be able to git Ashley off?"

Monroe smiled at the twenty-something young lady and answered, "I prefer to believe she's innocent. When someone's not guilty, you don't get them off, you prove their innocence."

"Well Mister, most of us who knows her, believes she's innocent," she told Monroe, and then strutted away.

Monroe chuckled.

Herm asked, "What's so funny?"

"Oh, it's just getting used to how people talk here. Don't get me wrong, I'm—"

"No offense taken. You're the ones who talk funny."

"What?"

"That nasal tone. Sounds funny to me," Herm said, popping a fry in his mouth. He then leaned across the table. Monroe looked at him, wondering what he wanted. "So, where did you come into money?" Herm asked curiously.

Monroe chomped a mouthful of his burger while pondering if he should tell Herm about the cash. He looked straight into Herm's eyes and said, "This stays between the two of us, got it?"

Herm nodded his head. "Sure."

"Someone, I don't know who, so don't ask,"—he lowered his voice to a quiet whisper— "sent me twenty thousand dollars. The note said it's for Ashley's case."

"Twenty thousand. Wow!" Herm exclaimed in a whisper. "That's all the note said?"

"Yes."

"Good for you, Monroe. Nothing says you can't keep it, right?"

"Nope. But here's the weird part. When I looked at the return address, it was *my* office."

"Odd," Herm said. "Postmark?"

"Jackson."

Taking a bite of his sandwich, Herm asked, "So, you sure you've got your head in this trial?"

"Yeah. Why?"

"Judge Harper calling you out. Not once, but twice."

"Oh that. I was listening. Besides, I want Breaux to get comfortable with thinking I'm out of my league."

"It has been a while since you were in a courtroom, you know. And when I saw Debbie's reaction, well . . ."

"Don't pay attention to her. She's a bit of a perfectionist at times. She likes to push me," Monroe said, chuckling as he popped a chip in his mouth. "It's why I love her. She wants the best for me, and from me."

The answer satisfied Herm, and he decided to focus more on his food than conversation.

After lunch, Herm told Monroe he would see him later, he had his agenda—unearth more muck, if any, on Marcus Butler, Sr. He knew trying to find evidence of criminal activity on this well-respected man would not be easy. A bank teller whispering something here, or rumor from an employee there is nice, but Herm needed facts, hard evidence. To get that meant calling up some former associates.

Departing Juanita's, Monroe took a stroll around the town square to clear his head before heading back to the courtroom. As he made his way down one side of the old square, he looked in a window. *Huh, a furniture store. I never noticed this before.* Laughing to himself, he thought, *Monroe, you need to get out more.*

Continuing his walk, he rounded a light pole and then crossed the street. Monroe stopped and looked through a pane glass window at the tools in the small hardware store.

"Mr. Lovett, how you are doing?" asked a familiar voice.

Monroe turned to see Jack. "Jack, how are you?" he asked with a kind smile.

Jack had exited the store carrying a small brown paper bag. "Ole Jack's doing well. Yes, sir, ole Jack is doing well, Mr. Lovett," he said with a big smile. "I sure hope you can help that Butler girl. Poor thing."

"I'm giving it my best, Jack."

"I believe you can help her. If anybody can, you can. I can feel it in my bones. You a good man, 'specially you being a preacher."

"Former preacher. But thanks for the vote of confidence, Jack. I believe she's innocent. The question is this. Who really did it?"

"Oh, that one's easy," Jack said, looking around to make sure no one was in earshot.

"It is?" Monroe asked, curious if Jack might have heard something.

"It's the person who did it, Mr. Lovett," Jack said with a boisterous laugh.

"Good one, Jack. Good one," Monroe replied laughing slightly.

Jack held up his small, brown paper bag and shook it slightly. The screws in it jingled a little. "Well, I got to be going. Mrs. Peels is waiting for me to fix her door."

"Alright," Monroe said, patting Jack on the shoulder.

Monroe headed back to the courthouse thinking, *Yeah, I do hope the truth will come out.*

Chapter 24

At 2:00 PM, Judge Harper called the court back to order. The young reporter, Amy, was in her seat glaring at Monroe. It was evident she had not forgotten their confrontation, and she was not happy with the defense lawyer. Monroe did not even notice her.

Debbie leaned forward and whispered into Monroe's ear, "Try to pay attention this time."

"Hilarious. Ha, you're so funny," he whispered sarcastically back at her.

Judge Harper tapped his gavel, saying, "Call your next witness, Mr. Breaux."

Standing, Breaux replied, "The prosecution calls, Fichard Roueché."

Roueché entered the courtroom wearing all black. His suit was solid black with a satin black shirt and black tie. Everyone watched him. No one knew him, and his testifying only raised curiosity. Word had leaked he was the prosecution's firearms expert. Even Herm couldn't find much about him. All anyone had on him was the credentials contained in the folder Carson gave Breaux.

While watching Roueché, one man in the gallery leaned over and whispered to a man next to him, "Wonder why Mr. Breaux isn't using Daniels? Everybody knows he is the go-to-guy for guns." A slight shrug was the only reply. A woman in the back of the gallery told her husband, "The style of his goatee makes him look evil." He nodded in agreement.

Ignoring the ogling, Roueché sat down in the witness chair.

Breaux asked, "Mr. Roueché, please explain to this court your findings concerning the shotgun entered into evidence, as to its use in firing the shots that killed the victim?"

"Ballistic fingerprinting of the buckshot pellets from firearms such as shotguns is not usually possible. In many cases, the shot rides inside a plastic sleeve that prevents it from ever touching the barrel. In the event where the shot does touch the barrel, the random movement of the shot down the barrel usually will not leave any consistent marks. But shotgun cases themselves can still be examined for firing pin marks," Roueché answered.

"Then, please explain to the court how you determined this shotgun was used to kill the deceased."

"I examined it for firing pin marks on the shells provided to me by the sheriff's department and local forensics," he explained.

"So, Mr. Roueché, in your expert opinion, can you say this shotgun murdered Julie Miller?" Mr. Breaux asked, beaming with confidence.

"No."

Mr. Roueché's response caught everyone off guard, especially Breaux and Carson. Carson snapped his head up and stared straight at Roueché.

Breaux turned around and glared square at Detective Carson.

Carson had a terrified and discomfited look on his face. Out of the corner of his eye, he could see Sheriff Austin looking at him. It wasn't a pleasant look.

Turning his attention back to the witness, the exasperated DA swallowed hard and asked, "Can you repeat that? And this time, please *explain* your answer."

"Objection, Your Honor. Asked and answered," Monroe challenged.

Debbie, relieved, mouthed, "Thank you."

Everyone waited for Judge Harper's response, especially Breaux. After what seemed like an eternity, Harper said, "Sustained."

"Your Honor! The witness should be able to explain his answer," Breaux complained.

"Then find another way to ask your question, Mr. Breaux," Harper responded.

Fretful, Breaux thought for a moment, and then asked, "Please explain how the shotgun entered into evidence could have been used to kill the victim."

"Objection," Monroe said.

"Overruled."

Mr. Roueché answered, "Any shotgun, much like the one entered into evidence, could've been used to kill the victim. However, I can't say with certainty, that that shotgun,"—he pointed to the shotgun entered into evidence— "was fired near the time of the crime. But I can state that that shotgun fired the shells recovered at the crime scene."

Roueché's explanation relieved some of Breaux's anxiety. Breaux asked several additional mundane questions, and then he sat down and said, "Nothing more, Your Honor." His anger was obvious. *This is Carson's fault.*

"Your witness, Mr. Lovett," Judge Harper said.

"Mr. Roueché, since the prosecution did not have you state your credentials, could you please tell the court what degrees you have in relation to firearms forensics, and where you have previously worked?"

"Objection," Breaux said.

"Overruled."

"I do not have any *formal* training in firearms forensics, if that's what you're asking," Roueché answered. "However, I do have an NRA certificate."

Moans and murmurs from the courtroom.

Harper tapped his gavel. "Order."

"So, what makes you a credible witness? A firearms *expert*?"

"I am a self-taught firearms expert."

"Self-taught? So, should the jury accept the testimony of a self-taught coroner?"

"Objection," Breaux exclaimed. "The defense is badgering the witness in an attempt to embarrass him."

"Your Honor, I'm just trying to make a point," Monroe countered.

"Overruled."

"The District Attorney and Sheriff's Department have my credential."

"Do you have a licensed business where you conduct any type of firearms training, forensics, or gun repair?"

"Objection. Having a business is not required to be an expert."

"Sustained. Move on with your questioning, Mr. Lovett," Judge Harper responded.

Monroe didn't argue the fact. He had made his point. He next asked Roueché, "How long have you lived this area?"

"Seven months."

"Seven months?" Monroe made a quick note. "Where did you live before moving here?"

"Your Honor. Is this necessary?" Breaux asked.

"Yes," Harper responded.

"Baton Rouge," answered Roueché.

"For how long?"

"Four months."

"And, before that?"

"In various places in southern Louisiana," Roueché answered as he squirmed a little in the chair.

"Can you provide evidence of your past residences?"

"I don't have those records with me. They were lost during Hurricane Katrina."

"How many court cases have you testified in?"

"This is my first."

"And who contacted you about testifying in this case?"

Breaux fought not to squirm in his chair. He slowly turned to get a look at Carson, but he was gone. *Coward.* He wanted to object, but he knew it would be pointless.

"Detective Carson," Roueché answered.

"And who told Detective Carson to contact you?"

"Objection. Calls for hearsay," Breaux said.

"Sustained."

Monroe jotted a note: *Recall Carson about Roueché.* He then asked, "In fact, you can't prove where you have lived for the past ten years, can you? You have no credentials. You have no background. You've never testified in a court case in your life, and you want this court to believe you?"

"Objection! The prosecution objects to this line of questioning, Your Honor. If you can even call this questioning. The defense is postulating, conjecturing, testifying, he's . . . he's . . . The defense is badgering the witness."

"Calm down, Mr. Breaux," Judge Harper said. "There're no Emmys given out here." He then looked at Monroe telling him, "Just ask questions, Mr. Lovett."

"Sorry, Your Honor," Monroe said. He looked over his notes, letting the previous line of questions and answers rest on the minds of the jurors.

"Mr. Lovett, do you have any more questions for this witness?" Judge Harper asked.

"Sorry, Your Honor. No, I have no further questions for this witness, at this time."

Judge Harper looked at the clock—it was 3:48 pm. He reached over, grabbed his gavel, and said, "Court is adjourned until 1:00 pm tomorrow afternoon."

Harper's early dismissal of the proceedings and late start caught Monroe off guard. He walked over to Breaux and asked, "Does he have somewhere he needs to be?"

Breaux chuckled, "Fishing."

"Fishing?"

"Yes. Fishing. He loves to fish," Breaux said, tossing his notes into his briefcase. "According to the fishing report, the bass are supposed to start biting at four-thirty and again at nine tomorrow morning." Breaux closed his briefcase and said, "You know, Mr. Lovett, for a preacher, you seem to know your way around a courtroom."

Monroe chuckled. "Well, let's put it this way, for many years I've been pleading cases *every* week, I guess you could say. I've also had to debate, not just another lawyer, but sometimes what seemed like several at once."

"I guess when you put it that way . . . but, that's not courtroom experience."

"No, I got that when I worked for Don Mecker."

"You worked for Don Mecker? Don Mecker, one of the country's top trial attorneys?" Breaux asked.

"Yes, that Don Mecker," Monroe answered. "I sat second chair a few times." Mecker's reputation had established him as the lawyer to turn to for some of the most important and high-profile trials in the country. "I learned a lot from him. And we have remained friends over the years," Monroe revealed. "If you had done a background check on me, you would've found that bit of information."

Breaux realized at that point that he was not dealing with an amateur. "Good for you, Monroe. Yeah, good for you," Breaux said, forcing a smile.

"So, Judge Harper likes his fishing, huh?" Monroe asked indifferently.

"Yes. And if I hurry, he won't leave without me. So, excuse me. I've got to go."

"Southerners," Monroe said under his breath, shaking his head as he watched Breaux hurry from the courtroom.

"Yep, and you better get used to it," Herm said, laughing and slapping Monroe on the shoulder.

"Give me time. Wait. I thought you were—"

"I was, and I've got some new info on Butler," Herm said quietly.

"Tonight. My place. Let's say around seven?"

"I'll be there," Herm said, turning to leave. He stopped. Turning back around, he asked, "Why not now?"

"Because I want to go see that Swatter guy again."

"Want me to come with you?"

"No. I think us being together only puts him on the defensive."

"Alright. Tonight then."

A couple of old pickup trucks sat parked outside in the gravel parking lot. Walking from his car and opening the joint's door, the smell of stale beer smacked Monroe in the face as he entered the small watering hole. The door closed behind him, and Monroe saw two good-ole-boys sitting in the far corner of the room nursing their beers. Both gazed at him, hard. Monroe was still wearing his suit. One thought came to mind as he eyed the men, *Deliverance*. He shuttered at the thought. Ignoring him, they went back to their chatting.

A familiar voice called to him from behind the bar. "Hello, Mr. Lawyer," Lisa said.

"Hello Lisa, how are you?" Monroe responded walking over to the bar.

"I'm fine. Can I get you something to drink?"

Monroe thought for a moment. "I'll have a beer."

"Any particular beer?"

"Something dark."

"Ever had Guinness?"

"No, but I like trying new things."

"Oh, you do, huh?" Lisa said, playfully and flirty. She turned, grabbed a glass, placed it under the spigot, and filled it with the black beer. She handed Monroe the glass making sure their hands touched as she said, "There you go. Hope you like it?"

Monroe took a sip thinking nothing of the hand contact. "Umm, now that's good," he said, setting the stout back on the bar. "Lisa, I've got a question for you."

"Okay. But you'll have to wait until I get off work," she quipped.

"Good one." Her remark caught him off guard. He blushed. The low light hid it, but the expression on his face said it all, and she saw it.

"You embarrassed, Mr. Lovett," she asked, teasingly.

"No. Just . . ." He took another drink trying to regain his composure, and then asked, "Did you see the argument between Ashley and Junior the night before Julie's murder?"

Before Lisa could answer Monroe's question, Swatter walked in from the back. "Hey there, Mr. Lovett. See you're having a beer. Are you here on business or just for the beer?"

"Hello, Mister—? What is your real name, anyway?"

"Swatter."

"I know you go by Swatter, but what if I was to . . . let's say, call you as a witness. What name would I—?"

Waving his arms like an umpire calling a base runner safe, Swatter insisted, "I *don't do* court. End of story. Me and court *do not*, don't get along."

"But I might need you to testify."

"I'm gonna be out of town."

"I haven't even told you when."

"Don't matter. When-*ever* it is, I'm gonna be out of town. Do you get my drift, lawyer man?"

"I can subpoena you."

Swatter defiantly told Monroe, "Subpoena me all you want. Your subpoena won't find me."

Not wanting to push his luck, Monroe backed off. He could see the tavern owner's patience thinning. "Okay, okay. I get it. 'Swatter' it is," Monroe said, lifting his glass. He took another swig. "I was asking Lisa here, about Marcus Jr. and Ashley's argument the night before Ms. Miller was murdered?"

"Haven't seen Marcus Jr.," Swatter answered, cutting his eyes to Lisa.

Lisa remained silent. Nervous, she slightly bit her lower lip and glanced over at Swatter several times. Monroe noticed her uneasy reaction. "Now, why is it I don't believe you? A witness has already testified confirming the argument. Even Ashley said there was an argument. I just want to ask you some questions to help me help her."

"Believe what you want, or don't believe. Don't matter to me what you believe, or what you want. I'm telling you, *we* haven't, have-not-seen Junior."

Monroe took another drink from the Irish dry stout, sat the half-full pint down. He realized he wasn't going to get anything from Swatter or Lisa. He definitely wasn't going to speak with the two rednecks sitting in the corner of the bar. Reaching for his wallet, he asked, "How much for the beer?"

Putting his hand up, Swatter said, "It's on the house."

"Thanks," Monroe replied. He smiled, tapped the bar, and left.

Swatter watched him leave and then walked to the back of the pub. Lisa stood there, unsure. Another man, one not seen by Monroe, who was sitting in another darker corner of the tavern, got up and walked over to the bar. Lisa asked him, "Would you like another drink?"

"No," the man said, as he left a twenty on the bar and walked out as Monroe's Camaro pulled away. He turned around and walked back to the bar. "Lisa, isn't it?"

"Yes."

"Can we talk?

Chapter 25

"Can you tell me what our friend, Mr. Roueché, did on the stand?" Butler asked Galliard, furiously. The two men were meeting that evening at the same vacant building as before. "He all but handed the case to the defense. You assured me—"

Galliard put his hand up and said, "Calm down, Marcus."

"Don't tell me to calm down. What the *hell* was he thinking? I stood in the hallway fuming, listening to him."

"He said you would be upset, but Mr. Roueché assured me he has everything under control. If he made an untrue statement on the stand, Lovett would have raked him over the coals. He couldn't lie about something that many people already know about shotguns."

"Under control?" Butler shouted as he began pacing. His anger radiated from him. "I have half a mind to bring him here for one of your little interrogations."

"That ain't gonna happen," Galliard stated dogmatically.

Butler stopped his pacing. He moved over close and with extreme animosity, glared into Galliard's eyes. "Then, what do you suggest, Mr. Galliard?"

Galliard had left his pistol in his truck and wasn't feeling his usual heavy-handed self. Butler towered over him by at least six inches. Seeing Butler's antagonistic stare, he stepped back a little. "Trust Mr. Roueché. What else can we do?"

"Trust? I don't know who I can trust right now. You? Him? Neither of you," Butler said, pointing his finger at Galliard. "One more misstep and I'm . . . I'll . . ." Galliard's uneasiness was evident to Butler. And his own loathing was just as apparent. The two men were out of answers. However, both realized griping about it in an empty building would not solve anything.

"I could get someone to, you know, take out the girl," Galliard suggested.

"In the Lane County jail? Who you going to get? Otis?"

"Who?" Galliard asked, not placing the name or the reference.

"No. I don't want no more killing," Butler said, walking to the door. "I'm working on my own plan right now."

"What kind of a plan?"

"None of your damn business. I'm trying another way to get to Lovett." He stopped and said, a little less ruffled, "By the way, we heard from Junior.

"How is he?"

"Told my wife he's fine. And I got a text right before I got here saying he'll see me after the trial."

"Told you not to worry," Galliard said, noticing Butler's calmness. He asked, "Now, when can I expect my money?"

"You serious?"

"Yes. I've done a lot here and should be compensated. One payment for a hundred grand should do it, and we'll be settled?"

"A hundred grand? I ain't got that much. Roueché milked me dry. I can get you . . . maybe ten."

"Naw, you can find a hundred. Sell something. Make it two payments."

Butler stared at Galliard with a look that could kill. The thought even went through his head, but instead, he scornfully replied, "I'm out of here. And we're done. Understand. Done."

Galliard didn't respond. He knew he'd get something. He wanted Butler to cool off before pushing him any further. He calmly removed a cigarette from his shirt pocket and lit it as he watched Butler walk to the door.

Butler stopped. Without looking back, he said, "Fifty for now. But give me two days."

"Two days works," Galliard said, laughing to himself while holding his cigarette in his teeth. He watched Butler leave and said under his breath, "I wonder what he's got going on?"

That same evening, Herm arrived at Monroe's home for their meeting. He parked in the drive and sauntered to the front door. As Herm raised his hand and began to knock on the panel steel entry door, it opened, and he nearly fell through the doorway.

"Hello, Herm," Monroe said, chuckling, seeing him nearly fall into the house.

Herm grabbed the doorjamb to regain his balance. "Monroe," he responded, embarrassed by his little dance. "Sorry for the . . . Well, hello," he said when he noticed an unfamiliar female standing in front of him. She appeared to be in her mid-forties, with light brown hair, wearing tight faded blue jeans, and a white blouse.

"No problem," the woman said, enticingly, as she eyed Herm from head to foot. "You can fall in my direction *anytime*."

Monroe rolled his eyes. "Herm, this is Mary . . . Mary Walters. She lives over in Taylorsville."

Not taking her eyes off Herm, she said, "I needed Mr. Lovett to help me with a small legal matter."

"It's a pleasure to meet you, Mrs.—"

"Mary is fine. I'm not married," she said with a wink and an alluring smile.

"Herm here is my investigator," Monroe tried to tell Mary, but she was more interested in what Herm had to say.

"Mary, it is nice to meet you. Sorry about my almost falling on you," Herm said apologetically.

"Oh, no problem. Like I said—anytime," Mary said, almost drooling.

"So, Mary, do you come to Peregrine often?" Herm asked, macho-like, as he leaned against the doorframe.

Monroe thought as he watched Herm, *Why not use the oldest come-on line in the book?* But it seemed to be working. However, after spending the last half hour with Mary, he wasn't surprised. Any line would've worked.

"Not a lot," she answered. "But, I'm sure if there were a reason, I could come here more often."

Monroe had enough of the flirting, and said, "Excuse me, but right now my air conditioning is working overtime to cool the whole county. So, if you two don't mind?"

"No, we don't mind, Monroe," Herm remarked with a playful chuckle.

"Oh, and funny too," Mary said.

"We have work to do. And, I'm sure Mary has someplace to be."

"Okay. I can take a hint," Mary replied. She grabbed the pen and small spiral notebook tucked inside Herm's shirt pocket. She opened it to the very back page and began writing, and telling him, "Here's my number, Herm. If you would like to continue this conversation without any *interruptions*,"—she bobbed her head in Monroe's direction— "give me a call, okay?"

Monroe smirked, rolling his eyes again.

"Sounds good, Mary," Herm told her. He took the pen and notebook from Mary, looked at the number with a smile, and then placed it back in his pocket.

"Ta, ta," Mary said, and then sashayed out the door and toward her car parked on the street.

Herm laughed to himself as he watched her.

"Come in and close the door, lover boy," Monroe said, waggling his head as he walked to the dining table. "And wipe that stupid grin off your face."

Herm patted his shirt pocket. "I might have to give Mary a call."

"Bad idea. She's not your type."

"Not my type?"

"Whose type?" Debbie asked, emerging from the kitchen with a carafe of coffee.

"Your husband thinks he knows my *type* of woman."

"*Believe* me, Herm," Monroe said, sitting down at the dining table. He pulled a stack of folders over to him. "I'm telling you, *Mary* is not your type. Not anyone's type."

"How do you know my type?" Herm asked as he sat down. "You've only known me for a few weeks."

"Yeah, how do you know his type?" Debbie asked, pouring a cup of coffee. She blew across the top of her cup. "Mary seemed like a nice woman."

"She seemed nice to me, too," Herm said, as he looked up at Debbie. "And wasn't it you who told me, not that long ago, that I should date?"

"Fine," Monroe said, raising his hands in the air as if surrendering. "Go out with the woman. What do I care?"

"Yeah, what do you care?" Debbie asked.

"Yeah, what do you care?" piped Herm.

Monroe exhaled as he shook his head. "Ashley's case. Can we?" he asked, exasperatingly. It was more important to him than continuing a stupid discussion about Herm's love life. "Deb, we need to get to work. So, please . . ." Monroe declared, motioning with his hand for her to leave. She huffed and then departed. Monroe watched her for a moment, and then he uttered, "Herm, go out with the woman. Marry her if you want. But for now, right now, we need to get to work on freeing Ashley."

"Thank you. That's all I'm asking," Herm said. He grabbed the coffee carafe. "I don't know though . . . maybe . . ."

"Herm, the case. What do you have on Butler?"

"Oh yeah," Herm said, pouring the coffee. "One of my contacts got me this," he said, opening a manila folder. There was a single sheet of paper inside.

"What do you have there?"

"Can't tell you."

"Why not?"

"Because I don't want to get you in trouble."

"Get me in trouble? What do you have?" Monroe asked, trying to get a peek at the sheet of paper. Herm pulled it back before he could.

"Let's speak in hypotheticals, okay?"

"Okay . . ." Monroe said, with his curiosity piqued.

Herm looked at the sheet of paper. "Let's say, hypothetically, some large, very large, sums of money were transferred from a person's business account into the same person's personal accounts."

"So? Your hypothetical business owner owns all the money."

"Hold on," Herm said, putting his hand up. "What if there were two large cash withdrawals? One for a hundred thousand and a second for, let's say, a hundred and fifty thousand."

"Still not much. But, I'll play along. When were these *hypothetical* transactions made?"

"The first—oh, perhaps—three weeks before the murder."

"And the second?"

"A couple weeks ago."

"But I can't introduce hypotheticals in court," Monroe explained. "Besides, you haven't shown any illegal activity."

"I know, but you can still use it, right?"

"Maybe . . . *if* we find the person your hypothetical business owner gave the money to. *If* it was given to a person. And, *if* we can show it was possibly criminal in nature. The withdrawals themselves are not enough to get a subpoena for bank records."

"Well, I believe there's something fishy going on."

"So, do I. Nonetheless, we need more. We need to connect that money to someone involved with the case. And figure out why it was given to them."

"Working on it."

"Working on what?"

"Finding where the cash went."

"Herm, how are you able to get this info?" Monroe asked, pointing to the manila folder.

"I have my sources. Twenty-five years as a cop, you get to know . . . people. Give me time."

"Time. Time isn't on our side."

"I know."

"Remember, I can't walk into court and begin spouting all of that— your hypotheticals. Judge Harper and Breaux will start asking me questions. Questions that could lead to my disbarment."

"You don't have anything to worry about. I don't work *for* you. *You* don't pay *me*. I work for myself as an independent investigator. You . . . you tag along with me from time to time, observing, learning investigative techniques."

"Well, it sounds borderline and shady."

"Yeah?"

"Yeah. I prefer to remain out of the gray areas."

"I know. You're pretty much a black and white kind of guy."

"Keeps me out of trouble."

"Don't worry. I would never do anything illegal. Maybe push a little into the gray areas from time to time, but never illegal." Herm put his hand up as if he was taking an oath, and said jokingly, "And I promise I will never pull you into the gray areas."

"Good."

"Anything else?" Herm asked, acting as if he was in a hurry to leave.

"Not that I can think of." With an inquisitive look, Monroe asked, "Why are you smiling?"

Herm stood up and tapping his chest pocket, "I've got a phone call to make."

"Mary?"

"Yep."

Monroe said, chuckling, "Don't say I didn't warn you."

Chapter 26

Rain poured as Herm stood outside the doorway of the Lane County Sheriff's Department. From under the awning, he watched the heavy downpour. It was what the locals called a frog-choker. A few cars drove by as he waited, but none were the ones he was expecting. He checked his watch. *Where are those two?* Herm was always early and thought everyone else should also be. The two he was looking for was Jason Daniels and Bryan Michaels.

A black four-wheel drive pickup truck pulled up and parked. Daniels opened the door, jumped out, and trotted through the rain over to Herm. "Michaels here yet?" he asked, shaking the water off.

"No. Not yet."

"Maybe the weather's got him held up in traffic," Daniels said, shaking the rainwater from his ball cap.

Herm checked his watch. "He's still got a couple minutes. Carson's probably having another doughnut anyway."

"Probably?" Daniels chuckled.

At straight up 9:00, a dark blue Jeep Wrangler pulled up and parked. Michaels got out and walked up nonchalantly to the two men. Looking at Herm, he said, "Mr. Hermann, I presume?"

"Yep. Call me Herm," he answered. He pointed at Daniels and introduced him. "And this is Daniels. He's our firearms expert."

"Daniels? You look familiar," Michaels said, brushing the water off his shoulders. He tried to place the face, but couldn't.

"You too," Daniels said. He couldn't figure out where the two might have met either.

"They ready for us inside?" Michaels asked.

"You might want to move your Jeep," Herm said, pointing to the vehicle.

"Why?"

"It's in a no parking zone."

"So?"

"So, you're in front of the *sheriff's department*," Daniels said with a chuckle.

Michaels shrugged as he walked past the two others, then opened the door and walked inside. Herm and Daniels looked at each other and then followed him. "It's your ticket," muttered Daniels.

Recognizing Daniels and Herm, Detective Carson spouted, "About time."

"What do you care? You've got all day," Herm responded.

"Follow me," Carson said, pushing the button to buzz the three men passed the front counter. "Our forensic guy is in the back, waiting."

All three followed Carson. The sign on the door read, Evidence Room. Waiting inside was a man standing next to a table with the 12-gauge shotgun on a table, encased in a large plastic bag. "This is Mr. Barnes, our forensics expert," Carson said, pointing to the man.

Daniels was already acquainted with Barnes.

"Bryan Michaels," Michaels said, introducing himself to Barnes.

"Oh, I know who you are, Dr. Michaels," Barnes said. "I've read several of your articles in—"

"Can we just get started and save the schmoozing for another day?" Carson asked gruffly.

Barnes cleared his throat and said, "Gentlemen, this is what you're here to see," Barnes said, motioning to the shotgun.

Herm leaned over to Daniels and said under his breath, "How does he see through those glasses?"

"Ask him," Daniels replied.

"Very clearly," Barnes said, glancing over at Herm. "And my ears hear perfectly, in case you're wondering."

"Oh. I was talking about—maybe we should get to what we came here for," Herm said a little red-faced. "Sorry," he said apologetically and feeling a little humiliated.

"Can we remove the shotgun from the bag?" Michaels asked.

"Sure," Barnes answered. He removed the tape and opened the bag. With gloved hands, he removed the shotgun, laying it on top of the bag. He made a note on the tag to indicate the date, time, and those present.

Daniels stated, "I just need to look at one thing."

"Go ahead," Michaels told him, gesturing to the shotgun.

"Thanks," Daniels said. He used a small wooden dowel sitting next to the shotgun and raised the end of the barrel so he could see it better. Pulling a LED flashlight from his pocket, he pointed the light down the barrel. "Cotton swab?" he asked without looking up. Barnes handed him one. He wiped the inside of the barrel and then lowered it back to the table. Next, he checked the receiver and asked, "Is this shotgun in the same condition as it was found at the crime scene?"

"Yes. Of course, it is," Carson said tersely.

Barnes nodding, "I bagged it myself, Jason."

"Then, I do not believe this shotgun, in its present condition, fired the shots that killed the victim," Daniels said, backing away.

Surprised by Daniels's statement, Carson and Herm looked at each other. Herm shrugged. Carson scowled back at him. "And you know this, how?" Carson asked, making a *yeah-right* face. "What, from just looking down the barrel?"

"It will be in my report *to* Mr. Lovett. Remember, you didn't want to use me for this case. You have your expert. At least that's what he said he was. Anyway, you can wait for my report and hear it when everyone else does. I'll know more after I investigate the crime scene."

Herm chuckled to himself as he listened to Daniels tick off Carson. However, he and the other men also wondered how Daniels could come to that conclusion.

Next, Michaels began his examination of the shotgun. Before looking at the weapon, he asked, "May I see the forensics report?"

Barnes handed him a copy of the report.

Michaels opened the folder containing the report and scanned it. He leaned over just a couple inches from the shotgun, looked at it slowly, and then stood up straight. "Were Mrs. Butler's the only fingerprints found on the weapon?"

Taken back by the question, Barnes answered, "Yes. There were a couple other smudged prints, but nothing usable. Why?"

"Funny?" Michaels said, raising his eyebrows. "Because there's another print on the shotgun." Barnes and Carson looked at each other. "Did you disassemble the shotgun?" Michaels asked.

Barnes, somewhat baffled, shrugged, answering, "No. I didn't see a need to. Why?"

Reaching into a large case he brought with him, Michaels removed a magnifying glass.

"Thought only Sherlock Holmes used one of those," joked Carson.

Herm laughed at the comment.

Not amused, Michaels ignored Carson's wisecrack and began a closer examination of the firearm, focusing on the barrel where it enters the receiver. He studied it closely for a couple of minutes. Looking up at Detective Carson, he asked, "This shotgun is exactly the way you found it?"

Flustered, Carson answered, "Yes."

Barnes interjected, "Like I said, I retrieved the weapon myself. Using extreme care, I placed the shotgun into a plastic bag. I sealed the bag at the crime scene and personally took it to the crime lab. I even took the prints before re-securing the shotgun. No one else has touched it."

"You're positive?" Michaels asked.

"Yes," Barnes insisted. He was growing irritated with Michaels by now.

Michaels pointed to the barrel, stating, "There's a partial latent print on the barrel, right here, where it enters the receiver. However, there is no mention of the print in your report." He looked at both Barnes and Carson, holding the report up, telling them, "We need to take the barrel out and get that print."

"Interesting?" Herm said.

Carson responded, "Why would anyone hold the barrel there? It's probably nothing."

"That print was not there when I checked," Barnes said.

"Shaking his head, Carson stated, "Could be that one of the guys at the scene or one of the techs in the lab touched it."

"You two need to get your stories straight," Herm said, looking at Carson and Barnes. "Carson just threw you under the bus, Mr. Barnes."

Carson did not find Herm's remark amusing.

Before examining the shotgun further, Michaels, with his smartphone, took several photos of the gun. Next, the others watched Michaels and Barnes carefully disassemble the shotgun. Daniels asked, "Why would anyone take the gun apart at the crime scene?"

"Whatever the reason, it's suspicious," Michaels said as reached into his case and removed a fingerprint kit.

"You know, we have all that stuff here," Carson told him with a contemptuous tone. "Then again, maybe Barnes should remove the print."

"No, it's okay," Barnes said, "he can lift the print."

With care, Michaels began to dust the partial print. "Looks like we have a pretty good thumbprint here," he remarked while lifting the latent print onto the fingerprint tape and transferring it to the fingerprint-backing card. He held it up for a better examination. "Yeah, it looks good. I'll take this print back to my crime lab in Madison and attempt to find a match."

Before he could do anything with the print, Carson reached over Michaels's shoulder and seized it from his hand.

"What?" Michaels asked, surprised by Carson's actions.

"It's state's evidence now," Carson said. "We'll gladly reimburse you for your supplies."

"I'll have Mr. Lovett get a court order," Michaels retorted.

"Fine. You do that." Carson placed the print in an envelope and then put it in the inside breast pocket of his sports coat. "But for now, it belongs to us. I'll run it for a match. Anything else?" Detective Carson asked. He could see the annoyance in their faces. It gave him delight.

Michaels looked to Herm for help. Herm shrugged and said, "He's right."

"Can I have a copy of that report?" Michael asked, pointing to the report Barnes had shown him.

Snatching the report from the table, Carson shoved it against Michaels's chest, telling him, "Here, take this one."

"Thanks," Michaels said. He wanted the print more than he did the report. "Mind if I take a few pictures of the shotgun?"

"Take all you want," Carson replied.

Michaels took several pictures. He focused on the barrel, especially where it entered the gun's receiver. "I'm done."

Herm eyed Carson and said, "I think we're done here."

"Oh yeah, we're definitely done," Carson said.

Daniels, Michaels, and Herm absconded from the room as Carson glared at them. After the trio was gone, Carson looked at Barnes and said, "Put the shotgun back in the bag."

"Sorry," Barnes said. "We didn't think—"

"Forget about it. I'll run this," Carson said, patting his pocket. "It's probably nothing. Anyway, you've got your hands full with the burnt body," he told Barnes and then walked from the room.

At the same time, back at the law firm, Debbie strolled down the hall and into her husband's office. She sat down on the couch, without saying a word. Monroe watched her from the corner of his eye, pondering her intentions. No doubt, they were not work-related.

She began playing with her hair, twirling it around her finger. Monroe noticed Debbie's slight shoulder shrug as she gently leaned forward grabbing her knees. She softly exhaled, "Hmm . . ." and then slowly ran her hand up her thigh while leisurely lying back into the couch. "Busy?" Debbie asked seductively.

Laughing to himself, Monroe noticed her exposed thigh. He replied, "A little. Just this . . . *trivial* murder case I'm in the middle of."

Debbie saw the desire in his eyes as he gazed at her leg. She giggled. With a breathy voice she asked, "Surely, you can take a *few* minutes off to spend time with your wife?"

Monroe thought for a moment. With a sheepish smile, he laid the file folder he had been reading on the desk. "What about someone coming in?" he asked, looking toward the main door.

"We'll hear the buzzer if anybody starts up the stairs," she said, softly biting her lower lip. Her eyes told him not to worry about anyone or anything else.

"You're serious?" he asked. Monroe wasn't sure just how far Debbie was willing to go. He'd seen these same signals from her before, but it didn't mean what he thought. Like a baseball player on first base staring across the diamond to the third base coach, he was wondering, *Are those the right signs, coach?* He gave another look into those green eyes. *Just go for it?*

"Uh, huh . . ." she said, invitingly curling of her finger, requesting him to come over.

Monroe got up, looked down the hall as if he expected someone to pop out from around the corner, and then closed his office door. Walking over to the couch where Debbie was hungrily watching him, he sat down. Leaning over, he gave her a long passionate kiss.

She moaned. He moaned, but in pain, as she wrapped her arms around his waist. "Your side?" Debbie asked, pulling back a little.

"My side? What side?" he said with a boyish grin, as he stared deep into her eyes, gently running his fingers along the outside of her thigh. He wasn't going to let a little tenderness in his side stop this. "I do believe it's time for us to christen the office," he said in his best sexy voice.

She said, giggling, "You're funny. But I *do* believe you're right," Debbie said, running her fingers through his hair as she pulled him close and kissed him.

With more passionate kissing, things were beginning to heat up between the two.

Bzzz . . . Bzzz . . .

"Dang!" Monroe exclaimed, followed by a sudden leap to his feet. "You have *got* to be kidding me."

Debbie stood up and adjusted her dress and blouse. Composing herself, she gave Monroe a quick kiss. "Maybe later."

"Maybe, nothing. Oh, there's no doubt about it. Absolutely, no doubt," he said with a quick dash to his desk, trying to stand naturally as he picked up a folder. She looked at him. Gesturing with her finger, she said, "You might want to sit down." Seeing why he dropped into his chair and scooted up close to the desk.

She opened Monroe's office door. "Herm!"

"Did I disturb something?" he said with a big smile.

"No . . . No, we were just going over some . . . looking over a file," Debbie replied, refusing to look at Herm. She hurried past him, staring at the floor as she walked back to her desk. Sitting down at her desk, Debbie realized her blouse was misbuttoned. *Oh great*, she thought.

Clearing his throat, Monroe said, "Herm, you have impeccable timing, you know."

"Hey, I'm sorry. I could leave and come back later. Let's say, what, ten minutes?" Herm chortled.

"What brings you here? Did our experts find anything useful?" Monroe asked, picking up his pen, still attempting to recover.

"I'm serious, I can come back if you two, you know—" Herm egged.

"Just give me something I can use, Herm," Monroe insisted.

Herm could see Monroe wasn't in a joking mood. "Okay. Got it," Herm laughed. He made a move to sit down on the couch and then stopped. He decided to take one more jab. Pointing at the sofa, he looked at Monroe and asked, "Did you two . . .?"

"Herm . . .!"

Herm laughed and then sat down in a chair. "Yes, they found something. But, they will only give their report to you."

"Did they say anything?" Monroe asked, unsatisfied with having to wait. He started clicking his pen feverishly.

"Daniels said the shotgun, in its current state, could not have fired the fatal shots. And Michaels found a partial print on the barrel not discovered by forensics."

"What? You're kidding?" He stopped clicking his pen.

"Nope."

"This is great news," Monroe said. "This opens the door for inconclusive evidence to convict. When can we expect their reports?"

"Didn't say. But, I'm sure it won't be too long. They know we need them quick. And I would agree about inconclusive evidence. But—"

"But what?"

"Carson took the print from Michaels."

"I'll file another discovery motion if I have to, to ensure we get a copy sent to us."

"Okay, but—"

"Again? What's with the buts?"

"But, you *are* in a small town. A small town where the accused's husband's family controls almost everything."

"What are you saying?"

"You need more than inconclusive. You need absolute, positive proof. Think about it. Ashley's not from here, Monroe. Butler and his family have been here for decades. His grandfather was from here. His dad was from here. It's an uphill battle."

"Thanks for letting the air out of my balloon," Monroe said, tossing his pen onto the desk.

"Hey, don't get down. Their reports might give us something. But, in the meantime, we need to look for more."

"You're right. Let's figure out who did this and why. Bury them." He looked at Herm and asked, "Any suggestions?"

"The burnt body. Why kill a witness?"

"I agree. We've been so focused on the murder weapon—maybe we should look at some other theories."

"Now you're talking," Herm said, rising to his feet. "You're starting to think like an investigator." He walked to the door. Stopping, he turned back telling Monroe, "Oh yeah, I'll be in Jackson all afternoon."

"Jackson?"

"Checking on a hunch about Butler."

"What kind of hunch?"

"Not sure, yet. Just something a little bird whispered in my ear. If it pans out, I'll let you know."

"I hope your little bird isn't leading you on a goose chase."

"Me too. Anyway, you can call Debbie back in here, and . . . you know," he said, pointing to the couch. "Maybe you should lock the office door and put a sign up that says, back in ten." Herm chuckled, "Or, better yet, go to the house."

"Or maybe you should take your act to the comedy club. The drunks might find it funny."

Chapter 27

Around 12:30, Monroe's phone rang. He was busy getting files ready for court. He pushed the intercom button. Debbie informed him Judge Harper's office was summoning him to chambers. His mind raced for reasons, but he had nothing, as he hurried to finish. With his files in a cardboard file box, he hastened out the door and across the street. Not wanting to wait for the archaic, rickety elevator, Monroe hustled up the stairs to the third floor, toting his box of records. The secretary waved him to go in. Winded, he entered the judge's office huffing and puffing. He dropped his carton on the floor.

"You okay, Counselor?" Harper asked.

"Y-yeah, I'm . . . I'm fine," Monroe stammered, bending over and sucking wind.

"While you're trying to catch your breath, I'm going to let Mr. Breaux here explain why he called this little get-together."

Breaux was sitting in a dark red leather chair off to the side. He snickered at Monroe for a moment. He then stated, "Judge Harper, it has come to my attention that our forensics personnel needs some additional time to re-examine the shotgun used in the crime."

"Re-examine? Why? They've had plenty of time to examine the thing," Judge Harper countered.

"I agree, Judge," Monroe said, still huffing. "The prosecution is trying to buy time because *my* investigator may, *or may not have*, found something that *might* or might not be of any importance." The extra time would help Monroe, but he didn't want to let the pressure off Breaux. He was placing his trust in Michaels and Daniels, and their ability to expedite their investigation.

"I don't know, Robert," Harper said. "The sheriff's department and the prosecution had plenty of time to analyze the evidence." Harper stood up and grabbed his robe from a hanger.

"But, Your Honor, what's a couple of days?" Breaux pleaded.

"Should've thought about that *before* you asked for an early trial date," Harper said while slipping on his robe. "Request denied."

Monroe, pleased with the judge's decision, asked Harper, "You catch a big mouth?"

"What?" Harper responded with a puzzled look.

"A fish? Did you, you know, catch a big mouth?"

Harper waggled his head as he stared at Monroe. "It's called a largemouth. A largemouth, it's called a largemouth bass. And, if it is any of your business,"—a big smile grew across the judge's face— "yes." Harper put up his hands to indicate the length, which grew longer as Harper's hands moved further apart. "A big one. Over seven pounds."

"Wow! Nice one, Judge. I'm happy for you."

"What about you, Robert?" Monroe asked. "You catch a big fish?"

"No."

Harper said, chuckling, "What he caught looked more like bait."

Taking the crack in stride, Breaux laughed, disingenuously.

"You fish, Mr. Lovett?" Harper asked, putting his hand on Monroe's shoulder.

"I did years ago. A little with my dad."

"What does he fish for?"

"Nothing now. He passed away three years ago."

Squeezing Monroe's shoulder, Harper said, "Sorry to hear that."

"Thanks, Judge."

"Maybe we can go sometime. It'll be good for you," Harper said. Then, his smile instantly disappeared from his face as he gave both men a quick glance. "Let's go gentlemen. We need to get a lot done this afternoon. I have a long weekend planned." Harper turned to the prosecutor, who was still sulking over losing the plea for more time. "C'mon, Mr. Breaux. Lick your wounds," he said, exiting the office.

"Yeah, lick your wounds, Robert," Monroe said not far behind the judge.

"Real nice, use the 'my daddy died story' to get in tight with the judge."

"It's true," Monroe said bluntly, and then walked out of the office with his box in hand, heading down to the courtroom.

The Lane County Courthouse was packed when Monroe arrived, the murder trial of Ashley Butler was about to resume. Blazing hot summer temperatures along with high humidity gave many a reason to search for a cool spot to get out of the heat. The Butler murder trial seemed to be the best show in town.

Ashley was sitting at the defense table when Monroe arrived. He sat his box down and then took his seat next to her. Harper made a short stop before going to the courtroom and was running late. Sheriff Austin tapped Monroe on the shoulder. He turned around. "Sheriff."

"Mr. Lovett. Thought I'd say hello."

Monroe stood up to speak with Austin. "You have something on my abductors."

"I wish I did."

"Sheriff, about the other day—"

"Think nothing of it. Anyway, see, here's the problem. We don't have much to go on. I got your picture of the van, but your neighbor could not say for sure if it was the same one he saw. Sorry."

"That's too bad. Bet his bank account grew a little."

"Between you and me—" Austin stopped, and pointed over Monroe's shoulder toward the judge's bench— "Looks like Judge Harper's coming in." He patted Monroe on the shoulder, telling him, "I'll keep you updated if we get anything more."

"Thanks," Monroe said, taking his seat.

"All rise," the bailiff called out.

Monroe huffed as he stood back up.

Harper sat down and, without looking up, said, "You can be seated." He began arranging his papers and folders. "Mr. Breaux, call your next witness."

Breaux stood up and announced, "The State calls Darrel Barnes."

Barnes took the stand. He appeared nervous, visibly jittery. In the back of his mind, he was thinking about the visit by Michaels and Daniels. He hadn't heard anything from Carson on the print Michaels discovered. He questioned his own findings a little, now.

Breaux looked right at Barnes, a little puzzled by Barnes's behavior. He wrote it off, thinking that maybe it was due to this case. He asked, "Would you please tell the court your name and your role in this case?"

Barnes cleared his throat and took a deep breath. "My name is Darrel Barnes. I am a Crime Scene Examiner for Lane County."

Breaux walked over to the evidence table and stopped next to the 12-gauge shotgun. He placed his hand on the weapon. "Mr. Barnes, can you please explain what you found when you examined the shotgun used to commit this crime?"

"Objection," Monroe said.

"May I inquire to what you are objecting to?" Harper asked.

"The shotgun is alleged to have been used to commit this crime. There is not any conclusive proof this particular shotgun was used in any crime, especially this one."

Breaux stood there with a dumbfounded look on his face, gazing squarely at Monroe.

"Sustained," Judge Harper stated before Breaux could even counter the objection.

Monroe slightly smiled at Breaux.

"Fine," Breaux said, annoyed. "*Allegedly* used." He gestured to Barnes and told him, "Please, go ahead and answer the question."

Barnes cut his eyes in Judge Harper's direction and then looked at the jury. They were all waiting for his testimony. He swallowed hard again and stated, "Lane County Sheriff's Department, they called me to the residence of Marcus Butler, Jr. When I arrived, I found, the police showed me, a 12-gauge pump shotgun, that shotgun,"—he said, pointing at the shotgun in evidence— "laying on the floor of the walk-in closet in the master bedroom."

Breaux turned to face Monroe, waiting for another objection. Monroe remained silent, sitting with his fingers interlaced below his chin; his index fingers extended upwards, with his chin resting on them. He gave Breaux a look that indicated he could proceed.

Breaux smirked vaguely and then turned back to Barnes and asked, "Did you find any fingerprints on the firearm?"

Barnes thought of Michaels's findings from earlier, but he knew that was not what Breaux was asking of him. He squirmed. With a shaky voice, he answered, "The defendant's, Mrs. Ashley Butler's. I . . . I mean, we found, discovered her prints on the receiver, and the fore-end of the . . . that shotgun."

A few additional technical and boring questions wrapped up Breaux's examination of Barnes. Once finished, he sat down announcing, "I'm finished with this witness, Your Honor."

"Mr. Lovett," Harper said.

Monroe stood up with notepad in hand. He paused for a moment as he looked over his notes, not because he didn't know what to ask. No, he wanted Barnes to sweat a little longer. He could see Barnes's anxiety. It worked. Barnes began fidgeting as he waited. Monroe looked up at Barnes as if to ask a question, and then paused.

Barnes inhaled and exhaled loud enough for everyone in the courtroom to hear. Monroe noticed as Judge Harper started to say something. Now Monroe was ready. He asked, "Mr. Barnes, did you find any other prints on the shotgun?"

"Objection," Breaux said, popping to his feet.

"Overruled."

Barnes rubbed his forehead in frustration. "Yes. We found Marcus Butler Jr.'s, they were also on the shotgun," he replied, red-faced. He took a deep breath.

"Any others?"

"Objection," Breaux said. "Best evidence rule, Your Honor. The forensic report has been provided to the court. The defense is asking this witness—"

"Sustained."

Breaux sat back down, relieved. He fired a quick glare in Monroe's direction. Monroe didn't see it. Didn't care. Getting under Breaux's skin made him happy.

Monroe continued with his questioning, "Mr. Barnes, did anyone else find additional prints on the shotgun?"

"Objection, Your Honor!" Breaux said, nearly leaping out of his shoes, jumping back to his feet again. "Objection! The defense is—"

"Sustained. Mr. Lovett," Judge Harper said, pointing the gavel at Monroe. "I do believe the defense has been given a copy of the forensic report. Unless you have some additional evidence entered into the record by presenting it to the court, then stay within the rules of evidence, Mr. Lovett."

"Yes, Your Honor," he answered, attempting to hide a cocky grin. "I ask the court's forgiveness?" Prior to sitting down, he said, "I'm still a little rusty, I guess. However, I have filed a new discovery request. Lane County Sheriff's Department is in possession of a new fingerprint obtained from the shotgun in question. However, we have yet to be provided a report, or access to the print."

With blind faith, he was putting his wager on Daniels's and Michaels's reports, believing they would give him what he needed to discredit the original forensics.

A quick glance in Breaux's direction gave cause for Harper to question either Breaux's or the Sheriff's Department in the handling of this case. "If this is true, then we need to see the evidence, Mr. Breaux," Judge Harper said. Breaux nodded that he understood. "Until then, we'll move on. And work the rust out, Mr. Lovett," Harper told him as he peered over his reading glasses. "Do you have any additional questions for this witness?"

"Not at this time, Your Honor."

"You may step down," Harper told Barnes, who was relieved to depart the hot seat.

Before Barnes could take his first step, Monroe remarked, "Yes, Your Honor. The defense does have one more question for this witness."

With a furrowed brow, Judge Harper told Barnes, "Mr. Barnes, please retake the witness seat." He then looked back at Monroe telling him, "Ask away, Mr. Lovett."

"Mr. Barnes, please accept my apology," Monroe said, flipping the page of his notes.

"No problem," Barnes acquiesced, uneasy again. He could only imagine what Monroe was going to ask him.

"Just a couple more questions. Was any additional shotgun barrels recovered from the residence?"

"No."

"So, the list of items recovered from the crime scene is, as they have been presented to this court, complete?"

"Yes," Barnes replied, convincingly.

"Nothing was left off the list?"

"No. Detective Carson and I went over the list more than once. We even went back to the crime scene to make sure we had everything."

Breaux looked over his copy of the list and did not see anything out of the ordinary.

Moving over to the evidence table, Monroe pointed at the shotgun, "And this shotgun that has been presented to this court in the same condition as when it was acquired from the crime scene?"

"Yes."

"Are you sure?"

"Asked and answered," Breaux said without looking up.

Harper, ignoring Breaux, said, "Overruled, the witness will answer the question."

"Yes, I am," Barnes answered.

"So, no one else could have handled the shotgun?"

"No. I'm sure. It's been secured in the evidence room."

"Thank you, Mr. Barnes," Monroe said, turning his attention to Harper. "Your Honor, I have no further questions for this witness."

"Mr. Barnes, you may now step down," Harper said. "Mr. Breaux, are you ready to call your next witness?"

"Your Honor, our next witness, the coroner, Dr. Angie Stevens, has been delayed."

Harper glared at Breaux, telling him, "Then it looks like we'll wait until Monday for Dr. Stevens's testimony. Mr. Breaux, take this as your one and only warning. Do not allow this to happen again, or I *will* hold you in contempt."

"Sorry, Your Honor. It won't," Breaux replied.

The judge turned to the bailiff and said, "Escort the jury from the courtroom."

With Barnes's testimony in the record, Monroe was ready to get his two experts additional time to prepare. He made a request once the jury was gone. "Your Honor, in light of the new fingerprint evidence, the defense would like a continuance?"

"What new fingerprint evidence," Breaux asked. "As we discussed earlier, forensics personnel did not present any additional prints."

"You stated, Your Honor, if it was true that additional prints were discovered, they could be entered into evidence. It is true prints were found. And, Mr. Barnes, Detective Carson, and three other individuals were present and witnessed the obtaining of those prints."

Harper asked Monroe, "How *much* time do you need, Mr. Lovett?"

"Thursday of next week should work," Monroe said with a shrug, asking for more than needed.

Breaux, upset, said, "Judge, this is highly prejudicial to the people's case. The evidence has been presented against the defendant. Nothing new has been presented in this case."

Judge Harper intently looked at Breaux and said, "You're correct, Mr. Breaux. If additional prints have been found, then yes, it is highly prejudicial for the prosecution, as it speaks to your preparation for this case." Breaux remained silent as he felt the eyes in the room looking at him. Harper, looking over to Monroe, said, "You've got until Tuesday.

We're adjourned until Tuesday morning at 9:00 am." Harper followed his comments with three smacks of the gavel.

For the first time in weeks, Ashley felt a sense of hope. She began thinking she might have a chance at freedom. Before the deputy retrieved her, she whispered to Monroe, "Thank you, Mr. Lovett."

Monroe smiled. "Don't thank me yet. We're not done, but . . . but I do believe things are looking up."

The deputy then escorted Ashley from the courtroom. Monroe turned to Debbie and said, "You think you could get her another dress?"

"Sure," Debbie answered.

"Get her one very similar to what she was wearing the day she first came to our office. I'm going to take a walk around the square. Clear my head. I'll see you back at the office later."

"Okay." She gave Monroe a flirtatious look. "And what about me?"

"What about you?"

"A dress?"

Monroe stood there blank-faced.

Debbie playfully pouted and then said, "Fine . . ."

"Just kidding, honey. You know I don't care. Get yourself something, too. But you know what this means."

"A round of golf."

"Uh-huh."

Debbie enjoyed the occasional shopping trip; although, like most small towns, there were few stores or dress shops for her to buy a dress. This meant a trip to the city. "Oh, I don't have my truck with me," she said, her hand out, wanting his keys.

"Not a single scratch on it," he said.

"I won't hurt your baby."

That afternoon, working off a tip given him by an employee of Butler Transportation, Herm made a trip to Jackson. The lunch rush was over, so not many people were at the Pearl Café. He walked in and quickly scanned the small restaurant.

A college-aged girl, thinking he did not see the Seat Yourself sign, said to him, "Sir, you can sit wherever you want."

"I need to speak with the owner," Herm replied with a gentle smile.

"Sir?" she asked.

"The owner. Is the owner here? I need to speak with the owner."

"Oh, okay. I'll go and get him."

Herm looked around as he waited. The place made for a nice little getaway to meet someone if you didn't want to be noticed. A few moments later, a man seemingly in his fifties, walked from the back. He appeared tired, and his expression said he didn't want to be disturbed. The young woman pointed out Herm to the manager. He walked over to Herm and said, "Kim said you want to see me." He didn't sound happy with the interruption.

"Yes, if you're the owner."

"I'm Dennis Anthony. And yes, I am the owner. And you would be?"

"Herm. Ed Hermann. Thanks for giving me a moment of your time, Mr. Anthony."

"Well, I haven't given you anything, yet. And it depends on what you're selling."

"Understood. But I'm not *selling* anything," replied Herm. "I work for an attorney. Monroe Lovett. And I would like to ask you some questions if you don't mind."

"Questions? What kind of questions?"

"Maybe we should speak somewhere else," Herm said, looking around the restaurant at the few patrons there. "This shouldn't take long."

Anthony thought for a moment. "Sure. We can speak in my office." He motioned for Herm to follow him, and the two men walked through the kitchen and headed to a small office in the back. Clutter filled the office. Receipts, food order forms, and several applications sat stacked on his desk and chairs. After Anthony had closed the door, he removed some of the clutter from a metal-folding chair and then sat down in his own desk chair. It leaned to one side. He asked, "So, Mr. Hermann, what can I do for you?"

Handing Anthony a picture, Herm asked, "Have you seen this man before?"

"Yes. That's Mr. Butler. He's a regular. Comes in two to three times a month." Anthony handed the picture back to Herm. "Why do you ask?"

"Does he come in alone, or with someone else?"

"Usually alone."

"Usually?"

"At times, there have been others. They have lunch. Talk, but nothing more."

"Men? Women?"

Anthony thought for a moment and then answered, "Both. A younger girl on several occasions. But the last couple of times, he had lunch with a man."

Herm reached into his breast pocket and showed him another picture. "Is this the girl?" he asked, holding up a photo of Ashley.

"No. She was a young black woman. She was more like light skinned. Very attractive."

Herm showed Anthony another photo. "Is this her?"

"Yes. Yes . . . she has been in here several times with Mr. Butler, but not lately, though. Why? Is there a problem?" Anthony asked.

"Yeah, she's dead," Herm answered, holding the picture of Julie.

Anthony swallowed hard. "Th-that's too bad." His face became pale.

"Do you know who the man is that's come in lately with Mr. Butler?"

Clearing his throat, he answered, "No. He's not a regular."

"Who paid? Both? Butler? Or—"

"I'm not sure. I'd have to check. That is if they used a credit card."

"Can you do that for me?"

"Sure, but it will take a couple of days."

"I saw surveillance cameras. Do you keep the video?"

"Yes. For sixty days."

"I sure would like to get a look at those tapes."

"I can get you copies. They're on our computer."

"Mr. Anthony, if you could get me that information, it will be a big help," Herm told him as he reached into his pocket and handed Anthony a business card. "Here. Call or email me when you have the information. The sooner, the better."

"Okay," Anthony replied as he looked at the card. "Is Mr. Butler in trouble?"

"Not that I know of. But your information may help someone else."

"Okay, sure. As I said, give me a couple days."

Herm stood up and said, "Thank you, Mr. Anthony. You've been a big help."

Rising to his feet, Anthony replied, "Denny. Just call me Denny. Everyone does." Before Herm left, Anthony said, "Oh, there's one other thing."

"What's that?"

"The last time Mr. Butler and that other man were here, I happen to be near their table. They seemed to have an argument. It was loud enough that others noticed. Mr. Butler seemed mad, really mad. I almost walked over to them to check, but he calmed down."

"Did you hear what it was about?" Herm asked.

"No. No, I didn't. Sorry."

"Thanks again, Mr. Anthony. You've been a big help." The two men shook hands. Herm left the Pearl Café and headed back to Peregrine.

While strolling around the square, the heat became too much, so Monroe decided to head back to his office. Arriving, he reached to open the door to enter the building when a hand grabbed his arm from behind him.

Monroe spun around. He was still a little jumpy from a few weeks ago. His heart raced. Lisa, from Swatters, was standing there. "Lisa, right?" he asked.

"Yes."

"What can I do for you, Lisa?"

"Can we talk, Mr. Lovett?"

"Sure."

"Inside? It's hot out here," Lisa said, pointing at the door.

"Of course," Monroe said, opening the door. He stepped inside but did not go upstairs. The door closed behind Lisa. Monroe stopped and said, "Alright, talk."

She glanced around, making sure no one was close by to hear them. "Mr. Lovett, I haven't been completely truthful with you or the police."

"What do you mean?"

Nervously, using a soft voice, she said, "That night, the night of the shooting . . . Ashley and Julie also had an argument. A bad argument at the bar. In the ladies' room. I had to step between them."

"Have you told Mr. Breaux this?" Monroe asked, suspicious. *Ashley hasn't said anything about this.*

"No," Lisa responded, looking away.

"Are you going to?"

She paused before answering and said, "Haven't decided."

"Okay?"

"Maybe you could convince me not to, you know," she said, licking her luscious red lips.

Her comment caught Monroe off-guard. He said, sweating, but not from the heat, "No. No, that won't be necessary." He took a breath and said, "I think you should go see Mr. Breaux. Tell him."

"You sure?" she asked, reaching over and caressing his arm. "I mean . . ."

He pulled his arm back. "If that's all, Lisa, I think I'm going to get something. Alone," he said, pointing inside Christi's Coffee House.

"No one has to know, Monroe," she said, licking her lips again as she eased closer to him.

"Yeah. I'm . . . I'm sure." Monroe said, stepping toward the coffee shop.

Lisa just looked at him, wondering why he passed her up.

Monroe walked into Christi's, leaving her standing in the entryway. *Better remember to tell Debbie about this.*

Chapter 28

Late that same Thursday afternoon, after court, Monroe was working alone in the office. Debbie was still gone shopping, and Herm was somewhere between Jackson and Peregrine. Monroe was looking over the coroner's report, searching for something he could use, but it was pretty much cut and dry. Soon, he began feeling overwhelmed with the thought of losing the case and Ashley not only being found guilty but possibly getting the death penalty. He dropped his head back and stared at the ceiling above. He tried to relax by closing his eyes. Then prayed silently, *Lord, you know, this was not exactly what I thought it would be. I do admit; my faith is being stretched.* He stared up at the ceiling. A verse from James 1:5 came to him. *But if any of you lacks wisdom, let him ask of God, who gives to all men generously and without reproach, and it will be given to him.* If there was a time he needed God's wisdom, it was now. *Lord, I need your wisdom.*

Taking a deep breath, he shifted his gaze out the window to the street below. There were a few people moving around the old town square. *Nice looking old Chevy truck.* He leaned back in his chair again as his anxiety got the better of him again. Letting his head lie back, he stared at the dropped style ceiling and prayed, *Heavenly Father, I'm not sure this was the right move to make. Maybe I got misunderstood you—got it wrong.* He began to relax. Peace and quiet, those two things were missing in Monroe's life as of late. In the stillness, as the anxiety gradually disappeared, Psalm 37:3 popped into his head: *Trust in the LORD and do good; dwell in the land and cultivate faithfulness.*

Buzz . . .

The sound disturbed Monroe's mental escape. The main office door opened and closed. He sat straight up and called, "Hello."

No one replied, only footsteps . . . heavy footsteps, the sound of boots coming down the hall. Was it Herm playing another little game? However, Herm never wore boots. A large framed man appeared in the doorway.

"Hello . . ." Monroe said, recognizing the man.

"Marcus Butler, Mr. Lovett," he said, taking a couple steps into the office. The look on his face said this wasn't a friendly visit.

"Mr. Butler. What can I do for you?" Monroe asked, standing to face him.

Butler helped himself to a seat and asked, "Can we talk, Mr. Lovett?"

"Sure, I guess," Monroe replied, easing back into his chair. "About what?" He could only imagine where this conversation was going.

"My daughter-in-law. Your case," Butler said firmly.

"You looking to help her?"

"Hell no," Butler stated. He looked at Monroe as if he was an idiot. "She killed that Julie girl. Why would I want to help, to help a killer?"

"In your son's home," Monroe reminded Butler. "So, you're more concerned about your son's dead girlfriend than your daughter-in-law?"

"If you're asking me to help a murderer, then you can forget it, Mr. Lovett."

Monroe suddenly connected Butler's voice to the one he was trying to discern the night he has snatched. It took everything in him to control his anger. Seething within, he focused his ire into probing for Junior's whereabouts. "Speaking of your son, where's the young man?"

"He's fine," Butler answered.

"How do you know this? Have you spoken to him?"

"Spoken? No."

His answer got Monroe's attention, but he didn't want to push too hard. "Why won't he come back and answer a few questions?"

"Why? What do you care?"

"I care about the truth. A woman was murdered in your son's home, and he is nowhere to be found," Monroe said, leaning forward. He heard someone enter the office. Butler sat resolute, listening to Monroe with a look of boredom on his face. By his appearance, he did not hear what Monroe did. Intently looking at Butler, he said, "And your daughter-in-law, Ashley, is on trial for her murder. Which—by the way—you haven't lifted a finger to help." Monroe kept an eye on the doorway.

"Put yourself in my shoes, Mr. Lovett. Would you help her?"

"I would," Herm said, who had eased into the office.

Butler yanked his head around, surprised by Herm's unexpected arrival.

"Herm, Mr. Butler is here for . . . Why are you here?" Monroe asked.

"Intimidation, most likely. That's what you're best at—isn't it, Marcus?" Herm remarked walking over to the couch. From there he could see both men, but more importantly, he could see Butler.

"Yes, I'm sure you're right," Butler chuckled mockingly, brushing off Herm's comment. "Look, what I'm asking is that you see things—from my perspective."

"Herm," Monroe said, waving his hand in the air, "I think Mr. Butler is trying to enlighten me. Maybe he's right. I should look at this whole situation, and how it affects him, only him."

Herm tilted his head as he gazed at Monroe. He didn't catch mockery at first.

Butler did. Flustered, he stood up. "Mr. Lovett, I'm not going to sit here while you ridicule me," he said, walking toward the door. Pausing, he said, "But, I can promise you, it is in your best interest to—"

"Do it your way?" Herm said.

Butler glowered at Herm.

"Mr. Butler, let me ask you this," Monroe said, leaning back in his chair. "Do you believe Ashley is guilty?"

"I'm not falling for that," Butler protested. "The next thing I know, I'm on the stand."

"Then, I think this conversation is over," Monroe said. In his mind, the man would be on the stand, but he wasn't ready to tip his hand. Why give Butler too much time to prepare? Let him think he's simply a bystander.

Herm kept his eye on Butler. He could see his face reddening, and he knew of Butler's reputation of having a quick temper, a temper he used when it benefitted him.

"Yes, I guess it is," Butler responded. However, he couldn't let the conversation end there. Pointing his finger at Monroe, he said, "Just know this, you've been warned."

"Are you threatening me?" Monroe asked, popping to his feet. "Maybe you'd like to deal with me without my hands restrained and a hood over my face," he said, moving from behind his desk.

Herm also stood and moved a little toward Monroe to intercept him. He could see the anger meter in the room reaching the boiling point. Two Bulldogs were facing off.

Butler looked hard at Monroe and told him, "Take it however you want, Mr. Lovett."

"Goodbye, Mr. Butler. I'm sure we'll meet again," Monroe assured, pointing back at him and stepping closer to him.

"Have the girl plead guilty and move on," Butler said, taking a step toward Monroe. "Things will go a lot better for you in Peregrine."

Herm glanced at both men, easing closer to act if need be. *This is going in the wrong direction. And I'm too old for this crap.*

"Oh, I've heard that suggestion before. Not going to happen, you hear me. Now . . . good-bye! Leave!" insisted Monroe, gesturing for Butler to leave.

Despite Monroe's insistence, Butler responded, "The evidence. The evidence. Her confession. It all proves she's guilty. Or, are you too blind to see it?"

"Really?" Herm resounded, moving to a position more central to the two men.

Butler shot Herm a smug glance.

"I think the man told you to leave," Herm said, not intimidated by Butler. "I might step back and let him loose."

Ruffled, Butler said, "I'm going to offer you some friendly advice, Mr. Lovett. Be careful where you poke around, and who and what you believe. You're starting to upset some people, people who might—"

"Kidnap me. Beat me up," Monroe said sharply as he rubbed his side where he had been punched. With fire in his eyes, he made another move toward Butler and said with a raised his voice, "Already been down that road—literally, Mr. Butler."

Herm put his hand on Monroe's chest, stopping his progress.

With a chuckle, Butler said, "Yeah, better hold your boy back, Herm." He glared at Monroe. "I agree. This conversation's over."

"For now," Monroe said, leaning hard against Herm's hand.

Again, someone entered. The tension in the office kept them from hearing the buzzer. This time, it was Debbie. She arrived to hear and see the scene between Butler and Monroe. The whole incident frightened her. "What's going on?" she asked.

Monroe relaxed his stance. So, did Butler, who then hastily exited the office, looking at Debbie, "Mrs. Lovett, you have a nice day."

Alarmed and rather frightened, she stood motionless. Debbie watched Butler leave and then asked, trembling and tears in her eyes, "Monroe, what is going on?"

He saw Debbie's fear and said, "Everything's fine. Don't worry. You know, I think we need a louder buzzer."

Debbie looked at Monroe with her mouth gaping open, not believing a word he said. She fired back at him, gesturing with her hand, "Fine? Don't worry? Mr. Butler just gave you a warning. Isn't it enough that they, or he, already . . . already beat on you?" Tears rolled down her cheeks as she remembered that dreadful night.

"Tell her, Herm. Tell her everything's going to be fine," Monroe said, looking to Herm for help. "Tell her there's no reason to get upset."

Herm reluctantly said, "Yeah, sure. There's nothing to worry about." Though he wasn't sure himself.

"You're just trying to placate me, Ed Hermann," Debbie said, pointing her quivering finger at him and then wiping the tears from her eyes.

Herm just stood there, speechless. However, his face said it all. He couldn't hide his own apprehensions from Debbie.

Seeing he was getting no help from Herm, Monroe asked him, "Did you find out anything from your trip to Jackson?"

"Yes. Yes, I did," Herm answered, still a little keyed-up.

"Monroe Lovett," Debbie said, now pointing at him. "Don't you ignore me."

Monroe walked over to her. Gently taking hold of her shoulders, he gazed into her eyes and said, "Babe, it's going to be okay. Everything's fine." He then kissed her forehead. "The conversation got a little heated. But it's okay."

She didn't say a word as she glared at him. Debbie simply turned, walked downstairs, and left.

Monroe walked back to his desk. Looking out the window to the street below, out of the corner of his eye, he saw Debbie get into his car and drive away. Without moving, he said, "She just took my car."

Chuckling, Herm said, "I'll give you a ride. And you wonder why I'm not married."

Monroe walked over to a cabinet waggling his head. "I love that woman." Opening the cabinet door, he asked Herm, "Want a drink?"

"Sure."

"Gentleman's?"

"Ah, the good stuff."

"On the rocks or straight?"

"Two cubes."

Monroe poured two drinks. Handing Herm his drink, he asked, "Alright, tell me about your trip to Jackson."

"Well, your new friend Marcus and Julie Miller were seen, on more than one occasion, at a small restaurant in Jackson. A place called the Pearl Café."

"Interesting," Monroe said, taking a sip of the Kentucky whiskey. "Interesting how you didn't bring that up a few moments ago while the man was here."

"I know. I wanted you to hear it first."

"Good point. What do you make of it?"

"Not sure, yet. But something about this whole situation seems cagey to me, mysterious."

Both took a sip from their glasses of whiskey. Glass in hand; Monroe motioned to Herm. "I was stopped by that Lisa girl."

"Oh yeah."

"She told me Ashley and Julie had an argument in the bar's bathroom that night. But, here's what puzzles me, why now? Why bring this up now? Just doesn't make sense to me. Maybe—"

"Hold that thought. I've got more," Herm said.

"More?"

"Marcus Butler has also been meeting with a man at the same place lately. The owner is going to get me some more info."

"A man? What do you mean by *meeting* a man?"

"I don't believe it's like *that*," Herm said, laughing, placing his glass on the end table. "I think it's—"

"I didn't mean it *like that*."

Both sat for a few moments in silence. Monroe finished his drink. "Get this. Lisa all but offered herself to me."

Shaking his head, Herm said, "You're right, things don't make sense."

"Hey—"

Herm laughed, grabbing his drink and downing what remained.

"I'm going to go see Ashley in the morning," Monroe said.

"Ask her about the argument?"

"Yeah, and," Monroe said, swirling the ice in his glass, "I'm going to tell her to come clean with me."

"What do you mean?"

"I don't know, Herm," Monroe said, setting his glass down. He deliberately stroked the condensation on the glass. "But I think she's hiding something. I'm convinced she's not telling me everything. Especially after my conversation with Butler."

"They never do. Do you believe Lisa?"

"Do you?"

"Nope. Seems fishy. I'm with you. Something about this whole situation stinks."

"Stinks it does . . ."

Both men sat, not speaking a word for a few moments. The wheels were turning. "So, what do you think of Butler's warning?" Monroe asked.

"You tell me," Herm said, pointing at Monroe's side.

"You think he'd do more?"

"Butler? Oh yeah. But he's smart enough to keep his hands clean. Wouldn't be surprised if he sent Lisa to see you. But on the other hand—"

"What about Breaux?"

"Him? Now him, I wouldn't put anything past Robert Breaux. He's all about winning, winning no matter the cost. But, breaking the law? I doubt it. Maybe bend the rules some. Unlike you."

"How about your friend, Detective Carson?"

"He's a loud-mouthed cop," Herm said, picking up his glass. He downed the water from the melted ice. "But, of course, I've been gone for a long time. Things change. People change. He and Marcus have been friends, close friends, for a long time."

"So, you're saying—"

"I'm saying, don't trust anybody."

"You?" Monroe asked.

"Oh, I'm different. You can trust me."

"You came to me, not me to you," Monroe said suspiciously.

Herm peered at Monroe. The statement caught him by surprise. "You know, that's not funny."

"Who said I was trying to be funny?"

"You're serious?"

Monroe stared at Herm.

Herm squirmed a little. He pointed at Monroe with the hand holding his empty glass. Flustered, he asked, "Are you serious? You think I—?"

"You know, for a retired cop, you sure are easily conned," Monroe said, laughing.

"Oh, ha-ha. Very funny."

The two sat laughing briefly, and then Monroe asked, "Can you meet me at eleven tomorrow morning at Christi's?"

"Sure. But why there? Why not here?

"Change of scene. Plus, I usually have coffee down there at that time." Monroe rose to his feet. "I think I'd better go talk to Debbie. I'll take that ride now."

Chapter 29

Early Friday morning, sunlight was peeking through the tall pines that lined the backyard of Monroe's home. Reaching for his cup of coffee, he took a sip, "Ah . . . That's good," Monroe said, opening his Bible. He didn't have a particular passage in mind. Any text would do. All he knew was it had been a while since he last read from the Bible. Chuckling to himself, *Funny, I used to tell people to read their Bible every day. And now, here I sit, not having opened mine for weeks.*

Flipping through the pages, he turned to the gospels thinking, *I need some red-letter words this morning.* Stopping at John, chapter eight, Monroe began to peruse the passage. His eyes slowed when he reached verse 31. He began to read, *"So Jesus was saying to those Jews who had believed Him, 'If you continue in My word, then you are truly disciples of Mine; and you will know the truth, and the truth will make you free.'"*

Meditating on those words, he focused on one sentence, "you will know the truth, and the truth will make you free." He reread it. He read it again. *Lord, what?* Looking up at the trees, he meditated on those words. First Peter 2:16 came to mind. Setting his cup down, he quickly turned to the passage and read, *"Act as free men, and do not use your freedom as a covering for evil, but use it as bondslaves of God."* The two verses stuck in his head. *These must be for Ashley.*

Monroe soon finished his coffee. Now, he wanted more than ever to have that conversation with Ashley.

Sitting in her dull gray 6 x 8 cell was becoming all too familiar for Ashley. She desperately wanted to get out. Hope, for the first time, seemed reachable as she replayed the previous court proceedings through her head. The more she remembered them, the more she gained confidence in her attorney. Sitting on the edge of the bed, she prayed, *God, thank you for helping me. And thank you for sending me to Mr. Lovett.*

"Mrs. Butler," the deputy called as the cell door opened.

Ashley, looking up, answered, "Ma'am?"

"Your attorney is here to see you."

Ashley, almost glowing, made the journey to the conference room. Observing Monroe when she entered, she noticed his expression did not have the same compassionate, sanguine appearance. After the deputy had left them alone, she asked him, "Is there a problem, Mr. Lovett?"

"Not sure?" Monroe said, snappishly. "You tell me?"

Taken aback by his brashness she countered, "What? What do you mean?"

"Ashley, something just doesn't add up here. Why would someone want to kill Julie? I can see why you would want her—but I believe you didn't—." Ashley sat, looking detached. Monroe's voice increasing in volume and intensity, he continued, "Where's your husband? Where's Junior? Haven't seen him since day one." The expression on his face became almost angry-like. Ashley was unsure why. He continued firing questions at her. "Why did someone kill Billy? I just had a witness come to me, claimed you and Julie had a loud argument at Swatters the night before Julie ended up dead? Why did your father-in-law have regular lunches with Julie? Why did someone beat me up? Why? Why? Why? More questions, but no answers—none," he said with a hard slap to the table.

Ashley flinched, recoiling.

Then, Monroe saw her confusion, and he said, "I'm . . . Look . . ."

Affronted, she said, "I . . . I don't know. I promise I don't know." She insisted, "And I . . . Julie and me never even talked at Swatters that night. I haven't spoken to her in like, forever. Why would I?" She sat back in her chair, pulling her legs up with her knees tucked underneath her chin. Her hope plummeted to the floor and rolled away, like the tears that were beginning to flow down her cheeks.

Monroe looked at her. This was not what he had envisioned. "Ashley, talk to me," he said to her.

She refused. Hurt and bewildered, Ashley would not even look at him. Sitting, staring at nothing, she did not respond.

"Now *that* . . . that right there, it tells me you do know something," Monroe said, gesturing at her with his hands as he leaned back in his chair. Sanctimoniously, he continued, "Ashley, this morning I was sitting on my patio, just spending some time with God. You know what I did. I asked him for help. Then I read, 'you will know the truth, and the truth will make you free.'" Monroe leaned across the table, lowered his head trying to make eye contact with her. She refused. He said, "Ashley, God was speaking to me about you."

She shifted her gaze away and slowly recoiling back in her chair, away from him.

Blinded, and misreading her, he believed he was making progress. "Ashley, you need to tell me the truth, the whole truth," he said unsympathetically. "Why are you being framed for this murder? Huh? I can't help you if you don't allow me to. What are you hiding from me?"

Monroe couldn't see his own insolence was building a wall, but, at the same time, breaking down another wall, constructed of trust and hope. Ashley sat frozen and unreadable for the longest. Monroe sat dourly, waiting for her to give him answers.

Breaking her silence, she choked through her tears, "I . . . I am telling you the truth."

He thought, *Finally, she's going to come clean.*

She continued, sounding more depressed, "But you . . . you . . . you're just like everybody else—no one believes me." His optimism vanished. She sniffed, wiping her tears with the sleeve of her striped jumpsuit, and said, "May-maybe I should just plead guilty and ya'll will be done with me. You can go back to . . . go back to—." Ashley broke down and began crying.

Monroe exhaled as if he had taken another punch to the gut. This was not what Monroe had anticipated. He pictured her giving him that last little piece of evidence, some tidbit of information leading to her acquittal. Did he misunderstand the biblical text? He thought not.

Both sat quietly for a couple more minutes/. Ashley soon regained her composure and stopped crying. Monroe spoke first. "Ashley—I don't know what's going on here, but I'm going to find out the truth, either from you or someone else." He grabbed his briefcase. Slowly rising to his feet, he said, "The other verse I read this morning was, 'do not use your freedom as a covering for evil, but use it as bondslaves of God.' I don't know if you believe in God, but he believes in you, Ashley. He sent you to me for help, but you won't let me help you. Help can't be on your terms. Maybe I shouldn't have—." He thought better of finishing his statement. "Look, you can't use your possible freedom as a blanket to cover up the truth of whatever evil has happened. People are dead. I've taken a beating, a beating because I am helping you. Now, do you want to tell me the whole truth?"

Ashley did not move. The words she had prayed just prior to Monroe's arrival came back to her. The distraught young woman would not look at Monroe. She just stared at the wall, tucked up like a ball in her chair.

Monroe walked to the door. He looked back at her, thinking she would open up to him.

She did. However, the quiet Ashley was gone. An ignited Ashley said, "You . . . you're just like every other Bible-thumping church-goer who's talked to me. Ya'll just . . . just a bunch of hypocrites. That's what you are, Mr. Lovett. A phony. You come in here . . . spouting your Bible verses at me." She glared at him. Monroe did not know what to say as he stood there seeing a side of Ashley he had not seen before. But he brought it out of her. She put her finger up, telling him, "Told me to trust you. Ain't met a man yet that I—Go. Go preach your sermons to someone else, Mister, or maybe I should call you *Reverend* Lovett." He didn't know how to respond, and she could see it. "What? You thought you could save me? Is that it? Check off, saved the poor little girl in jail, to make you better with God." Angry and agitated, Ashley, with a furrowed brow, became stone-faced. "Go. Leave me alone. You and your God."

He stood and took her tongue-lashing. What else was he going to do? Somewhat contrite, he said, "Ashley . . . I . . ." For once, he was speechless. Ashley had never spoken to him in that manner. He still doubted her honesty with him. Monroe banged on the door for the deputy to open it. A few seconds later, the deputy arrived. Before walking out, he turned back and said, "Ashley, when you're ready . . ."

"Go preach your sermons somewhere else," she indignantly muttered.

"So, you know, umm, Debbie got you a new dress." She didn't respond. "Okay, I'll see you later," he said, deflated and nonplussed before leaving her sitting there.

He turned in his visitor's badge and moped while leaving the county jail. As the door was closing, he heard someone yell from inside, "Counselor. Mr. Lovett."

Monroe grabbed the door and turned around, seeing a deputy walking at a fast pace toward him, he asked, "Does she want me to come back?"

"No. Here. You forgot your briefcase," the deputy said, handing him his attaché. "You left it at the checkout counter."

"Oh . . . Thanks," Monroe replied, forcing a smile.

Very few people were sitting in Christi's when Herm entered. The old geezers had their unofficial mid-morning gathering in a far corner of the coffee bistro. Most every small town has these gents, the ones who have all the answers, but no solutions. On the other hand, they have some neat and entertaining stories. Just grab a cup of that caffeine fix and take a seat. Herm wasn't ready to join their club. Looking around, Herm didn't see Monroe, but he heard the old guys laughing.

"He's over there," Christi said when she saw Herm. Pointing to a booth where Monroe was sitting, his back to them, she said, "He's been here for 'bout an hour. He hasn't said much. Kind of strange for him."

"Ah, it's nothing," Herm told her. He knew something was up. Starting to walk toward Monroe, he said, "Christi."

"Yes?"

"Coffee. Black. Please."

She nodded in affirmation.

Dropping into the booth opposite Monroe, Herm inquired, "Problem?"

"Why do you ask?"

"Christi said you've been here for an hour. Not talking. It's not like you."

Christi placed a cup on the table and poured Herm's coffee. "Thank you, ma'am," He said with a gentle smile. "Can I get one of those delicious cupcakes you make?"

"You bet," she answered and walked away.

"She won't talk to me, Herm?" Monroe said.

"Who? Debbie?"

"No. Debbie? She's fine," Monroe said downheartedly. "Who do you think? Ashley."

"I knew that. Just wanted to get your mind headed in the right direction," Herm said before taking a sip of java. "So, did you grill her? Tell her how she needed to *come* clean?"

"Yes. I even told her how God spoke to me this morning. How the verses I read this morning were for her."

"So, let's see, you raked her over the coals. Then pulled the *God* card out and preached a sermon. Told her, what? How the Scripture you read this morning was for her." Herm took another sip. "You know, I always find it funny how someone reads the Bible, and when it speaks to them, it is always for someone else and not them. What really irks me is—"

"Herm."

"Well, I don't understand why that didn't get her to open up. You know, you preaching to her and everything." He sipped his java. "That-doesn't-work, preacher-man."

"What?" Again, reminded of his preachiness.

"You have to be gentle. Be nice to the girl, Monroe."

"I needed to press her to get the—"

"You've watched too much TV. This is not an episode of Law and Order. It's real life, my friend. It doesn't work like that."

"What do you mean?" Monroe asked, ruffled by Herm's comments. "I've been nice. Every time we spoke. I was always nice to her."

"Until now. Today, what? Let's see if I can get this right. You walked in. Got a little aggressive—interrogated her." Herm laughed a little as he glanced out the window. He could see Monroe's body language out of the corner of his eye. Herm nailed him. "Monroe, you're her counselor. Her lawyer. Her advocate. Not today though. Today, you became her adversary. She's got a whole county full of adversaries. To her, you just joined them."

Monroe sunk back into his seat as a pit formed in his stomach. "Man . . . Son of a gun, you're right. You're right."

"I know."

"I so much wanted to get to the truth, that I—"

"Lost sight of your responsibility? Possibly lost sight of where the truth lies."

"Yeah . . . She called me a hypocrite."

"Is she right?" Herm asked. He let Monroe reflect on his conversation with Ashley for a couple of minutes. He sat up, stretching, and scanned the coffee house. "Where's my cupcake?"

Monroe rubbed his hand over the top of his head, his fingers running through his hair. After puffing his cheeks, he exhaled, "I'm an idiot. I'm an idiot. A stupid idiot."

"Yes, you are. But don't beat yourself up too much. We've all been there."

"You?"

"No," Herm said, staring at Monroe. Monroe sat, looking at him not knowing how to respond. "Of course, I have. Look, stop preaching," Herm said reassuringly. He leaned across the table. "You need to let Ashley know you're her defender, not her accuser. The poor girl has a world full of accusers. Take a close look at her. That girl's been through a lot. I look at her and see an ugly past. Convince her you're here to help her. She'll open up to you. Monroe, she has to trust you. You can't ask her to trust you and then turn on her."

Herm's comments struck a nerve with Monroe, a nerve that needed striking. He sat there, realizing he had taken God's message for him and transferred it onto Ashley. All he could think of now was how he had treated her. He recognized her response towards him was justified.

Christi returned with a coffee pot in hand and refilled their cups. Monroe didn't notice as he pondered Herm's advice.

"My cupcake?" Herm asked, trying to be cordial.

"Oh yeah. Sorry. I'll go get it," Christi answered. She looked at Monroe and asked him, "Is he okay?"

"Oh, he will be."

Christi left.

"Herm?" Monroe asked quizzically.

"Yes."

"We need to find out who Julie Miller *really* was?"

"What do you mean?"

"Well, she was black."

"At least half. So?"

"Her parents, the Millers, they're white. *Very* white."

"You have a point," Herm replied, straining his neck again to look for the whereabouts of his cupcake. "Oh, before I forget to tell you, I've got a date tonight."

"Do some background checks on Ashley. *Before* she married Marcus Jr."

"Okay, I can do that. I'll get on it first thing Monday." Herm kept looking for his sweet treat. "A date with Mary."

"Somehow, we've got to figure out why Marcus Sr. was taking the victim to lunches in Jackson," Monroe said, staring out the window over Herm's shoulder. "We need to figure out who really murdered her, Herm. And why?"

"That's what we're doing."

"Where's the connection between them?"

"That's what I'm working on."

"Herm, we need to find out who killed Billy, and why? What did he know? Or do? Was it just to get rid of Ashley's alibi? Was he involved somehow? If so, then it must be to protect someone. But who? And the money. Why?"

"Yeah, I know. I'm on it, Monroe," Herm said, rising from his seat a few inches to look around the restaurant. "Where's my cupcake? That Christi is nice, but a bit scatterbrained."

"You don't have time for a cupcake. Too much work to get done," Monroe said, dropping a five-spot on the table for his coffee.

"Did you hear a *single* word I said?" Herm asked.

"Yes. You're going out with Mary. The one I tried to warn you about," Monroe acknowledged, standing up. "And, I need to regain Ashley's trust. Thanks, Herm."

Herm looked at him, a little surprised Monroe had heard him. He replied, "I'll see you later—let you know what I find."

"Alright." Monroe chuckled, "Ought to be a fun date." Monroe left Herm and headed upstairs.

Entering the office, Debbie looked up at Monroe and said, "It's about time. Where have you been? I'm up here doing *your* job. And you, you're God knows where—?"

"I was down—" Monroe attempted to answer but to no avail. He knew to let Debbie rant. Thus, he stood and listened.

"But here I am, working . . . working hard. But you . . ."—She said, waving her hand around— "Well, who knows where?" Debbie took a deep breath and calmed herself. "Now that you're finally here, you need to see what I found."

"Found?" he asked.

"I got bored, so I started doing a little investigating of my own," she told him with an excited look on her face. "Digging for stuff."

"Digging? What did *you* dig up?" Monroe asked inquisitively.

"Julie Miller was adopted," Debbie said animatedly.

"And?"

"And, the adoption record is sealed."

"Adopted from where?"

"New Orleans. I called down to the courthouse, but they said we needed a judge to sign a court order to open the records."

"We? You're practicing law now?" Monroe asked, laughing.

"You know what I mean."

"I'll make a call. See what I can do."

"Why? I already got you in to see a judge, Monday at 4 pm. Her clerk said, 'don't be late.'"

"Four. Okay," Monroe said. Debbie's prowess happily amazed him. "You did all that?"

"Yes. Yes, I did," answered Debbie with a playful satisfaction.

"Good for you, babe. I think I need to promote you."

"Promote me? To what?" she asked, looking around. "There's only the two of us, unless, of course, you count Herm, then it's three, but I'm not sure if we can count him because he doesn't officially work for us, but—"

"Debbie, take a breath. Find a period," he said, putting two fingers over her lips. "To my personal assistant."

"I'm already that."

"Well, yes. But now, as my official personal assistant, you can sit at the table with me during the trial."

"Oh . . . okay. Can I do that?" she asked.

"You bet. Besides, I need someone who can take better notes. I can't read my own handwriting."

"Neither can I. Been taking my own anyway," she muttered, looking away slightly.

"What?"

"Nothing. Maybe we should go out and celebrate tonight?"

"Celebrate?"

"My promotion."

Monroe thought for a moment. Then he said, "You know . . . I've heard of this place, Tony B's. An Italian restaurant. It's supposed to be good."

"Italian . . . I like Italian," she said, licking her lips. "Sounds good."

Monroe leaned over within an inch of Debbie's face. "I love you, Debbie Lovett."

"I love you, too, Monroe Lovett." She kissed him on the nose and said, "I'm hungry. What's for lunch?"

"You want to go home for some . . . lunch?" Monroe asked, raising his eyebrows.

She knew what he wanted. "Yeah . . . Yeah, I think that is a *very* good idea," she said with a soft, breathy voice.

"Let me take care of a few things first," he said.

"Oh, I forgot to ask. How was your meeting with Ashley this morning? How's she doing?"

Monroe didn't answer her.

"Monroe, what happened?"

He recounted to her what he told Ashley and her reaction. Debbie listened, in shock. After he had finished, she looked at him and said, "Monroe Lovett! March yourself back over to that jail and apologize to Ashley."

"I don't think she wants to see me right now."

"And who can blame her? Monroe . . . sometimes . . . you can . . ."

"*I know*. Herm has already pointed out what I am."

"Well good for Herm. What are you going to do?"

"I'll give her time to cool off and then go back and see her. *And* apologize."

Ashley was sitting in her cell that afternoon, on her steel bed, curled up in a ball in the corner, and weeping. Feeling unloved, unwanted, and unbelieved, she sunk into depression. Even her own lawyer didn't believe her. In Ashley's mind, her husband had abandoned her along with his family, and her best friend was dead. Her thoughts flashed forward, as she saw herself standing while the jury announced, "Guilty." The death penalty handed down. The thought of dying seemed almost a relief to her as she felt completely alone and hopeless.

God, are you even real? Do you even care?

She cried harder. "Just let me die," she whimpered quietly through her tears.

One of the female deputies overheard her but was unsure of what she heard. So, the deputy went to check. Seeing Ashley, she asked, "Ashley, you okay?"

Ashley nodded yes, but only slightly. She didn't say anything. The deputy, knowing nothing about Ashley's conversation with Monroe, figured she was just upset, stressed.

"You sure?" the deputy asked. "I can call someone if you need to talk."

Ashley wiped her eyes and shook her head no.

"Okay," the deputy said, leaving.

Sitting with her body pulled into a tight ball, Ashley replayed her conversation with Monroe. "Why? Why? Why doesn't he—?" she whined quietly. Then she heard something, like a calm voice, in her thoughts— *Trust him.*

She didn't know what to make of it at first. *Trust who?* She thought about those two words. *But he doesn't believe me. Why trust him?*

Wondering whom to trust, she got up and started pacing in her cell. Running names through her head, the deputy returned. Ashley, seeing her, said, "I'm fine . . ."

"Someone's here to see you," the deputy said, opening the cell door. "Who?"

"Just come with me," the deputy said. Ashley's visitor asked the deputy not to reveal who was there to see her, in case she might not agree.

Walking through the hallway, all Ashley could do was wonder who was there to see her. Questions raced through her head. Was it 'the him' from her thoughts? If so, who? Junior?

Nearing the conference room, she became nervous and apprehensive. As the deputy opened the door to the conference room, Ashley's heart rate increased. The door opened slowly, and then cleared Ashley's line of sight so she could see inside. "No," she said, taking a step backward.

The deputy tried urging her inside, but Ashley struggled, pulling away. "Just go in and talk," the deputy said, trying to get her to enter the room.

Ashley refused with even more effort, stating, "No. No. I don't want to talk with him."

Another deputy, a sergeant, entered the jail area. Hearing the commotion, he asked, "What's the problem here?"

"Mrs. Butler, here, doesn't want to go into the conference room," the other deputy answered while gripping Ashley's arm.

The sergeant looked inside the conference room and said, "If she doesn't want to speak with him, then take her back to her cell. It's her decision."

"Okay," the deputy replied.

"And after you're done here, come see me," the sergeant said before walking away.

The deputy returned Ashley to her cell, where she spent the rest of the night lying on her bed barely sleeping.

Chapter 30

It was a warm and sticky evening, but Monroe and Debbie didn't care. Right now, Peregrine was in the rearview mirror, and they were out for the night—a much-needed date. The unexpected cash dropping into their hands allowed for a little celebration, a welcomed distraction.

After a forty-five-minute drive, they pulled into Tony B's in Madison. Walking in, a young woman, obviously of Italian descent, greeted them with a polite smile, "Hello. Welcome to Tony B's. How many are in your party?"

"Just the two of us," Debbie answered.

"We don't have a reservation," Monroe said, looking around and noticing the crowd.

"Oh, that's not a problem. We'll have you a table in about fifteen to twenty minutes if you can wait?"

"Yeah, that's fine," Debbie answered.

"Your name?"

"Lovett, Monroe Lovett," Monroe answered.

Monroe and Debbie sat down in the small, but picturesque waiting area. Two other couples were already there, lost in their own conversations. A band, three members, played soothing music in the bar area. On the light tan stucco walls, scenic oil paintings of Italian landscapes hung, interposed with black and white family photos. Potted trees, decorated with Christmas lights, placed around the eatery on the Tuscan-style tile floor, with green white and green colored canvas awning made for a cozy, old-world feel. The ambiance gave one the feel of being transported to Italy and sitting outside at an Italian café.

"This is nice," Debbie whispered to Monroe as she clung to his arm.

"Yes, it is."

The hostess called the other two couples to their tables, leaving Monroe and Debbie alone.

"Where did you hear of this place?"

"Honestly, I found it on the internet a few days ago."

"So, you were already planning this."

"Yeah. You deserve it," he said, gently squeezing Debbie's knee.

A few more people entered the restaurant.

Moments later, they heard a male voice call, "Lovett, your table is ready." Looking up they saw an older Italian man, standing slightly more than five feet tall. He had a warm smile and thinning solid white hair topped his head. "Please follow me," he said.

Monroe and Debbie followed him to a table situated next to a window overlooking a large water fountain and a multitude of blooming plants consisting of a variety of bright colors.

"Thank you," Monroe and Debbie both said to the elderly man as he gestured to their table.

Monroe pulled Debbie's chair out for her. "Well, thank you, honey," she said with a gleeful smile.

"No, thank you," Monroe said with a grin.

Handing them their menus, the kind man said, "Pam will be your server. She will be here shortly. Enjoy your meal." With a smile, he departed.

"What was that little goofy smirk for?" she asked.

"Lunch," Monroe answered, raising his eyebrows a couple of times.

Debbie blushed a little and said, "Monroe . . ."

LaPierre Restaurant was obviously busy when Herm pulled up at a little before 7 pm. He and Mary had agreed to meet here since they live some distance apart. First dates are always exciting because you never know what to expect. Will the person look or act as you remembered from that first brief encounter? Was this a mistake? Will they like me? Will I like them? A little nervous, the retired cop got out of his sedan. After taking a deep breath, and briefly considering leaving, he walked inside.

"Evening, sir," the maître d' said. "How may I help you?"

"I have a reservation for two."

"Your name?"

"Hermann. Ed Hermann."

"Ah, yes. Here we go. Your party has already arrived."

"Party?"

"You are meeting someone, aren't you?"

"Yes. I'm sorry. Just when you said party—never mind," Herm said, his nerves causing brain shut down.

"This way, Mr. Hermann," he said and sashayed away. Herm watched him for a moment, waggled his head, and followed the very colorful young man. *You'd think all those years in New Orleans I'd be used to this.*

Rounding the corner, Herm saw Mary sitting at a table.

The maître d' told him, "Here's your table, sir." He then flashed a smile and left the two alone.

Quickly looking around the dining room, he noticed most everyone was dressed up. Not him. Nope. Herm was dressed casual, whereas, all the other men had on sports coats, and many of them were wearing ties. "Well, I guess I didn't get the dress code," he mumbled, sitting down. His anxiety was visible.

Mary laughed, "There's nothing to be nervous about, Herm. We're just out for a night of fun. You do like fun, don't you?"

Looking across the table, he saw Mary's toothy smile. "Sure. Yes, I like to have fun," Herm replied. His idea of fun was usually a night sitting in front of his TV watching an old western while eating a microwavable dinner or take-out pizza. Not tonight. No. Fun had a different meaning. His cop instincts told him something looked different about Mary, but those instincts were fuzzy due to his elevated anxiety levels. So, he tried to relax.

A young female server approached the table and said, "Hello. My name is Cindy. Can I start you two off with some drinks?"

"A Bloody Mary," Mary said. She looked at Herm giggling, telling him, "Because my name is Mary. Get it? Bloody Mary."

Herm nodded, forcing a smile, supposing it was her attempt at wit—first date jitters.

"And, for you, sir?" Cindy asked.

"Gentleman's on the rocks, and make it a double."

"Thanks. I'll go place your drink orders as you look over the menu."

Herm opened his menu. He snuck a peek over the top of the menu at Mary. *Maybe Monroe was right.*

Before he could read the entries, Mary blurted out, "Oh, I love this place. The food is the best."

"It's nice," Herm said, giving the place a non-to-obvious look around.

A few moments later, Cindy returned with the drinks. After setting them down, she said, "Our special tonight is lobster-stuffed beef tenderloin with béarnaise sauce, served with red potatoes and a side for seventy-two dollars. It is one of my favorites. In addition, you can add a side salad if you like. So, are you folks ready to order?"

Herm stared back at her, trying to hide his alarm after hearing the price. All he heard was seventy-two plus. Dollar signs were flying through his head.

Cindy, seeing his reaction said, "Okay, maybe I'll give you two a minute to look over the rest of the menu."

"Yes, please," Herm said. His expression did not change as he watched Cindy walk away. *Seventy-two . . . You have got to be kidding me! How about a moment to go get a loan? Funny how she was quick to suggest it.*

"Yum-m-m, the special sounds dee-*lish*," Mary said, beaming from ear-to-ear. "I'm ready. And I'm starving."

Herm perused the other main dishes. He nearly choked when he saw the rest of the prices. *I don't want to buy the whole damn cow,* he thought as he looked over the steaks. *Maybe she's not very hungry. Most women don't eat a lot on a first date. Wait, did she just say . . .*

"I could eat a cow," Mary touted. "I'm thinking about having the special. What about you, Herm?"

He tried to control his shock. *I'm thinking pizza and beer back at the house would be better.* Herm bobbed his head from side to side, pretending to be considering his choices. *Maybe I can have a salad with bread and water. Somebody has to eat like a woman tonight. It might as well be me. How much is a salad?* He took a deep breath and answered, "Oh . . . I don't know. It all looks so good." *We should've gone Dutch.*

"Oh, this Bloody Mary is dee-*lish*," Mary said with a loud slurp.

Herm took a mouthful of his Kentucky Bourbon. *She seems older. Must be the light.*

"Slow down. You don't want to get drunk, now, do you?" Mary said with a loud cackle and a wave of her hand.

Cindy returned and asked, "Have you folks decided?"

"I'll have your special," Mary said. "My steak cooked medium-well. It just sounds so dee-*lish*. Oh, and a side of broccoli, light on the butter. No. Tell them no butter."

"Now, it doesn't come with a salad. Would you like to add one?"

"Oh, yes. Don't want to skimp on my leafy veggies," Mary said.

Herm looked at the salad menu and read, *"Side salad, $13.99"*. *For freaking lettuce!* He looked at Mary, attempting to hold a polite smile. His mental calculator was starting to run a tab. He felt a headache coming.

"What kind of dressing would you like, ma'am?"

"The fat-free honey mustard," Mary answered. "Edward, you have to try their fabulous honey mustard. It's dee-*lish.*"

"Just call me Herm," he politely told Mary.

Mary went on as if she never heard him. Looking up at Cindy, she said, "It's our first date."

Turning to Herm, Cindy asked him, "And, for you, sir?"

Between Mary's odd behavior and price-shock, he simply said, "The special."

"Broccoli?"

"Sure. But with butter. Lots of butter."

"Salad?"

"Yep, with your fabulous honey mustard dressing."

"The fat-free or the regular?"

"Oh, the regular."

"Anything else?" she asked.

"Another drink, please," Herm answered.

"A double?"

"Oh yeah."

After Cindy left, Mary began telling Herm her life story. Right off the bat, she told him, "You know, Edward, I'm a blessed woman. I've been so blessed to have been married to three great men."

"Herm," he said, but she never heard him. *Three husbands. She's probably a black widow.*

"Unfortunately, all three of them died un-expectantly. Can you believe it, a widow three times before I'm fifty?"

Yep. Killed them.

"The first had a heart attack. The second had a stroke. And the third, he also had a heart attack. I guess you can say," —she chuckled— "I'm the proverbial black widow."

Couldn't have said it better myself. Herm tried to come up with a snappy yet courteous response, but nothing came to mind. He sat, speechless, nodding as she gabbed away.

Rescued from his awkward moment, Cindy returned with their salads. Mary didn't miss a beat as Cindy did her job. Mary asked, "What about you, Edward? Any past wives?"

"Herm," he told her again. It was as if his correction went right past her. "Nope, never been married. Work kept me busy," he said, then taking a big bite of salad. The thought of being on the other end of the questions, having someone pick your life apart, was not an enjoyable concept for him.

"Work? What kind of work?" Mary asked him as she stuffed a bite of salad into her mouth.

Chewing, he answered, "police detective."

"Umm-hum . . ." She responded somewhat loudly. A couple seated close by clearly heard her. Discreetly, they turned for a glance but pretended not to notice Mary.

Herm looked at her, not knowing how to react to her animated response. He said, "I was a New Orleans police detective."

"Umm-hum . . ." Again, and exaggerated, Mary resounded. She took another rather large bite of her salad.

Herm stared at her for a second, before saying, "But . . . now . . . I'm retired."

"Umm-hum . . .!" she responded boisterously. This time, prompting more people to turned and look in their direction. Discretion was no longer a concern. Mary didn't see them, nor cared.

Dang, woman! Herm thought, attempting to hide any facial reaction to her gregarious ripostes. *Do you think you could umm-hum a little louder? I don't think they heard you in the parking lot.*

Much to his dismay though, the booming "Umm-hums" continued throughout their conversation.

Meanwhile, back at Tony B's, Monroe and Debbie were enjoying their meal. He ordered the cheese ravioli smothered with marinara sauce and she the seafood Alfredo over linguini.

"This is nice," Debbie said, holding her glass of Pinot Grigio.

"Peaceful. Something we've needed," Monroe said, then took a sip of his Chianti.

"I would like to go to Italy someday," Debbie said, admiring the decor. "Think about it—just the two of us, traveling through the Tuscany. We could explore Rome. Trek around the country. What do you think?"

"Sounds great. Who knows? Maybe one day I can take you on that dream vacation. You better start praying for a rich client," Monroe told her with a wink.

Debbie gave him a flirty little smile and then sipped her wine.

As they finished their meal, enjoying the quiet, tranquil ambiance, the older gent returned to their table. "How was your dinner?" he asked.

"Umm, it was wonderful," both Monroe and Debbie expressed. "This place is great. It has a certain charm about it," Debbie said.

"I'm so glad to hear that," he replied with a joyous laugh. "Well, my name is Tony. If there's anything—anything you need to make your experience more enjoyable, please let us know, okay?"

"Thank you, Tony. We will. But everything seems perfect," Monroe answered lifting his glass.

"You two have a very pleasant evening. And remember, if you need anything, anything . . ." Tony said, turning and walking away.

"He seems like such a nice man," Debbie said in a modest whisper.

"Yes, he does," Monroe said. "I bet he's Tony B."

"No doubt."

"He's a nice man," Monroe said, folding his napkin and placed it on the table.

Debbie looked across the table, and with a slight wonder in her voice, she asked, "How do you do it?"

"Do what?"

"How do you separate yourself from the case? You sit here, and have dinner with me as if none of that was going on."

Monroe reached across the table and took hold of Debbie's hand. Gazing into her eyes, he said, "When I'm with you, I'm one hundred percent focused on you." Debbie felt his love as he caressed her hand. "But, when I'm in court, or with my client, dealing with the case, I'm one hundred percent focused on the case. It's a matter of priorities." Leaning over the table a little, Monroe, gazing deep into Debbie's eyes, said, "And right now, at this very moment, my priority, my focus, is one hundred percent centered on you. Because you are the most beautiful, most gracious, hottest, sexiest woman I have *ever* known, or *ever* want to know. I love you, Debbie."

"Monroe, I love you, too. You're so sweet. You know, you just might get another *lunch* tonight," she said breathy, followed by a slow run of her tongue along her upper lip.

Over at LaPierre, things were going quite the opposite. Herm was enjoying his second double whiskey as he listened to Mary drone on and on about her life and dead husbands. Detail by detail she covered every aspect of all three marriages. He wondered why witnesses to a crime never had such good memories. Out of the corner of his eye, he saw Cindy coming with their food. *Thank God. Now we can eat, and she will stop yapping about her dead husbands.*

Cindy placed their food on the table. "Oh honey, you've got it wrong," Mary said. "This is his and that one's mine."

Stumped, Cindy frantically reached to switch the plates and said, "I'm sorry—I apologize."

Herm watched, stupefied.

Mary put her hand out, stopping her as she giggled, and said, "No sweetie. I'm just joshing you. They're both the same," she cackled.

Not amused, Cindy gave Mary a glance that said, "Lady, you're crazy." Herm rolled his eyes, taking another swig of his drink. Cindy saw him out of the corner of her eye and fought back a giggle, and then left.

Mary reached for her fork, but instead of clutching it, she knocked it off the table, and it fell to the floor. It landed about halfway between her and Herm.

"Let me get that for you," he said, starting to reach down.

"No, I got it," Mary responded, leaning down precipitously to retrieve the fork. Her forward motion was so hard that she did not notice that her wig, a short-style with large curls resembling a large ball, slide from her head and roll about six feet across the floor. Just as swiftly as she bent over, Mary popped back up, unaware her counterfeit hair had tumbled across the floor. What looked like some sort of white stocking cap was covering her real hair.

Herm froze. His mouth slowly dropped opened. He was unsure of what to do. *Should I say something? Maybe I can discretely point to her head.* He didn't want to embarrass her. That moment had passed. In his state of suspended animation, he thought, *Herm, you've got to say something.* With all the strength he could muster, he gradually raised his steak knife, pointing out the missing hairpiece. Sympathetically, he said, "Mar-ry . . ."

Giggles from nearby tables became louder.

"Yes, Edward."

It's Herm! With his steak knife in his hand and gesturing at Mary's head, "Mary, your . . . your hair, it—"

Suddenly, the rush of fresh air inundated Mary's head. She sensed her head felt a little lighter up top. Mary reached up with both hands to where her wig once sat. She looked over and saw Herm's tongue-tied expression. She glanced down and saw her wig lying in the middle of the restaurant floor. Unsure what to do, she glanced at Herm, who was still pointing with his steak knife. Then she looked back at the wig. Frantic, Mary exclaimed, "Oh my!" She jumped to retrieve the ball of synthetic hair.

Before she could grab the wig, a waiter, unaware of what was happening, walked briskly from the kitchen area carrying a tray loaded with four plates of food. In his peripheral vision, he noticed Mary's wig on the floor. Uncertain of what it was, he came to this abrupt stop. The tray of food did not. As hard as he tried to prevent it, he couldn't, and the food plummeted to the floor. Plates crashed, smashing into each other and breaking. Meals flew in every direction. A lobster and a steak went splat as they landed. People groaned as they watched in horror. Rolls tumbled and broccoli, asparagus, and green beans scattered. Others moaned at the sight that seemed to unfold in slow motion before their eyes.

One man bemoaned, "That's a waste of a good lobster."

Mary did not miss a step. In one quick swoop, she bounded over and snatched up the wig from the floor like a skilled shortstop fielding a groundball. She then hurried away to the women's room.

Herm went with his first thought. As people gawked at the mess on the floor, he eased up from his chair and headed straight for the exit. Walking across the parking lot, his steps slowed as he had second thoughts. Riddled with guilt, he stopped, turned around, and scurried back inside hoping to get back to his seat before Mary did hers.

Standing at their table when he returned was Mary, looking around for him. She saw him as he rounded the corner. He looked at her. His expression said it all—caught in the act. He swallowed hard.

Nonchalant, and somewhat affronted, Mary sat back down.

Herm had to decide—turn and leave, or go back to the table. Making the more gracious decision, he opted to take his medicine and ambled back to the table.

"Where were you going?" Mary asked him.

He did not have an immediate answer. Sitting down, he fought for the right words to say. "I thought I'd get another drink," he said unconvincingly. Her look said she wasn't buying it. "Look, Mary, I'm sorry. I panicked."

"Panicked?"

"You fixed your hair. It looks nice."

Her glare soon waned. She laughed, "*You* panicked? I freaked! Seeing my hair, my wig, lying there. Food flying. People staring."

Some still were.

"Point taken," Herm said repentantly.

The two of them finished their dinners without any additional catastrophes. Afterward, Mary and Herm walked out to the parking lot. "That's my car over there," she said, pointing at a silver Cadillac.

"Okay," Herm said as they strolled over. He was unsure what to say to her after the evening they had just shared. Sure, he thought she was a nice woman, but a bit too wacky for him.

Nearing her car, Mary stopped and turned to face him.

He gulped a little, wondering what he should do next.

"Edward, this evening was . . . well, interesting, to say the least," she said.

"Yes, that it was," Herm said, chortling. "And, I don't know if you heard me, but—"

"Oh, I heard you the first time. You like to be called Herm. But I like Edward," she said, placing her hand on his chest and looking up into his eyes.

Oh, crap! Call me whatever you like, he thought, wondering what she was about to do next. *Think fast, Herm. Should I kiss her? Does she want me to kiss her? Do I want to kiss her?*

"You're a . . . an interesting man," she said, "but, I don't think this is going to work. You're too—and don't take this the wrong way—a little too *stuffy* for me."

Mary stood there, looking up at him. He saw the awkward expression on her face. Relief engulfed him. *And you're zany.* Politely Herm said, "Yeah, I think you're right. However, I have to tell you—and how shall I say this—it *was* an *entertaining* evening."

"That it was," she laughed, reaching up to adjust her wig a little. "And the food was . . . dee-*lish.*"

Following their dinner, Monroe and Debbie took the back roads home. They put the car windows down and just rode through the dark. No radio playing and conversation was light. For the most part, the sound of the wind blowing through the car and the hum of the tires on the pavement was all they needed.

Debbie sat with her bare feet on the dash and her hand out the window with the wind blowing through her fingers.

Monroe reached over and clasped Debbie's other hand.

She looked at him with a content smile.

"I love you," he said.

Debbie scooted close to him and laid her head on his shoulder as they continued down the road. "I love you, too," she said.

Chapter 31

Saturday morning Monroe and Debbie were having breakfast. Talk had been light, mostly reflecting on their dinner the previous evening. After a short lull in their chat, she asked, "When are you going to see Ashley?"

"Don't know," he answered.

"Monroe, you have to go talk to her. What? Do you expect everything to just be magically better by Tuesday?" He sat there, looking at Debbie. His blank stare did not faze her. Grabbing their plates from the table, she stood up. "Go see her," she said, and then walked to the kitchen.

"Fine," Monroe said as he got up and grabbed his keys from the kitchen counter. "Love you," he said, walking toward the front door.

"Love you, too."

Driving into town, Monroe made a stop at Christi's. The thought of facing Ashley was a little unnerving. He wasn't even sure if she would see him again so soon.

"Hello, Mr. Lovett," Christi said as he walked in.

"Morning, Christi," Monroe replied, looking around. "Not very busy this morning, I see."

"Oh, it was earlier. The place was packed."

"Coffee, please," he said, walking to a booth.

"You got it," she said, motioning to a server.

The server sat his coffee down as she hurried by with a large pastry in her other hand.

He sat drinking his coffee, contemplating what he would say to Ashley. Going back home seemed more appealing. He knew if he went home too soon, Debbie would know he did go. He thought, *Maybe I should drive around for a while and then go home, then she will assume I went. It could work. Yeah.* Finishing his coffee, Monroe got up and headed to his car.

Sitting in his car, he contemplated what to do. His pride did not want him to go to the county jail. *Surely, Ashley will be okay by Tuesday. It will all be over, and we'll just move forward with the trial.*

Tired and weary, Ashley stared at her breakfast, not at the food, really at nothing. It wasn't that the food was bad. Juanita's supplied all the food for those in jail. Today there was Ashley and one other person, someone in the drunk tank.

This morning, Ashley had too much on her mind. Her hair was still wet from her shower as she sat, staring, feeling doomed. She sniffled as she poked at the scrambled eggs.

A female deputy, who had taken a liking to Ashley, opened the cell door and glanced at the untouched food tray. Ashley looked up at her and said, "I'm not hungry."

"You need to eat, Ashley. But it will have to wait. You have a visitor."

"Do I have to go?"

"I can't force you. But I really think you should."

Slowly standing up, Ashley ran her fingers through her hair trying to fix it a little. Reluctant to speak with anyone, she thought at least it got her out of the cell for a while. Her mind raced again wondering who might be in the conference room. "It's not the same person as yesterday afternoon, is it?" she asked. "I don't want to see him."

"Don't know. I wasn't here yesterday afternoon," the deputy said, opening the door.

As the door crept open, Ashley peeked inside. Monroe was sitting at the table. She froze at first. It was the last person she thought would be there. A mix of emotions rushed through Ashley, as she became anxious— anger, fear, and even annoyed. But deep within her, she felt a sense of contentment.

He stood up, slowly. "Ashley, I know I'm probably . . . the last person you want to see right now," he said contritely.

The deputy nudged her, whispering, "You need to talk to him."

Hesitantly, Ashley went in, just inside the door. The deputy closed it behind her.

Motioning to the other chair, he asked, "Please, come on in and hear me out?"

"Do I have a choice?" she asked.

"Yes. I'll leave if you want me to. But, you need to know, the judge isn't going to let you get another attorney. Not at this stage of the trial.

And I want to represent you. I still believe you're innocent. That hasn't changed."

Ashley stood, remembering those words she heard in her thoughts—trust him. She slowly walked over and sat down.

Monroe also sat back down. "Ashley, first, I want to tell you I am deeply sorry for how I acted toward you yesterday. I was completely out of line. I should have never, never spoken to you the way I did. There's no excuse. I was a total ass."

Got that right, she thought, sitting stone-faced, her gaze fixed on the wall over Monroe's shoulder.

Clearing his throat, he said, "All I know to do is to ask you to forgive me."

Ashley now fixed her gaze on him but remained silent.

"I know I should've believed— My job is to help you. Judging you, it was wrong."

Ashley still just looked at him.

"I'm supposed to be your attorney. Your advocate. Ashley, I'll ask you again, please forgive me?" Monroe asked, almost begging.

She didn't respond. She'd heard it all before from almost every man she'd been around. Monroe sat, waiting for her to respond, to do something. Ashley studied his face, to get a read while pondering his request. Once again, *Trust him*, rushed through her head.

The anticipation was killing Monroe. Getting up, he walked to a corner of the room. Turning back to her, he said, "Ashley, I know what I did . . . my actions were wrong. I – was - wrong."

This was the first time anyone had said those words to her. Looking up at Monroe, she said, "I didn't have an argument with Julie. I don't care what anyone told you."

Relieved she at least said something; Monroe walked over and dropped back into his chair. "I believe you, Ashley. I honestly believe you."

She considered telling Monroe of her visitor Friday afternoon, but changed her mind, thinking it didn't matter. She was too tired and didn't want a prolonged conversation. "Any more questions?"

"No," he answered, a little surprised by her question.

"Okay, cause I'm tired. Can I go back to my cell now?"

"Yeah. Sure," he answered. He got up and walked to the door to retrieve the deputy. Monroe watched Ashley as she was leaving the room. Before exiting, Ashley stopped. Turning around, she said, "Mr. Lovett?"

"Yes?"

"I forgive you. And, I trust you."

Monroe's eyes watered. Looking at her, with a smile, he said, "Thank you, Ashley. And I trust you, too."

Chapter 32

Early the following Monday morning, Herm entered Monroe's law office. Debbie, surprised, said, "Didn't expect to see you here today."

"Ask your husband. He sent me a text yesterday saying he needed to see me first thing this morning."

Debbie informed Monroe, who in turn told her to send Herm back.

Strolling in, Herm said, "Okay, I'm here."

Monroe didn't look up as Herm walked over to the couch. He was packing his briefcase, stuffing it with files he needed for court that afternoon in New Orleans. Herm dropped onto the couch with a sigh. Monroe, looking up, asked, "So, how was your date?"

"That's why you called me here?"

"No. Just curious." Monroe, looking around his desk, making sure he had packed everything, said, "That should be all I need—I hope."

"Let's just say, it was . . . an interesting evening."

"Interesting? Interesting how?"

Knowing he would not be able to stave off Monroe's questions, Herm decided to tell him about his eventful and unforgettable evening. Without sparing a detail, Herm relayed the events from Friday evening. The laughter grew louder with every detail as Herm recounted the occasion. He was nearly finished narrating his date with Mary when Debbie walked in the office.

"Knocking?" Monroe asked. "We might've been talking about the case."

"Well, with all of the laughing, I figured you two were just talking guy stuff," she answered.

"We were," Monroe said. He started chuckling. "Herm was telling me—" Monroe laughed harder as he pictured Herm's night— "telling . . . telling me about his date . . . his date Friday night."

"Oh yeah, so how was your night out with Mary?" Debbie eagerly asked Herm. "That was her name, right? Mary? And what is so funny? Herm, what did you do to that poor lady?"

"Umm . . . hum . . ." Herm answered. Both he and Monroe began laughing again. Monroe laughed so hard his eyes began to water.

Debbie gawked at both men, dumbfounded.

"Mary, freaking Bloody Mary. Or, maybe I should just say Crazy Mary," Herm said, then began laughing hard.

"*Crazy?*" Debbie asked.

Closing his briefcase, Monroe said, "We don't have time right now, dear. I'll tell you about it as we drive to New Orleans. And, I suppose you came in here for a reason?"

"Oh yeah, here," Debbie said, handing Monroe a note. "Dr. Michaels called and said he and Daniels are meeting Detective Carson at the Butler's house later this morning."

"Okay. Thanks, dear."

"New Orleans?" Herm asked.

"Yeah, I forgot to tell you. Debbie here discovered that our victim, Julie Miller, has a sealed adoption record. The thing is, it's located in New Orleans. We're driving down so I can request a judge to unseal the record. Who knows, possibly, it will give us some insight into what really happened," Monroe explained.

"Who's the judge?"

Monroe removed a note from his pocket. "Davillier."

"Judge Robin Davillier?"

"Yeah."

"She's a good judge."

"You know her?"

"Yep . . . You could say that," Herm said impishly.

Monroe saw Herm's slight smile but didn't have time for the details.

Herm eased up from the couch. "Since you two will be gone all day, I guess I'll try to find out some more about Marcus Sr. when I give him his subpoena."

"I'm just glad a federal judge in Jackson gave us some leeway to get those bank records," Monroe said, stepping from behind his desk. He loosened his tie and then grabbed his suit coat. Debbie reached out for him to hand it to her.

"Yep, you got lucky there," Herm said, walking to the door. He stopped, and dropping both hands into his pockets, said, "Who knows, maybe that restaurant owner, Dennis what's his name, will have something."

"Sounds good," Monroe said. "If you get anything noteworthy, call me, okay? I'm seeing the judge at four."

"Oh, before I forget. Ran into Sheriff Austin on the way here. Told me they've put out a BOLO on Junior. Since he's sending texts to his parents, Austin believes he's in the area and wants to speak with the boy."

"A what?" Debbie asked.

"Be on the lookout. It's an all-points bulletin," Herm explained to Debbie.

"Good," Monroe said. Motioning to Debbie, he said, "We need to go."

"I guess that's my cue," Herm said, exiting.

"Later Herm," Monroe said.

Chapter 33

Daniels stood patiently in the front yard of Ashley's home. Time passed, and he began to think Michaels and Carson were going to be no-shows. Then a familiar green Jeep came down the long gravel drive and parked next to Daniels's truck. Michaels got out, looked around, and then walked over to Daniels. "Detective Carson isn't here, I take it," he said.

"You suppose correctly. One thing you'll learn about Carson—he works on his own time and in his own way. He's a grouchy, cynical—"

"Very overweight—"

"Cop."

"Yeah, I got that from him the other day."

Minutes passed like hours as the two stood there. Michaels leisurely took in the view around the home. Finally, Daniels decided to chat. "So, how long you been in Jackson?"

"Madison. And six months."

"And, before that?"

"Texas."

"Texas is a big place."

"Yes, it is. Very perceptive of you."

"I just thought you could narrow it down to, you know, a city," Daniels said, chuckling sarcastically, raising his hands up in front of him, palms facing each other a few inches apart. Michaels watched him. Dropping his hands, he placed them in his cargo shorts pockets, Daniels said, "I'm just trying to pass the time here."

Michaels, without cracking a smile, replied, "Fort Worth."

"I've lived here my whole life. I married Christi two years ago. We're thinking about having a baby. What about you? Family? Married? Kids?"

"No," Michaels answered, cutting his eyes over at him.

Daniels stared at Michaels, attempting to figure this guy out. "You don't say much, do you?"

"I answered your questions," Michaels said, standing with his arms crossed, as he watched for Detective Carson. "You didn't ask me to elaborate. I could write you my life's story if you like."

"Hey, I'm just trying to make conversation. You don't have to be an ass about it."

Crunching of gravel under tires in the distance grew louder as a dark blue sedan eased down the drive. "I believe that's Detective Carson," Michaels said with a nod of the head.

"Yeah, that's him."

"Conversation over," Michaels said with a grin. "We should do this again."

"Sure."

After parking, Carson climbed from his car, grabbing hold of the top of the car's door and the doorpost, and then pulled himself out with a grunt. The look on his face said it all—irritable. He looked at the two men through his dark sunglasses and complained, "Gentlemen."

"De-tec-tive Carson, how are you this fine day?" Daniels asked. He knew Carson well and took every opportunity to get under his skin.

Carson ignored him, walking straight to the front door with his usual frown. Inserting the key, he said, "Let's get this over with."

Michaels said under his breath, "Nice guy. This ought to be fun."

"Told you," Daniels replied out of the corner of his mouth.

Following Carson into the house, the two began their investigation. They each made their respective measurements, took pictures, and examined the location of where the buckshot pellets penetrated the wall. It took a while for them to wrap up their investigation, especially as Daniels painstakingly checked the pattern of the buckshot.

Watching the two men, the surly detective grew weary and said, "You two chuckleheads about finished?"

"Just about done. Why, is there a special at Juanita's today?" Daniels retorted. He stood up from packing his gear and looked at the detective with a grin, "Okay, De-tec-tive. Maybe you should run your lights and siren to make sure you get there in time," he said, whirling his finger over his head demonstrating a police light while making the sound, "Woo, woo, woo."

Carson snarled. "You're such the comedian, Daniels. Why the attitude?"

229

"Oh, I don't know," he answered, no doubted ticked. "Maybe it has something to do with you changing to a new firearms expert. And, I use the word *expert* loosely. From what I saw, the man can barely tell you how a BB gun operates." He then zipped his gear bag closed.

Michaels laughed to himself as he listened to them. He shook his head as he packed his gear into his own bag. "I'm done," he said.

Carson started to fire a comeback, but he knew Daniels had a point. Walking toward the door, he barked over his shoulder, "Grab your stuff. Let's get out of here. I've got more important stuff to do."

Chapter 34

One thing was on Herm's mind, a face-to-face with Marcus Butler. Not only did he have a subpoena to deliver, but also after their conversation in Monroe's office a few days earlier, he had a bone to pick. A phone call later and Butler agreed to meet him at Butler Transportation. Easing into the parking lot and the only sign of life Herm saw was a shop worker walking around a semi-trailer truck at the far end of the large truck yard. He parked and got out of his car. From behind him, Herm heard someone calling to him.

Turning around, he saw Butler standing next to a dull yellow metal building, some sort of warehouse. Herm began walking toward him, keeping his cop awareness set at high. With each step, and being a tad uneasy, he checked out the buildings, glancing behind trucks parked on the lot.

"Herm," Butler said, as if the two were still friends, seeing each other for the first time in a long time. It was as if the exchange the other day hadn't taken place.

Butler's nonchalant attitude puzzled Herm somewhat. Cautiously he said, "Hello, Mr. Butler. How are you doing?"

"Mister? Why so formal?"

"Old habits, I guess," Herm said, still wary. Looking around, he asked, "What? You give most everyone the day off?"

"They're around. Probably hiding from me," Butler answered.

Who would blame them?

"Well, come in out of the heat. Follow me," Butler said, leading the way into the metal building. "We can . . . get caught up. Put the other day behind us."

"So, what's going on here, Marcus?"

"What you mean?"

"What do I mean? You know what I mean. Your daughter-in-law is on trial for murder. Your son is hiding out somewhere. And you, you seem to be going on as if nothing has happened. So, I'll ask you again, what's going on here, Marcus?"

Butler didn't say anything at first but just continued walking. "Herm, we're friends. You grew up in Peregrine. You need to understand something, that girl, she killed Julie Miller. She's a, a— I can't support someone like that. Wouldn't be the *Christian* thing to do."

"The Christian thing to do? We're not in church, Marcus," Herm retorted, chuckling. "You can't even say her name, can you? It's Ashley Butler. And the Christian thing to do is seek justice."

"I know her name. Like I said, she's a killer," snapped Butler.

"I disagree."

"Well, what you believe doesn't matter, does it?"

"Tell me about Julie Miller, Marcus. You were seeing her on the side, weren't you? Things . . . get out of hand? She threatened to tell Darlene?"

"That's stupid."

"Tell me something, Marcus. How is it that you and your son were both sleeping with the same woman?" Herm asked, seeing Butler's anger. It only encouraged him to press the issue. "Did the two of you have a fight over her, and one thing led to another? And what, Junior killed Julie?"

Butler stopped walking and turned to face Herm. Herm glared back. Through gritted teeth, Butler said, "Herm, I'm not going to dignify that with an answer."

But Herm did not back down. He wouldn't until he got what he wanted. He had done this a hundred times while in New Orleans, with hundreds of suspects. Without missing a beat, he asked, "Were you sleeping with Julie Miller?"

"No. Absolutely not" Butler answered adamantly and furiously. "That's just . . . disgusting. Where did you come up with something like that?"

"From you. You look guilty. Guilt's written all over your face, Marcus."

"Look . . . you listen to me, Herm . . . that's just, it's crazy. Crazy nonsense. You're way off base."

The two men remained locked in a stare-down. Herm leaned forward, getting close to Butler's face, he asked, "Tell me about the money, Marcus?"

Butler moved back a little and took a deep breath. "By the way, when did it become Herm?"

"You're not getting away from this that easy. The money?"

"I believe we're done here. I never would've agreed to talk to you if I knew you were gonna . . . going to speak such garbage. Harass me like some local thug."

Herm eyed Butler as Butler glared back at him. Neither man was going to give an inch. Keeping a close eye on Butler, Herm stepped back a little. He could see Butler trembling from his anger. He'd struck a nerve. Finally, Herm, pointing his finger at Butler, said, "Marcus, the truth is going to come out. You can't stop it. No matter how much money and power you have."

"If you're talking about the lies you and your, your new *lawyer* friend, Lovett, are making up—"

"Oh, speaking of Mr. Lovett," Herm said, reaching into the inside breast pocket of his sports coat. He removed a white envelope. "Here's something for you." He then handed the envelope to Butler.

"What's this?"

"A subpoena. See you in court, Marcus. As I said, the truth is going to come out," Herm said, turning and walking away.

Butler stood there fuming, squeezing the subpoena in his hand, as he watched Herm.

After getting into his car, Herm thought lunch sounded good after his fiery confrontation with Butler. Herm didn't like to miss a meal. It made him irritable.

Ding . . . Herm heard while driving back into town. He glanced at his phone. There was an email from Dennis Anthony from the Pearl Café. He pulled over to the side of the road to read it. Opening the email, he noticed two attachments—a pdf and a video file. He read the email:

Here's a copy of some receipts and surveillance video.
Hope this helps.
Dennis.

"Good. Maybe there's something here," Herm said, continuing his drive into town. Downtown Peregrine was tranquil as he drove into the square. It was the end of the lunch hour. Most were back at work. Herm parked in front of Juanita's. Entering, he saw an older couple was the only

233

patrons. Herm sat down at an out-of-the-way table where he could look over the pdf and watch the video without being disturbed.

"Hello, Mr. Hermann," a waitress said, greeting him with a smile. As a regular here at Juanita's, the servers knew him by now.

"Hello, Casey. I'll have a club sandwich—"

"And a glass of sweet tea."

"You got it."

"I'll bring it right out," she said.

With no one close by, Herm opened the email. He tapped the video file and examined the clip segments carefully. The quality wasn't too bad, and Marcus Butler, with another man, was perceptible. The final clip got his attention, as it showed the two men arguing, just as Anthony had told him, and the exchange of a briefcase. A second section of the video disclosed Butler having lunch with Julie Miller on six different days. *Interesting* . . . Herm closed the file. "Only one problem exists," Herm muttered to himself. "Who's the other guy? We need to find someone who can tell us who the man is."

"What's that?" Casey asked, holding his food.

Herm looked up. "Oh, nothing. Just talking to . . . it's nothing."

"Well, here you go," Casey said, sitting the sandwich and iced tea on the table.

"Thank you, young lady."

"Are you going to want anything else?" she asked.

"I might *want* something else, but I don't need it," he remarked with a pat of his belly. "Trying to keep my girlish figure."

She giggled. "Then I'll leave this with you," she said, laying the bill on the table.

Herm looked at the bill and then suddenly remembered the second attachment. He opened the pdf and studied the receipts. "Just what we need—dates and times," he said under his breath. After finishing his lunch, he placed a call.

"Herm?" Monroe answered.

"Monroe. Got the info from our restaurant guy, Dennis what-his-name."

"And?"

"The evidence isn't damning, but we've got video and receipts that put Butler at the Pearl Café."

"So?"

"He's there several times with Julie, and other times with some guy who he has an argument with after giving him a briefcase."

"I said to call me if you get something."

"It *is* something."

"Herm, you're too easy. I agree. The meetings with Julie are important. But, he could meet and argue with anybody. We need to find out who."

"I know. There's the briefcase."

"Does your video have an x-ray of it?"

"No."

"Too bad. Get some stills made and have them enlarged. Maybe there's something there."

"I can do that."

"Anything more?"

"No. Had that conversation with Marcus Butler."

"Bet that went well," Monroe said with a touch of cynicism.

"He got nervy and defensive. Didn't admit anything, but his body language told me something different."

"We can't admit body language into court."

"I know. But, if you push him, he'll lose control. I can guarantee it."

"Guarantee it. What, you selling suits now?"

"Yeah, how'd you know?" Herm answered. "Looks like some pieces of the puzzle are falling into place."

"Starting."

"Yep."

"Thanks, Herm. I'll see you tomorrow," Monroe said and then ended the call.

The diner's door opened and a woman with short dark hair and a shapely figure entered. She smiled in Herm's direction.

"Hello, Miss Dale," Casey said.

Herm returned the smile, but then had flashbacks to Friday night. With haste, he pretended to answer his phone. Wrestling to hold the phone next to his ear with his shoulder, he pulled some cash from his wallet and laid it on the table without looking. Wanting a quick abscond from the cafe, he did not notice when he failed to grab a ten-dollar bill and five-dollar bill but instead placed a twenty along with a ten-dollar bill on the table to cover his eleven-dollar lunch.

Casey picked up the money, saw what appeared to be a substantial tip, and softly said, "That Mr. Hermann sure is a nice man."

Chapter 35

"You're kidding," snorted Debbie, as she listened to Monroe relating Herm's Friday night date as they cruised south on I-55, just north of New Orleans. "The wig fell off her head, in the middle of dinner?" she asked, snickering.

"That's what the man said," Monroe replied with a nod of his head.

"Poor Herm. Is he going to see her again?"

"What do you think? After walking out, I'm surprised she let him sit back down at the table. Anyway, he said they both decided it wouldn't work," Monroe said, exiting I-55 onto I-10. "I tried to warn the man, but he wouldn't listen."

"Warn him?"

"Yeah."

"You did?"

"Remember, I told him not to go out with her the other night?"

"No," Debbie answered. Monroe shot her an incredulous look. She didn't see it. "Well, maybe you should've given him— Oh, wait. Mary was the lady he met at our house?"

"Yeah . . ."

"Oh, you should've told him about her, Monroe. I mean, that woman sat there umm-humming all evening. 'Bout drove me crazy."

"Me, too. But he wasn't listening to anything—" Monroe said, pointing to a highway sign. "There's our exit, Orleans Avenue. What's the judge's name again?"

Debbie reached into her bag, pulled out a piece of paper, and read, "Judge Davillier, Robin Davillier." She looked at Monroe. "You should have said something, Monroe."

"Looks like we're going to have a few minutes to spare," he said, looking at the clock. "I guess I could have told him something, but . . . we wouldn't have this good story."

"I don't think so."

"Don't think what?"

"Look at the screen. It's showing nothing but red," she said, gesturing at the traffic on the GPS screen. "You didn't really want to tell him. I know you."

"See if you can find us a way around that mess," Monroe said, a little frustrated.

"Okay." Debbie grabbed the phone from the dash mount and started searching for an alternate route. "It looks like most of the streets are the same."

"Just see what you can find. And hurry," Monroe snapped.

"I am. What do you think I'm doing over here, knitting a sweater?"

"I don't need sarcasm. I'm trying to drive," Monroe said, stomping on the brake pedal, attempting to change lanes.

Debbie felt the seat belt grab hold. "What are you—?"

"Trying to avoid being run over by a large dump truck."

She brushed her auburn hair from her face and quickly gave Monroe a dirty look. "I think I found a route."

"Tell me something," he exclaimed.

"Turn here, on Bienville. No,"—Monroe started to turn, but swiftly corrected— "it's one way, but the wrong way."

He huffed.

"I heard that," Debbie said.

"Just hurry. We're going to be stuck in traffic if we don't do something soon."

"I am. I am. Just hold on," Debbie said, blowing her hair out from in front of her face. "And I don't need your attitude," she said as tension in the car soared. "Take the next left, on Iberville. Here. Here. Here. Turn here," Debbie shouted, pointing to the street.

Monroe jerked the steering wheel to the left cutting off another driver. The driver honked his horn and gave a not-so-friendly hand gesture. Monroe smiled offering a friendly "I'm sorry" wave. Cutting his eyes with a quick glare at Debbie, he said, "Thanks for the heads-up."

"Hey, I'm doing the best I can over here. Just stay going on Iberville."

Neither said anything for a few moments.

"I'm sorry," Monroe said apologetically. It was something he was doing a lot lately. "I know you are."

"Take the next left onto Bourbon Street," she said. She knew the stress of the case weighed on him. "Apology accepted."

"Here?"

"Yes. Ooo . . . Look at all the restaurants."

"You look. I'll drive."

With traffic moving slowly, Debbie said, "Turn right onto Toulouse Street and then another right onto Royal." Without much difficulty, Monroe did as instructed. "The courthouse is just ahead on the left."

Monroe took a deep breath and exhaled loudly. He asked, "What time is my appointment?"

"Four."

"Four?"

"Yes. Four."

Monroe drove by the courthouse slowly down Royal Street. "So, we're early. I thought it would take longer to get here. We've got almost three hours. I guess the traffic wouldn't have mattered," he said sheepishly.

Debbie sat looking at him. Her all too familiar eyebrow was up just a little. "Then, what was all that about?" she asked, referring to the last few stress-filled moments.

"Sorry."

"Yes, you are."

"Look, I apologize. You know how I get in traffic."

"Yeah. So, what now?"

"How 'bout this? We park and walk around," he answered.

"Sounds fun." Neither had been to New Orleans before. Doing a little dance in her seat, she said, "New Orleans. Jazz music. Good food. Fun atmosphere. Par—taay . . ."

"We don't have that much time, dear. But we can get something to eat."

Monroe parked in a nearby parking garage not far from the courthouse. They walked out to the sidewalk. "Oh . . .! That stinks," Debbie said, stepping from the garage. She covered her nose and mouth. "That's some atmosphere," she said.

"Yeah," Monroe said, clearing his throat. "We must be near a dumpster or something." He looked up and down the street trying to get his bearings. "C'mon, Bourbon Street is back this way."

Monroe and Debbie walked, holding hands and admiring the old-world French architecture detailing some of the old downtown buildings. Debbie remarked, "Seriously, the buildings are neat, but this place smells like a garbage dump."

Monroe looked around and said, "I know, but I don't see a garbage truck anywhere. Maybe it's just New Orleans?"

"Doesn't make you want to eat here, does it?" she laughed.

"Unless you want to get away from the smell."

Just then, a man stepped out from a narrow alleyway between two buildings, blocking their way. Monroe and Debbie stopped in their tracks. His clothes were somewhat tattered, and he had an umbrella strapped over his shoulder held in place with a piece of twine. Everything pointed to him being a street person.

Shielding Debbie, Monroe took a position blocking the man from his wife.

"How ya folks doing?" the man asked, beaming a big smile.

"We're fine," Monroe retorted, quickly eying the man from head to toe. Surprised by the man's sudden emergence, Monroe did not return the smile, but just stared at him, wondering. Debbie remained silent, happy to let her husband deal with the man.

"Sir?" the disheveled man said, looking down at Monroe's shoes. He flashed his yellowed teeth again. "Sir, if I can tell ya where you got those shoes, will ya gives me three dollars?"

"What?" Monroe asked, caught off guard by the question.

Pointing at Monroe's shoes, he said, "I tell ya where ya got those shoes, and you give me three dollars." Not getting a response, he said, "Three dollars, ya see, will let me buy some chicken for my three children."

Hesitant, Monroe answered, "I don't think so. No."

"Sir, how 'bout two dollars?" insisted the man. "Surely, you don't want my two babies to go hungry, do ya?"

"What about the other one?" Monroe asked.

"Huh?" the man asked with a slight tilt of his head.

"You had three kids at first. Now it's two," Monroe said, holding up two fingers. "Besides, it's obvious where I've got my shoes. They're on my feet."

Realizing Monroe had called his scam, the man turned without saying another word and scampered back down the alley at a rapid pace.

Debbie clutched Monroe's arm and told him, "I'm so glad you're here with me."

"C'mon, let's look around for a place to eat," Monroe said with a calming smile. "I'm starving."

"It still smells here," she remarked, crinkling her nose. "Stinks."

"You already said that," Monroe chuckled.

"Judge Davillier will see you now," the administrative assistant told Monroe.

Monroe turned to Debbie and told her, "Be back in a minute."

Entering Davillier's office, Monroe walked toward her desk. She was rereading his petition. "Have a seat, Mr. Lovett," she told him, gesticulating to a chair across the desk from her. "I understad that you would like to have a sealed adoption record unsealed? Care to explain?"

Monroe cleared his throat as he sat down. He knew he had only one shot at this. He answered, "Your Honor, the young woman, the adopted child in the record, is . . . *was* a young woman who was murdered in Lane County, Mississippi. I am representing the defendant, Mrs. Ashley Butler, in the case. I believe the information in the adoption record may prove to be very beneficial for my client's defense."

"How?"

He expected her response. He also knew feeding her a line would likely cause Davillier to deny his request. Monroe decided on the honest route, answering, "To be honest, I'm not sure. That's why I need to open the record."

"Well, I'm not sure about this," Judge Davillier said as she sat back, pondering Monroe's application. She tapped her pen against her chin a few times, looking at him and then at the motion, and then at him again, and said, "I am not sure opening a sealed record, even if the person is deceased, is something we should do without the permission of the adoptive parents."

"But, Your Honor, the deceased wasn't a minor. She was in her early twenties. I believe the parental concern is a non-issue in this case. These are extenuating circumstances here. I believe justice in this case far outweighs anything else. My client's life is on the line here."

Judge Davillier lifted the pages of the legal petition, looking through it as she weighed Monroe's argument while considering any possible legal ramifications. Looking at Monroe, she said, "I'm going to grant your request, Mr. Lovett. I just hope it's worth it."

"Thank you, Judge Davillier. So, do I."

After signing the order, she held it out and said, "Here." As Monroe stood to take the court order, she said to him, "Please let me know the outcome of your case."

"I will, Judge."

"Oh, and tell Herm hello."

"Huh?" Monroe replied.

"He didn't tell you? He and I were . . . *close* for nearly a year," she said with a grin.

"No, no he didn't," Monroe replied, nodding while straining to fake a smile. Now Herm's impish tone from earlier became clear to him. "Did he call you about this?"

"Now, Counselor, my dealings with Herm are confidential," she answered humorously with a subtle smile.

"Confidential. I see."

Davillier said, laughing, "My secretary can point you in the right direction for Vital Records. You better hurry, though. They close soon."

Monroe gave a slight wave bye and rushed back out to the front office. Judge Davillier, shaking her head, said to herself, "Good ole Herm."

Monroe and Debbie were almost in a dead sprint to reach the Vital Record Department. When they arrived, both were practically out of breath.

"You two must be the Lovetts."

"Yes," Monroe answered, gasping for air.

"Judge Davillier's office called and told me you two were coming. Here's what you're looking for. I just need to see the court order," the woman said with a friendly smile.

Attempting to catch his breath, Monroe handed the court order to her and said, gulping for air, "Thank you. I'll try to hurry to read it."

"No, you can take it with you, honey," the woman said, stamping the order.

"With me?" Monroe asked.

"Oh, yes. That's your copy."

"Thanks," he said as he and Debbie left.

While they walked to the car, Debbie asked Monroe, "So, are you going to read it?"

"Not now. I'll look it over after we get back home."

"How can you wait? I would want to read it right now if it were me."

"Well, you're not me, are you?" Monroe joked as he closed the car door. "Let's enjoy the ride home. Maybe find some good country food for dinner."

Late that night, after Debbie went to bed, Monroe sat down at the kitchen table. Unsealing the brown folder, he removed the adoption record and began reading. Most of it was the typical legal jargon. "Wait," he softly said, reading a paragraph containing the name of Julie's birth mother. He read it again and then sat back in the dining chair, bowled over by what he read.

Once more, he looked at the birth mother's name. "I can't believe it. Darlene Butler? I never thought." Monroe studied her name thinking he'd missed something—he didn't.

Looking back at the document, he asked himself, *Birth father?* He read aloud, "Félix Roche." *So, Mr. Butler, your wife had an affair. Or, maybe worse.* He knew he was onto something. He began reasoning, thinking aloud, "I never saw this coming. Marcus Sr. wasn't having an affair with Julie. Somehow, he figured out who she was. Julie Miller was Marcus's stepdaughter. But it had to be an affair or rape. No wonder they wanted the records sealed."

Monroe rubbed his face with his palms as he tried to comprehend this new evidence. He knew, if made public, this would shake the foundation of Peregrine, all of Lane County. Then it dawned on him. He mumbled, "Marcus Jr. was having an affair with his *half-sister?* And he didn't even know it. Oh boy, oh boy. Oh—boy . . . this is Jerry Springer stuff here, Monroe. Herm's going to love this."

Monroe took a deep breath and puffed his cheeks as he weighed his little unearthing. Ashley's case was becoming something more than a simple love-triangle murder centered on adultery. Tired, he rubbed his eye. *This is getting crazy.* Astounded, he tried to figure out his next move. A long day and late night told him to sleep. He stuffed the document into his briefcase and ambled to the bedroom. Laying down he prayed, *Lord, some guidance, please.*

Chapter 36

"Where were you yesterday?" Breaux asked Monroe Tuesday morning, as the two men stood between their respective tables in the courtroom before the trial resumed.

"Gone. Why?" Monroe responded, suspicious of Breaux. "Like it's any of your business."

"No reason. Just heard this morning you left town and didn't get back until late last night."

"You need to get a life, Robert. If the best thing you've got to do around here is keeping up with my comings and goings, then—"

"Hey. I'm just making conversation, Monroe," Breaux said, chuckling, putting his hands up like a caught robber. "Remember, you live in a small town. People notice. They talk."

"Sorry. Long day and a late night. You know, trying to prove you're wrong," Monroe said with a slight smile.

"No use trying. Your client's guilty. What could you possibly submit proving she's not?"

"Now see, we were having a nice conversation. But you had to go there," Monroe said. He knew Breaux was fishing. "Good try, though. But you'll get my defense when I present it."

A deputy escorted Ashley into the courtroom. Taking the cue Judge Harper wasn't far behind, Monroe said, "Looks like we're about to start."

"Oh, I like your picture in the Ledger," Breaux said.

"Picture. What picture?"

Breaux turned his laptop around so Monroe, and anyone else, could see the screen. "Yeah. This picture."

There it was, a picture of Monroe, his face glaring with anger and his finger pointing at the camera. Above the photo was the story's title, **Defiant Defense Attorney Will Not Talk**. He didn't remember any camera getting close to him. Then he remembered; it was the day Amy asked him some questions. He didn't see it, but she had her cell phone in her hand when he stepped between her and Ashley and snapped several quick photos. "Not my best side," he quipped, trying to let it roll off his back. He stepped over to his seat.

Breaux did the same. With a slight waggle of his head, he said, "Some good stuff in the article."

Monroe looked around for the reporter. She was standing in the back of the courtroom. However, giving her a piece of his mind would not be a good idea, so he let it go. Ashley, his priority at the moment, sat down and Monroe took his place next to her. "Ashley," he whispered, "We okay?"

"Yeah. But I need to speak with you," she whispered back.

"All rise," the bailiff said as Judge Harper entered the courtroom.

"We'll talk later," Monroe told her as they both stood up.

After the jury entered and sat down, Harper tapped the gavel and said, "Mr. Breaux, please continue with the prosecution's case."

"Your Honor, the prosecution calls Dr. Angie Stevens, Lane County Coroner."

Dr. Stevens took the stand. After the formalities, Breaux asked, "Dr. Stevens, can you please tell us the cause of Julie Miller's death?"

"Yes. She received several gunshot wounds to the chest cavity, head, and extremities. One lead pellet penetrated her heart, the primary cause of death, along with the two that entered the brain, which would have also killed the victim. Of course, the point-blank shot to *her face* didn't help."

"Objection," Monroe said, tossing his pen onto the table to give the appearance of aggravation. "Your Honor, please ask the witness to refrain from using any *personal* sarcasm."

"Sustained," Judge Harper ordered. "The witness will refrain from any sarcastic remarks. Understood?"

"Yes, Your Honor," Stevens answered.

"Please continue," Harper instructed her.

A little embarrassed, Dr. Stevens said, "The remainder of the pellets did significant damage to the victim's face and body as well."

"The kill shots to her heart and brain, did they cause immediate death to Ms. Miller?" Breaux asked.

Most everyone looked to Monroe for an objection simply based on the question's inflammatory nature. Monroe sat still. He had his reasons.

"No. From the amount of blood found in the thoracic cavity, the victim would not have died immediately. She would have been alive until the shot to the face. That was the final cause of death. However, the shot to the heart would have ended the victim's life as well. It just would have taken longer for the victim to bleed out."

"Objection," Monroe stated. "Calls for speculation by the witness."

"This witness is an expert in the field of forensic medicine," Breaux countered, shooting a quizzical glance at Monroe.

"Overruled."

As Stevens testified, the jurors got an eyeful of how disconcerted the Millers were by her testimony. These were two grieving parents known in the community. They were churchgoers, having grown up here. Breaux made sure he stood so the jury could see them.

"Dr. Stevens, how long would you estimate the victim was alive?" Breaux asked.

"Anywhere from one—"

"Objection," Monroe said again.

"Overruled, Mr. Lovett," Harper stated, getting a little peeved at him.

Not only was the judge annoyed, but Monroe's constant objections were beginning to irk Breaux as well.

"But, Your Honor, there's no way for the witness to narrow down how long the victim was alive. It's outside the realm of—"

"What part of overruled do you not understand, Mr. Lovett?" Judge Harper asked, peering over his glasses. Monroe acquiesced.

"Could it have been longer?" pressed Breaux.

Monroe, surprised by Breaux's mistake of not realizing Stevens did not finish her answer, said, "Asked and answered."

"Sustained," responded Harper.

"Your Honor, the witness hasn't answered the question," barked Breaux.

Monroe laughed a little under his breath, and Breaux heard him. Heated at the chortle, Breaux said, "Your Honor, apparently the defense finds these proceedings to be funny."

"Is this true, Mr. Lovett?" Harper asked.

"Your Honor. I apologize to the court," Monroe answered. "But I do find the prosecution's handling of this case hilarious." Realizing he was getting at Breaux, he decided to continue playing head-games with him.

Breaux glowered at Monroe before looking down at his notes. Again, he failed to realize he had forgotten to revisit his last question. Monroe's strategy, much to his own surprise, worked. Breaux moved on to his next question. "Would Julie Miller have been alive when the shot to her face was fired?"

"Objection. I believe the prosecution has already dealt with this with the witness," Monroe said.

"Overruled."

"Yes," Stevens answered with an affirmative nod.

"Dr. Stevens, can you tell us the approximate time of death?" Breaux asked. As Breaux finished his question, the courtroom door squeaked open. Not unusual for a trial. However, the person who slipped into the courtroom stunned most everyone.

"Doctor, please answer the question," Breaux insisted. However, she stared past him at the person who just entered the courtroom. Dr. Stevens sat with a dazed look on her face, peering like many others at the young man. Slowly, she waggled her head in disbelief. Soon the courtroom was filled with several gasps and murmuring. The jury and Harper noticed the cause of the commotion, too. They all sat stunned.

Perplexed by the reactions of Harper, Dr. Stevens, and the jury, Monroe, Debbie, and Ashley turned to look. Ashley exclaimed, "Billy!"

The courtroom erupted into pandemonium as people simultaneously said, "Billy. Billy? I thought he was . . . Billy!"

Billy froze in his tracks, overwhelmed by the chaos surrounding him.

Smack – smack – smack. "Order. Order in the court," Harper said. *Smack! Smack! Smack!* "Order! There will be order!" he yelled. As much as Judge Harper smacked the bench, he could not silence the hullabaloo in the courtroom. Exasperated, the judge yelled, "This court is in recess until further notice!" He motioned to the bailiff, shouting, "Get the jury and the defendant out of the courtroom!"

Hearing Harper's order, deputies removed the jury. Another deputy took hold of Ashley and began ushering her from the courtroom.

"No!" she screamed, fighting the deputy's grip. Almost breaking free, she yelled, "I want to see Billy! Let me talk to Billy."

Monroe heard Ashley and turned to see what was happening. Her actions did not help her case. If it was Junior who'd just walked in, then her actions would be welcomed, but not for Billy. Rushing over, he told her, "Ashley. Calm down." He looked her in the eyes and said, "Look, he's fine. Okay? Don't fight them. You need to go with them. I'll come see you later and tell you everything."

She knew he was right. Unhappily, she went with the deputy, tears streaming down her face.

As the commotion continued, Monroe watched. *Now, this throws a monkey wrench into this whole fiasco.*

Pushing through the crowd gathered around Billy, three deputies whisked him away from the mob of gawkers.

"What are you doing?" Billy exclaimed.

Judge Harper got the attention of a deputy, and with an exaggerated gesture toward Billy, he waved his arm, motioning for them to bring Billy to his chambers.

Per the judge's instructions, two deputies took Billy straight to Harper's chambers followed by Sheriff Austin, Monroe, and Breaux. At first, all four just stared at Billy, as if they were looking at a ghost. He was still in a daze from the entire hubbub. Becoming uneasy as the men gawked at him, and wondering what was happening, Billy asked, "What's going on? Why all the fuss?"

"Billy. Billy," Judge Harper said, still dumbfounded. "Everyone . . . damn, the whole county, thought you were dead, son."

"Dead?" Billy gasped.

"Yes, Billy. Dead," Sheriff Austin told him.

"But, I ain't dead. I'm right here," Billy affirmed, patting his chest.

"Yes, we can see that," Austin said. The sheriff weighed the apparent resurrection of the young man. "Billy, where have you been?" he asked.

"Texas. Been fishing over in Texas with a friend."

"Fishing! The boy's been fishing," Breaux said with a wave of his arm that finished with a rub over the back of his head.

Monroe stood at a distance, taking it all in. He didn't know Billy, and Billy didn't know him. Why stick his nose in and throw another curveball at the boy?

"I got back this morning. Heard about Ashley being on trial," Billy said, looking around at those in the room with him. "So, I came straight here. Then everyone seemed so glad to see me when I walked in. It was like I had come back from the dead."

Monroe chuckled under his breath, "Talk about irony."

Billy heard him. With a quizzical stare, he asked Monroe, "Who're you?"

"Ashley's attorney," Monroe answered.

Breaux, thinking Monroe might use this as a reason to make a motion to postpone or even worse, requested, "Your Honor, I think we need to continue with the trial. To postpone would only allow for—"

"You're right," Harper responded. "I don't see how Billy's showing up changes anything."

"But Judge Harper, I've got questions for this young man," Monroe said. "Questions I deem are important to my case."

Harper looked at Breaux and asked, "Is the prosecution planning on calling Billy to testify?"

"Testify!" Billy bellowed. "Testify to what?"

Before Breaux answered, Monroe asked, "Billy, did Ashley and Julie Miller have an argument at Swatters the night before they found Julie dead?"

"Argue?" Billy asked, his head swimming from all the attention he was getting. "Yeah. No. I don't remember. But it wasn't uncommon for the two of them. Everybody knew they didn't like each other because of. . . Wait, no. I don't think so. But—"

"What about her and Junior?" Breaux asked.

"Yeah," Billy answered. "Anyway, when I heard about Julie from Chad, I called Ashley, told her the police were looking for her."

Breaux smiled as he listened to Billy. "Your Honor, the people are unsure if we will be calling Mr. Jenkins."

Monroe thought, *Doesn't necessarily eliminate him as a suspect, but—.*

"Mr. Lovett?" Harper asked.

"Your Honor."

"Will you be calling Billy to testify?"

"Not sure," Monroe answered as he dropped his hands into his trouser pockets, studying Billy as he sat there.

"Fine," Judge Harper said. "We'll resume at one this afternoon. That should be enough time for everything to settle down—hopefully."

Sheriff Austin looked around at the others and said, "That only leaves one question."

They looked back at him, curious.

"Whose body was it in the ditch?" he said,

They all nodded in agreement, except for Billy. He sat, appearing baffled and clueless. Breaux then made a quick exit.

Monroe followed him into the hall. "Robert."

Breaux stopped. "Yeah?"

"You still sure we need to proceed with this case? I mean—"

"You mean what?"

"I'll concede they were intoxicated that night. That an argument did *or didn't* take place between Junior and Ashley that night. Eyewitness testimony is dubious at best. But, you really think Ashley killed Julie? C'mon."

"That's why we're having a trial, Monroe. A trial in front of a jury. A jury that may not see things as you do. A trial—"

"Where the District Attorney allows an illegal confession? Where you allow a possible murderer to walk the streets also with the last name Butler. Or, for all we know, may have just walked into the courtroom moments ago and is sitting in Judge Harper's chambers," Monroe stated, pointing in the direction of Harper's office.

Breaux took a step toward Monroe. With his jaw clenched and nostrils flaring, he asked, "Are you accusing me of something, Monroe? Because, if you are, you're treading on thin ice—very thin ice."

Monroe didn't back down. Inside, he wanted to break Breaux's neck. Without blinking, controlling his emotions, he pressed Breaux. "Why don't you *just* drop the charges against my client, Robert? You and I both know she's not guilty."

"Then, prove it, Mr. Lovett. How many times do I have to remind you, your client *signed* a confession?"

"A confession she has retracted." Monroe leaned toward Breaux, stopping just a couple of inches from his face, and said, "You know—the way I see it—you've either made up your mind my client is guilty regardless of the facts. Or, you are protecting someone. Who are you protecting, Robert? Huh? Maybe someone making big contributions to your campaigns."

Breaux, livid, and looking up at Monroe, said, "Look—"

A worker stepped into the hall from an office. Seeing the two men, she hurried past them. Breaux backed away. "As I said, you're on thin ice, Counselor. I'll see you in court," he said, and then turned and walked away.

Monroe chuckled under his breath, crossing his arms as he watched Breaux legging it down the hall. "Guess he's upset," he muttered under his breath. Turning, he walked towards the stairs. *Best go see Ashley.*

"Hello, Ashley," Monroe said, greeting her when she entered the small conference room at the county jail.

Her mood was upbeat, more on the verge of excitement, from seeing Billy. "Hello, Mr. Lovett," Ashley said, sitting down across from him. "How's Billy? Where's he been? Did they hurt him?"

"Billy's fine, Ashley. He was in Texas, fishing. And no, no one hurt him."

"Good," she said with a sense of relief. "I'm glad he's okay."

Monroe gave her a strange look. "You sure you two are just friends?"

"Yes." She wasn't sure if he has serious or not. "He's like a brother to me."

"Alright." Her answer pleased him. He then looked her straight in the eye, contrite, he said, "First, let me start by apologizing again to you for the other— I shouldn't have jumped all over you the way I did. I was wrong. I didn't mean to come off as so—"

"Preachy."

"Yeah, preachy. I was preachy."

Ashley smiled, and said, "Thank you, Mr. Lovett."

Knowing he didn't have much time before court resumed, Monroe asked, "Ashley, do you know *anything* about Julie's background?"

"No," she answered with a slight shake of her head trying to recall anything. "She knew she was adopted. That was obvious," Ashley said with a duh expression on her face. "But she never talked about it."

"Ashley, I know I keep asking you this, but do you have any idea where Marcus Jr. could be?"

Her eyes filled with tears. "No. His daddy probably sent him away. That's how *Mr. Butler* does things. He'll do anything to protect his family, especially Junior."

"He's not helping *you*."

"*I'm* not family in his eyes," she said, tears welling up in her eyes at the thought.

Ashley's statement angered Monroe. *How could he not consider this girl family? She's his daughter-in-law.* "Why is that?"

"My past," she said ashamedly.

"Your past?"

"I was a . . . a dancer when Marcus Jr. and me met," she answered, her voice faintly choking.

"A dancer?"

"Yeah, I danced. In Jackson. But not nude, though," she insisted. Fearing Monroe's reaction, she looked away for a moment. Although, when she looked back at him, she saw caring eyes, a father's compassionate eyes. Not accusing or judgmental eyes like those she'd seen so many times from her father-in-law. "Junior came in the club one night, and we like—you know—hit it off. His dad tried to keep us from getting married. But, well, we did anyway."

Wow! "Okay. But that's your past. What's in the past is the past, right?"

"You don't know Mr. Butler very well, do you?" she asked. By now, Monroe was beginning to get a good picture of him, especially after his last meeting with him. Ashley said, "He *didn't* care. He . . . he just wanted us to stop seeing each other."

Monroe removed a picture from his briefcase, the picture Herm had printed from the video sent to him by the owner of the Pearl Café. He laid it on the table. "I know you can't see much of this man's face, but does he look familiar to you?"

Ashley leaned over to get a better look at the picture. She turned it several times, examining the face. Monroe could see she thought she recognized the man. "It sort of looks like—but I can't say for sure. With a ball cap and sunglasses, it's hard to tell."

"Who do you *think* it is?"

"Joe Galliard. But I'm not sure."

"Who is Joe Galliard?"

"He owns Smitty's. It's a club. The one me and Julie danced at."

"What? You and Julie? How come—why didn't you—" Monroe said, annoyed. "Ashley, I'm not upset with you, okay? But it's important. Why didn't you tell me that earlier? From the beginning?"

"You didn't ask."

"Okay. You're right."

"There's more."

"More?"

"He came to see me Friday afternoon."

"What?" Monroe asked, shooting up from his chair and started pacing. "What did he say to you? Did you tell him anything?" Monroe asked as his mind raced with a myriad of possibilities to him coming to see her.

"I didn't speak to him."

Monroe stopped his pacing and turned to face Ashley. "You didn't speak with him?"

"Nope. I hate the man."

"Why didn't you tell me before?"

"I was going to. But the trial started, and you said we'd talk later. It's later now."

"Good point. Okay. I have some things to do before court resumes in a little while. I'll see you then, okay?" he asked, standing to leave. He needed to call Herm.

"Tell Billy hello for me."

"Okay," Monroe answered with a smile. "But if he's in court, you can tell him yourself, if you want to."

She smiled and nodded yes.

"And don't speak to anyone but me," Monroe said, walking to the door.

"I know. You keep telling me that," Ashley said with a slight smile.

Chapter 37

Very few people were in Christi's. "Got a name for you," Monroe said, looking across the table at Herm. The two were grabbing a quick lunch.

"Yeah?"

"Joe Galliard."

"And Galliard is . . .?"

Monroe pulled out the same picture he had shown Ashley earlier and placed it on the table. "This is Joe Galliard," he said, tapping the photo.

"Who told you that?" Herm asked, taking a bite of his sandwich.

"Ashley. He owns the club she and—get this—Julie and she both danced there."

"You're kidding, right?"

"No, I'm not. And there's more."

"More?"

"He visited Ashley Friday afternoon. But our girl was smart enough not to talk with him."

"Good for her. But I do have to wonder why he wanted to see her."

"Oh, it gets better."

"Better?"

Lowering his voice just loud enough for Herm to hear him, Monroe leaned across the table, motioning for Herm to do the same, and told him, "Julie Miller. She was Darlene Butler's daughter."

"Son of a—!"

"Shh . . ." Monroe said, motioning with his hand for Herm to quiet down.

"The father?"

"Félix Roche."

"No doubt he was black because Darlene is very white, almost milky," Herm said.

"And where is Mrs. Butler?"

"Who knows? With everything that's going on, she's probably locked herself in the house."

"You're probably right," Monroe said.

"Do you realize how this is adding up?"

"Yes."

"Have you said anything to Breaux or Carson?"

"Haven't told anyone but you," Monroe said with a confident grin.

"You gonna tell them?"

"No," Monroe said, taking a slow drink of his soda, looking over Herm's shoulder and peering out the window. He looked back at Herm who was focused on his club sandwich and said, "You know, with Billy showing up, the more I think about it, my focus is on Butler. The kid just doesn't look like a killer."

"Senior or Junior?"

"Both right now," Monroe said, and then sighed. "It's probably unnecessary, but I need to go prepare my cross of Lisa. But I just don't think—"

"Lisa?"

"Remember. The girl from Swatters."

"Oh, her. Can't believe Breaux's still going to use her in light of current events."

"He's dead set. Bolsters his case, I guess. I don't know," Monroe said with a dismissive gesture of his hand. Instead of heading up to his office, Monroe stayed put, watching people, daydreaming.

Noticing Monroe wasn't going anywhere, Herm asked, "Got a second?"

"Yeah. Sure."

"I have a question for you, on a personal level."

"What?" Monroe asked, sitting up straight, as an invisible wall of self-preservation rose.

"Relax," Herm said, chuckling. "Just curious as to why you left church work?"

Laughing quietly, Monroe answered, "You just said it—Church. Work."

"What do you mean?"

"I spent more time umpiring debates about the color of the carpet or where to plant a bush." With a smirk and a head bob, he dryly said, "Like a bush is going to lead people to Jesus."

Without missing a beat, Herm quipped, "Maybe they thought someone might have a Moses experience."

"Good one, Herm. Good one. Your jocularity always has good timing."

"So, that's it?" Herm asked.

"Nah, I just got tired of people being more interested in buildings and programs than following Jesus and helping people. I don't recall Jesus saying, 'Go ye therefore and build buildings, and create a myriad of programs.' Or, 'Increase your staff to model a corporate institution,'" Monroe said. Herm saw the frustration in his face as Monroe stared straight at him, declaring, "I got fed up. Felt led to do something different. To help people. So, here I am."

There were a few seconds of silence as the two men sat. Monroe took a quick drink.

Herm asked, "Miss it?"

"No," Monroe said brusquely.

"Debbie?"

"Nope."

"Interesting."

"Why?"

"No reason. I just find your story interesting."

"How about you?" Monroe asked, wanting to shift the conversation away from him.

"You know my story."

"You've never said anything about God or Jesus. Are you, for lack of a better term, *religious*?"

"Religious? No. Jesus? It's simple. He leads . . . I follow."

"Can't go wrong with that, my friend," Monroe said, and then stood up. "Later, Herm."

Pointing across the table, Herm cited, "You haven't even touched your lunch." Gesturing at Monroe's sandwich, he asked, "You mind?"

Monroe reached down, picked up the sandwich, and took a big bite. "Nah, go ahead," he said, chewing. "You can have it."

"Thanks," Herm replied, smirking with a slight chuckle.

Across town in the DA's office, two other men were having a working lunch, although, theirs was not quite so euphoric. "So, what you gonna do?" Carson asked, slurping his nearly empty drink through a straw.

Breaux exhaled loudly as he leaned back in his desk chair. Placing his hands behind his head, he stared up at the ceiling. "I don't know. Billy popping up threw a monkey wrench in my strategy."

"I say forget the kid and press on."

"You say. You sound more and more like Marcus Butler every time I talk to you."

Ignoring Breaux's snide statement, Carson said, "Prosecute the girl and bury Lovett." For him, nothing had changed. "Beginning to think maybe she's not guilty?" he asked smugly.

"Just thinking out loud."

The last thing Carson wanted to hear was the prosecutor was now questioning his case. "She had a motive. Her prints are on the murder weapon. She *signed* a confession. And . . ."

"And a possible alibi just walked into the courtroom, for everybody to see—including the jury—in case you didn't notice," Breaux said sharply. Sitting up and, with an intent expression, he said point-blank, "You know what gets me? Monroe doesn't seem concerned. Not in the least bit." He reached over and picked up a sheet of paper. "Who's his first witness? Dr. Michaels, and then Daniels."

"What in the world does he expect to get from those two that we haven't already stated?" Carson asked with a huff. "The evidence speaks for itself. Right?"

"I don't know. You tell me. You said Daniels didn't agree with our findings. You've been around them. They say anything?"

Carson didn't respond.

"Yeah, that's what I thought," Breaux said spitefully. "Michaels?" Breaux asked, rubbing his chin. "Don't know much about him. Everything on him says he's good." He then stared hard at Carson, who had a complacent countenance. Carson's nonchalant attitude was beginning to wear thin with Breaux. "Look, your man, Roueché, better have not made a mistake," Breaux insisted, tossing the document back on his desk. "The man's credentials were—how shall we say—not what you told me. Made me look like a fool."

Carson made another loud slurping sound with his drink and then replied, "All the bases are covered, right? Don't you think the jury can see that neither Marcus nor Junior is in the courtroom? People see things like that. If her husband and daddy-in-law were standing by her side, then, well sure, we'd have problems."

"Let's hope you're right," Breaux said, and then leered at the detective. "Anything new on the burnt body?"

"Huh?"

"The body? You know, the one found charred, lying in a ditch. The one that *is not* the Jenkins kid."

"Oh, Dr. Stevens said she sent some samples for a DNA match. And she's checking for dental records. It's gonna be a few days before she hears anything," Carson said, and then stood up. Stretching, he said, "I've got to go before I fall asleep." Sauntering toward the door, he said, "I think it might have been a body dump by someone from Jackson. I've already alerted them."

"You know what I think?" Breaux said, glowering at Carson. "I think you shouldn't be thinking."

Lunch was over. The courtroom was pulsating with the latest news of Billy's return. A growing crowd packed the tiny courtroom, now abuzz with anticipation. Quietly, people debated the effect of Jenkins's supposed return from the dead.

Billy fought his way through the crowd to reach Ashley at the defense table. Seeing him, Ashley said, "Billy, I'm glad you're okay."

"Me? What 'bout you? Ashley, if they say you're guilty—"

"I'm confident in Mr. Lovett and Debbie. They've been so good to me. Mrs. Debbie helps me get ready every day. She even bought me this new dress," Ashley gleefully said as she showed it off. "And Mr. Lovett—"

"But that ain't gonna help get you off," Billy appealed.

Monroe butted in, "It's time to begin, Ashley."

"All rise," the bailiff called out." Billy took a seat behind Ashley.

Judge Harper took his seat on the bench. He scanned the docket for the afternoon session. People were still talking. *Wham* . . . Harper slammed the gavel down. The smack reverberated into the hallway. "Order! Order in the court," he bellowed. No doubt, he was still upset from the morning's outburst.

Instant silence imbued the courtroom. Every eye focused on Breaux, then on Judge Harper. Then back to Breaux. What would the prosecutor do? Continue track? Change strategies?

While they waited, Monroe motioned to Herm. Easing up close to Monroe, he asked, "What?"

"Move Billy back. I don't want him sitting this close to Ashley. It doesn't look good."

Herm turned, leaned over to Billy's ear, and quickly explained what Monroe wanted. Billy did as requested and joined Herm in the rear of the courtroom. With everyone's attention on Harper and Breaux, Billy's moving went unnoticed.

Dr. Stevens sat back down in the witness box.

"Mr. Breaux, do you wish to ask Dr. Stevens any further questions?" Harper asked.

"No. No, Your Honor. The prosecution does not have any further questions for this witness."

"Mr. Lovett?" Judge Harper asked.

"Dr. Stevens, was there any evidence Ms. Miller had sexual relations prior to her death?"

"Yes."

"Could you give an approximation as to how soon she had sex before she died?"

"Objection, calls for—" Breaux said.

"Overruled."

Breaux glared for a moment at Harper in disbelief.

Stevens answered, "Most likely within an hour before she died."

"Did you run a DNA test on the sperm?" Monroe asked.

"Yes. But there were no matches in the system."

Monroe made some notes. He then opened a folder and began scanning its contents.

"Do you have any further questions for the witness?" Harper asked impatiently.

"No, Your Honor. No more questions," Monroe replied, pondering Breaux's reasons for not asking these questions of Dr. Stevens.

"The witness is dismissed."

Apparently frustrated by the dismissal, she got up and left the witness box. Walking over to Breaux, she leaned over and whispered loudly, "*You should have asked me those questions.*"

Breaux snapped his head up, and asked, "What?"

"It made you look like you are hiding something," Stevens said forcefully.

"Is there a problem, Mr. Breaux?" Harper asked, gazing over the top of his reading specs.

No one heard the short conversation between Breaux and Stevens as they talked rather emphatically. Their faces said something was not right. Breaux, realizing Harper was irritated and everyone was watching, answered, "No, Your Honor. Everything is—everything's fine. Please accept my apologies." Breaux quickly pondered his situation. Billy showing up had him a little flustered. With a single jerk of his head, he motioned for Stevens to leave.

Shrugging, she walked away. Instead of leaving the courtroom, Stevens remained in the gallery.

"Call your next witness, Mr. Breaux," Harper ordered.

"The prosecution rests, Your Honor," Breaux said. His statement drew mumbling from the gallery as heads turned, people, looking at each other and wondering what was happening. Just as confused, Judge Harper gaveled, *tap, tap, tap,* instructing, "Order. There will be silence in this courtroom." The subtle mumbling ceased. Harper looked at Breaux and inquired, "Rests? You sure?" He knew Breaux had another witness.

He's not calling Lisa from the bar? Monroe thought as he studied Breaux. *Huh? Maybe he's come to his senses.*

"Yes," Breaux answered as he sat down.

If a glare could slap, then Carson's would have knocked Breaux from his chair. He had prepped her to testify of the supposed argument, but now no one would hear her testimony. He rushed to Breaux. Breaux put his hand up asking for a moment from Judge Harper, who allowed it.

Leaning over the rail, Carson whispered to Breaux, "You're not going to call Lisa?"

"No," Breaux replied motioning for Carson to leave. Turning back to face Judge Harper, Breaux said, "Thank you, Your Honor. But the prosecution does rest indeed."

Reluctantly, Carson did as Breaux wanted. He knew Marcus Butler would not be pleased.

Harper replied, "Okay. Mr. Lovett, I guess we will hear from the defense."

"Your Honor, I would like to ask the court to consider recessing until tomorrow morning. Since the prosecution's not calling his next witness, well . . . I was prepared to question that witness. But since she will not—"

"Agreed, Mr. Lovett," Harper answered. "The Court is recessed until tomorrow morning at nine."

"Guilty. She's definitely guilty," a man shouted across the table to his friend at Juanita's Diner. The eatery was packed with those wanting to discuss the trial. Who needed a movie when a real-life drama was playing out before their very eyes? The feature? Ashley Butler's murder trial.

"Not guilty," said the man on the opposite side of the table with a slight thump of his fist onto the table.

"Guilty," strongly replied his eating companion.

The same debate was taking place around other tables as well. The debate was mostly between those who worked for Marcus Butler and those who did not.

Juanita yelled, "Stop it! Stop all of this or get out!" Her staff tried to calm the diners, but their efforts were useless.

Opening the door of the diner, Monroe and Debbie stepped inside as the argument was reaching its pinnacle. Voices were loud and combative.

An immediate hush overcame the quaint restaurant as they all noticed the Lovetts. Every eye was now fixated on them. A single spoon clanged when it landed on the floor. Some of the faces appeared friendly, but others fired rigid, angry, dirty looks at Monroe. Juanita was angry, too. She was not angry with anyone, but at the whole situation. A full restaurant was not her issue. No, it was the arguing.

Monroe leaned over to Debbie and whispered in her ear, "Let's not eat here."

"Okay," she answered, amazed by the reaction of the patrons.

Before anyone could say a word, Monroe tugged Debbie's arm, and the two fled the eatery as Juanita stood with a scowl aimed at him.

As they hurried to their car, Monroe asked, "Fast food?"

"We better make it drive through."

"Definitely."

Chapter 38

Preparing his opening statement, Monroe had gone over it a hundred times in his head. Here was his moment to make a substantial impression on the jury. Saying he was nervous would be an understatement. His gut churned. Telling himself he'd preached a thousand sermons, and this was just another, wasn't working. Unfortunately, none of his self-calming techniques were working. He tossed his notes into his briefcase. It was time to go, ready or not.

"Monroe, you will do fine," Debbie assured him, walking into his office. Nearing him, she checked his tie. She could see his anxiety.

"I know. That's what you keep telling me. I've been telling myself the same thing all morning. But this is different."

Debbie rose to her toes, kissed Monroe's cheek, whispering, "Well, I believe in you, Monroe Thomas Lovett."

"Now you sound like my mom," he said with a cringed.

Tugging his suit coat lapels slightly, Debbie then ran her hands down them until she reached the top button. "Well, I *do* believe in you. And I love you," she said, buttoning his suit coat.

"I love you, too, dear," Monroe said, picking up his attaché. Glancing at the clock, he said, "I've gotta go."

"Go. I'll see you later."

Monroe walked to his office door, but then stopped. He looked back at Debbie.

"What?" she asked while standing next to his desk.

He then walked back over to her and set his attaché on the desk. She watched him with curiosity. Reaching up, Monroe brushed Debbie's hair back from her face, then ran his fingers just so lightly down her cheek. Gazing into her eyes, and she into his, he leaned over, giving her a long, arousing, deep, sensual kiss. After kissing her, Monroe softly stroked her cheek with his thumb, telling her, "Thank you, Debbie Lovett."

"Go," she said with a seductive smile, "or you're going to be late."

"Later?" he asked, caressing her cheek again.

"Later. No doubt about it," she answered, kissing his finger. He gently smiled. She could see the love in his eyes. She also knew he didn't have much time before court resumed. "Now go," she told him, rising to her toes and giving him a quick kiss.

"Love you, sweetie," Monroe said before hurrying away to the courthouse.

Left standing, still feeling fancifully woozy from their kiss, Debbie said under her breath, "Oh yeah, that man knows how to get me going."

Walking into the courthouse, Monroe went straight to Judge Harper's chambers. Reluctant, Harper agreed to see Monroe. "What couldn't wait, Mr. Lovett?" Harper demanded, without looking up from his desk. He was busy signing some court papers.

"I'm adding a witness. I need a subpoena issued."

"Tell me why my clerk could not handle this?" Harper retorted, still not looking up at Monroe.

"It's Joe Galliard."

Harper's head popped up. "Who's Joe Galliard? And why are you adding this witness at such a late date?"

"I just discovered he may provide some crucial evidence to my case. I believe his testimony, along with the rest of my case, will prove my client's innocence."

Harper weighed the request and then answered, "Alright. You've got your subpoena."

"Thank you, Your Honor."

Judge Harper's gaveling echoed over the hushed crowd. "The defense will now present its case," he said.

Suppressing his nerves, Monroe stood in the courtroom, which was as silent as a funeral home at midnight. The Lane County Courthouse could have sold tickets, and people would have paid the asking price to watch this. Monroe glanced over at Debbie, having arrived moments before court began. She gave an assuring smile.

"Your Honor, members of the jury, and all those in this court," Monroe said as he began, "I thank you for listening to me this morning as

I offer you this simple statement. Ashley Butler is innocent. I know, many of you are saying to yourself, 'Sure, that's what the defense is required to say. And some of you are thinking, 'Your client signed a confession.' And, you'd be correct.

"Yes, it is a sad thing Julie Miller is dead. But I will prove Mrs. Butler did not commit this crime. I acknowledge the prosecution has presented some very compelling evidence, most of it, at best, is purely circumstantial. However, I am so confident in Ashley Butler's innocence, which I will not stop with simply proving it. No. The defense, by demonstrating Mrs. Butler's innocence, will reveal the person who did, in fact, commit this heinous murder. Someone who had a more incontrovertible reason to brutally murder Miss Miller."

Faces of shock suddenly appeared across the courtroom. Breaux looked at him as if he was crazy. Judge Harper looked at him with a quizzical expression. And, he wasn't the only one.

Monroe continued, "I will prove Mrs. Butler was forced to sign her confession." He paused. *I can't believe I just said that.* He had removed the statement from his notes days ago.

Breaux, smirking, shook his head.

Harper looked at him with a "Say what?" expression.

With a quick mental recovery, Monroe resumed, "We live in a time in our nation when things are no longer what they *used* to be. America was always a nation known for doing the *right* thing, leading the world in truth and honor, and standing on the integrity of our word—a nation demanding justice. However, today, that integrity is almost gone, nearly having vanished from the American landscape." His enthusiasm grew with each word as he said, "Nonetheless, it does not have to remain that way. You, the members of this jury, have the opportunity to set things right, to help restore that honor—that integrity." With one hand on his hip and the other emphatically pointing to the floor in front of him, he stated, "See, it can all start right here. Here in Lane County. Here in Peregrine, Mississippi. Here in this courtroom."

Monroe paused, as he gazed at the jurors. Eying them, lowering his voice, he persuasively said, "All I ask of you is to honestly and truthfully look at the evidence, at the testimony presented to you. To look past the smoke and mirrors of the prosecution's flimsy case. Then, and only then, make the right decision, a decision of integrity, justly finding Ashley Butler not guilty."

Monroe walked back to his seat. From the corner of his eye, he could see several heads nodding in agreement in the gallery. He looked at Debbie and Ashley sitting, looking back at him. Both were smiling. Breaux sat emotionless, unfazed. He'd heard defense attorneys preach on their client's behalf numerous times.

"Thank you, Mr. Lovett," Judge Harper said. "Please call your first witness."

"The defense calls Dr. Bryan Michaels," Monroe said.

Michaels entered the courtroom and took the witness stand. After his swearing in, Monroe asked him, "Dr. Michaels, please tell this court what your credentials are?"

"I have a Ph.D. in forensic science from the University of Texas. For the past ten years, I have assisted law enforcement with major crimes in the cities of Fort Worth, Dallas, and Austin. I recently moved to Madison, Mississippi, about six months ago upon accepting the position as Chief of Forensics Research at the newly-established Mississippi Forensics Labs in Madison."

"Dr. Michaels, did you examine the shotgun presented as the murder weapon by the prosecution?"

"Yes."

"Can you confirm the fingerprints found by the state forensics lab as belonging to Ashley Butler?"

"Yes."

People turned to each other in the gallery, surprised. Someone in the back turned to the person sitting next to him and whispered, "I thought he was a defense attorney?" Chuckling under his breath, the other man nodded in agreement.

Monroe asked, "Did you find an additional fingerprint on the shotgun, not on the initial fingerprint report?"

"Yes, I did."

Mumbling from the gallery softly rolled across the courtroom. Harper cleared his throat to quiet the noise.

"Please tell the court what you found?" Monroe asked.

People were now leaning forward in their seats to listen.

"A partial right thumbprint. I also observed some smudged prints, but nothing that could be used for a match."

Detective Carson stared over at Barnes, who was in the gallery to listen to Michaels's testimony. Both had a look of surprise because Michaels never said anything about the smudged prints.

"Did you point out these to Detective Carson or Mr. Barnes from forensics?"

"The thumbprint, the one I lifted, yes. But the smudges, No, I did not."

"Why not?"

"At the time, I didn't think the smudges were important. However, after I thought about them, and after conferring with Mr. Daniels, I changed my mind. I then informed you."

Picking up the shotgun, Monroe handed it to the bailiff. "Your Honor, I would like this handed to the witness for a demonstration."

Judge Harper nodded his head in agreement, telling the bailiff, "Give it to the witness."

Michaels took possession of the shotgun.

"Dr. Michaels, could you please indicate to the court where the print you discovered—the one not found by forensics—was located?" Monroe asked.

Sheriff Austin glowered over at Carson, who saw him and then snapped his gaze straightforward. He could still feel Austin's angry stare.

Michaels pointed to a spot on the section of the barrel that fits into the shotgun's receiver. "Here," he said, showing, first the jury, and then Judge Harper.

People in the gallery strained to get a look, as did Breaux.

"Dr. Michaels, could you now demonstrate how someone would have gripped the barrel in order to leave the smudges you found?"

"Objection," Breaux said, standing. "Calls for speculation."

Monroe turned to rebuff the objection, but before he could say anything, Harper retorted, "Overruled."

Michaels, standing, grabbed the barrel with his right hand and the stock with his left, holding the shotgun in a horizontal position, across the front of his body. "Like this," he said, holding it for everyone to see.

"Was there *anything* special about the smudges on the barrel?"

"Yes. It was as if someone was twisting the barrel."

"Why did this raise your suspicion?"

"Because none of this was in the initial forensic report. Therefore, it led me to believe they were either overlooked or—"

"Objection," Breaux, again, barked. "Calls for speculation, Your Honor."

"Sustained."

"Dr. Michaels, do you believe someone altered this shotgun?"

"Objection."

"Sustained."

"Dr. Michaels, do you believe the partial thumbprint you discovered was overlooked by the forensics lab or left there—"

"Ob—jection!" Breaux declared.

"Sustained, Mr. Lovett," Harper said.

Monroe asked, "Can you please tell the court about the thumbprint?"

Michaels paused before answering, waiting for Breaux to object again. Breaux didn't. "Yes. I found a partial print," Michaels replied. "But, it was confiscated by Detective Carson."

"Have you received any report from the Sherriff's Department or forensics pertaining to the print?"

"No. No, I have not."

Michaels handed the shotgun back to the bailiff.

"Were you able to determine a match for the new print?" Monroe asked Michaels.

"No. As I said, Detective Carson took them from me after my examination."

"He did?"

"Yes."

Monroe asked, "So, you're saying the print, the one never mentioned in the report you received from the sheriff's office, *nor* the prosecution, has not been identified?"

"Objection," Breaux declared.

"To what?" Monroe questioned Breaux. "It's a simple yes or no question, Your Honor. The defense is simply attempting to establish that someone else besides my client may have handled the shotgun. And, and that person needs to be identified."

Harper looked to Breaux, who did not have an immediate response. Without any further reason for his objection, Harper told Breaux, "Overruled. The witness may answer."

Michaels replied nonchalantly, "No."

Monroe asked, "So, you've received nothing from the Lane County Sheriff's Department concerning the print?"

"No."

Carson became red-faced. His anxiety increased as Austin made his way toward him. The sheriff's face said it all—he was not thrilled. In fact, he appeared downright mad.

"Your Honor," Monroe said, "I would like it entered into the record the defense has not been provided a report concerning the unexplained print."

"Noted," Judge Harper said with his own suspicions. He saw Austin in the back of the courtroom. "Sheriff Austin," he called.

"Yes," Austin answered, caught off guard by Harper's beckoning.

"The court *requests* you and the forensics lab expedite the results on that print."

Austin felt like slipping under the door while being lectured by Harper. Everyone felt the tension. He glowered hard at Carson, who would not return the stare. He simply nodded, answering, "Yes, Your Honor."

Harper motioned for Monroe to continue.

"No more questions. Thank you, Dr. Michaels," Monroe said, and then sat down.

Debbie reached over and flipped the page on Monroe's notepad. She ardently pointed out additional questions.

"Mr. Breaux, do you have any questions for this witness?" Harper asked.

"Just one, Your Honor," responded Breaux. "Dr. Michaels, did any of your findings disprove the defendant fired the shotgun?"

"No."

"Thank you," Breaux said, self-satisfied. "Nothing more. Thank you."

"Redirect?" Monroe asked, realizing his mistake, thanks to Debbie.

"Go ahead," Harper instructed Monroe.

Monroe stood up, and asked, "Dr. Michaels, did you find anything proving Mrs. Butler fired the shotgun?"

"No."

"Did you find anything in the forensic report indicating Ashley Butler fired that shotgun?" Monroe asked, pointing at the murder weapon.

"No."

"Please explain."

"Even though the defendant's prints were on the shotgun, there was no indication a GSR test was performed on her. Therefore, there is only proof she, at one time, held the shotgun."

"Is there any way to date the prints?"

"No."

Monroe opened a folder and removed pictures from the day Ashley was booked into custody. They were the official arrest photos. He displayed them so the jury and Judge Harper could get a good look at the photos. "Dr. Michaels, what type of shells were fired from the shotgun used in the crime?" Monroe asked.

"Three-inch magnum buckshot."

"How tall is the defendant, Ashley Butler?"

"I measured her at five feet, four inches."

"How much does Mrs. Butler weigh?"

"As of yesterday afternoon, 118 pounds."

"How would you describe her complexion?"

Breaux stood up. "Your Honor, is there a reason the defense is asking this witness to describe someone we can all *clearly* see?"

"Mr. Lovett?" Harper asked.

"If the court would please bear with me," Monroe answered.

"Hurry to your point," Harper told Monroe. He then said to Michaels, "You may answer the question."

"Fair, or light skin. Caucasian."

Monroe stepped back for the jury to see Ashley, and asked Michaels, "In your opinion as a forensic specialist, if someone you just described fired this weapon"— he reached and lifted the shotgun— "wearing that dress"—he pointed to the pictures showing Ashley wearing a dress with spaghetti straps— "would there be any evidence?"

"Objection. Calls for speculation from the witness. The defense is asking this witness to draw a conclusion. At the very least, this testimony lacks foundation," Breaux insisted.

"Your Honor, may I remind the prosecution the witness has a doctorate in forensic science. If the prosecution can offer forensic science to attempt a conviction, then the defense must be allowed to do the same to substantiate its case."

Judge Harper glanced at the pictures. He looked at Ashley sitting at the table wearing a similarly styled dress. He mulled over the testimony just offered, and replied, "Denied. Denied. Denied, to all three objections offered by the prosecution. And, from now on, Mr. Breaux, please keep your objections to one at a time."

Breaux dropped back into his chair, visibly not happy with Harper's ruling.

"Dr. Michaels, please . . ." Monroe said, instructing Michaels to come around to a tripod holding the photos.

Picking up a felt-tipped marker, Michaels indicated, "After firing five times, there would, in all likelihood, be a contusion on her shoulder from the shotgun's kick, here." He drew a circle around the front of her shoulder. "Unless she is an expert user, a shotgun of that size would be difficult for her to handle and hold tightly against her shoulder. Or, to her side. And even then, she would have some light bruising." A couple of the jurors nodded in agreement. Monroe and Ashley saw them. Michaels said, "The result would most definitely have left a dark bruise, some very visible discoloration of the skin. Especially, with the defendant's light complexion."

Monroe walked toward Ashley, holding the shotgun in front of her.

Breaux cut his eyes over at Monroe. *Please pull an OJ. Let her hold the gun. I'll show she can hold it correctly. I know I can.*

"Thank you, Dr. Michaels," Monroe said, as he then placed the shotgun back on the table and sat down. "Nothing else, Your Honor."

"Mr. Breaux?" asked Harper.

Smirking, Breaux answered, "No questions."

"You're dismissed, Dr. Michaels," Harper said.

Michaels got up and left the courtroom.

Monroe stood to call his next witness.

Harper looked at the clock. "Before you call your next witness, let's take a break."

Monroe sat back down.

"We will be in recess for thirty minutes," Harper declared.

Breaux walked over to Monroe. "Not bad, Mr. Lovett."

"Thanks."

"Where did you find Michaels?"

"I didn't. Ed Hermann did."

"Well, his testimony was good, but not persuasive."

"Not persuasive? You were in the courtroom, weren't you? Anyway, I'm not trying to convince you, am I?" Monroe said with a wink and then turned to speak with Ashley. Breaux knew Monroe was correct. He turned to consult with his assistant.

Sheriff Austin caught up to Carson who was attempting to sneak from the courtroom. "We need to talk, Detective."

"About what, Sheriff?" Carson asked, working to appear naive.

"You know what. But not here. My office in ten."

"Okay . . ." Carson said, realizing he better get his story right.

As Monroe was conversing with Ashley, Debbie checked her email. One email caught her eye. She tapped it to open it. After reading the message, she said, "Monroe. Monroe, you need to see this."

He looked at her. "See what?"

"This. You need to see this email," she insisted, pointing to her phone. "Come over here," she said, motioning for him.

"Excuse me, Ashley," he said and then walked over to Debbie.

Ashley turned to talk with Billy.

Monroe and Debbie moved to an out-of-the-way corner of the courtroom. She handed him her phone. After reading the email, he asked Debbie, "What made you check?"

"Mostly, just curiosity."

Monroe walked back to Ashley. She was sitting with her back to him. Tapping her gently on her shoulder, he said, "Ashley?"

"What?"

Monroe looked at Billy, and said, "Billy, please excuse us, but I need to speak to Ashley."

"Okay," Billy said as he turned and walked away.

Monroe asked Ashley, "Why didn't you tell me you grew up in foster care?" He needed answers from her, not for Ashley to clam up again.

"You didn't ask. Didn't think it was important." Only answering questions asked her was something she learned growing up in and out of foster care.

"True," Monroe said.

"Does it matter?" she asked.

"I'm not sure." He thought for a moment. "Ashley, do you remember any of your foster parents?"

"No. Not really. When I was 'round ten, they put me in a children's home."

"Do you remember the name?"

"New Life Children's Home. I'll never forget it."

Monroe wrote it down and asked, "What is your maiden name?"

"Good question. My mother was a rape victim, and I'm not sure who my real father was. She gave me up when she couldn't take care of me. I ended up in foster care, and in and out of homes." Tearing up, she said, "One of my foster dads . . . he, he abused me. But I don't remember his name either."

Wow! Monroe then asked, "Her name? Your mother's?"

Taking a deep breath to regain her composure, she answered, "Dorothy Xavier. I don't even remember her face. I only know her name, because they gave it to me when I left the home."

"Did he go to prison?" Monroe asked, writing down everything.

"Who?"

"The man who, who abused you?"

"Don't know. They took me away after it happened. And I never heard anything more."

He compassionately placed his hand on Ashley's shoulder and said with a kind smile, "Thanks, Ashley." Monroe then took his notes over to Debbie. "Here," he said, handing her the information. "See what you can find out."

"Okay. You don't want Herm doing this?" Debbie asked, looking at Monroe's scribbles.

"You seem to be better at the computer stuff than he is," Monroe said with a trustworthy smile. "Computers and him . . . they don't get along."

"True."

"And I think she needs your womanly prudence with this."

The mood in Austin's office was heavy with mistrust and apprehension on the part of the sheriff. "Detective, would you like to explain to me what is going on here?" Austin asked.

"Sheriff, I'm waiting for the prints to get back," Carson answered. He shuffled his feet a little, as he stood in front of Austin's desk. "Nothing's come back on it."

"Then, I want Barnes in here."

"He's not working on it."

"Then who is?"

"Sent it to Jackson."

Austin was leaning back in his desk chair glaring up at Carson with an incensed expression. "Do you realize how incompetent you have made this department look? People have to trust us, Carson."

"Sheriff, I'm—"

Austin wasn't sure if he should believe Carson or not. The detective had become more evasive lately. He told Carson, "I don't want your apologies. What I want is for you to do your job. Got it?"

"Got it," Carson replied.

"Now go do your job. And you better not make me, or this department, look like fools again."

Chapter 39

It didn't take long for the thirty minutes to pass. Debbie was gone, and Monroe was ready to move forward. Judge Harper gave him the nod to proceed. Monroe called his next witness, Jason Daniels.

"Objection," stated Breaux as Daniels entered the courtroom.

Harper gestured for the bailiff escorting Daniels to stop.

"Objection?" Monroe inquired, with a puzzled look on his face. "Objection to what? I haven't even asked him a question. Besides, you knew before today I was calling Mr. Daniels and never objected."

"Yes, Mr. Breaux, I'm wondering the same thing myself," Judge Harper commented.

Breaux stood up and said, "Your Honor, why does this witness need to testify to what we already know. The proof has *clearly* been established. By presenting two witnesses, one for the prosecution and one for the defense, affirming this shotgun was indeed used to commit the murder of Julie Miller is unnecessary. Why do we need a third? It's a waste of the court's time."

"Mr. Lovett, the prosecution has a valid objection," Judge Harper said. "Is there a reason we need to hear from this witness?"

"Sidebar, Your Honor?" Monroe requested.

"Escort the witness from the courtroom," Judge Harper said, waving for the two attorneys to approach. Harper asked, "Mr. Lovett, do you have a good reason to have Mr. Daniels testify?"

"Yes, Your Honor. Mr. Daniels will provide additional testimony that neither of the previous two witnesses provided to the court. His testimony is crucial to my client's case. And, I do believe the defense is allowed to rebut the prosecution's case."

"Judge, there's absolutely no need for a third expert to tell us what we already know," Breaux reiterated.

"Judge, the state has already shown their inability to provide proper fingerprint evidence," Monroe countered. "And the state's expert was anything but."

Judge Harper considered Breaux's objection. Having a case overturned by the appellate court concerned him. Resolutely he ruled, "The witness will testify."

The bailiff brought Daniels into the courtroom. Several of the jurors had questioning expressions, likely wondering why Breaux had not used him. What evidence did he have? Why try to suppress it?

Daniel's sat down as Monroe opened his notes. Monroe inquired of him, "Mr. Daniels, could you please state your credentials for the court?" Of course, this was customary for the court record because everyone in town knew of Daniels's impeccable credentials.

"I have been a certified NRA firearms expert and instructor for nearly ten years. I have advised on and testified in numerous cases throughout Central Mississippi. And I have worked with the Mississippi Bureau of Investigation on two separate cases."

"No doubt, you're much more qualified than the prosecution's expert?"

"Objection."

"Withdrawn," Monroe said, slightly smiling in Breaux's direction. Gesturing to the shotgun, Monroe asked, "Did you examine the shotgun presented in this case as the murder weapon?"

"Yes, I did."

"Would you say that shotgun, in its present condition, as submitted to this court, was used to commit the crime?"

"No."

Moans from the gallery followed Daniels's answer. Even Breaux and Harper appeared stunned by his brazen response.

"Please explain," Monroe urged him.

Pointing at the shotgun, Daniels said, "The shotgun, in its *present* condition, could not have fired the shots that killed Julie Miller." He looked at Judge Harper, requesting, "May I demonstrate?"

"Yes," Harper answered.

Whispering arose in the gallery, which brought another throat clearing from Harper. Even Breaux leaned forward in his chair, awaiting Daniels's explanation. This was not the repeated testimony he had anticipated.

Judge Harper sat up straight to get a good look. Everything he and the court had previously heard was how that shotgun murdered Julie Miller. Now, Daniels was refuting previously offered testimony, at least part of it. Everyone waited with anticipation. Ashley stopped her doodling. Sheriff Austin fired another harsh look at Carson, whose face was beet red. Their conversation during the break left Austin with a bad taste in his mouth.

Monroe handed Daniels two cut out pieces of a shotgun barrel.

Daniels pointed at the firearm lying on the evidence table. "The barrel on that shotgun did not fire the buckshot rounds used to murder the victim. The barrel on the shotgun in evidence is like this one,"—Daniels held up one of the cutout pieces— "a smoothbore. This type of barrel is used to fire rounds like buckshot, or birdshot."

"Mr. Daniels, did you examine the shotgun shells obtained from the Butler home?" Monroe inquired taking the display barrel from him. He handed the cutout piece to the jury for examination as Daniels continued his explanation. The jurors passed it around as they listened to the testimony.

"Yes," Daniels answered. "The type of buckshot loads recovered from the crime scene has no shot cup or buffer material which means it usually spreads quickly," he said, spreading his hands in a forward and outward direction indicating how the pellets would spread out in a wide circular pattern.

"Did you perform an examination of the crime scene?" Monroe asked, taking the smoothbore cutout from the jury forewoman.

"Yes. The pattern of the buckshot fired at Julie Miller, after measuring the distance to the most probable spot the shooter stood firing the first shots, indicates the barrel used had to be a rifled shotgun barrel like this one," Daniels said, lifting another cut-out piece of the shotgun barrel. The barrel's rifling was highlighted with bright red coloring to make it easier to see.

"Unlike the one on this shotgun?" Monroe asked, pointing to the pump shotgun entered into evidence.

"Objection. The prosecution believes the witness is using conjecture," Breaux stated, feeling like he needed to say something.

"Your Honor, if we could just let the witness finish his explanation," Monroe responded.

Judge Harper was enthralled with Daniels's testimony, much like everyone else in the courtroom. "Overruled," he stated.

"Mr. Daniels, please continue," Monroe said.

"Yes, like that one," Daniels answered. "The rifled barrel will create a broad, donut-shaped shot pattern. And, it will increase in size the further it travels."

"How does all of this affect this particular case?" Monroe asked, handing the second cutout to the jurors.

"The shotgun used in this crime, much like other shotguns, has interchangeable barrels. One is a smoothbore, like the one on the shotgun now. The other barrel is a rifled bore, used to fire slugs. If someone shot the type of buckshot recovered at the crime scene through the smoothbore, the pattern of the shot would be much tighter. Causing more damage to the intended target."

"The victim?"

"Yes."

Monroe took the cutout barrel from the jurors.

"However," Daniels said, "if someone were to fire that buckshot through the rifled bore, the pattern would be more spread out due to the centrifugal force, thus producing a wide spread-out pattern, like that at the crime scene."

Several moans and murmurs once again came from the gallery. A couple of people mumbled, "Yep. That's right, I have one of those."

Judge Harper heard the murmurings and grabbed his gavel. *Tap-Tap-Tap*. "Quiet. I'll have silence in this courtroom, or I will clear it. Understood?"

Knowing the judge meant business, and he would do as stated, everyone complied.

Monroe removed several photos of the crime scene. "Your Honor, the defense would like to enter these photos into evidence. They show the scene, highlighting the entry points of the buckshot on the walls. Thus, demonstrating what this witness is stating corresponds to this crime." He handed the photos to Harper.

Judge Harper glanced at the photos and then handed them to the bailiff and said, "Show them to the jurors."

"Mr. Daniels, in your expert opinion, are you stating that shotgun, as it has been presented to this court by the prosecution,"—Monroe asked, gesturing in Breaux's direction— "did not kill Julie Miller?"

Almost in unison, those in the tightly packed courtroom leaned forward as they waited for Daniels to answer the question.

"Yes."

Monroe allowed Daniels's answer to hang in the air. He knew the effectiveness of a good pause. Preaching had taught him so. "Mr. Daniels, did you check the barrel on the shotgun, in its present condition, for gunpowder residue?"

"Yes. The barrel was clean," responded Daniels. "However, there is gunpowder residue in the receiver. That indicates to me the shotgun had not been cleaned after it was last fired, but someone changed the barrels."

Ashley fought to hide her smile. She knew she was not out of the woods yet, but it was looking much better than it did a few weeks ago.

Monroe next reached over, picked up the shotgun, and said, "Mr. Daniels, would you please demonstrate for the court how someone would go about changing the barrels on that shotgun?" He handed it to the bailiff. The bailiff, in turn, handed it to Daniels.

Daniels stood up and while demonstrating, "Locate the shell tube which is underneath the barrel. There will be a knurled knob at the end. Rotate the knob counterclockwise and continue to unscrew the knob from the shell tube." He then grasped the barrel in the same manner Michaels did in his elucidation of the smudges.

"Could you please stop for a moment so the court can see how you are holding the shotgun barrel?" Monroe asked.

Daniels did so. Many endeavored to get a view.

"If the court will notice," Monroe said, "the witness is holding the barrel in the same manner Dr. Bryan Michaels testified as to where he saw the smudged prints."

"Noted," Harper said.

Pulling another set of photos from a folder, he said, "The defense would like these photos taken by Dr. Michaels entered into evidence. These were taken in the presence of Detective Carson and Mr. Barnes."

Again, Austin glared at Carson.

Judge Harper examined the pictures and then said, "Enter the photos into evidence."

"Please, continue," Monroe said, gesturing to Daniels.

"Okay. P-u-l-l the barrel from the shotgun . . . with a sli-ight twisting motion to help the barrel assembly—there we go—break free from the receiver."

People watched as Daniels, a gun expert, struggled slightly to remove the barrel.

"Next, pull the barrel straight-off-the-gun," Daniels said, continuing his explanation. Monroe handed another barrel to him. Taking the barrel,

Daniels said, "Then, slide the replacement barrel into the shotgun receiver, making sure to line up the metal retaining loop onto the shell tube. I would like to point out, the bolt needs to be slid back just a little to allow the barrel to slide into place, or it won't fit into place. No matter how hard you try. For someone not familiar with this, it can take some time to figure it out," he said, assuring the barrel was in place. "Then, replace the knob. Make it snug, but do not over tighten. There."

Daniels handed the shotgun back to the bailiff. After receiving the shotgun from Daniels, the bailiff handed it back to Monroe. He held the large firearm in front of Ashley for a moment, providing a mental picture for the jury, as he did with Michaels, before handing it back to the bailiff.

"How easy would this be for someone to do?" Monroe asked.

"For a person unfamiliar with this type of shotgun, not so easy. Besides, you would have to know the barrels are interchangeable. It would have to be someone familiar with the firearm," Daniels answered.

"What about someone in a hurry, having just shot someone?" Monroe asked.

"Objection."

"Sustained."

Having planted the question in the minds of the jurors, Monroe continued. "Your Honor," he said, "the defense would like to point out the list of items retrieved from the crime scene does not contain any other barrels or shotguns."

"Noted," Harper said.

"The defense has no more questions for this witness, Your Honor."

"Does the prosecution wish to question the witness?" Judge Harper asked.

Sitting, a little dispirited, Breaux responded, "Yes." Slowly standing, he asked, "Mr. Daniels, could the defendant if properly taught, change the barrels?"

"I guess. But—"

"Please answer yes or no," Breaux demanded.

"Sure. If she were properly taught. But those conditions would change in a highly stressful situation."

"Just answer the question *without* elaboration," Breaux said.

Daniels gave Breaux a look that said, "Are you kidding me?"

"Do you have any other formal training besides what you have stated to this court?"

With a slight chuckle, Daniels answered, "My training has been enough for you in the past. But, to answer your question, yes. I have a degree as a gunsmith from Ashland College."

"Didn't the Sheriff's Department release you as their expert on this case?"

"Yes."

"Does that mean they do not see you as being qualified to examine the evidence in a case like this?"

"Objection. Calls for hearsay," Monroe said. "In addition, the prosecution is badgering the witness."

Daniels just sat there lightly chuckling at Breaux. He knew most everyone in Lane County was familiar with his expertise.

"Sustained," Judge Harper replied. "Move it along, Mr. Breaux." Breaux stood there for several seconds not say anything. "Mr. Breaux, do you have anything else you would like to ask this witness?" Judge Harper asked.

"No, I guess not," Breaux responded. He turned and looked directly at Detective Carson. Carson was standing in the back of the courtroom, expressionless, staring into space.

Sheriff Austin slipped out of the courtroom when he saw the silent exchange between the two men.

"The witness is dismissed," Judge Harper told Daniels.

As Daniels made his way out of the courtroom, Monroe offered a motion to the court, "Your Honor, I do believe it is imperative to this court, so that the truthfulness, in this case, can be revealed, that everyone who is known to have handled the shotgun presented as the murder weapon, to be fingerprinted."

"Objection! Objection, Your Honor," Breaux stated fervently.

"Your Honor, Dr. Michaels testified there is an unidentified print on the barrel," Monroe said, pointing to the shotgun. "A print yet to be identified by the Sheriff's Department. Also, Mr. Daniels has just testified the barrel, on the shotgun in its current state, *is not* the barrel that fired the fatal shot. Therefore, it is obvious the barrels were changed. And it is likely the unidentified print is the print of the person who changed the barrels, or who possibly fired the lethal shots. Therefore, it stands to reason—"

"Judge, is this really necessary?" Breaux interjected, exasperated by Monroe's prolonged request. "The defense is grandstanding."

"Maybe Mr. Breaux is not interested in the truth, Your Honor. But I do believe this court is. Aren't we here to discover the truth? To seek justice? To make sure we put the true murderer behind bars?" Monroe proclaimed, knowing he had Breaux on the ropes.

Jumping in to stop the two attorneys, Harper said, "Well, if the defense is *grandstanding* as you claim, Mr. Breaux, then he's doing a good job at it. I agree with the defense's motion. He has a valid point. This court *is* interested in the truth. And justice."

"Thank you, Your Honor," Monroe replied.

"But—" Breaux interjected.

"But nothing. This court is in recess until each person known to have handled that shotgun has been fingerprinted, and the results of those fingerprints are identified," Judge Harper stated, much to Breaux's disappointment. "We're in recess until further notice. Sequester the jurors," he declared with a tap of the gavel.

The looks on the jurors' faces said it all—not happy. A deputy led the jury from the courtroom.

Those previous undertones heard from the gallery due to Daniels's testimony, soon became a loud commotion. Nothing precarious came from them, but just intense discussions, as local citizens began debating the legitimacy of his testimony. Those agreeing with Daniels far outnumbered those opposing him.

Amy, the young reporter from the Ledger, hurried to finish her notes and then rushed to speak with Breaux. He didn't seem as anxious to chat with her as he did in their first encounter. After breaking free from Amy, Breaux made a beeline to Monroe. "What are you up to, Monroe?"

"Doing my job. Defending my client. Maybe if you hadn't been so *eager* to prosecute this case, you would have discovered this instead of me having to do it for you."

"You're cocky now, but you haven't won," Breaux said as he stood up, fuming. The funny thing, Monroe was not the true cause of his anger, but more him looking like a buffoon in the eyes of the people.

Monroe grinned while chuckling under his breath. He said, "I'm just trying to get my client acquitted. To do that, all I need to do is convince one juror, just one, of my client's innocence. And I do believe I'm on the way to accomplishing that goal. How many hunters do you think are on that jury? How many knew what Daniels was talking about? And how many know Daniels and trust him? Yeah, that's what I thought," he said, seeing Breaux's reaction. "Now, how many do you believe know and trust Roueché?"

Stung, Breaux brewed for a moment. "If you think a single print, and—there's still motive. And your client had . . . never mind," Breaux said, waving his hand, turning and walking back to the prosecution's table to gather his files. Many still in the courtroom saw his theatrics and giggled.

Amy took another stab at Breaux. "Mr. Breaux, is the defense right? Have you made a mistake in prosecuting Mrs. Butler?"

"No! No, absolutely not," Breaux fired at her. Glowering at Amy, he yelled, "Now leave me the hell alone." He looked around to see several people staring at him.

Ashley was standing behind Monroe listening to the conversation with glee. When Monroe turned back, he noticed her. "Oh, I thought you were gone."

"No," she said with a smile. "They told me it would be a few minutes."

"You seem happy."

"I'm starting to believe this might work, that I might—go free," she said.

"I told you to trust me. We still have a ways to go. But, I believe when we're done, you will walk away a free woman."

A deputy gave a slight tug to Ashley's arm and said, "Let's go, Mrs. Butler."

She left with a smile.

Chapter 40

Detective Carson did not wish to speak with the impatient prosecutor. He was there, not because he wished to be, but because Breaux had summoned him.

"Close the door," Breaux curtly told Carson, who had just entered.

Carson flopped into a large chair with a forceful exhale. Breaux looked up from the notes he was making. He was trying to figure out how to turn the jury back in his favor. "Problems?" Breaux asked acerbically.

"Got better things to do besides being here," Carson griped. He wouldn't even look at Breaux.

"Don't care. Fingerprint?"

"We've got a problem," Carson said.

"Problem? What *kind* of problem?"

"Fichard Roueché."

"What about him?" Breaux asked, laying his notes down.

"Can't find the man."

"What do you mean, you can't *find* the man? Is he out-of-town?"

"Nope, he's missing," Carson nonchalantly answered. He became more concerned with a food stain on his shirt than speaking with Breaux.

"Forget about that damn stain and tell me what is going on, Detective."

Continuing to pick at the stain, he replied, "His phone, disconnected. His residence is empty. He's vanished, just . . . vanished."

Irritated, Breaux pointed his finger at Carson. "This was *your* expert. *Your* guy. *You* convinced me to use him, but now . . . now, I look like a fool. Not you. Me," he said loudly, turning his finger back to himself and tapping his chest. Breaux's face was red and his eyes bulging with anger.

"But, Marcus said—"

"Marcus?" Breaux asked, rising to his feet. "Do you take your orders from Marcus Butler, or from Sheriff Austin? Don't answer that. I wouldn't want you to self-incriminate." Breaux began pacing like a caged lion. All he could see was a case crumbling before his eyes and the chief cause of him losing was sitting in his office.

Carson didn't say a word. He sat there, slumped in his seat, his eyes fixed on the floor in front of him, and his hands clasped at his waist.

Breaux stopped pacing. With fire in his eyes, he turned and glowered at Carson, yelling, "All I know. You screwed up. And now, I'm the one who will clean up your, your . . . damn mess. I pushed Judge Harper to move fast in this case. Why? Because of you, you Detective Carson, you assured me it was open and shut. But now . . . now I've got Monroe Lovett—he's making me look like an idiot, a blooming idiot!" Everything in the extremely exasperated prosecutor wanted to obliterate the detective. With all the anger he could gather, he put his finger in the detective's face and told Carson, "But you're the idiot! Not me. You are!"

Taken back by Breaux's outburst, he retorted, "Hey, you wanted evidence. I gave you what you wanted. So, don't try to make me your scapegoat. We're all in this together."

"What do you mean by '*we*'?" Breaux asked probingly.

Stumbling to answer, Carson, choked out, "You know . . . law enforcement. Us."

Resuming his pacing, with a brisk wave of his hand, Breaux austerely said, "Just find me Roueché. Search under every rock. Call every law enforcement department within five hundred miles, a thousand miles if you must. Call Interpol," Breaux said with an exaggerated swoosh of his arm. He put his hands on his hips and stood for a moment looking out his office window trying to gather himself. "I don't care what you have to do, Detective, but find me that man. Do you understand me?"

"I can put out a BOLO on him. Besides, I don't know what else we can do."

"Austin know?" Breaux asked.

"Oh yeah. I called and told him. He ain't happy with me right now."

"Count me in that group."

"He said he wants to see me later, to *talk* about it. These talks are becoming routine now."

"Maybe I'll give him a call."

"Thanks. I need all the help I can get."

"Oh, it won't be to help you. I can promise you that," Breaux said, fixing his stare on Carson. "And get me something on that print before Monroe gets Judge Harper to declare a mistrial. Or, even worse, drop the charges."

At the same time, across the town square, Debbie hurried into Monroe's office. "I've got something," she said, swiftly sitting down. With her hand, she brushed her hair behind her ear.

"What kind of something?" he asked, watching her. "You know, it's so sexy when you brush your hair back like that."

"Hey,"—Debbie snapped her fingers— "stay focused, Mr. Lovett," she said, giving him that motherly look.

Monroe, seeing her poker-faced, fought back his laughter.

"Ashley's background. You're not going to believe this."

"It's still sexy," Monroe said with a wink. Now Debbie remained blank-faced. He motioned to her and said, "Well, go on. Tell me."

Not amused with his antics, Debbie told him, "I may have found the name of two men associated with Ashley's past."

"Okay."

"One is Fichard Roueché. You know, something about him made my skin crawl."

"You're kidding," Monroe said, sitting up straight. "You're telling me, the very man, who offered expert testimony on the firearm used in this murder case, is linked to Ashley, our Ashley?"

"Looks like it," she said, beaming with self-confidence.

"But she didn't recognize him."

"Maybe—"

"But why? We need to find out—I wonder if Breaux—we need to get Roueché back on the stand," he said with the gears turning in his head.

"You want *me*—?" Debbie asked, unsure. She knew she was already stretching her abilities, even though it was fun for her.

"No," Monroe answered, seeing his wife's apprehension. "No, you've done plenty, honey. This is more of Herm's expertise."

"Okay, I'll give him this," she said, holding up the folder.

"You said two?" Monroe inquired. "Who's the other person?"

"Oh yeah. The other was an uncle on her mother's side."

"Uncle?"

"Yeah."

"Huh," Monroe said, wondering how Roueché played into the scheme of things. "Good job, sweetie. Give what you've got to Herm."

"I'll do," Debbie said, getting up and walking around to Monroe. "So, you think my brushing my hair back is sexy?" she asked seductively.

"Hey, Debbie. Stay focused," he said, motioning back and forth from his eyes to her eyes with two fingers. "Alright?"

"Fine . . . but it's your loss," Debbie said and sauntered back to her desk.

"No doubt *about* it," he said under his breath, watching her walk away.

Not long afterward, Monroe's phone rang. Debbie said, "Robert Breaux wants to speak with you."

"Put him through." Monroe pushed the speaker button and said, "This is Monroe Lovett." He grabbed a baseball on his desk and started tossing it up in the air and catching it as he chatted with Breaux.

"Monroe, this is Robert," Breaux said.

"What can I do for you, Robert?"

"Can you come to my office?"

"Sure," Monroe said, rolling his eyes as he caught the ball. "When?"

"Now?"

Monroe paused for a moment. He tossed the ball up again and then after he had seized it said, "Give me fifteen."

Suspicious, Monroe entered the DA's office. He noticed the familiar, yet exasperated, faces of Breaux and Austin. With Carson sitting in silence a little off to himself.

"Thanks for coming," Breaux soberly told him. "Please, close the door behind you."

"Okay . . ." Monroe said, with a sense of uneasiness in his spine. "I feel like I've been called to the principal's office."

"No, it's nothing like that," Breaux expressed.

"Then, what?" Monroe asked.

"We've got a slight problem," Austin answered, clearly upset. "Or, maybe I should say, the *district attorney* has a problem."

"Only one?" Monroe responded, chuckling. Breaux let the comment roll off his back. He had bigger problems at hand.

"Fichard Roueché is missing," Austin said.

"Hmm . . . Yeah, I'd say *you guys* have a problem," Monroe replied, gesturing to the three men.

"Please, Mr. Lovett, have a seat," Breaux requested, motioning to a chair. "There's no need to get testy."

Monroe sat, laughing to himself. "Get testy? Now, all of a sudden, you want to play nice. So, why am I really here?"

Breaux glanced at Austin, and said, "We thought . . ."

"Hey, don't include my office in this," Austin said, putting his hands up signifying a wall.

"Okay . . . I was hoping you might be of some assistance?"

"Assistance? How?"

Breaux took a seat on the corner of his desk. "I'll get right to the point. Since Judge Harper has stopped this trial because of your motion for the fingerprints, and the only person we can't locate is—"

"And, you want me"—Monroe interjected, pointing to himself— "to help you, so the trial can quickly resume?"

"Yeah, *something* like that," Breaux answered.

"You guys are a bunch of nuts," Monroe declared, standing up.

"Not me. Him," Austin said, pointing at Breaux.

"And him," Monroe said, his finger pointed directly at Carson, who remained silent.

The tension in the room quickly rose as Monroe neared Breaux. "You've got a lot of nerve . . . a lot of nerve, Robert."

"Stay calm, Monroe," Breaux said. However, it was too late for that.

Monroe put his finger in Breaux's face, telling him, "First, you charge my client without completing a thorough investigation. And now, now— when I'm about to blow the lid off *your* case—you want me, *me* to help you do *your* job. Why so you can finish railroading this poor girl? A girl you know is innocent."

"Monroe, please—" Carson said.

"Monroe? It's Mr. Lovett to you, Detective," Monroe retorted, again pointing his finger at him. "Personally, I think you're a step above a rookie." His voice began to increase in volume with each word while Carson's face reddened. "But maybe, just maybe, you were more concerned with helping your friend, Marcus Butler, than solving a murder . . . than doing your job. How far will you go to help him? Huh? How far? Force her to sign a confession? Tamper with evidence?"

Carson leaped to his feet, taking a step toward Monroe. Monroe held his ground. Carson said, "Look here, Counselor. You're about to cross a line."

"Detective Carson!" Sheriff Austin yelled. Austin knew Monroe was right about Carson.

Aiming his finger dead at Carson, with outright contempt, Monroe told him, "I believe you've already crossed that line."

The expanding balloon of tension was about to pop. Austin knew he had to do something before things got out of hand. He stepped between the two men and said, "Both of you—both of you, go back to your corners and calm down."

Breaux watched stunned by what he was witnessing. Several moments later, tempers began to calm.

Looking around at the men, Monroe said, "Mr. Breaux, your problem is not my problem. The way I see it, you can drop the charges against my client, Robert. And then find the guilty party and prosecute them. Or, take it up with Judge Harper. Personally, I . . . don't . . . care. But I will not, will not, do you a favor to get your butt out of hot water. You forget—I've played some ball in the big leagues. Either put your big boy pants on or get off the field. This isn't community softball. This is the majors. And rest assured, this is just the beginning. It's only the beginning." Monroe quickly stared down each of the men and then stormed from the office. He knew he had Breaux on the mat, and he wasn't about to let him up.

"That went well," Breaux said. He stared at Austin and Carson. "Find Roueché."

"What did he mean by the big leagues?" Austin asked.

"He worked for some big-name lawyer years ago," Breaux answered derisively.

"Huh?" Austin said. He looked at Carson. "Half hour. My office. And have me something. I don't care what it is. Because right now, your job is on the line."

"I'll try, Sheriff," Carson said, scornfully cutting his eyes at Austin. However, the sheriff didn't see him, having already turned his back to him.

Austin walked to the door and said, "And don't be late."

Already down to the sidewalk, Monroe hustled to get back to his office. *This is getting interesting. I'm not sure I want Herm to find Roueché now.* He reached for his phone to call Herm, but he had left it on his desk.

Chapter 41

Two days later, Friday morning, and still, the search for Roueché has come up empty. Judge Harper, at the request of Sheriff Austin, scheduled a meeting with Monroe and Breaux. Both attorneys and the sheriff were waiting for the judge outside of his chambers. Harper was twelve minutes late. It was unlike him to be late. All three sat, in silence, as they watched the clock. Monroe wasn't in the mood to converse with Breaux after their last meeting, and Breaux felt likewise. Sheriff Austin sat reading a magazine, ignoring the two lawyers.

At last, at a quarter past, Harper arrived wearing fishing pants and shirt, and a cap. Monroe, Austin, and Breaux all glanced at each other with similar looks of surprise. The judge walked past them motioning with a slight head nod for them to follow. Along with Harper's clerk, they obeyed.

Tossing his hat onto the desk, Judge Harper rubbed his mostly bald head, and said, "Mr. Breaux, Sheriff Austin, it seems we have a problem with obtaining a set of prints from one of *your* witnesses."

Contritely Breaux replied, "Yes, Your Honor. We cannot locate Mr. Roueché."

"Surely his prints are on file with the FBI, or the NRA, if he's a licensed instructor?" Monroe asked, knowing there was more to Roueché than any of them knew.

Breaux stood, with his hands in his pockets, like a scolded schoolboy, not saying anything. His whole appearance had the look of a child caught with his hand in the cookie jar.

"Well?" Harper pushed, wanting an answer from the prosecutor.

"There's . . . well . . . see, there's no Fichard Roueché registered with the NRA, nor—"

"Judge?" Monroe interrupted. He was ready to slam Breaux onto the legal mat and pin him. Before he could, Harper put his hand up, stopping him. Monroe backed down, reluctantly.

Breaux awkwardly said, "I'll let Sheriff Austin explain."

Monroe started to speak again. Judge Harper abruptly stopped him again. "Hold your horses, Counselor." Monroe did as told, but with a slight huff. Then, Judge Harper, staring straight at Breaux, with no reading glasses blocking his intense glare, began admonishing the DA, "So, you're telling us—" Austin started to interject, but the judge held up his hand to him also "—that you, you, the District Attorney, had an expert witness testify in *my* courtroom without checking his credentials? What has gotten into you, Robert?"

The prosecutor wanted to hide under the carpet if he could. Breaux timidly responded, "Y-yes, Your Honor." He waited for Harper's wrath.

Monroe stepped forward again, and once more Harper stopped him. Monroe sighed loudly but complied. He wanted in this fight.

The perceptive judge said, "Mr. Lovett, I know what you're going to ask. Your motion to exclude the witness and all associated testimony of Fichard Roueché is granted. It will, will be stricken from the record." Harper's glower said it all as he refocused his attention on Breaux. His jaw muscles tightened as he struggled to keep his cool with the DA. Through clenched teeth, he said, "I'm considering slapping you with a contempt charge, Mr. Breaux. And maybe having the bar consider taking some sort of disciplinary actions." Harper then turned to Austin and said, "Sheriff, please enlighten us?"

Austin cleared his throat. The last thing he wanted was to be in the judge's crosshairs. "Our Fichard Roueché is not on file anywhere with any government agency," Austin answered moderately. "There are several Fichard Roueché's alive and well, but none we can find who resembles our man. One works for the FBI, he's an African American, but not our man."

"Yeah. . . not our guy," Breaux tentatively whispered.

Judge Harper asked, "So you're saying you have no clue who our Fichard Roueché is?"

"Correct," Austin answered.

"Your Honor," Monroe interrupted, "I would like to restate my request to dismiss all charges against my client."

"Denied," Judge Harper replied. "There's still enough circumstantial evidence, albeit very thin,"—he said, glaring at Breaux— "and I *emphasize*, very thin, to charge your client. But, unfortunately for you, the girl signed a confession. That alone is merit to continue with the case."

Monroe knew the judge was right, "But she has recanted the confession. And its procurement is dubious at best."

"Then prove it, Mr. Lovett," Harper said.

"So, what do we do, Judge?" Breaux asked.

"We resume first thing Monday morning at 9 am. Be ready to call your next witness, Mr. Lovett."

Monroe gave a slight nod, indicating his agreement. Sure, he could argue for more time, but why put Ashley through it. He was ready to continue his attack.

"I'll have the Sheriff's recent findings entered into the record," Harper said.

"What about the fingerprint?" Monroe asked.

"Carson told me there were no matching prints found when he ran them against those we took," Austin said.

"And you believe him?" Monroe countered.

"Yes, we do," Breaux replied.

Austin glanced at Breaux, thinking, *Speak for yourself*. "At this time, I don't have much of a choice."

"And the railroad of my client continues," Monroe said, waving his hand.

"Mr. Lovett," Harper stated.

"Sorry, Your Honor."

That afternoon, Monroe and Herm were discussing Ashley's case. Monroe watched the bourbon and ice as he swirled it in his glass. "What do you make of our fake Mr. Roueché?"

Herm shrugged, as he answered, "To be honest, I don't know. It's a first for me."

"But he's somehow connected to Ashley's past."

"You asked her about him yet?"

"No. But I will."

"Well, whoever he is, he must've stolen an identity."

"Means he's good."

"Means the man had some alternative motive," Herm said, pointing at Monroe with his glass in hand.

"What could it be?"

"Don't know. Wish I did."

"That's it?" Monroe asked, surprised by Herm's comment. "Don't know? That's your best response?"

"I don't know, Monroe. I really don't," Herm asserted, throwing his hands out, his drink almost spilling.

Debbie walked in carrying a plain white envelope. "Here," she said, handing it to Monroe. She glanced over at Herm as he sat with his hands still out in front of him. She could see his frustration.

He slowly lowered them.

"What's this?" Monroe asked.

"Don't know. But it's from you to you—*again.*"

"Don't know. That's everybody's answer," Monroe said with a fleeting look at Herm.

Herm grinned and then took a drink of his bourbon. Monroe chuckled under his breath.

"What is?" Debbie asked.

"Never mind," Monroe said, sniffing the envelope. "I don't smell money."

"What if it's laced with ricin?" Herm remarked.

"Not funny," Monroe answered, hastily withdrawing the envelope from his face.

"Well, you're the one sniffing it," Herm said, chuckling. "I'm just saying . . ."

"Just open it, Monroe—but carefully," Debbie told him, thinking of Herm's warning.

Monroe eased a letter opener under the flap. Debbie watched, holding her breath. Herm took a casual sip of his drink. As he removed the single sheet of paper with care, Monroe gradually shook it open over his trashcan while turning his face away. Nothing fell from it, no killer powder. Convinced it was free of anything harmful, he then read it to himself.

"Well?" Debbie impatiently asked.

"Well, what?" Monroe replied, knowing it was driving Debbie crazy. "Maybe it's confidential."

She crossed her arms and gave him the raised eyebrow. She knew he was just trying to annoy her, she said, "What, you sent yourself a confidential letter?"

Herm saw Debbie's expression and said, "You better read it to her."

"Alright, alright." Monroe looked back at the letter and read aloud, "Dear Mr. Lovett, You continue doing your job. I will not reveal my identity to you, nor to anyone else. So, forgo any efforts to find me. I cannot be found. Sincerely, Fichard Roueché."

"You just made that up, didn't you?" Herm said.

Monroe smiled. "No, it's real. Here," he said, refolding the letter and tossing it to him.

Herm looked it over and said, "The man's a screwball. We know what he looks like."

"And yet, no one can find him, can they?" Monroe declared, pouring a little more bourbon. He offered the bottle to Herm.

"Sure," Herm said, leaning back and crossing his legs. "No. No, we can't, to answer your question." He motioned to Monroe with a nod of his head. "Is there a postmark?"

Handing the bottle to Debbie to give to Herm, Monroe then flipped the envelope over. "Jackson," he said, pitching the envelope back onto his desk. A small piece of paper slid out when it landed.

Debbie noticed it first. "What's that?" she asked, reaching for it.

Monroe snatched it up before she could get to it. She shot him a pouty-face. "Give Herm the bottle," he said, ignoring her reaction. She grabbed a glass and poured herself a drink first before giving it to Herm. Monroe read the three words printed on it aloud, "Until next time." He looked at Debbie and Herm holding his arms out with his palms up and asked, "Until next time? What does that mean?"

"Who is this guy?" Herm questioned.

"Means he's whacky," Debbie said, sipping the bourbon. Clearing her throat from the burning of the drink, she said, "As I said, something about him made my skin crawl."

"Give the letter back," Monroe said, his hand outstretched, motioning for Herm to hand it to him. Herm complied.

Monroe placed the letter along with the note back into the envelope. He taped the envelope shut, and then locked it in the bottom drawer of his desk. After placing the key back in his pocket, he looked at both Debbie and Herm. "This letter never existed. Got it?" Both acquiesced. With a stern tone, Monroe said, "Herm, stop looking for him for now, okay?"

"Got it, boss."

"Why?" Debbie asked.

"Because I don't want anything to happen to Ashley," Monroe answered. "This letter might be a warning. So yes, I'm taking it seriously."

"Oh . . ." she said.

"You gonna tell Breaux or Judge Harper?" Herm asked.

"Was it addressed to them?" Monroe asked.

"No."

"There's your answer then," Monroe replied as he finished the last of his drink. "Now, I plan on taking the weekend to relax with my beautiful wife, here—"

"You are? Where is she?" Debbie jested, looking around.

Smiling at her, he continued, "Need to clear my mind. I need to be ready for Monday. It's time to attack."

Putting her glass up to her mouth to take a drink, Debbie smiled at Monroe, quickly raising her eyebrows a couple of times. He knew the alcohol was starting to get to her.

Monroe smiled at her, almost laughing, but then looking over at Herm asked him, "So, Herm, you going out with Mary again this weekend?"

"No," Herm snapped.

"But I thought you had such a good time. According to you, you can make a woman's hair fly *right off* her head. Or, in your case, flip her wig," Monroe said teasingly while swooshing his hand over his head and laughing.

Debbie covered her mouth as she began laughing.

"Maybe you should give up law and go into comedy," Herm said with a sniping chortle. He sat just glaring at Monroe, but couldn't hold a straight-faced any longer as he began laughing. "Man, that night—oh, it was funny. Yep, it was funny. She . . . she didn't even realize it was gone—there it was, lying on the floor. Looked like one of them critter things in the movies when they rolled across the ground. The woman, she just sat there with that . . . that stocking thing on her head. Looking at me like nothing had happened."

"Oh . . ." Monroe laughed, wiping a tear from his eye. "Let's get out of here. We've got a busy week ahead of us."

Chapter 42

Monday morning

The first witness on the docket was unknown by most of those in the courtroom. However, one person knew him well . . . Ashley. Monroe gave his young client a look of reassurance as the bailiff announced, "The defense calls Joe Galliard to the stand."

Reluctant, Galliard took the stand. He stared at Ashley. He gave her a slight sneer. She looked away. Most of the jurors detected the exchange between the two, as did Harper and Breaux.

"Your Honor," Monroe asked, "permission to treat this witness as hostile? He is here under protest."

"Granted."

"Mr. Galliard, please tell this court what you do for a living?" Monroe asked.

"I own a bar in Jackson."

"Actually, it's a gentlemen's club, correct?" Monroe asked for clarification.

"Yeah, you could call it that."

"We will," Monroe said. "Please explain to the court your relationship with Marcus Butler?"

"Don't know the man."

Monroe opened a folder and removed three 8 x 10 glossies and showed them to Galliard. Galliard glanced at the pictures dismissively. Monroe asked, "Isn't that you in the photos?"

"Hard to tell. But yeah . . . it could be. Could also be any number of people. I've got one of those faces, you know."

"I'm prepared to call the owner of the restaurant, Dennis Anthony, who will testify that is you."

"Do what you gotta do."

"Since it's you, please tell the court who is sitting with you at the table?" Monroe asked, removing another photo and presenting it to Galliard.

"Objection," Breaux interjected. "The witness did not state positively it is him in the photo."

Quickly reflecting on the trial, Harper replied, "I'll allow it."

"Mr. Galliard?" Monroe asked, still holding the photo.

"I . . . I don't . . . I'm not sure," Galliard answered, rubbing his hand over his mouth and then down his goatee. Lightly scratching his beard, he appeared to be thinking, but it was obvious to all he was doing a bad acting job.

"Isn't that Marcus Butler?" Monroe pressed.

Mumblings arose in the gallery with the mention of Butler's name.

"Objection, Your Honor," snapped Breaux. "Please ask the defense to get to the point."

"Overruled," declared Harper. "The witness will answer the question."

Scratching his beard again, Galliard answered, "Sure, if you say so."

"It is," Monroe confirmed. "So, I will ask you again, Mr. Galliard. What is your relationship with Marcus Butler?"

Galliard was cornered, and he knew it. The last thing he needed was for Judge Harper to throw a contempt charge at him. He thought for a moment as his beard rubbing increased, and then answered, "We're . . . business associates."

Almost immediately, word of Butler's association with a known club owner advertising girls dancing on stage began to spread from the courthouse and into the town. An upstanding, church-going community leader, a man like Butler, wasn't supposed to associate with the likes of Galliard. People began to wonder why Butler would even know this man.

"What kind of business associates are you?" Monroe asked.

"Just business. Nothing major. Small stuff, you know."

"No, I don't," Monroe replied. He saw Breaux ready to object to his answering a witness and said, "Withdrawn."

Breaux relaxed.

Monroe turned his attention back to the witness. "Mr. Galliard, your real association with Marcus Butler, is that he paid you for some information?"

"No, he didn't pay me for information."

"Then, why did he give you money?"

"I don't know what you're talking about," Galliard nervously chuckled.

Reaching into a file box, Monroe removed a couple items and said, "Your Honor, the defense would like to enter into evidence a video of Marcus Butler giving the witness a briefcase. Along with the video, we would like to also have entered copies of several withdrawals and transfers from the personal and business bank accounts of Marcus Butler."

"Objection, Your Honor," Breaux stated. "How did the defense obtain these without your knowledge?"

Before Harper could say anything, Monroe stated, "Your Honor, since Mr. Butler's accounts are held by a national bank, I filed papers with a federal judge in Jackson to subpoena Mr. Butler's bank records. After explaining the circumstances of this case, the judge granted my petition."

Harper looked at the prosecutor and said, "There you go, Mr. Breaux. The defense's request is granted."

"Mr. Galliard, should I play the tape?" Monroe asked.

Galliard thought for a moment. Prison wasn't something he desired to experience, and feeling the walls closing in on him, he answered, "Fichard Roueché."

That name drew a loud stir from the gallery. Amy from the Ledger feverishly scribbled her notes. Judge Harper gaveled, calling out, "Order."

Breaux turned to look at Carson. A little fearful, Carson glanced at Sheriff Austin, who was not far from him. Austin shifted his glare equally between both men. What were the odds it was a different Roueché?

Monroe never lost his focus. He asked, "What kind of information?"

"All I know is that it was something about a daughter. I swear . . . that's all I know."

Mumbles rolled across the courtroom like soft thunder. Some whispered, "Daughter? The Butlers only have one child."

Judge Harper gaveling quieted the courtroom.

"Do you know the name of this so-called daughter?" Monroe asked.

"No. I swear that's all I know," Galliard insisted. "All I ever knew was that it made Butler mad, really mad."

"You're positive you never peeked, not even once, at the name?"

Squirming in his chair, Galliard answered, "Uh, what, what was the— Oh yeah, I remember now. It was—I think her name was Julie something."

The courtroom erupted with loud whispering. Harper shouted as he smacked his gavel, "Order. Order in the court."

The gallery was still buzzing as Monroe asked, "Mr. Galliard, where is Fichard Roueché?"

"I don't know. He . . . he just left town, I guess. Disappeared."

"Do you know his real name?"

"Huh?"

"His real name?"

"I thought that *was* his real name," Galliard answered with a bemused appearance.

"One last question. Why did you try to see the defendant in the county jail?"

"I plead the fifth."

"You can't," Harper said. "Now answer the question."

"Just a friendly visit," Galliard answered, visibly anxious.

Taking a few steps toward Galliard, Monroe asked, "Were you trying to intimidate Mrs. Butler?"

There was a pause as Galliard sat, staring at Monroe. "Well?" Monroe asked.

"No. Like I said, it was a friendly visit. But she wouldn't see me."

"Mr. Galliard, did you murder Julie Miller?"

"No."

"Do you know who did?"

"I guess your client," Galliard answered, chortling.

"Your Honor, I ask the witness's response be removed from the record. He gave an opinion."

"Objection, the witness answered the defense's question," Breaux said.

Judge Harper ignored Breaux and replied, "Strike the witness's answer."

"Your witness," Monroe told Breaux, and then sat down. He held his breath as Breaux began his cross of Galliard.

Breaux stood up, buttoned his coat, and shook his head a little, attempting to appear unbelieving of what he had heard. With an air of smugness, he asked, "Mr. Galliard, do you expect us to believe your elaborate story?"

"It's the truth," he answered.

"What? The truth that you and Mr. Lovett cooked up? I mean, the two of you should put your act in the local theater."

"Objection," Monroe said.

"Mr. Breaux, refrain yourself," Judge Harper said.

"My apologies," Breaux replied. "Mr. Galliard, just to be sure, do you know who killed Julie Miller?"

"No."

"Did you know of Julie Miller *prior* to gathering this so-called information that you *claim* was obtained for someone else?"

"Yes."

Galliard's answer was not what was expected. Breaux froze in his steps. Peering at Galliard, he asked, "You did?"

"Yes. She used to dance at my club. Her and Ashley."

Monroe exhaled, realizing the cat was out of the bag. However, he'd half expected it.

All eyes fixed on Ashley. She felt them. Wanting to comfort her, Debbie reached over and grasped her hand. "Don't let them get to you, Ashley," she whispered.

Monroe remained focused on Galliard, as did Sheriff Austin from the back of the courtroom. Austin also wanted to keep an eye on Carson.

"Her and *Mrs. Butler*? The same Mrs. Butler sitting at the defense table?" Breaux asked, swinging his arm around, stopping with his finger pointed directly at Ashley.

"Yes. They were good friends. At least it seemed like it."

"Did they ever have any disagreements?" Breaux probed.

"I'm sure they did, but—"

"Objection," Monroe said. "Nonresponsive. Calls for speculation."

"Sustained," stated Harper. Then he told the prosecutor, "Rephrase your question, Mr. Breaux."

Breaux considered his options. He looked at Harper and concluded, "No further questions." He had planted the seed of Ashley's long-time relationship with Julie for his closing arguments, and that was satisfying for now.

"Let's take a twenty-minute break," Judge Harper said. He knew the next witness would draw even more attention and he thought he, and the court, needed a break.

Galliard stormed from the witness stand straight to the defense table.

Herm saw him coming, moved from his seat just behind Monroe, and stepped in front of Galliard. Putting his hand on Galliard's chest, Herm told him, "I don't think so."

Stopping, Galliard lifted his hands a little, and said, "Hey, just a word with Mr. Lovett."

Herm looked to Monroe.

"What do you want, Galliard?" Monroe asked.

Galliard, while chuckling and rubbing his goatee, asked, "How're the ribs?"

Monroe stepped closer to Galliard. Rage filled him as he stared intently into Galliard's dark eyes. With his jaw muscles flexing, he said, "You're pretty tough when a man is tied up with a hood over his head. Maybe we should see how you do mano-a-mano. And no duct tape this time."

Herm wasn't sure whom to hold back at this point. Even one of the deputies saw the scene unfolding and took a few steps toward them. Ashley quickly moved behind Debbie as she was backing up herself. A few people in the gallery saw the altercation and stayed to watch. Amy watched, taking notes for her article.

Galliard moved back, putting his hands up like someone being held at gunpoint, retorting, "Hey . . . I was only asking, man."

"Maybe it's time for you to leave," Herm insisted, pushing Galliard even further back.

Taking a few steps closer, the deputy assumed an assertive posture.

Galliard gave a slight tug at his sport coat lapels and strutted away like a cocky rooster. He looked back over his shoulder, raising his eyebrows a couple of times, provoking Monroe.

"Herm, that guy . . . the guy who— He—"

"Yeah, I know. Let it go, Monroe. Calm down. Focus on the case. Focus on the case, buddy," Herm said, both watching Galliard swagger away. "His day's coming. His day is coming . . ."

Realizing what had just happened, Monroe spun around to Debbie and Ashley. Both of their faces were showing fear. He walked to them and said, "Everything's fine. Don't worry about that idiot."

Gently taking hold of Ashley's shoulders, Monroe said, "Forget about him, Ashley."

Ashley, still nervous, nodded yes.

"Ashley, I need to ask you a question. Did you recognize Roueché? Have you ever seen him before? Ever?"

Trying to remember, she answered, "No. I've never seen him. Why?"

"Just wondering," Monroe said with a reassuring smile.

Chapter 43

There was this uneasy electricity in the courtroom. More people than any previous session were in the gallery. Galliard's' testimony had circulated around town, and word of the next witness had leaked out.

Ashley did not want to be in court for this part of the trial. She sat with her shoulders drawn in, her hands tucked between her knees, and her eyes fixed on the notepad on the table in front of her. Debbie sat next to her with one knee bobbing up and down at an accelerated rate.

All the key personnel was in place, except for Judge Harper. Monroe sat calm, anticipating this witness. Herm leaned forward and asked Monroe, "So, what do you think is going to happen?"

"Either one of two things. He will give up Junior. Or—"

"All rise," the bailiff ordered.

Monroe turned back and stood before finishing his thought. Herm wanted to hear the rest but knew he'd have to wait like everyone else. All watched as Judge Harper settled into his chair. With his trademark peering over his glasses, he lifted the gavel and smacked it down. He said to Monroe, "Mr. Lovett, if you are ready, please call your next witness." Harper took a deep breath.

"The defense calls Marcus Butler," the bailiff said. It echoed through the extremely hushed courtroom. It was as if someone had hit the mute button, as everyone waited with anticipation.

Cr-e-eak . . . as the door opened.

People rubbernecked to get a glimpse.

Emerging through the doorway was the most powerful man in Lane County. Visibly perturbed, Marcus Butler walked in with the air of a domineering CEO, ready to take control, to fix the problem, to set things right.

Monroe leaned back and quickly whispered to Herm, "He's on my turf now." Amy from the Ledger overheard Monroe and scribbled the quote down.

Thump. Thump. Thump Butler's western boots boomed as he marched across the old wooden floor. He sat down in the witness chair. Heavy-browed and smug, appearing as the local kingpin, he looked over at the jurors. He grunted at them with a sneer. Most did not return his stare. Intimidated, they looked away or down at the floor.

One factor Butler failed to estimate—Monroe saw him as nothing more than just another witness sitting on the stand. The former preacher had dealt with richer, more powerful men than Marcus Butler during his years as a pastor and law associate. Moreover, the two had already had a private confrontation, which in Monroe's mind, he won.

Monroe opened the folder containing his questions for Butler. He glanced at them and then closed the folder. Debbie saw it and wondered what he was doing. *Wing it*, he thought. He pushed his chair back as he leisurely stood up. The sound of the grating chair legs over the wood floors was the only thing penetrating the friction in the room. Walking out from behind the defense table, Monroe stared straight at the middle-aged honcho.

Butler adjusted his position a little in the chair. Not being in control was a new feeling for him, but he believed he was ready for the battle. Monroe continued his gaze at Butler as he took a position in front of the table. For him, this battle would end the war.

Breaux fixated on Monroe, wondering.

Judge Harper cleared his throat as he glanced at Monroe. Monroe took the hint with a slight nod of his head. He smiled at Butler and said, "Mr. Butler, thank you for coming here this morning."

"Not like I had a choice," Butler rancorously replied.

"That wasn't a question," Monroe said.

Breaux sat, ready to interject with a swift objection. He and Butler might not be friends, but he liked the campaign contributions. All he saw were dollars flying out the window.

"Mr. Butler," Monroe said, "I would like to offer my condolences for your loss. How are you coping?"

Looking around, confused, Butler answered, "What? I don't understand. Condolences? Condolences for *what?*"

Monroe leaned back against the table, crossing his arms he said, "Condolences for the death of your step-daughter, Julie Miller, or should I say, Julie Davillier."

An eruption of gasps, loud moans, and sounds of amazement filled the previous silent courtroom. One juror muttered, "Oh my."

Judge Harper began gaveling and stating, "Order. Order. Order in the court or this courtroom will be cleared." He shot a quick glare at the discomfited juror and said, "The jury will remain silent."

Breaux popped to his feet yelling, "Objection! Objection, Your Honor! The prosecution objects to this line of questioning!"

Unable to grasp the meaning of all of this, the Millers sat, stunned, motionless.

Monroe, undaunted by what was going on around him, stared at Marcus Butler. As much as Butler tried to hide his reaction, Monroe could see he had hit a nerve, a nerve of truth as he noticed Butler's jaw muscle flex several times.

People continued to mutter their opinions.

Judge Harper was slapping the bench with his gavel—*Wham-Wham-Wham*. It was a wonder it didn't fly apart as hard as he hammered the bench. It took several minutes for the deputies to get everyone settled back down.

Fumes from Harper were almost visible. "Mr. Lovett," he said, pointing his gavel at Monroe, "this had better be going somewhere, or I will sustain the prosecution's objection."

Breaux glared at Judge Harper, taken back by his allowing Monroe to continue. It seemed that no matter what he objected to lately, Harper overruled him. Before the judge caught a glimpse of his gaze, Breaux flopped back down with a clunk. In a lowered voice, he told his associate, "This is ridiculous. Total absurdity." The associate nodded in agreement.

Butler squirmed in his chair

"It is, Your Honor," Monroe answered.

"Well, it better be," Judge Harper insisted.

Monroe turned his attention back to a red-faced Butler, who was now nervously gnawing the inside of his cheek. Still leaning against the table, Monroe asked, "Isn't it true the victim, Julie Miller, is the illegitimate daughter of your wife, Darlene Butler?"

Once more, the courtroom burst forth in bedlam, even louder this time. People sat, many with their jaws having dropped to the floor. Like before, Monroe didn't take his eyes off Butler. Beads of perspiration were breaking out on the man's forehead and upper lip. Moreover, it wasn't warm in the courtroom. Monroe leered at the man thinking, *Welcome to my interrogation, Mr. Butler.*

Ashley sat, dumbfounded. Her anxiety began to ease, a little. She couldn't believe what she was hearing. And neither could anyone else. A woman in the back of the courtroom muttered, "You can't make this stuff up."

Butler dropped his smug stare, shifting his gaze to the courtroom floor. He would snap an occasional glance up at Monroe like a nervous dog as he waited, looking as if he might chew a hole through his cheek. The truth was coming out, a past veiled from the public for over two decades.

Smack-Smack-Smack sounded the gavel. "Or-der! Order in the court!" the judge yelled. Butler's blood pressure rose equal to the volume of Judge Harper's gavel pounding. This time the outbreak carried into the halls of the courthouse where people had gathered to listen. Deputies rushed about, demanding everyone to settle down. It took more than ten minutes to regain order in the cramped courtroom. Monroe was enjoying every minute of it.

Debbie saw Monroe's calm demeanor. Leaning back to Herm, she told him, "He never had this much fun in church work." Herm laughed as he shook his head.

Judge Harper gave Monroe a nod to continue, maintaining a tight grip on his gavel. Monroe motioned to Butler, "Please, answer the question, Mr. Butler."

Butler, with his hands, firmly clasped together below his waist, and wringing his fingers, answered quietly, "Yes."

"What was that, Mr. Butler? I didn't hear your answer," Monroe said, looking to Judge Harper.

Harper looked at the court recorder. She shrugged shaking her head indicating she did not hear the answer either. Turning back to the witness stand, Judge Harper said, "Mr. Butler, please answer the question loud enough for the court to hear."

"Yes. Yes. There you have it. Yes, Julie is my—She was my, my step-daughter," Butler answered.

Mrs. Miller jumped from her front-row seat behind the prosecutor and ran from the courtroom. Her heals galumphed the floor with each step. People gawked at her as she dashed by, tears streaming down her face. Mr.

Miller didn't move. He sat dazed by the announcement. They didn't know. It was by mere coincidence they adopted Julie.

Monroe watched Mrs. Miller flee the courtroom, and then moved to his next question. "Then, is it true your son, Marcus Jr., whom no one has seen for weeks,"—he said, holding his arms out to his side in a quizzical gesture— "was allegedly having an affair with your wife's illegitimate daughter, his half-sister, unbeknownst to the young man?"

Moans, groans, and gasps preceded yet another chaotic outbreak in the courtroom. Heads shook in astonishment. Others sat open-mouthed. Ashley dropped her head to the table. Her forehead made a clunk sound when it landed. Monroe had not said anything to her. He wanted her raw reaction as she heard along with everyone else.

Like the previous vocal discharges, Harper began his gaveling and calling for the court to settle down. More deputies moved in to quiet the gallery.

Monroe walked around to Ashley and sat down next to her. Leaning over to her, he said, "It's going to be okay."

"This is just crazy," she said. "I mean . . . I never thought— Please tell me this isn't happening."

Stepping over at Debbie, Monroe covered his mouth so only she saw him and said, "Take care of her. This is going to get worse." Debbie nodded yes, as she wondered what else would come out. Monroe had not told her either. Only he and Herm knew what was about to become known.

Jurors stared at each other, at Butler, at the commotion breaking out before their eyes. They were as surprised as everyone else was. One female juror leaned over to another and whispered, "I can't believe we have to decide this case?"

"I know. This is crazy," the other juror replied, shaking her head as she ogled the disorder.

Monroe resumed his position in front of the table. Several jurors noticed his confident demeanor.

Some of the people standing outside, eavesdropping, took off running throughout the town, spreading the unfolding of proceedings in the courthouse. This brought more curiosity-seekers to the courthouse, filling the halls. Others gathered outside, waiting for the broadcast of the latest piece of news. A few people even attempted to listen through the windows. Amy, from the Ledger, frantically jotted her notes. This was front-page stuff in her mind.

Sheriff's deputies worked feverishly under Austin's directions to keep the public under control as the crowds increased. After several minutes had passed, the deputies restored calm around the courthouse and in the courtroom.

With order reinstated, Breaux declared, "Objection, Your Honor. The question calls for speculation on the part of the witness. The defense is assuming an affair occurred."

"Your Honor," Monroe retorted, as he reached around and snatched up a piece of paper from a folder on the table. He had anticipated Breaux's objection. Holding the sheet of paper up, for all to see, Monroe said, "I have a copy of the prosecution's opening statement, Your Honor. It says right here in the highlighted section, and I read, '...the defendant had a motive to murder Ms. Miller because of an *alleged* extra-marital affair between Ms. Miller and the defendant's husband and this *alleged* affair drove the defendant to commit the heinous act of murder.'" Monroe placed the sheet of paper back on the table. Gesturing in Breaux's direction, he said, "The prosecution, from the very beginning of this trial, introduced possible sexual missteps by this witness's own son." Monroe waited for Harper's decision as several groans came from the gallery.

"He's right, Mr. Breaux. You introduced the affair yourself," Judge Harper said. "Your objection is overruled."

Breaux's resentment boiled over. He shot straight up to his feet. "Dang-it, Judge! What's the point of me even being here, if you're not going to at least give the prosecution a chance?" No sooner had those words sailed from Breaux's mouth than he realized he said them aloud, for everyone to hear. All eyes promptly locked on him now.

Judge Harper's face said it all—his eyes bulged at the prosecutor. The thought of throwing the gavel at him flew through his mind.

Breaux immediately appealed, "I beg the court's forgiveness, Your Honor. I do deeply apologize for my statements. I . . . I . . . ." Breaux said remorsefully. He feared a night in jail and a hefty fine.

Controlling his own wrath, Harper was scowling at the very embarrassed prosecutor and scolding him said, "The prosecution had its chance, Mr. Breaux." He thought for a moment, and said, "I have half a mind to find you in contempt of court, and slap a fine on you as well. Now, sit down." Breaux took the deserved scolding and did as told. After reprimanding Breaux, the judge said, "Mr. Butler, you will answer the question."

"Yes," Butler answered.

From the hallway, a young man yelled to those outside the courthouse, "Old man Butler just admitted Marcus Jr. was sleeping with his half-sister."

Judge Harper yanked his head up when he heard it, demanding, "Close those doors—completely. I don't care how warm it gets in here, keep those doors closed."

Monroe drank it in as he asked, "Mr. Butler, where's your son?"

Butler flung his arm up and pointed at Ashley and yelled, "You have a signed confession from that, that—"

"Your Honor," Monroe said, "the witness's answer is nonresponsive."

Judge Harper looked at the jury and instructed, "You will disregard the witness's statement, and it will be stricken from the record." Shifting his gaze to Butler, he told him, "Mr. Butler, you will, I repeat, will *only* answer the questions *asked* of you. Or, I will hold you in contempt of court. Do you get my drift?"

Butler nodded yes.

"Now, answer the defense's question. Do you know where your son is?"

Shamed, Butler answered, "I . . . I don't know. Hiding out somewhere, I guess. I, we've only had a few texts from him."

Monroe accepted the answer and asked his next question. "Did Marcus Jr. murder Julie Miller, Mr. Butler?"

"No," Butler answered unequivocally.

Hearing his answer, Monroe decided to head down another road, another line of questioning. "Did *you* murder Julie Miller?"

Seeing the gallery ready to react to the answer, Harper gaveled with a single loud smack. It was enough to preempt another outburst.

"No. Of course not. Why would you ask—that's a stupid question?"

Pausing briefly, Monroe thought, *Maybe I should ask him if he had anything to do with the confession.* He took a quick glimpse at Butler. That little voice in his head told him to stay on track. So, he pulled out a photo and handed it to Butler. "Is this you in this photograph?" he asked, passing out additional photos to Harper, Breaux, and the jury.

"Yeah, sure . . . I guess . . . it looks like me," Butler answered.

"Looks exactly like you. Who's that at the table with you?" Monroe asked.

"I'm not sure. It's kind of hard to tell," Butler answered without taking a second look at the photo.

"Maybe I can help you remember," Monroe said. Butler swallowed hard, wringing his hands. "Isn't that you at the Pearl Café in Jackson, Mississippi, and the person sitting across from you is Julie Miller?"

Loud mutterings came from the courtroom gallery. Not wanting another uproar, Judge Harper tapped his gavel a couple of times. Everyone knew the drill and calmed down. The spectators wanted to hear Butler's answer.

"Yes," Butler said.

More whispering arose from the gallery. A couple more gavel taps from Judge Harper, as he said, "Shh . . ."

"Isn't it true the two of you met at the Pearl Café on several occasions?" Monroe asked.

Realizing Monroe had the proof, Butler answered, "Yes." Leaning forward in his chair, and glaring at Monroe, Butler asked, "What are you getting at, Mr. Lovett?"

"That you, you, Mr. Butler"—Monroe said, pointing his finger at Butler— "killed Julie Miller? In fact, in the photo, it appears you and Julie were having an argument."

"Objection!" shouted Breaux rising to his feet. "Mr. Lovett cannot testify on behalf of the witness."

"Sustained," Judge Harper responded. "Strike the witness's question to counsel, and strike Mr. Lovett's response. The jury will disregard those remarks."

"Mr. Butler, I'll ask you again, did you kill Julie Miller," Monroe asked loudly.

"Objection!"

"No!" Butler declared.

"Overruled!"

Frustrated with his courtroom becoming a circus, Harper looked at the clock and said, "It's 11:42. This court is in recess until two this afternoon. I want two deputies to escort Mr. Butler to a holding room and no one, I mean no one, is to have contact with him until we return." Judge Harper looked to the rear of the courtroom, "Sheriff Austin, I need to see you in my chambers."

Sheriff Austin acknowledged the invitation with a nod and purse of his lips and then cut his eyes over at Carson. Carson stood, leaning against the wall, staring up at the ceiling.

Monroe smiled at Breaux who was none too pleased.

Chapter 44

Judge Harper removed his robe, placed it on a hanger, and then turned his attention to Sheriff Austin. Austin was clueless about his summoning as he stood, waiting.

"Sheriff. Detective Carson?" Harper asked, sitting down in his high-back reading chair.

"What about him, Judge?" Austin asked, still standing.

"What about him? Have you brought any disciplinary actions against the man for his multiple mistakes in this case?"

"I suspended him without pay for a week until I decide my next move. So yes, I have."

"To be honest, I'm wondering if charges are called for against the man."

"You too?" Austin asked.

"What do you mean by that?"

"Everybody in town is talking about how this lawyer, Lovett, is making me and Breaux look bad."

"Your point?"

"So, you agree then? Have *you* taken Lovett's side?"

"Mind yourself, Sheriff." Austin knew he should tread lightly and regained his composure. Harper went on, "You didn't see his face, Sheriff. The whole time the court was in chaos . . . Lovett, he just stood there, with this, this confident demeanor. He's got more. I don't know what else he and Ed Hermann have on Marcus Butler, but—well, let's just say . . . Butler might want to think about getting his own lawyer."

"What? Have you convicted Butler already?" Austin asked, walking over to the window. The thought of possible corruption in his department weighed heavy on him as he watched people below stroll by on the sidewalks. "Look, I've got nothing against Lovett. I even like the man, but—"

"But he may be onto something. And, Marcus Butler may be guilty of some, some improprieties. That's all I'm saying, Sheriff. You sure your department and Detective Carson didn't move too fast in arresting the girl? Did it ever cross your mind her husband might have committed the murder?"

Sheriff Austin turned around and faced the judge. Fighting to control his anger, the sheriff didn't take kindly to Harper's inference. Crossly, but measured, he said, "Judge . . . a word . . . a word of . . . advice. I run the sheriff's office. And, and you, Judge . . . you run your courtroom. That robe," he said, pointing to Harper's robe, "doesn't give you the right to . . . to tell me how to do my job—period. Do I make myself clear, Your Honor?"

Harper, not normally one to back down, knew Austin was correct. He politely responded, "Understood, Sheriff. Point taken. I was only trying—"

"I know, Judge. It's just this case I guess," Austin said, calming down by taking a breath. "Well, if nothing else, this whole thing is putting Peregrine on the map."

"Just the kind of publicity we *don't* need."

The ringing of Austin's phone paused their conversation. Looking at the screen, he read at the caller ID. "It Dr. Stevens," he told Harper. "Sheriff Austin," he answered. He listened to the caller. Judge Harper watched as the blood drained from Austin's face. "No. I'll handle it. Don't tell anyone. And I mean it, not a word, Doc," he said.

"Okay," she said.

"What's wrong?" Harper asked, seeing Austin end the call.

Discernibly shaken, Austin answered, "As I said . . . it was Dr. Stevens—"

"Don't tell me, she made a mistake in the case?"

"No. It's nothing like that. It's the burnt body."

"What about it?"

"She's got . . . got a DNA and a dental match."

"Yeah?"

"Judge, it's, the body is Marcus Jr."

"Oh, my," Harper remarked, stunned by the news. "Marcus and Darlene are going to be crushed."

"I should go tell him," Austin said, stepping toward the door.

"No," Harper said. "Don't tell him. At least, not yet, anyway."

"Why not?"

"I don't want him to be dealing with the death of his son until after he's done testifying. It's best he doesn't know until he's done."

"Okay. If you think it best?"

"I do," replied Harper trying to soak in the news. "And, think about Ashley too, Sheriff." Harper looked out the window across the street to Juanita's Diner below. "I wonder what's taking lunch so long to get here. Usually, Juanita gets it right over."

Sheriff Austin shrugged off Harper's lunch statement. Walking to the door, he said, "Yeah, poor girl."

"Poor girl, indeed."

"Well, it appears I've got a new murder to solve."

"Let's keep it quiet, Sheriff. We don't need any additional excitement in this town right now." Harper turned to Austin and asked him, "And, Sheriff?"

"Yeah, Judge?"

"Carson?"

"I'll get someone else to work the case. Don't worry."

"Good."

"It's gonna eventually come out, Judge."

"I know. Just keep it under wraps for as long as you can. Until Butler is off the stand, at least," Harper said, turning back to the window, facing Juanita's. "Where's my sandwich? I'm starving."

"Yeah, me too. My stomach's starting to eat my throat," Austin said, reaching for his own neck. As he opened the door, he said, "Till after his testimony, Judge. But after that, I'm going full steam ahead. And Carson, I've got it under control."

"I trust you, Sheriff."

Austin started to leave, but then stopped and turned back. Harper noticed and asked, "Forget something?"

"Yeah. Butler testified Junior had been sending text messages. Last I checked, dead men, don't text."

Harper's head snapped up, as he stood speechless, staring at Austin.

Juanita's was jumping with a larger than normal lunch crowd. "Wow," Debbie said as she, Monroe, and Herm entered the diner.

"This place is packed," Herm said, looking around for a table.

"You guys hurry up!" Juanita yelled in the direction of the kitchen. "People are getting restless out here." Walking over to the trio, Juanita eyed Monroe, but not in a *good-to-see-you* kind of way.

"Hello, Juanita," Monroe sheepishly said. "Kind of jam-packed, I see."

"No thanks to you. We can hardly keep up," she sniped. She wouldn't let it out, but she was happy for the extra business. Griping was her way of showing it.

"Then I guess I can expect some sort of compensation," Monroe said, chuckling.

"Ha!" she countered. "No. But you can expect to *not* find a table. And from what I hear, Christi's is the same."

From across the small restaurant, a man called out, "Hey, it's that lawyer, Mr. Lovett." Monroe looked in the direction of the voice. "Mr. Lovett, you guys can sit with us," the man said, waving for them to join his table.

Monroe gave Juanita a questioning look.

"Sure. Go ahead. I'll have someone find some chairs for you. But count this as your *compensation*," she said, cracking a small smile. "Now, I've got to get the judge's lunch to him. He's probably standing at his window watching for me." Then she headed to the kitchen.

Monroe, Debbie, and Herm walked over to the table amidst stares. The trio could feel all the eyes on them and tried their best to ignore them. "Hello, Mr. Lovett," he said. Offering a handshake, the man said, "I'm Pastor Keith."

"Hello," Monroe replied, returning the handshake. "This is my wife, Debbie. And this is Ed Hermann."

"Just call me Herm," Herm said politely.

"Oh, everyone around town knows who you guys are," Pastor Keith said excitedly.

Monroe looked at him and said, "Thanks for the offer." He looked at the woman sitting with Pastor Keith, and with a courteous smile. "And, who might you be?"

"Oh, I apologize. This is my wife, Barb," Keith replied. "I'm the pastor at Peregrine Community Church. You guys should come visit with us sometime."

Monroe dodged the invite. Church was the last thing on his mind right now. "Well, it's a pleasure to meet you, Keith and Barb," Monroe said with a smile.

A restaurant worker walked up with three folding chairs. "Here you go," he said, opening them. All five crowded around the table and placed their orders with the flustered waitress. Her hair kept falling into her face as she wrote down their orders.

Keith leaned across the table toward Monroe, animatedly telling him, "Do you realize the uproar you've brought to Peregrine? I mean, look around. There hasn't been this much excitement in years, shoot, for decades."

"Well, I'm just representing my client—doing my job," Monroe responded.

"So, who did it? You know,"—Keith lowered his voice— "killed the Miller girl? I mean, in your opinion?"

Debbie cut her eyes at Monroe with an anxious look. *Maybe we should have gone home to eat.*

"That's not my concern," Monroe responded. "My job is to defend my client."

Another man, an older man, walked up from behind Monroe. He had a harsh scowl on his face as he tapped Monroe on the shoulder. Monroe turned around to see who it was. "Yes?" he asked, not recognizing the man.

"You're destroying a good man. Marcus Butler has done great things for this community. You can't treat him like a, a common criminal. Like some thug. You're going to get a killer off, let that . . . that harlot go free. I sure hope you can sleep."

Debbie sat there astonished at the man's brazen attitude. *Yep. Should've gone to the house.*

Herm struggled to hold back his laughter.

Monroe listened. Once the older gentleman finished his little tirade, Monroe said, "I understand your feelings, but I'm just doing my job. And yes, I sleep just fine."

"Damn Yankee lawyer," grumbled the man as he glared at Monroe.

Monroe didn't want an argument. He had been down this road before. Ruffling people's feathers was something he had done for years. "Well, you have a nice day, sir," Monroe said, turning back to his table hosts.

The old man continued his dirty look for a couple of seconds. He then huffed and walked away.

"See," Pastor Keith said, bright-eyed. "Like I told you, you've stirred things up around here. That's the most life I've seen from that man in five years."

"You're the new town sensation, Monroe," Herm said, chortling.

"Just what I didn't want," Monroe countered. "So, you know him, Keith?" he asked, gesturing over his shoulder with his thumb.

"Oh sure. He's an inactive deacon in our church."

Debbie covered her mouth, almost spitting out the water she had just sipped. Doing her best to swallow the mouthful, she then asked, "*Deacon?*"

"Yeah . . . he wasn't always like that, though," Barb said.

"Well, he seems very active now," Monroe chuckled.

Turning to get a good look around the small diner, Monroe noticed the crowd seemed evenly split. Half glowered in his direction as they glanced up from eating their lunches. They looked away when they noticed him looking back at them.

Others offered him gentle smiles and nods of approval. *Yeah Monroe, go to a small town. Open a small law practice. Enjoy the laid-back life of a small community. Yeah, how's that working out for you?*

"Mr. Lovett? Mr. Lovett?" a young woman's voice called to him.

Lost in his introspective state, he didn't hear her. She tapped his shoulder. Turning, he recognized the face, and said, "You're that reporter from, from . . ."

"Yes, Amy Byrd from the Ledger."

"Yeah, the Ledger," Monroe said.

"Mr. Lovett, I was wondering if I might speak with you about the trial and its impact on Peregrine. It'll only take a few minutes and will really help my story."

"Well, Amy . . . right now I'm getting ready to eat my lunch. Besides, there's not much I can say, except my client is innocent of the charges levied against her."

"But, what about your questions for Marcus Butler? How do you think he fits into this case?" she asked.

Monroe looked past Amy and said while pointing, "There comes our lunch. Now, please excuse me, I'm hungry."

"But—" Amy attempted to ask again.

"But nothing," Monroe retorted. "I've given you all you're going to get from me. Now, please let me eat my lunch," Monroe said, turning around. He felt bad for being rude to her. Turning back to Amy, he said, "Look, after the trial, I will gladly sit down with you for a one-on-one interview. It's the best I can offer you."

She stood there, not happy with his terms. Wisely, she agreed and walked away.

"Well, now you've got the press on your side, Monroe," Herm said, laughing sarcastically.

Chapter 45

People were rushing back from their lunch break to get a good seat in the courtroom before the trial resumed. Those who couldn't get a seat inside endeavored for the choicest spots in the halls. An even larger crowd than earlier was gathering outside the courthouse to hear tidbits from the proceedings. No doubt, there was a buzz in the air around Peregrine. Word had spread about Butler's family secret.

Ashley entered the courtroom. Self-conscious of everyone ogling her, she walked with poise to the defense table. Sitting down, she whispered to Debbie, "I can't believe all this."

"Me neither," Debbie said. "The whole town has gone crazy. You should see outside."

Monroe made some last-minute notes as Herm sat down behind him. Amy readied her notepad and pen.

Sheriff Austin got an email. After reading it, he motioned for Deputy Reed to join him while walking over to Detective Carson in the rear of the courtroom. Carson saw Austin coming and said to the sheriff as he neared him, "Problem, Sheriff?"

"Not here," Austin said intently looking at Carson. "Let's find somewhere, less crowded." He nodded for Carson and Reed to follow.

Sque-e-e-ek as a door opened. The courtroom went silent.

Breaux glanced over his shoulder, surprised by the reaction. Julie Miller's parents were both sitting in their usual spot. Mrs. Miller sat stoic, as she struggled to hold back her emotions. Her whole world was crashing down around her.

Through the door in the corner of the courtroom, Harper's clerk entered the noiseless room followed by Judge Harper. Everyone stood up in unison. They knew the drill. "This court is now back in session," announced the clerk.

Judge Harper resumed his spot on the bench. He gaveled lightly once. Everyone was waiting for the drama to recommence. Even outside the courthouse, no one made a sound. The only sounds were the chirping of birds.

A deputy escorted Butler back to the witness stand. His expression said it—displeasure.

After finding a spot at the far end of the courthouse where no one was present, Sheriff Austin stopped and said, "This is good."

Reed glanced at Austin and then looked at Carson. "What's going on, Sheriff?" Reed asked.

"Oh, I think Carson knows," Austin answered, moving closer to the detective. Stopping a couple feet away, he stared intently into Carson's eyes.

"Don't have a clue, Sheriff," Carson said, returning the stare.

Austin held up his phone with the email opened for Reed to see it. "Read this out loud," Austin said, still glaring at Carson.

Reed focused on the email and read, "Sheriff Austin. The fingerprint you sent us is an eight-point match for Detective Benjamin Carson." Stunned, Reed slowly shifted his gaze to Carson.

Austin eased even closer to the nervous detective. He firmly whispered, "I've got the state forensics telling me you tampered with evidence, Detective."

Carson began slowly moving away from Austin. Deputy Reed moved to block his progress. He then smoothly reached over and removed Carson's pistol from his belt.

"You're under arrest, Mr. Carson," Austin said, grabbing Carson's own handcuffs and then placing them on him.

A few people down the hall saw the arrest and began spreading the news to others.

"Let's go," Austin said, pulling Carson's arm.

Dropping his head, Carson sighed heavily as the reality of his crime flooded over him.

Harper glanced over at Butler. Taking a deep breath, the judge said, "Mr. Lovett, you may continue your questioning of the witness."

"More like an interrogation," complained Butler under his breath.

Harper looked at him, "I'll advise the witness to keep his opinions to himself."

Butler returned a single indignant nod.

Monroe rose and return to his former position in front of the table. He peeked at his recently handwritten notes, and he said, "Mr. Butler, I know these questions must be hard for you, but believe me when I say, they are necessary if we are going to prove the innocence of your daughter-in-law, the defendant."

"That's your opinion," Butler growled. "Didn't she sign a confession?"

"Yeah, everyone keeps telling me that. And that's what bothers me," Monroe replied.

Rising to his feet, Breaux said, "Objection, Your Honor. Please instruct the defense to only ask questions."

"I've warned both of you already," Harper said. "Mr. Lovett, just ask your questions. And Mr. Butler you answer the questions. Understand?"

Butler responded with a scowl.

Monroe nodded he understood. "Yes, Your Honor," He removed three copies of a photo from a folder. He handed the first to Judge Harper, the second to Butler, and the third to the jury.

"Mr. Butler, can you tell the court the identity of the man sitting with you at the Pearl Café in Jackson, the setting of this photo?"

"Your Honor, the prosecution would like to see the photo," Breaux requested.

"I apologize, Mr. Breaux," Monroe said, removing the fourth photo from the folder. With a wry smile, he handed it to Breaux.

"Thanks," Breaux said, snatching the photo from Monroe.

"Mr. Butler?" Monroe pressed.

"I don't know," Butler answered. He shrugged, "I have lunch with several people."

"I didn't say it was a lunch," Monroe said.

Butler set the photo on the rail in front of him saying, "Not sure."

"Not sure? Unsure? Or unwilling to say?" Monroe asked, raising his arms to his side.

"Your Honor, the defense is badgering the witness," Breaux interjected.

"Your Honor," Monroe said, "this witness is not here to testify on behalf of my client but to offer testimony proving the innocence of my client. Permission to treat the witness as hostile?"

"The prosecution's objection is overruled. The defense's request is granted."

"Mr. Butler, is this Joe Galliard in the photo?" Monroe asked.

"You tell me?" Butler responded.

"Your Honor—?"

"Mr. Butler, answer the question," Harper ordered.

"Yes. Yes, it's Joe Galliard. So, what? What does it matter?"

"Oh, it matters, Mr. Butler," Monroe said. Before another warning came from the bench, he asked, "What is Joe Galliard's type of business?"

"He operates a . . . a gentleman's— a club—Smitty's," Butler answered.

"Do you know of anyone who does or did work at Smitty's?"

"Maybe."

"Yes or no, sir."

"Yes," Butler answered with a quick look at Ashley.

"Who?" Monroe insisted.

Butler remained silent.

"Who, Mr. Butler?" Monroe urged. "You have to answer the question."

"Ashley," he said, pointing at her.

"And?"

Butler squirmed. "Julie. Julie Miller," Butler answered, resuming his gnawing of the inside of his cheek.

"Why were you meeting with Galliard, Mr. Butler?"

"Personal."

"Did you ask him to kidnap, interrogate, and beat me?"

"Ob-jection!" Breaux exclaimed, jumping to his feet. "The question has nothing to do with the current case, Judge."

"I'll withdraw the question," Monroe said. Nevertheless, he had made his point.

Breaux sat back down as people in the gallery and the jury looked around at each other, confused by Monroe's question.

Butler fidgeted in his seat again as he leaned his head back, taking a deep breath.

"Mr. Butler, I am prepared to call a witness, the owner of the Pearl Café, who will testify he saw you on more than one occasion giving Mr. Galliard a briefcase. Were you giving money to Mr. Galliard for information?"

Butler leaned back in his chair and crossed his arms. He would not look in Monroe's direction. He reached up and gave a squeeze and rub to his nostrils, drawing his hand over his mouth and down his chin. He crossed his arms again and remained silent, exuding defiance.

"Your Honor, please instruct the witness to answer the question," Monroe requested while reaching for several sheets of paper, fastened with a large metal binder clip. Before Harper ruled, he asked, "Mr. Butler, we have your financial records. Did you buy information about Julie Miller?"

"Objection, Your Honor," Breaux hollered, leaping to his feet again.

Butler became red-faced as he sat there listening. His anger was evident. Fueled by Monroe's questions and his own pride, his blood pressure soared. His personal life and family secrets were now public knowledge.

"Overruled."

"Your Honor, the defense also requests Mr. Butler be fingerprinted, and those prints be compared to the prints on the shotgun used in this murder," Monroe requested, standing with one hand on his hip holding his suit coat back and pointing at Butler with the other hand, flapping the bank records for all to see.

Butler's rage was beginning to reach a flashpoint. He was wringing his hands even more than earlier. Beads of sweat were popping out on his forehead and upper lip. Feeling strangled, he reached up and loosened his tie.

"Your Honor," Breaux declared, waving his hands in the air. "Your Honor, the defense has lost his mind. His demands upon this court are preposterous, at best. Maybe he has forgotten who is in charge here?"

Butler's handwringing morphed to him gripping the arms of the chair, squeezing them—white-knuckled. A vein was visibly bulging from his forehead as he was now sweating.

Judge Harper watched and listened to the two attorneys going at each other like two pit bulls. Part of him wanted to stop the whole fiasco and declare a mistrial. However, down deep, he wanted to let this play out.

"And the prosecution's handling of this case has been laughable from the beginning as his office, along with the Lane County Sheriff's Department, have tried to railroad my client," Monroe said, as the gallery and jury watched like spectators at a tennis match.

Outside, people were rushing to the courthouse to get a glimpse of the show inside.

Wham! Harper gaveled. "Enough, you two. Mr. Breaux, sit down and shut up. Mr. Lovett, continue."

Dropping into his chair, Breaux was perceptibly humiliated and upset.

Tossing the bank records onto the table, Monroe asked rather forcefully, "Two hundred and fifty thousand dollars, Mr. Butler. Where did it go?"

Radiating rage, Butler indignantly answered, "Not sure. Business."

"Business?" Monroe asked, removing a sheet of paper from a folder. Holding it up, he said, "Here is evidence, Mr. Butler, a sworn statement that you met, on several occasions, at the Pearl Café with Joe Galliard, to which Mr. Galliard confirmed in earlier testimony." Increasing in loudness, Monroe asked, "Can you please explain to the court why you were meeting with Mr. Galliard? And, why the two of you had a loud argument the last time you met? Was it about the money?"

"I renew my objection," Breaux stated. "What does any of this have to do with this case? The defense is only dragging this witness's life through the mud."

Butler, red-faced, even sweatier, and incensed, gritting his teeth, rose to his feet shouting and pointing his quivering finger at Ashley, "She signed . . . a confession!"

Several people in the back began yelling, "She's guilty! She's guilty! She's guilty!"

Becoming red-faced herself, Ashley wanted to crawl under the desk. Debbie put her arm around her.

Herm looked around in amusement as Sheriff Austin directed several deputies to move toward those chanting.

Sma-ack! Sma-ack! Smack! "Order! Order in the court!" Harper hollered repeatedly. *Smack! Smack!* "I said, order!" Judge Harper whacked the bench with his gavel once, so hard, it cracked the head of the gavel. His court was nearly out of control. Rising to his feet, and pointing with his gavel, the normally even-tempered judge roared, "Remove those people from my courtroom!" The deputies did as ordered.

With courtroom quiet again, Monroe said calmly, "Your Honor, the defense requests the witness's last statement be stricken from the record."

Breaux began to speak, but before he could, Judge Harper, who was still standing, replied, "So moved. The jury will disregard the witness's last statement." Sitting down he said, "There will be no more outbreaks in this courtroom. Do you hear me? One more uproar and I will empty this courtroom."

Butler sat down. His breathing became heavier by the second. His nostrils flared with each breath. He could feel all those eyes focused on him as the perspiration poured down his face.

"Mr. Butler, the money?" Monroe pushed. "Did you pay for information concerning your wife's illegitimate daughter, Julie Miller? The same Julie Miller who was sleeping with your son?"

"Objection!" Breaux bellowed.

"Overruled." Harper then turned to Butler and said, "The witness *will* answer—"

Butler rose to his feet again, shaking from head to toe as he tightened his body in rage. His face was blood red and his eyes bulging. Looking as if he might explode, he started yelling, "I did it! I did it! I killed that whore! I killed Julie Miller! That half-breed child of adultery was having sex with my son, her half-brother. No—!"

All eyes locked onto Marcus Butler, standing, trembling with rage.

Harper's jaw dropped.

Ashley locked her unbelieving stare on him.

"I could no longer allow it," Butler said, staring at Monroe, who stood, happy to let the man speak. "I told Junior to get out of the house when I caught, caught them—the boy didn't have a clue about who she was."

Harper and Breaux could not believe what they were hearing. Each sat flummoxed, dazed. Harper wanted to stop him, but couldn't bring himself to do so. He did muster up enough composure to say, "Mr. Butler, maybe you should speak with an attorney."

"Don't want no *damn* lawyer," Butler snapped.

"It is your right," Harper told him.

Ignoring the judge, waving him off, Butler continued his rant. He wasn't looking at any one person. It was more like he was watching a movie play out in front of him. "I told that whore," Butler said, briefly shifting his gaze to the Millers, "to stop seeing Junior. But she said, 'No.' She laughed at me. Dared me to tell Marcus Jr., and to tell her parents. Junior had no clue what she was talking about, as we stood there in the bedroom, both of them half-naked. That's when I saw the shotgun. Propped inside the closet. I grabbed it and pointed it at her."

"What about Junior? Did he—?" Monroe asked.

"Told him to get out. To leave the house."

Ashley looked on, her mouth wide open, in total disbelief at what she was hearing.

"What happened next?" Monroe asked.

Butler remained focused, as he answered, "Dared me to do it. 'Go ahead old man,' she said. 'You ain't got the guts to shoot your half-nigger step-daughter, do you?' She mocked me. *Me*, Marcus Butler."

"What did you do next," Monroe asked, taking a couple steps toward Butler.

"Then I pumped a shell into the chamber. She looked into my eyes and realized I was serious. That's when she began begging me not to kill her . . . that little bitch begged for her life as she backed away."

"And," Monroe asked.

No one in the gallery made a sound. They all sat still watching, listening.

"She pleaded with me, 'No . . . Please!' as she held her hands up. Now I had her attention. She begged, 'Why are you doing this? We can talk. Sure, let's talk.'

"I told her, 'You. Have. Ruined. Ruined my family!'" Butler said, waggling his head. "She said, 'I'll l-leave. Go away—yeah—far away. You'll never see me again. Please don't kill me.' She began to cry, to weep like a baby. She said that she never thought it would go this far. I laughed at her and said, 'Too late.' I gripped the shotgun even tighter and told her, 'No. No, I'm going to make sure I never see you again.'" Butler paused and stared into space.

Everyone in the courtroom could see Butler's rage as he relived that moment. Judge Harper could not believe what he was hearing. Part of Ashley was happy that people could see the man she knew, although she was mostly sad for Julie and what she had lived through. Like her, Julie's life had been a mess.

"Mr. Butler?" Monroe asked.

Butler slowly looked at him.

"How did Ms. Miller react?"

"She was trembling, clutching her fists tight. Scared, she begged, "No . . . Please . . . I don't want to—

"I pulled the trigger. Sh—she fell to the floor. I could see the life draining from her body. She was alive, but just barely. For a moment, I thought of Darlene. This was her daughter," Butler said, almost sounding remorseful. Then his tone reverted to anger, and he said, "But then I remembered what that little bitch had done to my family."

"Her? What *she* had done?" Monroe asked.

"Yes. Her! I couldn't let that secret out. I pumped another round into the chamber. I shot her again. And again. And again."

Everyone in the courtroom jump as Butler described the shots. They watched in horror as they listen to the pillar of the community confess his heinous act.

"That's when I walked over and—put the last one in her face. The sight of her disgusted me."

"Then what," Monroe asked him.

"Looking at the shotgun, I saw it was empty. Blood was everywhere. Standing there, I realized what I had done. I became nauseated, almost throwing up. Nervous and wanting to get out fast, I went into the closet and attempted to remove my fingerprints from the gun by wiping it with a nearby shirt. Then pushed it under some hanging clothes."

"Why kill her? Couldn't you have—?" Monroe asked, stunned by what he was hearing.

"I didn't want to at first. I went to talk. But then, then she just laughed, *laughed* at me. No one laughs at Marcus Butler. Not like she did."

Harper, Breaux, and everyone else hung on his every word, in aghast, as he recounted the murder of Julie Miller. Butler scanned the courtroom. By now, he didn't care. The truth was out, ugly as it may be, and he couldn't—wouldn't stop it. He slowly sat down.

Someone in the gallery uttered, "Psychopath."

"The barrels, Mr. Butler?" insisted Monroe. "Did you switch the barrels on this shotgun," he asked, gesturing to the murder weapon.

"Barrels? I didn't switch any barrels. No. I told Ben to do it."

Breaux turned to get a look at Detective Carson. He was absent from the courtroom. Not seeing him, Breaux scanned the room for Sheriff Austin, but he too was gone. *Why aren't they here?* He turned back to listen to Butler.

"Are you happy, Mr. Lovett?" Butler asked. "Are you? My family is ruined, and it's your fault. It's your fault," Butler bellowed, pointing his trembling finger at Monroe. "Everything would have worked out. But you—you . . ."

Everyone in the court sat still, their mouths agape, watching Butler's actions.

"No, Mr. Butler. It's your fault," Monroe replied as he pointed his finger back at Butler. "You have no one to blame but yourself, sir. You committed murder in trying to cover a sin and disgrace—a simple family secret. You should have faced the truth. Accepted your daughter-in-law, and dealt openly and honestly with your son and stepdaughter. But no, you chose to cover-up your secrets, using deceit, and hiding from the truth. You chose murder and intimidation. Dragging your family and friends down with you," Monroe told him, staring down the guilt-ridden Butler.

Breaux considered an objection but changed his mind as he tried to comprehend what he was hearing.

As the truth sank deep into his soul, Butler slumped back into the witness chair and continued, broken in spirit, and said, his lip starting to quiver, "All I saw was a problem, not a person—she was threatening to expose my, my. . ." With anger returning to his face, he sat up straight and said, "I just couldn't take it any longer. I couldn't take it any longer!" Butler dropped his face into his palms and began weeping. His crying was the only sound heard in the courtroom, in the whole courthouse. Through his sobbing, he said, "Now . . . now, my wife, she's left me. My son, he's . . . he's gone into hiding."

Monroe eased back to his own chair. Before he sat down, he said, "Your Honor, the defense . . . rests. And I renew my request for all charges against my client to be dropped and Mrs. Butler receives the justice she's due."

Harper looked at Breaux. He asked in a rather shaky tone, "Does the prosecution wish to cross-examine the witness?"

Breaux, stunned, rose slowly to his feet. Puzzled, and a little unsure, he shifted his look to Harper, then to Monroe, and finally to Butler. "Umm . . ." he said as a multitude of questions raced through his mind. All he could muster was, "Your Honor, Judge Harper, the prosecution agrees with Mr. Lovett's motion. That all charges against the defendant, Ashley Butler, be dropped. And that her confession be withdrawn from the evidence."

Ashley stared at Judge Harper as she waited for his answer. Her wait seemed like an eternity.

Judge Harper, still trying to comprehend what had just occurred, looked at Marcus Butler and replied, "I have never, in all of my years on the bench, witnessed such an unthinkable, unimaginable scene as I—we all, have just observed. I am shaken, shaken to my core, Mr. Butler. My advice to you is, get a lawyer, a damn good lawyer." Harper glanced at Breaux but said nothing. His rebuke would have to wait. Next, the judge shifted his gaze to Ashley. She sat motionless, anxious, waiting for him to rule. Both Monroe and Debbie held her hands. Herm was leaning forward with one hand on her shoulder and the other on Monroe's.

The only sounds heard were breathing. If the judge agreed, the trial was over. The jurors would gladly accept him deciding.

"Mrs. Butler," Judge Harper said sincerely, "please accept the apologies of this court and all it has put you through. The justice system let you down. All charges against the defendant are dismissed." She struggled to contain her excitement, as did Monroe, Debbie, and Herm. Harper said, "Ashley Butler, you are free to go. I hope and pray you can somehow find a way to put this all behind you." Harper gave a slow shake of his head, took a deep breath, and lifted his gavel. With one final slap of his gavel, he declared, as a piece of it broke off, "The jury is dismissed. These-proceedings-are-over. Court is adjourned."

Immediately, the court erupted in a loud uproar. This time Harper didn't care. It was over.

Ashley leaped to her feet, elated. Turning to Monroe as he stood up, she reached up and gave him a big hug. "Thank you. Thank you. Thank you," she said as tears of joy rolled down her cheeks, framing her beaming smile.

Debbie was next on Ashley's list to receive a hug. She clung to Debbie like she would a mother. Debbie looked at Monroe, who had a smile of relief and satisfaction on his face.

Herm patted Monroe on the shoulder, offering his congratulations to him.

Monroe looked at him and said, "Good job, Herm. Good job."

Herm leaned over and whispered, "Austin arrested Carson."

Monroe gave him a wink and thumbs up.

While the defense team rejoiced, Breaux motioned for a deputy to come over.

"Yes, Mr. Breaux?" the deputy asked.

With a head gesture in Butler's direction, Breaux said, "Take Marcus Butler into custody."

Obeying Breaux's request, the deputy retrieved two additional officers and did as told. They handcuffed Butler for all to see. Butler didn't seem to notice the cuffs as the deputy placed them on his wrists.

Pandemonium soon became silence as people perceived the arrest of Marcus Butler. Here was this man—a man who had provided jobs and, at times, used bullying tactics to get his way—humiliated for all to see. Word of Butler's confession soon spread through the small Mississippi town. The excitement that once enveloped the quaint town was, in an instant, transformed into somberness.

Pushing their way through the crowd, the three deputies ushered the formerly influential man through the courtroom. Sure, they could take him out the back door, but they too had just listened to his admittance. No, it seemed more appropriate to parade Marcus Butler, a constrained man, through the mass of people, out the front door, and down the main steps of the courthouse for all to see.

Not far behind the handcuffed Butler, Monroe and Debbie led Ashley from the courtroom and out the front of the courthouse. Ashley beamed as she walked outside to freedom.

Having retreated to his chambers, Judge Harper was sitting on the couch attempting to come to grips with what he had witnessed.

Knock-Knock

"Come," Harper said.

As the door opened, Sheriff Austin walked in and said, "Hey, Judge."

"Sheriff, come on in." Harper pointed in the direction of the courtroom and said, "I needed to get away from, from—"

"Yeah, me too."

"Is there something I can help you with, Sheriff?" Harper wasn't in much of a mood for conversation.

"You're not going to believe this."

"Now what?"

"I got a text from a Highway Patrol officer I know. Joe Galliard was involved in a single-car accident on Highway 32. He was found dead in the vehicle. Get this. Junior's cell phone was in the car. Explains the text messages."

"And the burnt body, I hope."

"Me too."

"Our county?" Harper asked.

"No. He was in Porter County."

"That will be Judge Tucker's case."

"Seems odd to me, don't you think?"

"This whole ordeal seems odd to me, Sheriff."

"Yeah, I guess you're right, Judge. There's more."

"More? I'm not sure I can handle more, Sheriff."

"Carson. I arrested him."

"You did?"

"For tampering with evidence. But I'm sure the list of charges will increase. Sent the print on the barrel to the state for them to check it. Got an email before court resumed. A near perfect match to Carson's."

"What made you check it?"

"Taking care of my department, Judge," Austin said with a grin.

Out front of the courthouse, as Butler was waiting to get into a patrol car, Amy, the reporter from the Ledger, yelled over the clamor of the onlookers, "Mr. Butler, who do you think killed your son?"

Word was now out. Someone had leaked the news. All eyes turned to her and then back to Butler. He did not hear the question, only his name.

"What?" he asked.

With a blanket of silence covering the former chaos of voices, Butler heard her just fine when Amy asked again, "Who do you think killed Marcus Jr?"

Like a punch to the gut, Butler melted like butter on a hot summer day when he heard her question. Two deputies had to clutch him under his arms to keep him from falling to the ground. Butler said nothing as he panted under the emotional pain and grief. Just then, a patrol car pulled up, and the deputies placed Butler in the back seat.

Ashley also heard the news of her husband's death. Her glee of regaining freedom, in an instant, turned to grief. Tears of sorrow replaced tears of joy. Ashley's legs became rubbery as she began to break down. The emotional roller coaster was screaming fast down its largest, steepest hill, and she was in the back seat being jerks as the emotional ride yanked her along.

Monroe and Debbie took hold of her and led her away from the hoard of people who were now staring at her.

Amy, the reporter, headed straight for her. Herm blocked her, as Monroe and Debbie absconded with Ashley back into the now empty courthouse. Amy wrote in large letters at the top of her notepad, "Article Title – Butler's Justice."

The three walked hastily through the building, Monroe assuring the grieving widow, "Ashley, we are here for you."

"We're going to help you through this," Debbie said comfortingly.

Ashley did not respond. Only sobbing moans of heartache came from her.

Debbie checked a door. It was unlocked. It opened to a small empty conference room. They rushed inside, closing the door behind them. Herm, not far behind, saw them and stood guard outside.

Debbie assisted Ashley into a chair. She told her, "Ashley, we're so sorry. You can count on Monroe and me, okay?"

Ashley wept.

Chapter 46

The trial was over. As the days passed by, Peregrine began to return to normal. Monroe, Debbie, and Herm were sitting in Christi's having a cup of coffee. Christi walked over to them. "Is there anything else I can get ya'll?"

Both Monroe and Debbie shook their heads, no. Herm answered, "I'd like one of those *delicious* cupcakes you make."

"You got it. I'll go get you one," she said, and then scampered away.

"So, what did you two do over the weekend? Go out and celebrate?" Herm asked.

"Sort of. We started to go back to Tony B's, but decided to go to this other place we heard about, Burgers and Blues," Debbie answered.

"Best hamburger I've ever had. I mean the meat, oh—" Monroe said, rubbing his belly.

"I've heard about that place," Herm said.

"Yeah, and the music was nice," Debbie said, leaning on Monroe's arm. "We'll definitely go back."

"You hear about Carson?" Herm asked.

"Just that he was arrested," Monroe answered.

"He confessed to everything. Breaux is seeking charges," Herm said.

"Must be why Austin wants to see me," Monroe replied. "Maybe he has something on my case."

"I sure hope so," Debbie said.

Each of them took sips from their coffee. Herm did a scan for the whereabouts of his cupcake.

"How about you, Herm? What did ole Herm do? Sit around the house all weekend eating pizza?" Monroe asked.

"Had a date."

"A date?" Debbie asked, excited.

"Yep. A woman named Wanda Dale," Herm said with a sparkle in his eye.

"Ah . . . did you see that ?" Debbie asked, nudging Monroe.

"See what?" Herm replied.

"That little twinkle in your eye when you said her name," Debbie said, pointing at Herm. His reaction told her everything. "Oh, you like her."

As much as he tried, Herm could not hide his boyish grin.

"Dale? Of the Dale Dairy family?" Monroe asked.

"Yep. Her late husband started the dairy," Herm answered. "He died a few years ago leaving Wanda a boatload, I mean a *boatload* of money. Word has it he was a tightwad. Now, she's got it all, and he's well . . ."

"Dead," Monroe said.

"How was the date?" Debbie asked with a look that said *give me details*.

"We went out to eat, and everything was going great. Then, she started to remove her silverware from her napkin and dropped her fork."

"No . . ." Debbie exclaimed, putting her hand over her mouth to hide her laughter.

"Yep. She bent over to pick it up."

Both Monroe and Debbie start laughing, remembering Herm's last date, and the whole wig incident.

"And . . . nothing happened. No wig. Everything went great. We're going out again this weekend," Herm said. He stretched his neck to look around. "Where's my cupcake. Christi always tells me she's going to get me one, but never does. I don't think she really makes cupcakes."

Finishing their coffee, Monroe said, "I need to head up to the office. Ashley's stopping by later."

"I'm done," Debbie said.

The three got up and left Christi's, but without Herm's cupcake. Before reaching the staircase, Monroe heard, "Wells, hello Mr. Lovett."

Turning, the trio saw Jack standing, having just entered the building. "Hey, Jack. How are you?" Monroe asked.

"Hello, Jack," both Debbie and Herm said.

"Oh, I'm doing just fine. Yes, sir. Ole Jack id just fine," Jack said with his toothy smile. "Mr. Lovett, I told you, did I?"

Unsure of what Jack was alluding to, Monroe asked, "What's that Jack?"

"Who did it, remember?" Jack asked, laughing a little.

"Oh yeah. Yes, you did," Monroe said, remembering their sidewalk chat. Gesturing up the stairs, Monroe said, "Jack we need to go upstairs, but would you like to have a cup of coffee tomorrow morning here at Christi's?"

"Oh, that would be great, Mr.—"

"Monroe, Jack. Just call me Monroe."

"Okay, Mr. Lovett. How about eight?"

"Eight it is, Jack. I'll see you then," Monroe said, turning to go upstairs.

"Bye Jack," Debbie said.

"See you then, Mr. Lovett. Good to see you, Mrs. Debbie. And you too, Mr. Hermann," Jack said, walking into Christi's.

Herm gave Jack a friendly pat on the shoulder as he walked by him. "Good to see you, Jack."

The three of them went upstairs. "Something's wrong," Monroe whispered as he came to an abrupt stop after entering the office.

"What is it?" Herm asked, lowering his voice as his cop antenna went up.

"My office door,"—Monroe said, pointing down the hall— "was closed before. Now, it's open."

"But you had to unlock the door," Debbie remarked in a breathy voice.

"I know," Monroe said, easing down the hall with Herm and Debbie just behind him. Debbie was wondering why Herm was not taking the lead since he was a cop. They all listened for noise, but it was quiet. Of course, the creaking of the three of them walking on the wood floors would have alerted someone.

Peeking into the office, Monroe quietly said, "Nothing appears to be disturbed."

After checking the office, they didn't find anything missing. Monroe sat down in his desk chair. "What's this?" he asked suspiciously, seeing a small note on his desk with a handwritten message.

"What's what?" Herm asked.

Debbie walked over to get a better look.

Monroe lifted the small piece of paper from the top of his desk. He read aloud, "Until next time. F. R. PS. Darlene."

"Darlene? Why Darlene?" Herm asked."

"Do you think—? No," Debbie said.

"Think what?" Monroe asked. He thought for a minute and then, shaking his finger at her, said, "You might be right. Just hold that thought."

"Hold what thought?" Herm asked, confused. "What is this, husband-wife telepathy?"

"F. R . . .? F. R . . .?" Monroe muttered, thinking hard. Holding the note, he was rapidly flapping it in the air as he combed his memories. "No. No way. It couldn't be," he said as he stopped fluttering the note.

"Couldn't be what?" Herm asked, appearing clueless.

Snatching his keys from his desk, Monroe unlocked the bottom drawer. Reaching in, he removed the letter he had placed in there a few weeks before. After unfolding the letter, he studied the name. "Look at this," he said, laying the note on top of the letter to compare.

Herm and Debbie moved close to get a look.

"Yeah?" Debbie said.

"F. R., Fichard Roueché. It's the same person," Monroe said, his finger on the name.

"That's a stretch, isn't it?" Herm responded.

"Is it?" Monroe replied. "Look at the F's and the R's."

Herm bent over so he could get a better look. "Dang . . . They're identical."

Monroe thought for a moment. "Debbie, work your magic on my laptop and see if you can find out how Fichard Roueché died."

"Died?" Herm asked.

"Yes, I believe the original Roueché is dead," Monroe answered.

With a small wave of his hand, Herm said, "Okay, I'll play along."

Opening the laptop, Debbie began searching the internet while Monroe and Herm continued to talk.

"Just bear with me," Monroe said. "Want a drink?"

"Sure," Herm answered.

"Yeah, me too," Debbie said, typing away.

"No, you search," Monroe told her. She briefly cut her eyes at him as he walked to the cabinet. He poured two glasses of bourbon. After he had handed Herm his drink, Monroe sat back down as he waited on Debbie.

"Got it," exclaimed Debbie.

"And?" Monroe asked.

"Burned," she said. Reading the article aloud, she summarized it for them, "It says here his body, Roueché's, was found severely burned. DNA and dental records were used to determine identity."

331

"So, our guy stole Roueché's identity," Monroe surmised, slowly swirling his drink.

She wrinkled her face as she leaned back. "Eww . . ."

"What?" Monroe asked, setting his drink on his desk.

"His genitals were cut off and left on the bed. It says they were unburned."

"Yep, same guy," Herm said, taking a sip.

"But, why didn't they find this when they were looking for him?" Debbie asked, quickly taking hold of Monroe's drink. She took a sip and set it back.

"Because they were looking for someone still living," Herm answered. "When is the article dated?"

"Three years ago," she answered.

"There you go," Herm said.

"He's been working this for a while," Monroe said, picking up his glass of bourbon. He saw Debbie's lipstick she had left and smiled a little.

"There's more," Debbie said, scrolling down the page. Something caught her eye, and she said, "Huh?"

"What is it?" Monroe asked.

"There's a photo of the man believed to have committed the crime. The name under it is Félix Roche.

"Félix Roche?" Monroe asked, leaning forward.

"What is it, Monroe?" Herm asked.

"That's the name of Julie Miller's real father."

"*Holy* . . ." Herm said. "Darlene and that guy—"

"So, that means Ashley's uncle was Julie's *father*?" Debbie asked.

"It does seem so," Monroe said.

Debbie looked back at the screen and said, "The last update on the article says his whereabouts are still unknown." She turned the screen around for Monroe and Herm to see.

"See, he's black," Monroe said.

"But Ashley's not," Herm replied.

"Does it say anything about his family?" Monroe asked Debbie.

Rotating the screen back around, she quickly scanned the article. Debbie said, "It says authorities spoke to his step-sister. Dorothy Xavier."

"And that would be Ashley's mom," Monroe said.

"Explains the race difference," Herm said, finishing his drink. Setting the glass down, a questioning expression came over his face as he asked, "But why did he risk being recognized by Darlene?"

"That is weird," Monroe said. Remembering Butler's testimony, he then pointed at Herm, and said, "Wait a minute. Didn't Marcus say while he was ranting, that Darlene had left him?"

"You're right," Herm replied. "Do you think she and Roche—?"

"But would she run off with the man who killed her son?" Monroe asked.

"But I thought Galliard killed him?" Debbie asked. "In her mind, he was the bad guy, not Roche. Besides, all she knows is Galliard and her husband killed people, not Roche."

"Debbie makes a good point," Herm said.

"Does the article say anything else?" Monroe asked.

"Says Dorothy hasn't had any contact with Roche for more than ten years," Debbie said. Quickly scanning further down the article, she said, "You're not going to believe this."

"What?" Monroe asked.

"It says here, in Roueché's obit, that his only heir was a cousin. Roy Galliard."

"How much you want to bet that Roy's son was our own Joe Galliard?" Herm asked rhetorically.

Throwing back the remainder of his drink, Monroe wiped his mouth and said, "This is starting to make sense now. In a weird, sort of, kind of way."

"And, you would be correct," Debbie said. "Did a quick search on Joe Galliard. It says his father's name was Roy. There's an article in the Ledger from two years ago," she said, clicking the link. Both Monroe and Herm waited for her. After a fast perusal, she said, "Apparently, Roy Galliard was found dead in his home with three gunshot wounds to his chest and one to the head."

"Does it say anything more?" Monroe asked.

"Hold on, I'm reading," Debbie answered.

"Guess she told you," Herm said, chuckling.

"Listen to this," Debbie said. "He had served three stints in prison. He was a known gambler. It says the paper made numerous attempts to speak with Roy's estranged son, Joe Galliard, but he refused to speak with them."

"We should give this to Breaux," Monroe said, leaning back in his chair. "Man, think about it, Roche got his revenge on Butler. He walked away with the two hundred and fifty thousand dollars he extorted from the man who killed his daughter, and possibly slipped away with his wife."

"And Butler confessed in front of everyone," Debbie said.

"Plus, he killed the only man who can finger him for any of it," Herm said.

"You think he killed Galliard?" Debbie asked.

"Oh yeah," Herm answered. "Odds-on, both of them. Roche kills anyone he deems necessary."

"But we have a face and name now," Monroe said.

"But why?" Herm asked. "That question just will not go away."

"I've got a theory," Monroe said.

Herm gestured for Monroe to explain.

"I see it like this. Darlene Butler somehow figures out who Julie is. She contacts Roche. Who knows, maybe the two of them stayed in contact over the years. Darlene tells him where she's working and that's where he meets Galliard."

"It's a small world," Herm said.

"For him? Yes," Monroe said. "But in the process, Darlene enlightens him regarding her daughter-in-law's past."

"And he begins putting two and two together and realizes he's Ashley's uncle," Debbie said.

"So, he takes the *name* of the man who *molested* Ashley?" Herm asked.

"Yes. Why not? He's dead," Monroe replied. "It's not that uncommon. Ashley didn't know the real Roueché's name. And it meant nothing to Julie. Did anyone dig into Roche's past? No."

"There was no need to," Herm said.

"Right. His secret was safe . . . until now," Monroe said.

"I buy it," Debbie said.

"You'll buy anything he says," retorted Herm. "He's your husband."

She shot a playful dirty look at him.

"Do you realize the odds of something like this—? I mean, for him to—"

"There's probably something we're not seeing," Monroe said. "The only thing I can figure is after he found out Ashley's last name, he knew. He didn't want his own daughter sleeping with his niece's husband."

Debbie reached over and picked up the note. "What do you think 'Until next time' means?"

"Beats me," Monroe answered.

"Let's hope there ain't no next time," Herm said. "I hope they find this lunatic."

"I agree," she said.

Herm popped to his feet declaring, "*Dadgummit!*"

Startled, Monroe asked, "What?"

"My cupcake. You know . . . the last time I asked Christi for a cupcake, she never brought me one. And she's done it again. I'm going to get my cupcake."

Monroe and Debbie watched Herm leave, both laughing as he stormed from the office.

Chapter 47

Putting away some files from the case, Debbie asked, "You going to tell Ashley about what we were discussing?"

"Nope," Monroe answered. "If she asks, then I will. But that girl's been through enough," he said, placing the note in the envelope with the letter and locking them in his desk.

"What time is she coming?" Debbie asked, closing the box.

"Any time now," Monroe answered, glancing at the clock.

"Hello?" Ashley called out.

"Well, speak of the girl," Debbie said.

"Come on back, Ashley," Monroe said.

"Hello Ashley, "Debbie said.

Monroe walked over to welcome Ashley. Unexpectedly, she gave Monroe a daughter-like hug. He returned the hug while looking at Debbie with a puzzling appearance. Debbie smiled at him, thinking since they didn't have children of their own, *He'd be a good dad.*

After the warm embrace, Monroe kindly said to Ashley, "Have a seat, young lady."

Instead, she walked over and gave Debbie a hug. Stepping back Ashley said, "I just love you two. Ya'll help me more than you know." She then sat down.

"How are you doing, Ashley?" Monroe asked, walking to his desk chair.

"Better. I've been taking care of Junior's—" she said, choking a little on her words, her face showing her grief.

"It'll take time," Monroe said. "You've been through a lot."

"I know. I just thought after everything . . . well, I still miss Junior in some sort of *weird* way."

"That's understandable, sweetie. It's not weird," Debbie said caringly. "You'll never fully get over him, but after some time, you'll work through it and move forward with your life."

"Have you made any plans?" Monroe asked.

"Think I'm gonna leave Mississippi. Too many bad memories. Maybe move up north. A new beginning. Maybe go to college. Billy wasn't thrilled to hear it."

"Try Ohio," Debbie said. "I think you would love it up around the lake."

"Ohio sounds nice," Ashley said.

"Debbie's got family there. I'm sure they'd be happy to help you get settled," Monroe suggested.

"Sure. I have a niece, Amanda. I think the two of you would hit it off," Debbie told her.

"Well, I have some other things I need to do, but I've got a question for you. Mr. Lovett, can you help me with some estate planning before I leave here?"

"Sure," Monroe answered, shrugging with a nod.

"Good. I also wanted to give you this," she said, handing an envelope to Monroe.

"What's this?" he asked.

"Payment for—"

"Ashley, I said you didn't owe me anything."

"I know, but now I have access to the bank accounts, and Junior's life insurance was well, let's just say—I'm set. His dad took it out on him. And when we got married, Junior made me the beneficiary. Didn't tell Mr. Butler. Bet he'd be mad now. Anyway, what ya'll did for me . . . you're worth every penny," she said with a smile.

"It was our pleasure to help you," Debbie said.

"You believed me. That meant so much. I don't know if you remember, Mr. Lovett, but you told me to trust God?"

Monroe nodded yes.

"Well, anyway, I decided to do that. I put my trust in God. If it wasn't for Jesus, well . . . I don't know—he gave me the strength to trust you."

"We're happy for you, Ashley," Monroe said, smiling.

Standing, Ashley pointed to the envelope and said, "Don't look at it until after I leave your office. And no, I won't take it back. But you have to promise something."

"What's that?" Monroe asked.

"Do something nice for Mrs. Debbie."

"Thank you, Ashley," Debbie said.

Strolling toward the door, Ashley said, "I'll call later to set up an appointment for help with that estate stuff. Ohio, I'll give it some thought. Maybe get your niece's info."

"Sounds good," Monroe said.

"I'll have it for you, sweetie," Debbie said.

She took a step through the doorway and then stopped. Turning around, Ashley stood still, looking at the two of them.

"Yes, Ashley? Forget something?" Monroe asked.

"You know, I've never really had a momma and daddy, but if I did . . . I'd want them to be just like the two of you."

Monroe and Debbie were unsure of how to react. They both looked at each other. Debbie became teary-eyed. Monroe humbly said, "Ashley, thank you."

Through her watery eyes, Debbie said, "Ashley, that's the sweetest thing anyone's ever said to us."

"Well, I mean it. I really do. I'm glad I trusted you," she said. Ashley then rushed over to Debbie, wrapping her arms around her neck and squeezing. Debbie hugged her back and gave her a soft kiss on her cheek. Slowly backing away from Ashley, Debbie wiped a tear from her cheek.

"What's wrong, Mrs. Debbie?" Ashley asked.

"Nothing. I'm just happy for you," Debbie said.

Ashley then gave Monroe another hug. Feeling awkward, Monroe attempted to hug her. Debbie held back her giggling as she watched him. She knew he didn't do well with mushy stuff when it came to anyone but her. I'll see ya'll later," Ashley said, backing away from Monroe and then turned to leave.

"Bye Ashley," Debbie said.

"Bye Ash," Monroe said.

"Ash?" Debbie asked.

"Yeah. I kind of think of her like a . . . a niece," he said with a smile, walking towards the couch. He dropped down with a sigh. "I hope everything works out for her. That girl has been through hell and back."

Sitting in a chair next to him, Debbie leaned forward with a big smile, staring at him.

"What?" Monroe asked.

"I love you, Monroe T. Lovett. You're a good man."

"I'm glad you think so."

"I do."

"You miss not being able to have children, don't you?" he asked.

"Most of the time I'm okay with it. But, then there are other times, when . . . you know."

"Yeah, I do," he said as the two sat there for a few moments. Monroe then patted Debbie's leg and said, "You know, I feel like getting out of here." Standing up, he grabbed her hand, and said, pulling her up, "C'mon, let's get out of here."

"Woo . . .," Debbie said as Monroe pulled her to her feet. She grabbed the envelope Ashley gave them from Monroe's desk and handed it to him and asked, "Want this?"

"Oh yeah." He peeked inside as they were walking out of his office. "Not bad. I can't believe—she shouldn't have," he said. Placing the envelope in his pocket, he took a deep breath and said, "No doubt about it, we definitely need to go put this in the bank."

"So, you gonna tell me?" she asked, turning Monroe's office light off as they walked into the hall.

Stopping in the hall, he turned, facing her, and said, "Um . . . well, let's just say we could . . ."

"Could what?" Debbie asked, amazed.

Holding up one finger, with an excited look, he said, "Now, add six zeroes."

Falling back against the wall, her knees buckling a little, Debbie asked, "Are you serious?"

He didn't answer.

"Monroe . . . honey, do you, do you know what this means?"

"Yes," he said, giving her a kiss. "It means I got you."

Debbie glared at him and said, "You're mean."

Laughing he said, "You're so easy."

"I know. I know," she said, pouting.

"Will you still be happy with thirty?"

"Thirty dollars?"

"No . . . thirty thousand."

"Yes. I was happy just to help her."

"I know. But it was fun seeing your face when I told you—"

"Ha! You're so funny," she said, starting to giggle. Then Debbie threw her arms around Monroe's neck and started kissing his face as he continued to laugh. She fell back against the wall again, looking at him and him at her, their eyes locked.

Leaning over, he gave her another more loving kiss, as he slowly ran his hands down her back, stopping at her rear. After a tender squeeze, he reached over and switched off the hallway light, leaving the hall dimly lit.

No longer giggling, Debbie slowly ran her index fingers down his chest and said, "What are you doing?"

"Just turning the lights out," he said, reaching over and playing with her hair.

"You silly man," she said, gazing up into his eyes, throwing her arms back around his neck. "I love you so much, Monroe," she breathed.

He whispered, "I love you too, Debbie. Very, very, much." He gave her an even longer, slow, heated kiss, pulling her tightly against him.

She ran her nails ever so slowly over his shoulders and down his arms, wantonly gazing up at him. "Monroe, what are you doing?" she asked impishly.

"What do you think?"

"Lunch?"

"Yeah . . . *lunch*," he replied with a frisky grin.

"No . . . Really. Lunch. Food. Why, what were you thinking?" she asked, giggling. "See two can play that game."

Laughing, he popped her rear. "You're hilarious."

"Hey!"

They both started laughing. After locking up, holding hands, the two sauntered from the office. Walking to the car, Debbie snuggled under Monroe's arm, and suggestively said, "But, after lunch . . .

Made in the USA
Middletown, DE
29 November 2019